Praise for Jody Wallace's
A Spell for Susannah

""A Spell for Susannah is absolutely fantastic. Exceptionally told with the look and feel of a fairy tale, but this is no story for children. With exceptionally detailed prose, the author creates a sensuous fantasy world complete with romance, fairies, spells and intrigue. ...This is one highly entertaining and original novel. I would not ever hesitate to read anything by Jody Wallace."

~ *Bonnie-Lass, Coffeetime Romance*

"Jody Wallace has truly done a fabulous job of telling a story surrounding the princesses....Out of all the men that come to visit, Jon Tom is the one person that Susannah finds intriguing and makes her angry at the same time. As they come together to solve the true curse, emotions between them heat up unbelievably and the ending will have you cheering for everyone."

~ *Goddess Minx, Literary Nymph Reviews*

"With her delightfully quirky brand of humor, Jody Wallace gives an old story a wonderfully new and unique twist....Ms. Wallace is a bright new talent who shines in both the elements of fantasy and romance. A Spell for Susannah makes a memorable first impression as you laugh and cheer the main characters on to their well deserved happily ever after."

~ *LeeAnn, Fallen Angel Reviews*

"This is a tongue-in-cheek romp (think, oh, Piers Anthony's fantasy stories). ... Ms Wallace has achieved a very nice balance between the story and the humorous elements in A Spell For Susannah. The storyline is pretty strong and coherent without being buried under a mountain of jokes. Everything comes together very nicely here, making it a pleasurable story to read and laugh with."

~ *Mrs. Giggles*

"This enjoyable adaptation of the Twelve Dancing Princesses fairy tale is clever and intriguing. Jody Wallace gives the story a new face, adding some modern elements that spark the plot and provide the reader with plenty of smiles along the way. She has a great feel for her characters, a nice sense of comic timing, and a contagious sense of humor. ...This is a great read when you want something light and entertaining, but truly satisfying."

~ *Miranda Lee, ParaNormal Romance Reviews*

"With a gentle humor that is akin to, but not as bald as Gregory Maguire's, Ms. Wallace sweeps us away to magical lands populated by witty women and somewhat clueless, for the most part, men that they love. It's an interesting place to visit, and I'd enjoy seeing how the other eleven girls find their way to romance."

~ *Amanda Killgore, Huntress Reviews*

Look for these titles by
Jody Wallace

Now Available:

Survival of the Fairest
Liam's Gold

A Spell for Susannah

Jody Wallace

A Samhain Publishing, Ltd. publication.

Samhain Publishing, Ltd.
577 Mulberry Street, Suite 1520
Macon, GA 31201
www.samhainpublishing.com

A Spell for Susannah
Copyright © 2008 by Jody Wallace
Print ISBN: 978-1-59998-987-7
Digital ISBN: 1-59998-872-0

Editing by Bethany Morgan
Cover by Christine Clavel

First Samhain Publishing, Ltd. electronic publication: January 2008
First Samhain Publishing, Ltd. print publication: November 2008

Dedication

I'd like to thank the Brothers Grimm for transcribing the tale of the shoes that were danced to pieces in the eighteen hundreds. And since the Brothers aren't around to tell me I'm welcome, I'd like to thank my family, for giving me the time to write, edit and complain—the complaining being a Very Important Part of the process, you understand. My local RWA chapter, Music City Romance Writers, definitely shouldered some of the griping, so they are to be praised as well. Other folks who helped bear the burden of my quest for publication include my agent Laura Bradford, Cathy Pegau, Joanna King, Natalie Damschroder, Julie Wellons and Sierra Donovan. And of course, I'm grateful to my publisher and to my editor, Bethany Morgan, for seeing the possibilities in fairy tales for grown-ups.

Prologue

The final sovereign of the Middle Kingdoms signed the petition with a flourish and then fanned the ink to dry it before handing it to the footman. The youngest of the thirteen kings, he was a handsome man with dark brown hair and a neat beard.

"Well done!" The Emperor accepted the completed document and unrolled it to its full length, nodding his head in approval. The charmed parchment, when signed by all thirteen human kings and their Emperor and witnessed by three representatives from the Fairy Alliance for Ethics, would bind the fairy Malady from the human lands, in particular from attending any more christenings with her nasty little gifts.

"It was your child upon whom Malady bestowed her final curse, so it is fitting you be the one to summon the Fairy Alliance to hear our judgment." The Emperor handed the pearl and ruby conch shell to the youngest king.

"Thank you, Your Splendor." The man raised the device to his lips and blew several short, eerie blasts. Almost immediately, three fairies materialized in the center of the golden throne room. The breeze of their arrival ruffled the heavy crimson hangings along the long walls and set the tiered chandelier tinkling.

"We've been expecting your summons," Pleasentia said, swishing her gauze dress and smiling at the men gathered in the darkened room.

"Hurry and get this over with." The fairy Budbud snapped her wizened fingers, and in them appeared a large gold seal. "Recite the document, sprinkle on the fairy dust and let us ratify it. We've better things to be doing during the blue moon's night."

The third fairy held a crumpet dripping with jam. "Is this about Mali?" Gary asked, licking his fingers. "You know, her gifts really don't—"

"We don't want to hear any more of your excuses!" thundered the Emperor. "We have the right to bar specific fairies from our midst if we so choose. In fact we have the right to bar all fairies from the human lands, and then where would you get your precious gold?"

"Oh, do shut up, Hubert, and get on with it," Budbud said. "We all know you aren't going to ban all the fairies. You want our spells as much as we want your gold."

The Emperor flushed and cleared his throat. He began to recite the document, which cast the first threads of the spell that would prohibit Malady from entering human lands until the parchment was burned three times with the feather of a red gold phoenix.

"We the people..."

"They always start their documents that way. Why do they do that?" whispered Pleasentia.

"Hush, dear." Gary patted her hand. "Let them have their fun."

"We the people, in order to maintain a more solid union, to provide for the common defense of ourselves and our posterity, do hereby declare the fairy Malady banned and barred from the Middle Kingdoms forthwith. She is forbidden from attending the christenings of any human children, be they noble or common, even if those christenings take place outside the Middle Kingdoms, and should she seek to harm, injure or otherwise take revenge upon any human, let her—"

In a blast of light followed by a billow of reeking smoke, the fairy in question exploded into the vaulted throne room, her wiry hair standing on end. She stamped her feet upon the crimson carpet and the walls trembled.

"What charade is this?" she cried. "Banning me, the great Malady, from your puny human lands?"

The Emperor stared at the wicked sprite in dismay, his mouth hanging open, as the other occupants of the room coughed and waved tendrils of smoke from their faces.

"Keep reading, Your Splendor!" insisted the youngest king.

"We shall not traffic with her. Let her see how she likes bargaining with the Sun Demons for her precious gold." But the Emperor let the parchment droop in his grasp.

"Better not make that face, Hubert." Malady cackled, raised a hand and an icy globule of magic appeared in it. She hurled it at the Emperor, striking him in the head and immobilizing him. "It might freeze that way!"

Budbud harrumphed. "Always butting in where you aren't invited. You leave these humans be!"

"I will not!" screeched the black-haired fairy. "I curse these humans! I curse them and the horses they rode in on!"

"Can't we leave the horses out of it?" asked Gary. "What did they ever do to you?"

"Okay, scratch the part about the horses." Malady sketched some glowing runes in the air before she wiped them out with a quick hand. "But as for these foolish humans, these so-called nobles who reject my gifts, let them be forever cursed!"

Since the other kings were too intimidated to move, the young king beside the Emperor snatched the document from his limp hands. "We the people, yes, yes," he said, racing through the text.

"Let them never bear another male child—" shrieked Malady.

"If she should seek revenge, blah blah, let her be banished by the representatives of the Fairy Alliance who stand here—" shouted the king.

"Let them bear only female children from this day forward—"

"Banished to east of the sun and west of the moon for a thousand years and a day!"

"Only girl babies for every king, every duke, every single noble in your stupid, pitiful lands!"

"So be it rote!" The young king snatched the philter of fairy dust from a gaping footman and doused the parchment.

"So be it rote," echoed the twelve kings.

"Mmmfh!" rasped the Emperor.

"So be it rote," agreed the three fairies, who'd observed the chant-off with great interest. Budbud hopped onto the Emperor's dais and stamped the document with the golden seal. A ripple of pale light bloomed outward from the paper, dissipating as quickly as it appeared.

Upon the completion of the banishment, Malady doubled over with hateful laughter. Still chortling, she exploded out of the throne room in much the same way she entered, leaving a burned patch on the crimson rug.

With a gasp, the Emperor tore the icy skein from his face. "Surely that curse won't stick," he panted. "Will it?"

Chapter One

And so it came to pass that the noble inhabitants of the Middle Kingdoms bore no more male children. Ten, twenty, thirty years, and still no male children were delivered to swell their ranks and inherit their lands. The aristocracy tried, how they tried, but daughters alone did they have. Daughters who had fewer and fewer men to marry each year. Daughters trapped by the Kingdom Laws, which decreed women could hold no property nor titles independent of men. Daughters who must remain at home until married. Daughters who grew restless.

Susannah groaned when the Queen slammed open the closely guarded door to her bedchamber and punched the button that made the wrought-iron oil lamps pop on. Their penetrating light joined with the bang of the door and squeak of the hinges to wake her from some much-needed slumber.

"Mother," Susannah said, "do you have to be so loud?" All twelve sisters, from oldest to youngest, shared a room so they could be guarded more efficiently.

The Queen clanged her toad-headed cane on the closest iron footboard in the two rows of beds. "Yes, I do." The cane bounced off the footboard and into Susannah's toes.

Susannah curled her legs up and sighed. Tendrils of a pleasant dream about waltzing with the enchanted princes in the secret land below the castle unraveled before her tightly closed eyes.

As usual on the mornings when the twelve princesses lay abed, Susannah's mother was not pleased. "I don't suppose any of you ladies will tell me why you're so tired this morning?"

Several of her sisters stuck their pillows over their heads. Eyes gummy from lack of sleep, Susannah rolled out of bed, but none of the rest moved.

The Queen whacked her cane on the next footboard in the row. "Get your royal bottoms out of bed!" She rapped out their responsibilities for the day. "Calypso, Peter, Hortense—shopkeeper visits. Fay, Esme, Lilly—library. Annabelle, Nina, Temple—castle accounts. Fay, Ella, Rosa—herb gardens."

No one budged.

The Queen stalked to the middle of the long room. The square stones and wooden beams of the ceiling echoed her words with chill precision. "If you persist with this disobedience, I'm going to start giving you away to the first men who ask for you, commoners or no."

At that, Hortense sat up. "Kingdom Law Number 333 states that those of noble blood cannot be wedded to those of common blood unless that individual performs some quest or feat which earns him or her elevation to the ranks of nobility."

"Besides, Papa won't let you," Susannah reminded her mother. "You've been trying that for years."

"You devious girls haven't been sneaking off in the middle of the night to exhaust yourselves into a stupor until recently. Your dear Papa is getting extremely frustrated."

"It's not our fault Malady cast the Female Curse," Ella said. Susannah cast the teenage troublemaker a "shut up" glance behind her mother's back, but Ella ignored her. "You and the other kings and queens brought it on yourselves when you banished her from attending any more christenings."

While Susannah agreed with her sister, she did so in silence. Antagonizing their mother in the morning was unwise. Antagonizing her at other times was foolish, as well, but not so much as after one of their prolonged snoozes.

The Queen shook her cane at Ella. "Curse or no curse, you are going to put your lazy selves to work doing something constructive. Idleness will turn you even more wicked than you already are."

Susannah took her corset off the hook on the tall cedar armoire beside her bed and began snapping it over her night rail that doubled as a chemise. The Queen hadn't yet assigned her a task, which struck her as ominous. "Mother, what am I to do today?"

The Queen, ignoring her comment, bent down to the cool, gray floor and snatched up a pair of ruined silk slippers. "Look at this rag. Do you girls think shoes grow on trees?"

Susannah gave her mother a mild look. "We keep the shoemaking elves in business. Otherwise, they'd be haunting the unemployment office."

"That doesn't stop you from putting many guards out of a job. You know good and well your father fires every one who lets you wicked girls keep doing...whatever it is you're doing. I should have you all put in the stocks in the public square."

Hortense, voice muffled through her workaday dress as she slid it over her head, cleared her throat. "Kingdom Law Number 432 states that no one of noble blood shall be stocked, hided, whipped, tortured or imprisoned in the lesser dungeons at any time. They also cannot be disowned, denounced or otherwise demoralized without indisputable proof of treason, immorality or misallocation of kingdom funds."

"Shut up, Hortense." The Queen turned to Susannah. "Today, Miss, you'll be helping me select the next batch of sentries. The guards shall know it is you personally, Susannah, who causes them to be thrown from the castle in disgrace. Your father has agreed when more guards lose their jobs, you'll be responsible for apologizing to their families and finding them employment outside the castle."

Temple, one of Susannah's youngest sisters, lay down on the floor and scrabbled under her bed. A pair of tattered silk dancing slippers skidded into the middle of the room, then another, and then a red croquet ball. Her head under the dust ruffle, she asked, "Couldn't Father just quit firing the guards? None of them succeed. It's not fair to make them suffer."

At Temple's naive comment, Susannah froze in the middle of her hasty ablutions. So did her sisters. Their shoulders hunched as they prepared for an onslaught from their aggrieved mother.

Temple leapt up and knocked her shins into her bed frame. "I mean, there's nothing for them to be guarding us from, after all, so how could they succeed?"

More frightening to Susannah than the harangues, more painful than the whacks and smacks, was the calculating expression that crossed the Queen's face. Her bright blue eyes narrowed and her thin lips curled up in a sneer.

"I wasn't going to tell you this, but your father has decided enough is enough."

The Queen had such a look about her today that an ill-omened pressure built in Susannah's stomach. She and her siblings had always thwarted their mother's attempts to catch them when they crept off at night to dance with the enchanted princes. She knew how dreadful it would be if the King and Queen discovered what their daughters had been doing at night, and how they managed to get there. So far, they'd been lucky. But luck always ran out.

The Queen strode down the bed-lined, narrow chamber and tested the iron bars on the sunny windows at the end of the room. She stamped the iron heating vents, covered for the warm season the past fortnight, while Susannah and her sisters stood in silence. Despite the fact she never found anything, the Queen often turned the room upside down in a search for secret doors or magic items. She used her cane to flick aside the brightly colored velvet tapestries adorning the outer walls, sniffed and stalked back to the middle of the room. Her skirts brushed against the pale stones of the floor with a faint shushing.

"Too many pairs of ruined slippers. Too many torn chemises and spilled bottles of cosmetics." She struck her cane against a footboard to emphasize each point, the sharp clang making Susannah flinch. "Too many guards dismissed for failure to perform and too many mornings twelve perfectly healthy young women slumber abed. Most especially, there have been too many episodes of disregard for the commands of your parents!"

Tendrils of the Queen's smooth blonde hair escaped its careful twist as she paced. "Your father and I are not monsters, my dears. We realize your position entitles you to certain luxuries. We realize that, unwed as you are, cloistered as you are, as old as some of you are, it was inevitable you get up to mischief. In fact, we consider ourselves lucky we had thirty-five years of relative harmony, unlike some of our neighbors.

"But this ends now. Whatever it is you're doing, we're going to find out, put a stop to it and punish you accordingly."

The Queen stopped pacing in front of her eldest daughter.

"Susannah, be in my office in fifteen minutes. I have breakfast waiting, so no dawdling in the kitchen." With that, the Queen swept majestically out of the room, reminding Susannah her mother was, indeed, a force to be reckoned with. She tended to forget that fact in her obsession with the enchanted princes.

Chapter Two

With more speed than finesse, Susannah shoved her mass of hair into a knot at the nape of her neck. From her carved wooden armoire, she grabbed a white blouse and a dark, sensible overdress in hope of convincing her mother that she could be a prudent woman. A quick trip to the nearby bathing chamber, where she splashed face and hands in cold water, and she raced to the Queen's office.

She closed the door softly behind her. "Hello, Mother."

The Queen grunted. She sat in a brown leather chair at the plain sturdy table she preferred to the massive desk shoved into a far corner of the room. To an outsider, the room was a cheerful, tapestried chamber with lush blue carpets and elegant shelves of books and curiosities, but Susannah knew it as the place she and her sisters were frequently brought to task. Susannah nibbled on ham, rolls and currant jelly, and sipped peach nectar and water. Her mother's large quill pen scratched across a stack of parchment.

"Now, Susannah," the Queen began, setting aside her quill, "you can put a stop to all this if you just speak with me, woman to woman, about what you do every night."

Susannah swallowed a lump of bread. "You know what we do, Mother. You spent the night with us only a week ago."

Susannah hated lying and wished she could confide in her parents. But she knew how much trouble she'd be in if the King and Queen discovered their precious daughters cavorting with ensorcelled men several nights of the week, entirely unchaperoned.

More importantly, she knew what kind of an uproar it would cause if anyone found out how she'd discovered the princes in the first place—she, mortal woman, had learned to use fairy magic. The fairies bequeathed christening gifts, warded the Middle Kingdoms' borders and bespelled many devices for humans in return for the coveted gold they were unable to mine or work, but mortals weren't capable of the magical arts. It was an unspoken law of nature nobody questioned. Yet Susannah had found a way to do it. That knowledge could destroy far more than her relationship with her parents.

The Queen sighed. "You sleep, indeed, but what else do you do? What wears out brand-new slippers in one night and sprinkles fairy dust all over your skin?" Susannah glanced at her chest, where her modest blouse revealed a few tiny glints on her neck from last night's revelries. There was probably more on her bosom, for she'd worn a low-cut chemise. Her partner for the evening, one Prince Agravar, had been covered in the insidious stuff.

She tried for nonchalance. "Someone threw a powder puff at me."

The Queen raised an eyebrow. "I've heard that one before. Do you know what I think? I think there are men involved."

"You must be joking. How could there possibly be men involved? No way in and no way out? All locked up from dusk till dawn in the most secure room in the castle?"

"Hardly dawn," the Queen said with a snort. "I can smell men on you. I can see certain looks growing in your eyes, looks no unpromised maid should have."

Susannah rolled her eyes. "I'm hardly a maid. I'm thirty-five, even if I've never been anywhere or done anything my whole life. What man would you promise me to in this accursed land? The butler? The baker?"

"It doesn't take a titled male to spark a gleam in a lady's eye. What do you do, seduce the guards? Do they all deserve to be turned out?"

If only her mother knew! "No, Mama, of course not. We know our place."

"Then what do you do?" The Queen picked up her pen and stabbed it into the inkwell. "Susannah, I'm your mother. You

19

can tell me anything and I'll still love you, you know that."

The Queen helped their father run a tidy little kingdom. Susannah figured her mother could forgive their dancing with hundreds of adoring men, but if she knew Susannah had learned to defy nature's laws, how far would that love extend?

She never wanted to find out. "We sleep. We stay up late talking, but eventually we sleep. We discuss how unfair it is there are no men for us to marry. We talk of how we think the Middle Kingdoms should solve their inheritance troubles. I'm of the opinion the Kingdom Laws—"

The Queen laughed, breaking the tension. "I'm aware of your opinions. Don't get sidetracked bashing all the hidebound old men in charge of things."

"I should think you would be able to influence Papa," Susannah began, but her mother interrupted her again.

"It won't do, Susannah." The Queen tapped a tapered finger against her chin. "I've switched your bedchamber, I've separated you, I've spied on you through the night. I've stationed a maid on a cot in the center of your room. I don't suppose an appeal to your love for your distraught parents would do the trick?"

"Mama, there's no cause for distress. I promise you, your concerns are groundless." Susannah stared at her mother's finger as it tapped against that elegant, determined chin. She sincerely hoped her mother didn't separate them again. That had certainly been a challenge.

"But you're doing something, aren't you?"

Sometimes Susannah opted for a half-truth when the lump in her deceitful craw grew too large. "We aren't doing anything to disgrace you or ourselves."

In truth, the princes were no threat to the princesses' chastity, considering the effects of the enchantment—or curse, as it were. Something kept the princes impotent as well as amnesiac. Despite the best efforts of certain siblings, not much was even possible. Perhaps that was a kindness to the men. They were trapped in a timeless place with nothing to do but dance and play games. No women, except the princesses, and no telling how long their curse would last.

Unless Susannah could break it.

"One might actually believe you were telling the truth, for you've never been able to keep secrets from me. There is always someone willing to tattle on the others."

"There's nothing to tattle." A trickle of sweat slid between Susannah's breasts. "We practice our dance steps quite a bit, and the flagstones in this palace are not exactly smooth. Not to mention you have us running enough errands to spoil hundreds of slippers."

"Susannah, Susannah." The Queen shook her head. "I don't believe that for a minute. You don't wear dancing slippers for everyday errands. If I forbid the elves to deliver any more, no doubt you'd ruin your everyday slippers instead." She picked up an uneaten roll from the serving plate and eyed it as if it contained answers. Susannah held her breath.

The Queen replaced the roll and dusted her fingers. "I don't know how you've managed to cow all the other girls, but I'm going to find out, starting today. Half a year of this nonsense is more than enough."

"Whatever you say, Mama. Now let's choose some guards." Susannah always cramped with guilt when their guards were fired. Finding them new jobs was hardly a punishment, even if most of them would have preferred to remain employed by her father.

The Queen signaled a maid to clear the breakfast remains from the table. Sunlight filtered through the clear glass windows, and the office hummed with authority and power. While the King spent his days settling his subjects' disputes in the Justice Chambers or traveling to other kingdoms on missions of diplomacy, the Queen ran the kingdom from her office. She functioned as a chatelaine for the entire land. Her room wasn't positioned behind the throne, but it might as well have been.

"Today we'll interview guard applicants from outside the castle." The Queen eyed Susannah as she waited for a footman to place her chair beside her mother's. "Your father employed a talent scout to find these candidates. I plan to hire as many as I deem necessary."

"You mean a headhunter?" Susannah's eyes widened as she settled into her seat. "Mama, royals don't use headhunters."

"They do now." The triumphant grin on her mother's face unsettled her.

The first man to interview was a bearded giant. "Aye, I'll see to it the little missies don't go scampering out of their room at night." The giant grinned, showing several gaps between his large teeth. He crouched on the ground in front of the table instead of sitting on, and crushing, the chair positioned for the candidates' use.

"How tall are you, sir?" Susannah asked. Giants rarely came to the Middle Kingdoms, and even crouched upon the rug he was as tall as she or her mother.

"Tall enough to see whatever it is you're up to." The giant let out an unmanly titter. He dug his fingers into his wiry beard and scraped his chin with a sound like a carpenter's sander.

"Where have you worked before?" The Queen scratched down notes with her pen, the feather dancing this way and that.

"I did siege work with the late King Nobbyknees, more siege work with King Torrance and some gate bashing with King Phillip, who hired me right out from under King Torrance's nose during the siege, he did."

"Are you an employee who cares most about gold?" the Queen asked. "If, say, my daughters offered you a great deal of money to look the other way, would you take it?"

The giant again scratched his chin. "It would depend on if His Highness offered me more."

"He'll do quite well," Susannah whispered to the Queen. "Considering we have never bribed anyone, his loyalty will never be tested."

The Queen pursed her lips. "You might not be the right giant for this assignment, but you may talk to the steward to see what other positions are open."

The giant rose to his full height and nearly crashed into the ceiling. His huge navel, eye level with the seated ladies, looked exactly like a bathtub drain. "Thank ye, Your Highness." A footman flung open both doors so they were wide enough for him to exit.

The second man was a tiny brownie whose head was level with the top of the table. If brownies weren't reputed to be so sharp-witted, Susannah would have welcomed the chipper man onto the castle staff. They hadn't employed a brownie in years.

In a surprisingly deep voice for such a small fellow, the brownie said, "Greetings, Your Highness! Greetings, Princess!" He hopped into the chair and swung his legs. "I've come about the job. The princesses can't possibly pull one over on me."

The Queen inclined her head. "That's what we hope. You do realize the punishment for failure is dismissal from castle service with no letter of recommendation?"

"Aye, everyone knows that. The guards hoodwinked by the princesses are talking about forming a union. But I shall not fail."

"There has been no hood to wink." Susannah sniffed. "What jobs have you held?"

"I guarded a sheep farm for many a year before setting off to seek my fortune. Besides, I was tired of the smell of sheep."

This wasn't going to be as bad as she thought. Susannah whispered to her mother, "If I'm the ringleader and the other girls my flock, you should indeed hire him."

The Queen sighed. "Guarding sheep isn't like guarding twelve girls too clever for their pantaloons. If you'd like to visit our steward, he may have other positions open."

The next to interview was a haughty young man with golden hair. He reminded Susannah of Agravar from the enchanted palace.

"Mr. Finder," the Queen said. "What skills can you offer for our special project?"

"I always choose the correct door," the man claimed. "It's my christening gift. If the princesses evade my watch I'll always know what door they hide behind."

Susannah wondered if the man could detect what magical door they hid behind, but the door didn't exist. She used her powers to create it each time. In fact, she could do it from anywhere in the castle, though it was easiest through Calypso's armoire. Hers had the fewest clothes in it.

"Where have you worked before?" Susannah asked him.

"I worked with Pete & Benjamin's Animal Circus in the funhouse," he admitted, shamefaced. "I helped children find their way out of the mirror maze. But I did a little sideshow work—lady and tiger stuff."

With a spare quill, Susannah scribbled her mother a message.

Choose him! He will know at all times we're behind the door of our bedchamber.

The Queen drew an "X" through Susannah's note. "Mr. Finder, your skill might be better put to use in our Lost and Found department. If you will go into the hall and turn to the left...well, I'm sure you'll know what door to open."

As the day progressed, Susannah and her mother interviewed a seamstress with a directional needle, a cook who never burned the broth, a soldier who could talk to fish, a man with seven-league boots and a minstrel whose lute playing would soothe the princesses into deep slumber. They interviewed a centaur, a giant badger and a coachman who was down on his luck and just looking for a job. Susannah grew more light of heart and the Queen more surly.

"Come, Mother," she said during their teatime break. "I have never known a talking badger before."

"I'm leaning toward the minstrel. He can sleep all day and play his lute all night."

"Shall I call him back?" Susannah suspected she could dig up a counterspell to lute-induced slumber in one of the tomes in the castle library's archives. She could create the door to the enchanted land, see and hear through walls, cast illusions, light candles, defeat truth spells, inspire slumber, make beds and heal aches and pains, and her powers were expanding daily.

She wished she could also read minds, although she doubted that would be on the safe list of ethical uses for magic Hortense and several of her sisters had worked out with her when her powers first surfaced. The Queen shook her head. "The headhunter inventory says we have one more candidate. I'll interview him and then make my decision."

Susannah straightened the skirt of her somber brocade overdress and brushed a few crumbs onto the carpet. Her hair tickled her neck and face, escaping from her hasty knot, and she shoved it behind her ears. "What is his name?" she asked her mother.

"Jon Tom."

"Jon Tom what?"

The Queen frowned. "It just says Jon Tom."

"But that is two first names and no last. What does he do?"

"It says he is a...detective."

Clapping her hands, Susannah laughed. "A detective! What does he detect, stolen sheep? Burning broth? Anyone who needed something detected would come to the King's Lost and Found department."

The Queen shot her a sour look and rang the silver bell. The tall double doors swung open and Jon Tom the detective walked through. Susannah examined him, as she had the other applicants, for potential threats. He had a swarthy face, dark hair and white teeth, which gleamed brightly in the afternoon sun streaming through the tall, thin windows.

"My Queen, my Princess," he said, executing a low and graceful bow.

"Greetings, Jon Tom," the Queen said. "Please, make yourself comfortable. I understand you're a detective?"

"Yes, Your Highness."

"What exactly is a detective? What is it you detect?"

"I detect solutions, Your Highness. Solutions, answers, reasons and culprits."

"Solutions to what?" Susannah wanted to know. The man had a wily look she didn't like. His dark eyes glanced about the room, assessed everything and everyone in it.

The man regarded her coolly, almost insolently, as if he knew her secrets. "Solutions to who killed Cock Robin. Solutions to what happened to the Queen's tarts. Solutions to where twelve naughty ladies go every night when the sun is down and the night is full."

The Queen stopped scratching her quill on her notepaper and leaned back in her chair. "Do you indeed?" A smile spread across her face.

"Not every city has a Lost and Found department as assiduous as yours," Jon Tom complimented the Queen. "Not every kingdom has a king who puts his own daughters to work solving the citizens' problems and caring for the community."

"Have you been detecting solutions for long?" the Queen asked.

"Many years, Your Highness. I hail from Pavilion, where the late ruler's failure to produce a male heir has resulted in near anarchy. The kingship has gone to a baronial cousin who isn't bearing the burden particularly well."

"We would like to avoid Pavilion's troubles, but first we must control our daughters."

Susannah pressed her lips together. As if she wanted this strange man thinking of her as out of control!

"You seem to know quite a bit about our situation already." The Queen steepled her fingertips near her chin. "Perhaps you would like to share your theories at this point?"

"Oh, no doubt there is a man involved." Jon Tom winked at Susannah.

Had her mother noticed this bourgeois man, this detective, wink at a royal princess? Susannah turned to her mother to protest.

But the Queen's face was lit with pleasure. "That's exactly what I said."

"And I told you, Mother, there isn't a man involved," Susannah snapped.

Jon Tom smiled, seemingly pleased by the outburst. Her eyes drifted away from that face, from that hawk-like nose and strong chin, to his broad chest, two strong arms crossed over it as he lounged in his chair. Down to tan trousers encasing a fine pair of legs. The man was as attractive as any of the enchanted princes in the land beneath, but he had such an air about him, such a dangerous air, as if he'd sooner snatch her up and eat her than dance a reel.

"So tell me, Your Highness, about your daughters. The more information I have, the more easily I can solve the case."

"Well, you have met Susannah. At five and thirty, she is the eldest and I fully believe she is the ringleader of whatever is going on."

"I make no mistake about that," the man agreed. "Princess Susannah." He rolled her name around in his mouth like a toffee. "I am charmed to make your acquaintance."

Susannah sniffed and turned her head to one side. Out of the corner of her eye, she saw the man smiling a strange, slow smile.

"My second eldest is Calypso," continued the Queen. "She is a tomboyish gel who loves horses and polo. She hasn't the sort of trickery about her to instigate this matter, but she's game for any adventure. My third daughter is Peter."

"Peter? That's an odd name for a princess."

The Queen inclined her head regally. "His Highness was convinced an amulet he acquired on the black market could defeat the Female Curse and named her Peter before the doctor could say, 'It's a girl.' It wouldn't do to tease Peter about her name, though. She's very sensitive about certain things."

"She's as sensitive as your wooden cane," Susannah muttered.

"Hortense is next. She's a law-abiding woman who isn't the type to go along with escapades."

"Never be surprised the lengths to which a lady will go when there is a man involved," the detective assured the Queen. "Even a proper girl can have her head turned by a handsome man...or a very determined sister."

Susannah focused an intent glare upon Jon Tom. It would be nice if she could use that pincher spell and needle him in the...but she didn't dare. Her hostile regard didn't discomfit him. He gazed back at her knowingly until she looked away first.

Why did her mother not notice the things this man was saying to her with his eyes? "Mother," she whispered, "I don't think this man will suit. He's disrespectful."

The Queen ignored her and continued to catalog her daughters.

"Do you mind if I write this down?" The detective took some tiny paper and a black crow's feather out of a small pocket on his tunic.

"Do you need ink for your quill?" The Queen gestured to her inkpot.

"Oh, this is an enchanted quill—never runs out of ink. A fairy gave it to me when I aided her on a confidential matter. Please continue. I'm learning a great deal."

Susannah rested her chin on her hands as her mother described Susannah's sister Lilly. "She would make a lovely bride," the Queen said. "Not that there are any men for her to meet and marry."

"No men you know of," Jon Tom commented. "I'm willing to bet Princess Susannah knows differently." He wrote another note in his book and tapped his mouth with the dark quill.

Susannah twisted about in her chair. "Mother, do we have to hear any more? This man is clearly a fraud."

"You seem anxious to get me out of here, Princess."

"I'm anxious that my father not waste his gold hiring a charlatan. Who has ever heard of a detective, anyway?"

"Susannah!" exclaimed the Queen. "That was very rag-mannered."

The strength of her annoyance surprised Susannah, but she didn't back down or apologize. There was something about this man that activated her hackles.

Jon Tom held up a strong brown hand. "Don't worry about my feelings, Your Highness. The Princess's discomfort is natural when the end of her clandestine revelry is so near."

"You don't know anything about it. Or about me." Susannah crossed her arms over her chest, echoing his posture. "Mother, you shouldn't allow a commoner to speak to one of royal blood in such a way. Father would be most displeased."

"I think your father will be delighted."

"What do you mean, 'Father will be delighted'?"

The Queen twitched a single finger in a silencing gesture but didn't otherwise acknowledge Susannah's interruption. First her mother said she was out of control. Now she shushed her like a child. When Susannah peeked at the detective, he twitched his own finger in a similar fashion, and it was all she could do not to jump up from the table and pull his stupid, shining hair out by the roots.

"My twelfth child," the Queen said, finishing her litany, "is Rosa, my baby. She was twelve this past Snow Faire."

"I'll enjoy meeting all your children, Your Highness."

His assumption he'd meet all her sisters was overconfident. Susannah's ire rose. "This man shouldn't be introduced to my sisters, much less Papa."

"Your father is going to enjoy meeting Mr. Tom and discussing possible theories with him. Tonight."

"Tonight? You're hiring this man?"

"I am."

"Mother, please. I don't like the look of him. He will

probably be gone in the morning with half the crown jewels."

"I'm wealthy already, Princess. I have the luxury to choose my cases based on which ones interest me. This one interests me very much."

Susannah clutched her mother's arm and lowered her voice. "He winked at me. He keeps intimating things that aren't proper."

"Don't be silly, Susannah. I intended to hire the candidate to whom you most objected. By the strength of your objection, Jon Tom will do a wonderful job. You have outsmarted yourself, my darling."

Susannah's mouth opened and closed like a fish, and at that moment a flicker of fear scampered across her skin. Could Jon Tom truly use these detective skills to discover her use of fairy magic and the enchanted realm beneath? Just what were these skills? Had he some magic mirror which answered questions? Had he some djinn in a bottle bound to obey its master's commands?

"Your Highness," Jon Tom said, "I'm flattered by your quick decision, but you've yet to hear my terms."

That seized the Queen's attention. "You would barter with the Queen?" The regal lady's eyebrows flew up toward her hairline.

"I would, Your Highness. I have certain requirements for proper detective work. One, that I not be dismissed until the princesses evade me at least three times, as according to the common rule of three. Two, that royal chaperonage customs be relaxed so I can spend time with the ladies alone. And three, when I succeed, I wish a house and fertile lands instead of gold."

It was the Queen's turn to gape like a landed fish. "We'll talk to the King," she finally said. "You may discuss your terms with him. And you, Susannah, may repair to the library for the rest of the day."

Susannah rose and stalked as far away from Jon Tom's chair as she could get without being too obvious. Not that obvious mattered at this point, for she'd expressed her disapproval of the man clearly enough.

"Princess Susannah," Jon Tom said, just as she gained the safety of the door. Reluctantly she turned. Jon Tom had risen from his chair and stood facing her, a glint in his coal-dark eyes.

"It was a pleasure to meet you," he said. "I look forward to discovering your secrets, no matter how you hide them."

"My only secret is I wish the headhunter had never found you."

"The headhunter didn't find me, Princess, I found him. I found him, and soon I'll find out about you."

Chapter Three

Susannah welcomed the quiet of the library after her unsettling encounter with the detective. Although several of her sisters had been assigned there as well, they seemed to sense her turmoil and left her to her thoughts. Pale sunlight from the strategically placed skylights reflected off the dust motes in a restful fashion, though it didn't relieve the gloom between the many aisles of tall shelves.

She and her sisters sat among stacks of books at the large wooden table near the entryway. She was tempted to search the archives for mention of detectives—perhaps in the mythical-creatures section—but instead she fetched a few spell books from their hiding places. Not that they were recognizable as spell books, but thirty-five years of poring over the same volumes definitely gave one the ability to see beyond the surface. The only obvious one was the tiny fairy primer, and one could easily mistake it for a book of rhymes. All the sisters had great faith Susannah could discover an answer to the Female Curse, even if they didn't all agree about her dabbling in magic.

Her sister, Esme, sighed heavily and slammed a book shut, making everyone jump. "Is it time for dinner yet?" she said.

"Not even close." Susannah turned another delicate, crackling page in *The Seven Habits of Highly Effective Curse Fairies*. She had found the strange volume stuck in the wrong section, between jam recipes and herbology.

"What are you reading?" her sister Lilly asked her. "Is it about...the curse?" She lowered her voice to a whisper on the last phrase.

"A book in Ancient Dullish." Susannah tapped the squiggly writing with a dusty forefinger. "Not even the ancient Dulls

31

wrote in Ancient Dullish. I suppose that's why the fairies used it for their book. They have no written language of their own."

"The Female Curse stinks," Esme said. She didn't lower her voice to a whisper. "I'm damned glad Malady was banished before I was born. Too bad about you, Suze."

"Too bad," Susannah agreed. At her christening, Honoria had given Susannah canniness, Pleasentia had given her excellent vision, Budbud had given her nice breasts, Gary had given her a way with jams and jellies, but Malady had said, "This child Susannah will not marry a man of her choosing."

Which created a paradox. Who would she not marry, considering it would save her birthright? She'd choose anyone—anyone legitimate. She'd marry a fellow with a swan's wing for an arm if it meant having a husband and children and a kingdom to rule from behind the throne.

"I like the new guard you and Mother chose." Lilly smiled and leaned toward Susannah in a conspiratorial manner. "I met him at second tea when he was chatting with Papa. He is so handsome, don't you think?"

"Handsome is as handsome does. He's going to be trouble. I can tell." He was also the first guard Susannah would enjoy putting out onto the cobblestones of the street when he failed. The look on his face when the King fired him would go down in her memory as one of life's pleasant moments.

Esme tossed a book to the floor. "Nobody is marrying anybody, so what should Susannah's stupid curse matter? If Mama and Papa hadn't been so prickly about their precious firstborn, none of us would be old maids anyway."

Lilly picked up the book Esme discarded and straightened the pages. "We would have acted against Malady eventually. She gifted the Emperor's son with body odor, after all. Susannah's curse was merely the last in a long string of spiteful behavior."

Esme rolled her eyes. "Books aren't going to do the trick. Everybody knows the fairies only let you break one curse. If she's going to break anything, Susannah needs to concentrate on getting us all some men, not just herself."

Susannah ignored her sister's negativity. She had slogged through the title, prologue and first chapter of *Seven Habits*, and Susannah was eking her way through chapter two, envisioning the solution to a curse as you created it. The book probably wasn't supposed to be in a human library, but there it was. If only she could travel to other libraries for further study! The Kingdom Law Library in Emperator City was reputed to be exceptional. But she was an unwed princess, so studying abroad wasn't an option. Leaving home for any length of time wasn't even an option if she didn't marry, which wasn't likely to happen if she couldn't break the Female Curse. And then there were the poor princes beneath the castle. Why did she have to choose just one curse to break?

"Look at this picture," she said, sliding the book to the center of the table. "This gleaming castle surrounded by miserable-looking men. The picture has a border of cracked hearts. What can this be but a representation of our princes?"

Her sisters leaned in for a closer look. Surely it was a clue to the mystery Susannah sought to unravel, if only she could unravel the text.

"The cracked hearts would support your theory the men are being punished because of bad choices in love," Lilly said. "Didn't you decide they tried to seduce fairy women and got banned to a lonely land of impotency for their presumption?"

Esme snorted. "Most fairies are hussies. They wouldn't care if humans tried to get under their skirts. That theory is goat dung."

Susannah rested her chin upon her hand. Esme was probably right, but the picture made sense if she interpreted it that way. Randy human men, propositioning the wrong fairies and getting banished as a result. It made sense. It was circular. Fairies liked circles.

The question was, how to break a curse put upon men who'd been too fresh? What was the key? Should one of them fall in love with the right woman? Should she ask a certain question or open a certain door?

Esme poked the illustration with a pudgy finger. "These lads have on too many clothes. They're dressed like us, like Middle Kingdomers. Ours dress like harem boys in Seelan."

"Remember when we first met them?" Lilly tapped her pink lips with a quill pen. "Their clothing was so shocking! I'm glad we decided to wear our chemises now instead of court finery. It makes returning to bed easier, and the princes don't notice one way or the other."

Esme twirled her finger beside her temple. "Because they're idiots."

Susannah spread her fingers over her mouth to conceal a smile as Esme continued. "Good-looking idiots. I bet Jon Tom isn't an idiot. I bet he would know what to do with his—"

"Hush, Esme." Susannah didn't want to think about Jon Tom and his whatever, yet her sisters kept bringing him up. "Quit talking about that annoying man."

"What's your fuss? There's no way he can follow us." Esme plopped her elbows on the table. "We're too smart for him."

Susannah managed a smile. "Not so smart as all that. As you know, this whole spell was supposed to be a door to the fairy's realm where we could plea bargain with them."

"I like the door you opened better," Esme said with a leer. "The fairies would have fried us as soon as we set foot on their precious Ulaluna. Instead, we got half-naked men."

"Maybe so." Susannah rubbed the small of her back. At her age, she could no longer bend over the tiny print for hours without repercussions. The library chairs were hard, with straight backs and no give. "Maybe I just need to study more."

"We'll help you find time." Lilly stared at Susannah's book with a frown. "Especially if it means you keep taking us to dance with the princes."

"Speak for yourself," Esme said. "Pig's eye, but I loathe these chairs. I'm done for the day. I'd rather find out how the unnaturally lascivious *Polydame* Misha trains her new boy." She cackled and pulled out a bawdy harem novel, currently all the rage with the nobility's female offspring, for obvious reasons.

Susannah tapped her pencil on the novel's red cover. "Those books are unrealistic. Seelan's *polydamen* don't sexually subjugate their harems."

"How would you know, Miss Virginal? Been there, done that?" Esme squirmed her plump self from side to side and slumped until she was barely eye level with the table. "It makes for damn fine reading."

Susannah wished she could toss aside her cares as easily as Esme, but her burdens shadowed her like dark clouds. She laid her head on the table, thoughts roiling. Malady had been barred from the Middle Kingdoms, but her parting shot was going to destroy them if something wasn't done. The Emperor, her father and the other kings tried to barter with the Fairy Alliance for curse relief, but the fairies refused to touch Malady's work, citing professional ethics. A boycott of fairy products never got off the ground. So hundreds of noble daughters grew bitter and cantankerous, trapped by the inheritance section of the Kingdom Laws to remain unwed and home with their parents.

They couldn't inherit because they couldn't marry. They couldn't marry because there were no suitable men. As female nobles of this generation well knew, gardeners and grooms, chefs and tailors, and, Susannah supposed, detectives, were good for some things, but you couldn't marry them. Taking them to bed was also a bad idea. The herbal and magical solutions to prevent conception weren't reliable, and commoners, it had been observed, were unusually potent of seed. The consequences for failure, or success, depending on how one looked at it, were severe. Having relations with a commoner was a quick trip to banishment.

Banished female aristocrats, most of whom weren't trained to do anything besides run a manor house and catch a husband, had few choices of how to support themselves. Primarily they ended up doing the thing with men that got them banished in the first place.

Most kingdoms had taken to encouraging non-aristocrats to attempt great feats, as allowed in the addendum to Kingdom Law 333, and so be elevated to the nobility. However, the practice killed off more young men than it ennobled. Moreover, the ones it did promote to a baronetcy had demonstrated no ability to produce male offspring with their noble mates. A couple minor earls and barons had attempted to pass boy children off as their own, but a quick parental testing by a fairy had nipped that subterfuge in the bud.

It would have been more sensible to allow unmarried noble women to inherit, not to mention move out of their parents' castles before bloodshed occurred. Unfortunately, the Consortium—the thirteen kings plus the Emperor—had yet to be sensible about much of anything. And Kingdom Law 134 was certainly clear on the subject of who could and couldn't inherit noble titles and wealth in the Middle Kingdoms: legitimate sons or, failing that, the legitimately noble husbands of legitimate daughters.

Susannah sighed and lifted her head. A page of notes stuck to her cheek and she pulled it off with a wince. Lilly scanned a scroll, researching Justice Chamber issues, and Esme sniggered over her novel. The men in charge would never alter the laws that gave them their power. When all the noble men died out, things would change, though not for the better. She just hoped the middle class and gentry folk managed to band together and defend the Middle Kingdoms against the Hinterlanders to the west and the Sun Demons to the east. Managed to find the gold to pay the fairies who warded their borders and kept the Middle Kingdoms safe.

Their kingdom had more of a chance than most. It was small, and Susannah and her sisters were trained to help run it. If Susannah's christening curse prevented her marriage, the logical solution was for one of her sisters to wed instead. However, all potential mates who visited the kingdom looked to Susannah, as first in line to inherit.

None stayed. There was always a finer union to be had, a richer noble in need of a man to marry his daughter. Her curse acted so subtly to drive them away that few in the Middle Kingdoms remembered Malady had burdened her with it. Few remembered she was the last princess Malady had christened, the precipitant of the curse that rid the world of noble men.

Witch. Hag. If she ever got her hands on that fairy, she had a spell or two just waiting to be tested! But that was as likely as her marriage, and cursing Malady would reveal to all and sundry she knew how to work magic.

Chapter Four

"Mama is mad at you for skipping dinner," Rosa informed Susannah that evening in their room. "We had a guest at the table."

Susannah had remained in the library until late, putting aside the frustrating *Seven Habits* to search for references to "detectives" and what powers they might have. She found a crumbling tome about a knight named Magnus who performed Justice Chamber duties with few tools besides his intellect. But everybody used their intellect in the Justice Chambers, so she had no clues as to how Jon Tom planned to spy upon them. She cast a discreet aural dampener over the room, just in case.

"He was very nice, Susannah, not at all like you said in the library," Lilly said. "And even more handsome up close."

"Those black eyes, that curly dark hair, those full lips—he'll be highly entertaining to have around." Peter stretched on her bed, catlike, bare feet digging into the fur lap robe at the bottom. "He hinted that he wants to become better acquainted with me during his stay, and I know what a man means when he hints at that."

"Said he's ventured into the Hinterlands," Calypso added. "You have to respect that."

The detective seemed to know exactly how to appeal to her siblings. Well, she wasn't so easily cozened.

"Mr. Tom is our guard, you ninnies," Susannah reproved them. "He calls himself a detective and claims he has skill at finding things which are hidden. He's sitting outside our door as we speak. Open it up and check if you don't believe me."

"It's not like he's allowed in our room to see where we go." Calypso gestured at the door. "Cast that illusion of us in bed— the one that fools Mother when she pulls back the covers. It should fool any magical viewer he has as well."

"It's not that easy." Susannah paced up and down the room between the beds. "That particular spell takes a lot of power. Don't you remember the time I cast the solid illusion on all twelve rooms when we were separated? I was exhausted."

"You shouldn't have any power at all," Hortense pointed out.

"I stick to the safe list," Susannah said. "I don't cast spells that hurt anyone."

Hortense's lips tightened. "It's still dangerous and unnatural."

"I haven't seen you turning down Susannah's offer to go beneath." Ella, from Calypso's bed, grinned impishly. "We all benefit from Susannah's discovery. I can't wait until I figure out how to access the fairy power, too."

"Dragon save us!" Calypso cuffed Ella on the side of the head, though not hard enough to hurt. "One mutant in the family is enough."

Susannah quit pacing in front of the door and used her magic to look through it at Jon Tom. She enjoyed the feeling of the power surging through her, but that wasn't the only reason she spied on him. He'd had the gall to seat himself on a huge stack of cushions, instead of the wooden chair the other guards had used. In fact, he appeared to be asleep.

Surely he was playing a trick. Susannah pressed her forehead against the door. Jon Tom stretched across several cushions, a green cap over his eyes and his head upon a dark brown wad of shabby fabric. He showed no evidence of a magic mirror, listening tube or other spying device. He couldn't have an invisibility spell. Even the most seditious fairies refused to give those to humans for any amount of gold. In fact they said invisibility wasn't possible. The fairy lights in the corridor dimmed, as fairy lights do when they aren't needed, but the man didn't stir.

Susannah tried another spell. She put her ear against the door and squeezed shut her eyes to focus her sense of hearing. This trick was one she hadn't mastered as well as seeing through walls, but she was able to make out a raspy snore.

Asleep! Asleep on the job, and it was early yet. Perhaps he assumed he'd intimidated her so much she wouldn't dare try anything. The cocky swine.

Susannah let the bloom of energy inside her die away and resisted the urge to cast a slumber hex on the man. Normally she restricted her use of her powers, but it was so exhilarating to hone them—as exhilarating as deceiving the arrogant detective would be.

She turned to face her sisters. "The fool is sound asleep out there. Let's go dancing!"

Ella gave a whoop and Peter sat up on the bed with a smile. The other sisters, although tired after a late night and a long day, were still more than willing.

Rosa stood beside Ella's bed, twisting the hem of her gown around her fingers. "I don't want Mr. Tom to get fired," she whined. "He promised he'd come see my pony."

Susannah sometimes felt she had raised Rosa as much as their mother had, but a baby sister wasn't the same as a child of her own. Her instinct to comfort the girl overcame her annoyance. "He doesn't get fired until we elude him three times. You can still show him your pony."

"Time enough for me to get what I want from him, too," Peter said with a smile. "I grow tired of our impotent friends in the land beneath."

Susannah frowned at the thought of Peter, her perfect, black hair and white skin, oozing charm all over Jon Tom. Surely she wouldn't be that foolish? Jon Tom was no enchanted prince or humble tailor she could toy with like a pet. The man was subtle, even dangerous, and Susannah suspected not even Peter, with all her wiles, was a match for him.

"Just don't let him trick any of you into answering certain questions," she responded. "You know the kinds of questions I mean."

"We're not idiots," Peter said.

Susannah held up her hand. "Regardless, we should prepare a defense. For starters, Ella, can you find time tomorrow to ask around about Mr. Tom?"

"Gladly." Ella rubbed her hands together. "I'll find out all the gossip."

Satisfied, Susannah signaled her sisters to begin dressing.

As one, the princesses leapt up from their beds and opened armoires, dressing table drawers, trunks and chests to draw forth their chemises and slips. Full court regalia made undressing for bed in the wee hours a hassle, especially when haste was needed. Susannah enjoyed a certain wicked freedom wearing her chemise in the company of men, even if those men never noticed the particulars of their appearance.

Some primping, however, she and her sisters enjoyed. They styled their hair, dabbed on perfume, chose earrings and jewels. Even better, they left their corsets hanging on armoire doors, the bones and strings and tight straps superfluous in the land beneath. Even Rosa was allowed a spot of lip rouge and a dusting of face powder, although Hortense insisted she wear a double chemise to conceal her garters and stockings.

"What harm can the princes do?" Peter lazily inquired when Rosa complained, as usual, of the restriction. "It's not as if they can ravish her." Peter's peach silk chemise was so diaphanous her nipples darkened the fabric and so short the hem's swirling folds revealed a portion of her calves. Susannah had her suspicions as to how Peter had convinced the tailor to design the chemise but didn't voice them.

"Hurry up, sisters." Susannah's own chemise was a flame red, which made her wild hair look nearly black and her gray eyes pale and interesting. It swooped low over her breasts, the most impressive of all the sisters' thanks to her christening gift. Of course, she wished the fairy Budbud had seen fit to add moderate thighs and hips to her blessing, but her scarlet shift drifted lightly over the worst of her figure while exposing the best.

The last blossom was tucked behind an ear, the last stocking tied to a garter, and the sisters lined up at Calypso's armoire behind Susannah. Last in line, Rosa flicked out the room's lights with the switch beside the door.

By touch, Susannah opened the armoire doors, shoved aside Calypso's few gowns and laid her palms upon the wooden back. She breathed in and out deeply and focused on the tiny bud of power inside her until it blossomed. The power curled out through her fingertips and the outline of a door appeared, rimmed with pale light. It was nearly effortless as long as she created the door in the same spot every time.

"I'm through," Susannah said. She gave the door a push, and it swung open. Carefully, each sister stepped into the dark, rough room behind the armoire, where they linked hands while Susannah returned to the room to cast a practiced glamour over the empty beds.

In the dark, she fumbled back through to her sisters. In the dark, she didn't see the single door to their room, the one way in and out, crack open and softly close, without a single squeak of the hinges.

Chapter Five

From the room behind the armoire, Susannah led her sisters carefully down the stone staircase. She gripped Calypso's hand and shuffled forward. "Step," she whispered. With practiced ease, the chain of sisters tiptoed down the first flight of lightless, narrow stairs.

From the back of the line, Rosa let out a shriek. "What was that? Someone tugged on my scarf. Ella, are you playing tricks on me?"

Susannah stopped upon the stairs and leaned against the rough wall. Muffled curses echoed through the dark as the princesses bumped into each other. She gritted her teeth. "Ella, stop teasing your sister."

"I'm in front of her. How could I pull her scarf?" Ella's indignant complaint held no hint of mischief. "She's a big baby."

"Am not," Rosa muttered.

Susannah tugged on Calypso, and the chain of princesses started down the stairs. Again Rosa shrieked. "Someone tread upon my gown!"

"You caught it on a rock, crybaby," Ella said. "Why are you so jumpy tonight? Are you afraid the giant badger is coming to get you?"

"I'm not afraid of the giant badger," Rosa sniffled, her voice quivering.

Would they ever reach the light switch at this rate? Perhaps Rosa was overtired. Perhaps this was a bad idea after last night.

"Grrrrrunt, grunt, grunt," Esme snorted, farther down the line. "I'm a giant badger coming to eat Rosa up!"

"Shut up!" Rosa yelled. "Susannah, make them stop."

"We can turn around right here and go back to our bedchamber." Susannah stepped up one step, beside Calypso.

"Yeah, shut up, you little jerks," her sister added.

Once her sisters subsided, she continued. With great relief, Susannah located the first landing. She searched the wall for the magic button, and the fairy lights along the wall came to life, flickering a soft glow down the next section of steps. From here to the land beneath, the rough-hewn staircase was chiseled into the rock face, and a wooden handrail bordered it on the right. The rest of the stairs curved down the cliff, and no end to them could be seen.

"Is there a giant badger?" Rosa asked. Everyone looked behind her. The only thing visible was the narrow staircase they had just vacated.

"Somebody did grab my scarf," she insisted. She pushed through her sisters to Susannah and buried her face in her sister's chest. "I want to hold hands with you."

"All right, dear, you can walk between me and Calypso." Susannah stroked her baby sister's smooth brown hair.

The sisters commenced the remainder of the descent, Susannah still in the lead. The murmur of voices and scuffle of slippers on raw stone echoed through the vast, dark cavern. Traversing the hundreds of steps so frequently the last few months had improved her stamina. The first weeks, she'd barely made it back to her room. Now she could take the stairs at a trot, although the climb at the end of the night would never be a breeze.

Susannah smiled to herself as they traipsed downward. This was the first movement toward booting Jon Tom from the castle so she could concentrate on the various curses. She didn't need an enigma like the detective on her threshold when she had a kingdom to preserve.

After the second landing, the stairway broadened and the ceiling disappeared in distant shadows. Points of light speckled the blackness on the other side of the handrails. The fairy globes shone more brightly. Here the chilly stairs were smoother and less likely to chafe or trip.

"Race you!" Ella cried and darted past the others to gallop down the stairs. Calypso hiked up her skirts and trotted at a more sedate pace past Susannah and Hortense.

"May I run, too?" Rosa bunched her double white chemises in her hands. "Wait, Ella!"

"Go ahead." Susannah sighed, straightened her chemise and followed at a more sedate pace. After all, she was the eldest. At first the visits had been the grandest adventure of her life. Now it felt like a chore, a chore she wasn't even performing efficiently. She'd made little progress breaking the curse on the princes, but with the *Seven Habits* volume it was more than she'd made with the Female Curse. If it weren't for the fact most of her sisters would mutiny without the visits, she wouldn't come unless she had some theory to test or new spell to try.

Very soon, the twinkling lights became strings of fairy globes draped from tree to tree. Rare fruits and flowers and even jewels hung from the branches of a marvelous orchard, and the velvety green lawn was unmarred by weeds or thin spots. The enchanted place appeared to be a vast cavern, but some aspect of the enchantment ensured they wound up where they started whenever they veered off course. Susannah suspected it was another plane, like the fairy realm of Ulaluna, because any cave this gigantic would have caused vicious sinkholes all over her father's land.

The sisters in front floated across the ground in the lane between the carefully pruned trees, silk chemises billowing behind them like wings. At the end of the lane by the shores of a glistening silver lake waited twelve enchanted princes, standing at attention beside twelve translucent boats that looked for all the world like giant tortoise shells. The sky remained black as tar with lacy skeins of mist floating above the uncountable multitude of fairy globes gleaming in the trees. And in the center of the silver lake stood an elegant white castle, with myriad crenellations glowing and tall, red-capped spires.

Susannah drew in a deep breath. The exotic odor of flowers from climes not found in the Middle Kingdoms permeated the entire land beneath, a scent she'd grown to associate with sexual titillation, if not the sexual fulfillment she might have wished. Another reason the visits had palled after only a few months. She enjoyed the dancing, but what was the point otherwise?

The point was relieving stress. Pleasing her sisters. Defying her parents, when they wouldn't convene the Consortium and lobby to change the inheritance laws.

And now, getting one over on Jon Tom.

Beside her, Hortense rolled her head on her neck, loosening up. "I wish they wouldn't run across the grass. It's not dignified." However, when she saw the bronze and muscular Prince Cuchalain beside her boat, clad in flowing silken trousers and a dark blue vest, even she stepped toward the lake more smartly.

Prince Humbert stood manfully by Susannah's own boat, his brown hair tied back by a red ribbon. A satiny red vest strained across his upper torso and barely brushed the waistband of his simple trousers. No popinjay like Agravar, Humbert wore her scarlet colors in a tasteful manner.

Excellent. She'd been afraid Agravar would be her escort again. The prince who rowed a princess across the lake was entitled to as many dances as he wished, and last night's experience with Agravar had been annoying.

"Be still my heart!" Humbert declared. He took her hands into his. "You look as lovely as a dancing flame this eve." He drew her hands to his lips, his biceps flexing.

"Thank you." Susannah freed her hands. He'd have complimented her had she been wearing sackcloth and mud on her face. He assisted her into the boat where she sat on the padded seat. The rounded bark rocked more than usual in the mild surf, and she clutched the sides until Humbert settled himself and pushed the boat off the shore.

As her escort rowed, she trailed her hand in the sparkling water. Bubbles fizzed gently around her fingers like champagne.

A frown marred the handsome prince's brow. "I wonder, do you carry an anvil with you this eve? The boat moves strangely heavy."

Susannah pulled her hand out of the water and eyed Humbert askance. "Are you saying I've gained weight?"

The prince inspected her consideringly. "You are as luscious as a ripe plum, my heart. But you are not so large as to sink our vessel." The boat lay low in the water and a slight wave sloshed over the edge, wetting Susannah's red silk.

"Oh, drat!" The fabric stuck to her legs in a clammy manner, and she flapped it in a futile attempt to dry it.

"Forgive me!" The prince cursed and pounded his fist upon

his thigh. "I have damaged your beauteous gown! I am a clumsy oaf and not worthy of your attention." He dropped the oars and pulled his long hair.

"It could have happened to anyone." The vehemence of Humbert's dismay surprised Susannah.

"I am a churlish lout. I do not deserve the pleasure of your company."

"Nonsense!" Susannah's exclamation carried across the water to the other boats, closer to the castle than her own. "It's just a little water."

"I hereby relinquish the right to the princess's hand!" he declared in a loud voice. "Instead of delighting in her presence, I must punish myself for such a grievous error."

"Don't be silly! I want to dance with you."

The prince took up the oars and plunged them into the water like a madman, obviously beginning the punishment by breaking his back. Susannah tried again. "There's no need for punishment here. What do you intend to do?"

The prince, his face set in fiendish concentration, didn't answer. The boat skidded across the water with the force of his mighty strokes. It ran onto the beach, and the prince leapt into the water, splashing Susannah. Without a backward glance, he steamed into the castle.

Susannah picked her way out of the boat onto the white beach, mystified by her escort's behavior. The first time they'd visited the land beneath, nervous, dressed in their court regalia to negotiate with the fairies, they'd found the princes instead—the eager, fawning princes. Working out the unwritten rules those first few trips had been, well, interesting.

Every time they ventured below, the men awaited the princesses on the beach and wore the princesses' favorite colors. Though their eyes glazed over when anyone violated the unwritten rules, mostly the princes behaved like performers in an eternal dinner show. Greet princess. Row her across the lake. Dance. Flirt. Eat and drink. Row princess back. Try to steal a kiss.

The sameness had been noteworthy. And then it had just been sameness. Prince Humbert's erratic behavior was disturbing—or was it a breakthrough?

"What was all that about?" Calypso and Prince Daemon

walked with an astounded Susannah up to the castle.

"I have no idea," Susannah said. She held her clinging chemise away from her body.

"Prince Daemon, can you tell us what that was all about?" Calypso turned to him hopefully. He shrugged. The princes never knew much about anything except dancing, drinking and courting the princesses, however unproductive that was.

Susannah indicated her gown. "I got splashed with water and Humbert acted like a mad fly had bitten him."

Prince Yarrow trotted down the steps of the castle. He wore a black silk vest and trousers like most of the unaccompanied princes, and the fabric clung to his sleek waist and hips. His golden hair brushed his collar, and a neat moustache outlined his upper lip. The princes changed clothing, but never their basic appearances. Their hair never grew. Their faces, unless they sported moustaches or beards, were always freshly razored.

"Well met, Prince Yarrow," she said. "Will you escort me this eve?"

"That devil Prince Humbert has insulted your ethereal beauty," Yarrow declared. "I will challenge him and regain your honor, milady!" He clapped a hand to his waist, where a sword would have been had these men possessed blades. His face turned a mottled red shade, and he, too, plunged into the castle, shouting, "Cur! Dog! Come back here, you cowardly swine!"

"My honor is intact," Susannah muttered. "It's not as if my chemise, even wet, is any less decent than Peter's."

"You can have your pick of princes tonight," Lilly commented. "We never get to pick. They always pick us." She turned a sour look on Prince Agravar, her escort. He yawned and buffed his fingernails on his lilac satin vest.

"I suppose," Susannah said. The princesses and escorts marched up the grand marble staircase. She studied her wet silk. "Maybe I could dry the gown faster if I tried a—"

"And maybe you could let nature dry it," Hortense interrupted. "Nature can accomplish some useful things, if we've the patience to let it."

Her sister's sharp comment echoed through the vaulted antechamber. Pale marble veined with traces of gold echoed the gold roses embroidered along the edges of the plush carpet. Suits of unlikely armor stood in alcoves. In the ballroom, spare princes lounged on cushions, eating sweets and drinking nectar from jeweled goblets. Some played a game of dice in the corner near a gigantic fireplace, a game none of the princesses had ever been able to figure out. Humbert and Yarrow were nowhere in sight.

"Everything seems in order." Hortense tugged her dark blue chemise higher on her breasts. The musicians on the small dais, also princes, took turns playing the various instruments. At the moment seven or eight of them strummed an elegant waltz. The floor of octagonal golden tiles gleamed under the huge chandeliers.

"We came here to dance, so take me to the dance floor, darling boy." Peter fluttered her eyelashes at her entranced escort, Prince Tennyson. Gradually all the other sisters gave in to the lure of the waltz. Susannah stood there, alone, and shook her wet gown, a wallflower for the first time in the land beneath.

It wasn't as if she lacked experience being a wallflower. The King and Queen hosted numerous balls to which they invited men from town. The merchants and tradesmen and their families welcomed the opportunity to hobnob with the King and Queen. At those balls, Susannah remained on the sidelines. Her mother would smack her silly if she commandeered one of the young men to dance. She'd never known if it was her appearance or her personality that put off the fellows in town, but put off they were.

The allure of the enchanted princes was that each and every one was happy to fawn over whichever princess he could. They competed for the attentions of all the ladies, even Rosa. Susannah appreciated the plethora of dance partners, the lively atmosphere, the reams of charm directed at her old-maid self. She had no idea how they lived during the day or how they knew when to cross the lake. Nor did the princes have any idea, or any curiosity, about the land above.

Indeed, they cared nothing for solving the puzzle of their lives. They only cared that they got to dance with the princesses, whiling away their time in decadent idleness. There was little jealousy among the princes for the attentions of the women. The scenes of breast-beating rivalry seemed practiced and false. The princes had no concept of what they might have been before they were enchanted. In fact, in the permanent dusk of the land beneath, it could be said they didn't know night from day.

But now as she stood there, water stains blotching her chemise, tendrils of damp hair curling out of her upswept coif, Susannah contemplated the awful feeling of being left out. The other princes, and there seemed to be over a hundred tonight, glanced beyond her as if she didn't exist. Why didn't they flock around her? Why did none ask her to waltz? Frequently one of the unattached men would contrive a dance with one of the other princesses, but no one even greeted her. This was quite unprecedented.

"Yoo-hoo!" Susannah waved to a tall, tawny man with a square jaw. "Prince Fabio!"

He ignored her.

She walked across the smooth floor of the ballroom to stand beside a short fellow she thought was Prince Garamon. She tapped him on the shoulder. "Would you like to dance?"

He cast her a startled glance and hastened out one of the balcony doors.

When she reflected upon the issue—standing alone gave her time—she recalled another example of puzzling conduct. Last night Prince Agravar had declared his wish to ask for her hand in marriage. That had never happened before. Kisses, sure, and other things, but the princes never acknowledged the future or the past.

She should have asked her sisters if they'd noticed anything unusual. But her irritation today with her mother, with Jon Tom, knocked her off balance.

That annoying guard! Her worries about detectives took away from her study time. Her anger at his sleeping habits sent her dancing for the second night in a row, when she was tired and irritable—and hungry from skipping dinner. Too bad Papa didn't put him to work solving the Female Curse instead of the mystery of the twelve slipper-killing princesses.

Susannah hugged her midriff. Perhaps she'd suggest it when the man was fired. True, it was a castle job, but Jon Tom had already changed some of the rules.

"All alone, gorgeous?" A husky voice, barely more than a whisper, tickled her right ear.

Susannah leapt to the left, looked around and saw no one. The nearest princes were sprawled on a mass of silken cushions far to the right, and they weren't watching her.

"What's a nice princess like you doing in a place like this?"

Susannah whirled. No one. Were the princes becoming jokesters? She gazed around the room with growing unease.

"Who's there?"

"Don't be afraid. I won't hurt you." The voice came from her right.

"Where are you? What kind of trick is this?" Susannah reached out her hand, tentatively, and touched nothing.

"Show yourself!" she demanded.

A warm finger, a warm and very invisible finger, touched her lips. "I'm called Prince, ah, John." The husky timbre of his voice played up and down her backbone like a harp string.

She grabbed the finger on her lips and found it connected to a hand, and that to an arm, and that to a body. The ghostly prince's finger left her lips and his hand took hers, holding it away from his chest.

Susannah tried to speak, but the prince said, "Shh!" and led her across the room into one of the side chambers.

There was definitely something up with the enchantment. Either it was so powerful it bent the laws of magic and made the impossible possible—invisibility—or the fairies had been lying about invisibility all along. On the other hand, if this gilded prison was an extension of Ulaluna, perhaps the rules for invisibility were different.

Either way, it didn't explain why this was the first time he'd made himself known.

Once they were in the room, hidden from the view of the others, he dropped her hand. They were in the flower chamber, several miniature fruit trees in pots along the walls and a low balcony that overlooked the palace gardens. The room smelled of roses and a whiff of spice. Mirrors in gold frames hung on the walls, reflecting only her face and form.

Where was he now? Wary, she spun in a complete circle. Why had she come into this empty room with a strange, invisible prince?

None of the princes had ever harmed her, ever forced their

attentions on her, so she wasn't nervous—yet. She stared at a potted plant as if it were him. "Why can't I see you? Invisibility isn't possible."

"Because I'm a mystery." The teasing comment sent another shiver up her spine. Something brushed against her arm. "A mystery you haven't figured out."

A sharp thrill not unlike the feeling of her powers coursed through her. "I haven't? Or no one has?" Was he circling her? Was he behind her or in front? A moist breeze, or a breath, stirred the tiny curls on the back of her neck. She turned again and made herself dizzy.

"You. And no one." He was close enough to reach out and graze her arm, or her cheek, or her hair, but never let her place her hands upon him. It was like a game of blind man, only playing with a man instead of her sisters added a certain element of tension.

She backed toward the door of the room. "Why are you invisible? How is it done?"

"It's part of my..." the voice paused.

"Part of the enchantment?"

"Ah, yes. It's part of the enchantment. I was going to say part of my charm."

Susannah narrowed her eyes. He probably had no idea how it was done. Mortals rarely understood magic. They just accepted it. Accepted when the fairies told them things weren't feasible. "No one else here is invisible. None of the others even know they're enchanted."

"I'm not like the other princes." Prince John chuckled quietly.

"Why are you whispering?" she asked.

She heard the sound of a throat being cleared. "I don't want to attract anyone's attention but yours." One of her curls received a sharp tweak. She smelled the faint spicy odor more.

She clapped a hand to her hair. "Quit doing that!" She spun to rush out the door but came up hard against the man's invisible form.

His hands grasped her arms to keep her upright. He seemed tall, and his palms were rough, callused. She could see the doorway in front of her, and the ballroom beyond that, but

51

every nerve in her system told her she was smack against a warm, male body.

"Dance with me," he whispered.

"Let me go."

His hands slid up and down her bare arms. One dropped to grasp the curve of her hip and the other took her hand, holding it against his chest. His body was hot and hard. Not like the other princes, not like them at all. The scent of warm skin and musty cloth tickled her nostrils.

"Princess," he said, "close your eyes and pretend you're with a normal man, a man enchanted only with your beauty." The hand on her hip caressed her with slow, mesmerizing circles. He continued to the small of her back, where his hand seemed to burn through the thin silk.

Susannah grabbed at the rough cloth over his forearm and halted the liquid progression of his hand upon her body.

"All the princes," she pointed out, "are enchanted with my beauty and my sisters' beauty. That's how it works."

"Why were you all alone out there?"

"I don't know. That has never happened before. We always have dance partners."

"You have a very willing dance partner now, milady. All you have to do is cooperate." His hand resumed its massage of her lower back, and the muscles in his forearm shifted.

He felt so real, as real as any other prince. Perhaps it was because she couldn't see him and could imagine he was anything she wanted? If she lost her hold on him, she might not find him again. He was just a man, another poor, enchanted man. He piqued her interest because he was different, perhaps representative of a change in the enchantment.

If he knew about the enchantment, he might reveal more information about it.

"You tell me why I stood alone, Prince John. If you're so unlike the other princes, tell me who you are, who they are and why you all languish here in this place."

"We languish here in anticipation of your presence."

That silly answer was on par with the type of things the other princes told her. She tried again. "Why did the fairies enchant you? Are you being punished?"

"I have no more knowledge than what I explained, fair one. All I know is I'm here with the others, yet they aren't aware of me. All I know is I've watched you from afar, as graceful as a lark, and wanted you. And now I have you."

Her stomach fluttered, and she twisted in the prince's grasp. "Don't be ridiculous. You do not have me."

"Ah, but I do!" He tightened his arms around her and pulled her against him. A smooth, unseen face buried itself in her neck, and silken hair brushed her jaw. He inhaled deeply and disregarded her struggles.

"Close your eyes, my sweet. Close your eyes and this will be as real to you as it is to me." His hot mouth opened upon her skin, suckling the tender join of shoulder and neck.

Susannah realized she'd gotten herself into a precarious situation. Yes, she sometimes kissed her princely escorts at the end of the night, and yes, she at times allowed further caresses, but the princes never pushed, never took anything that wasn't offered. This man was taking, and she feared she might offer if she didn't put a stop to his clever tongue very quickly.

The King had seen to it all his daughters received training in how to deal with unwanted attentions. Susannah's knee rammed between the prince's legs.

This prince was formed like other men, if his immediate reaction was anything to go by. His arms jerked away from her and she assumed he clutched himself. She could tell where he was by his gasping moans.

"Was that real enough?" she shouted as she flounced toward the ballroom.

At the doorway, a hand on her arm stopped her, turned her. "Princess," he said, his voice strained. "Another part of my enchantment is you can't tell anyone about me."

"What do you mean?"

"If you tell your sisters, if you tell anyone, something horrible will come to pass."

"How do you know this? What will happen?"

"I'm not certain. I just know, as surely as I know I'm different from the others, if you tell anyone about me, I'll suffer greatly for it. Have pity, Susannah."

He called her Susannah. Had she told him her name? She

couldn't recall if the princes ever called her by name.

"I'm sorry I frightened you." His voice moved closer to her and his whisper grew even softer, more insidious. "I'm sorry I held you close and tasted your delicious skin. But the provocation was too great to resist."

"I did nothing to provoke you," she said. "I don't even know you."

"You wore that clinging scarlet chemise. You put your hair up in curls just so. You scented yourself with vanilla and jasmine. You painted your lips with tender roses. Why else do you do these things, why else do you come to this place, if not to provoke me?"

"To have a pleasant evening," Susannah retorted. Heat flared across her face. His accusation hit close to home, for she enjoyed being sought after. Were the men here all tortured by what they couldn't have? All but Prince John seemed cheerful and happy. "I come to please my sisters and to dance. But not with you."

"I'll see you again, Susannah. Princess." He dropped her arm and his voice moved away. "I'll see you again and next time we will dance. But remember. You cannot tell anyone about me." A calloused finger touched her cheek and then nothing.

Chapter Six

A breeze from the balcony blew the scent of honeyflowers into the room, yet the chamber remained vacant. The trees along the walls rustled. She heard only the sweet strains of a waltz.

"Prince John?" Her voice quavered. "Hello?"

"Who are you talking to?" Calypso asked suddenly and goosed Susannah in the rear. Susannah leapt into the air with a shriek.

"No one...nobody." Susannah stumbled over her own tongue.

"So jumpy!" Calypso chortled. "Is the giant badger after you?"

"We should go now," Susannah said. She rubbed the bruise on her buttock. "This night is far too strange."

"I agree." Her sister nodded. "Daemon played a prank on me by pretending to twist his ankle. He lured me into the naughty room—you know which one I mean—and got fresh. I poured my champagne on his head, and he went wild with regret and ran out of the room."

"Just like Humbert." Susannah contemplated how to describe her experience while obeying Prince John's aspect of the curse, just in case. "I had an encounter with a strange prince myself. He was aggressive."

Hortense bustled up to her sisters, her dark gaze snapping with ire. "Was it Prince Theodorix? He's gone quite mad."

"You, too?" Calypso laughed at Hortense's brown hair, which had fallen out of her no-nonsense coronet.

"What's gotten into our princes tonight?" Hortense shoved tendrils of hair from her face.

"I hope it's something I did, but I'll have to research further." Susannah's unease increased, and she turned to the ballroom and counted sisters. She wanted to tell them about Prince John, but who knew what would happen if she did? "Let's round everyone up. Peter is missing, of course. Where's Rosa?"

"Out on the lawn playing one of those nonsensical dice games with Ufta and several other lads." Calypso stuck her thumb in the direction of the front of the palace. "She's fine."

Hortense finished straightening her hair. "Not all the princes are behaving oddly." The remaining princesses were waltzing gracefully about the ballroom, oblivious to the concerns of their elders.

"Well, round them up," Susannah said. She straightened her shoulders and wondered where Peter could be. "I'll start looking for Peter."

"I don't think you should go alone." Hortense's brow furrowed. "Let's go together."

It took some time, but they found everyone without mishap and without encountering Prince John again. Although Peter seemed annoyed, none of the others reported any strange doings. However, once the ladies reached the shore of the silver lake, Susannah, Calypso and Hortense had no one to row their boats.

"Prince Ufta! Yoo-hoo!" Hortense waved to the tow-headed prince, who had just finished a dice game on the close-cropped lawn.

The prince looked up, a startled expression on his face, and gamboled over to the beach. The other princesses were already being rowed across.

Hortense pointed at her boat. "Prince Ufta, we require your assistance. Pray escort us across the lake."

The prince looked at Hortense as if she'd spoken a foreign language. He shuffled from one foot to the other. "I...I cannot do that, milady."

"Whyever not?"

"I do not have your colors."

Hortense shook her finger at the young man. "All we need is someone to row us across the lake. If you can't do it, I'll ask someone else."

"They do not have your colors."

"Where are the princes with our colors, then?"

The prince twisted his hands together. "I know not!"

"Can't you just change clothing?"

"I do not have your colors!"

"What a piece of work!" Calypso gestured rudely at the man.

Ufta, a frantic look in his eyes, took Calypso's movement as his cue to leave. He hastened up the bank and passed the other princes playing the dice game.

"They're useless, useless!" Hortense paced up and down the smooth beach, casting aggravated glances at the dice-tossing men. "Confront them with one minor change, and they go soft in the head."

Watching Hortense's anxiety, Susannah thought the princes weren't the only ones who had trouble dealing with change but wisely kept that comment locked behind her teeth. This change energized her even as it disturbed her. Why had the enchantment shifted? Was it the book? Was it the words of love Agravar had spoken? Words of love had broken curses before. Was it Prince John? What was it?

"The princes were already soft in the manhood," Calypso said. "Perhaps the enchantment is progressing the rest of the way up their bodies."

Hortense shook her head. "This whole evening has been a travesty."

Not how Susannah would describe the evening. "If the enchantment is changing, I wonder what's causing it. The fourth guideline in the second chapter of *Seven Habits* says something about curses in transition once the cure is nigh."

"We can discuss this later." Hortense frowned. "How are we going to get across the lake?"

Susannah sat on the prow of her little red boat and wiggled her toes. Could Prince John be convinced to row them across the lake? Perhaps the calluses on his hands came from doing just that. Perhaps he'd explored and knew more than he was telling. Perhaps...

"Susannah, are you falling asleep?" Calypso kicked the side of her boat and nearly sent her tumbling to the sand. "We can't stay here. Our sisters need you at the top of the stairs to open the door unless you think Ella has figured it out."

"Let's hope not," Susannah muttered. Ella, with her abundant sense of mischief, wouldn't restrain herself from using the magic prankishly.

Hortense gazed across the lake to the little cluster of boats on the surface. The others had turned in their seats to watch their sisters on the beach in front of the glowing castle. "Will we have to wait until tomorrow night for an escort?" she fretted. "Mother and Father will be frantic if we disappear entirely. And who knows what these pudding-headed princes will do?"

"We'll row ourselves." Calypso hiked up her chemise and stepped into her boat. "Come, sisters, I'll go first."

Susannah helped Hortense into Calypso's boat. "Are you sure three would be safe in these tubs?"

"This isn't controlled by the rule of three, Sister. They could hold four. Got seats for four," Calypso said.

"I haven't rowed in ages, but I'm sure I remember how." Susannah climbed into her own boat. It rocked wildly, and she barely saved herself from a tumble into the shallow water.

Calypso laughed. "Yeah, you still have it," she teased. "Hortense and I will be close in case you decide to take a swim. Can you still swim?"

"Of course," snapped Susannah. "There's something wrong with this boat."

"Whatever you say." Calypso pretended to get her oar stuck in the water with an expression of mock horror.

Susannah balanced on the rower's bench as the boat tipped from side to side and pulled an oar out of the lock. It took nearly all her strength to nudge the leaden boat. Of course, she'd never tried this before. Perhaps it was always awkward.

Finally she scooted the boat off the beach and fumbled the oar back into the lock. She grabbed the handles and swung them forward. The flats of the paddles splashed into the water and she heaved back, but the oars skipped along the surface. Susannah peered toward the castle. Was Prince John on the beach, laughing at her?

"Are you sure you don't want to get in our boat?" Hortense called. From the echo of her voice, their boat was a good distance into the lake. "Cal seems to have the hang of this."

"I'll get it." A few more awkward splashes and she managed to move the small vessel across the water.

"Steer to the right, Susannah," Hortense called. "No, my right."

"It doesn't shift easily," Susannah panted. Her arms and shoulders grew tense with the strain. She wouldn't be doing much lifting tomorrow, she could tell already.

With encouragement from Calypso and Hortense, the two little boats floated across the silver lake. Was the water safe to drink? Sweat soaked her back, and she was parched. The spicy scent of Prince John left over from their embrace kept tantalizing her nose. When they made it to the bedchamber—she didn't even want to think of the stairs—she'd drink a whole pitcher of juice. Too bad she didn't know a breeze spell to cool her overheated body.

Her hair tumbled down her neck and shoulders, a hot blanket on her perspiring skin. She continued to tug on the oars. Calypso, she noticed, wasn't even breaking a sweat.

It seemed like they rowed for an hour. Calypso paused frequently to allow Susannah to catch up. It had never taken this long with a prince at the oars. Hortense continued to call out directional advice until Susannah wanted to throttle her. Did it matter where she landed, as long as she got there? Raw spots opened on her palms and perspiration drenched her chemise.

When they neared the far bank, she could hear her sisters cry encouragement. She stopped rowing and glanced around. The princes who'd escorted the sisters sat in their little boats like statues. She rowed a bit more until she bumped against the bank.

Ella splashed into the water and helped Susannah drag the boat onto the shore. "Thank you, dear," Susannah panted. "I think my arms are going to fall off."

"I'll rub your shoulders when we get upstairs." Lilly brushed Susannah's hair back from her face. "You poor thing!"

"Did you manage to drive off even the enchanted men?"

Peter asked.

"Yes, Peter, that's exactly what happened." She rolled her shoulders to work out some of the cramps. Raising her arms above her head pained the muscles in her chest and back. Oh, for her lost youth and resiliency!

Brimming with energy, Calypso strode over and patted her back. "Good job, Sis."

It pained Susannah to realize Calypso, so near to her in age, was unaffected. "Aren't you even a little tired?"

"Sure." Calypso worked her arms back and forth. "That was a tidy workout. But I don't sit around on my duff all day reading books and eating jam."

By the time they reached the top of the stairs, several sisters were dragging Susannah. The princesses huddled in the dark room outside the bedchamber like lost sheep. She leaned against the place where she would create the door, panting. The stair climb at the end of the evening had never been pleasant but never this much of a trial, either. Not even at first. Her sisters milled around in the dark, complaining and yawning.

Susannah concentrated. Light flickered around the door, which took longer than usual to coalesce. She felt no thrill using the magic, not when she had so little to give. What if she hadn't been able to summon the strength to open it? They'd have had to remain here until her powers replenished. Her vision blurry, Susannah stumbled through the armoire and straight into her bed.

"Would some wonderful sister fetch me a gallon of juice?" she begged. "Jon Tom hasn't been instructed to prevent us from basic necessities, and right now juice is necessary for me to remain in the land of the living."

"Call a maid and have them deliver it," Esme suggested.

"They're all sound asleep." Susannah twisted and tried to find a more comfortable position, but no matter how she turned, her shoulders and back ached. "There's no reason to wake a maid when one of us can do it. Just be careful when you open that bedamned squeaky door that you don't wake our snoozing guard."

"Do you suppose Jon Tom used a magic mirror while we were out?" Lilly slipped into a robe.

"If he did, Mother and Father would already be in here with the padlocks and chains," Susannah managed to groan out.

Lilly peeked out the bedchamber door. "He's gone! Mr. Tom is gone."

"What?" Susannah propped herself up on rubbery arms. "Where is he?"

Lilly left the door standing open and walked out into the corridor, looking right and left. Ella scampered out the door, too.

"What are you doing out of your room?" Susannah heard a man's voice call from somewhere outside.

Lilly shrieked. "Mr. Tom! We were... I was...going to the kitchen for a glass of juice!"

Ella raced back into the room and slammed the door. Everyone leapt into bed in chemises and paint, earrings and slippers, and pulled the covers to their chins.

Susannah tried something she'd never done before. She exerted the last of her energy to focus her powers on listening from her bed. She was amazed it worked, considering her recent adventures.

"Milady," she heard Jon Tom say, "do you expect me to believe that?"

Susannah frowned. Why shouldn't he believe it?

"Yes?" Lilly said uncertainly.

"Perhaps I might peek at your sisters and make sure everyone is accounted for." Even through the stone, Susannah heard amusement in Jon Tom's voice.

"They're asleep," Lilly said. "Where were you? Our other guards didn't leave."

"Milady, even a guard has to use the necessary on occasion."

Susannah could sense Lilly's embarrassment through the wall.

"Perhaps, Princess, you might want to go back in your room and put on some warmer shoes before gallivanting about the castle. If you say your sisters are there, I'll have faith in your honesty and goodness." Susannah released the last trickle of her power and sank more deeply into the soft bed, her ears ringing. It wasn't at all pleasant, she observed, to use her store of fairy magic down to the last drizzle.

Lilly reentered the room. She kicked off her dancing slippers and donned a pair of fleece bed shoes.

"Thank you, Lilly," Susannah whispered. "That was very brave."

Lilly smiled. "My heart nearly pounded out of my skin when Mr. Tom came striding down the corridor. Normally I'd be happy to set eyes on such a handsome man, but he startled me. I'll be back in a trice."

They were safe, after the closest call in the history of their nocturnal visits. It had been a strange, disturbing evening, and Susannah hoped she slept without dreams, dreams of invisible princes, dreams of endlessly rowing across a gleaming silver lake.

Chapter Seven

"I'm not getting up today," Susannah informed her mother when the Queen woke her. Why she could never send a sweet, soft-voiced maid to get them from their beds, Susannah didn't know. Or perhaps she did.

Her mother paused in mid-harangue and regarded her incredulously.

Susannah took a deep breath and flexed her shoulders against the mattress. Her muscles screamed, and her ears rang faintly from her magical overextension. "I believe I may be ill."

The Queen turned to Esme. "Is Susannah ill?"

"Yep," Esme said. "And I am too." She climbed back into bed.

"That won't work when you've already rolled out of bed." The Queen chuckled, but not with amusement. "Get up."

Esme opened her mouth, probably to say if she wasn't sick then neither was Susannah, but Calypso sat upon the end of Esme's bed and grasped Esme's ankle.

"Susannah is ill," Calypso said. "Esme is not."

"It might be catching," Esme grumbled. "I might get it tomorrow."

"I doubt that," Susannah said. Was there any way she could go to the court healer without having to reveal the reason for her muscular discomfort? A hot bath and healing draught would be wonderful, though she had no idea what would remove the bees from her head.

Inspired, she explained, "My muscles are sore like I have influenza. I can barely raise my arms or turn my head."

The Queen walked to Susannah's bed and yanked her arm into the air. Susannah yelped as pain lanced the cramped muscles. The Queen placed a cool hand on her forehead. "You feel hot, and that was an honest wail. I'll notify the healer. Perhaps a spring physick is in order."

Susannah shook her head against the pillow. "There's no need for a purge. Really."

"No one else is ill?" The Queen's eagle eyes speared everyone in the room. "This has no connection to your clandestine activities?"

"What clandestine activities, Mama?" Calypso looked up from plaiting her hair.

The Queen's lips pursed. "All right, Susannah, you may stay abed today. But if you're not well by tomorrow, you'll have a physick."

Susannah heaved a grateful sigh. Even though her sisters rose and took no particular pains to be quiet, she fell dreamlessly asleep and woke only when a young maid brought a cup of salts from the court healer for her bath.

"Reynald says to drop these in a bath you've run as hot as you can stand it," said the child as Susannah rubbed her eyes. "If the ache doesn't go away, send for a tincture of willow bark."

"Thank you, Emily." Susannah lurched out of bed and accepted Emily's help pulling her robe over her night rail. The maid accompanied her to the finely appointed bathing chamber down the hall and manipulated the porcelain levers until hot water poured from the magic spigot into one of the animal-footed tubs. Washbasins on dainty white pedestals and gold-framed mirrors lined the other walls. Several sundry chests completed the room's accoutrements.

"Thank goodness we have enchanted taps. I'd hate for all this water to have been lugged from the kitchens," Susannah said. The salts Emily poured into the bath smelled of the sea. Susannah swished her hands in the water to dissolve the grains and slumped down the back of the smooth tub. The delicious water soothed her sore arms and shoulders, and after her extra sleep, her headache was gone, as was the buzzing in her ears.

"Can you fetch that tincture of willow bark? Have Cook make it into sugared tea."

Before leaving, Emily placed a towel and some vanilla and

jasmine soap on the stand next to the tub as well as the silver bell that matched the one on her girdle.

"Ring if you think of anything else," she said and then skipped out of the room with the cheerful good health of a child.

Steam rose about Susannah as she soaked, eyes closed, enjoying the heat and the delicate tang of magic from the spigots, something she could sense now that she'd found the magic inside herself. Her thoughts strayed to the previous night and her discoveries.

Ah, privacy. A rare and delightful possession in a household of eleven nosy sisters and two suspicious parents. She wriggled against the back of the tub and sighed with bliss.

As if on cue, the bathing room door creaked, and Susannah's eyes popped open. Here in the tub, nude and sore, she was completely vulnerable. Surely Jon Tom wouldn't...

Ella slipped into the room and closed the door. "I thought I might find you here."

Susannah inhaled a deep breath of the flowery steam to calm her startled heartbeat. "Aren't you supposed to be working?"

"I have some ideas about last night. Plus I have a report on Mr. Tom." Ella settled on the smooth tile floor beside Susannah's tub and gazed up at her.

Ella with ideas about last night, Susannah thought. One of the last things she needed, right next to Jon Tom walking into the bathing chamber.

"What have you found out about the detective?" Susannah began to scrub her arms and legs. She wasn't going to get the peace and quiet she longed for, after all.

"I'll trade information for information." Her sister flashed a cheeky grin. "Aren't curses often broken when true love is involved? Do you think somebody has fallen in love?"

"Are you in love with Prince Fabio?" Susannah teased. She stretched, wincing, to scrub her feet. The hot water of the bath stung the raw spots on her palms.

"Of course not!" Ella flicked her fingernail against Susannah's tub with a clicking sound. "Men are all right, but I like magic better."

Ella was like a puppy with a purloined stocking when it

came to magic. "We've discussed this, dear. Magic isn't like learning to shoot a bow and arrow or dance a reel. I don't know why I can do it, but no other humans can. It's probably not safe, and can you imagine what Hortense would do if she had to agonize about us both?"

"Hortense is a worrywart. She and the others shouldn't restrict you." Ella scowled and fiddled with the bottles on the little table beside the tub.

Susannah sighed. "We all agreed on the safe list. There are certain things I can't do and shouldn't try. Even the fairies have a FairFairy Oath, or so it's rumored." As far as she was concerned, the safe list was settled and she didn't want to whack on that dead horse. Thinking about Hortense's unwavering disapproval depressed her because it was the exact reaction the rest of the Middle Kingdoms was likely to have.

Not to mention the fairies.

She changed the subject. "What did you hear about Mr. Tom?"

Ella made a snorting sound. "First tell me what's in that curse book."

Should she give Ella specific information? She'd been wishing for another mind to think through the strangeness of last night, and Ella's was razor sharp.

"The first chapter of *Seven Habits* is about planning your curse. It covers the ripple effects that must be taken into account. The second chapter involves creating a curse mission statement and outlining how the curse will behave once the cure is enacted."

"You're right. That's not helpful. A mission statement? Come on. What are the exact guidelines?"

Susannah frowned and rubbed the cake of soap over her legs underwater. "It's hard to say. The text reads like a self-help book instead of a practical rulebook. One of the things it advises is to consider how the curse will come to an end as it's constructed. Then something about keeping your strands robust. In chapter two, I figured out guidelines one, two and four."

Ella touched a tongue to her upper lip. "So casting a curse causes ripples. That's obvious. Look at the Female Curse. It has tidal waves, not ripples. Maybe Malady never read the *Seven*

Habits book."

"Or maybe she wrote it," Susannah said with a laugh. "There's no way to tell."

"Does it say if there are ripples when a curse starts to break? Like how Briar Rose's thorn wall let the prince in after a hundred years? Maybe the princes have been there a set amount of time."

Ella was so astute! Though it didn't mention ripples, the fourth guideline read, "Figure out how the curse will act once the cure has begun, which places the curse in transition." Unfortunately, Susannah's sister rarely applied her mental acuity to anything constructive. "I have no idea if the time factor comes into play and no idea if the princes' behavior is indicative of an end to the curse. If it's caused by something we've done, I'm at a loss. Our behavior hasn't changed, and I haven't tested any spells recently."

"Have you noticed anything else strange or just Humbie's freak-out?"

Besides Prince John the Mysterious and his hot, hard, invisible body? Susannah realized she was washing her breasts for the second time and snatched her hands out of the water. "Agravar said he loved me and wanted to marry me the night before last."

"That's it!" Ella shot to her feet. "Aggie loves you! Who'd have thought?"

Why wouldn't a man love her? Susannah pursed her lips. "That's not it. He's already forgotten. Hand me that shampoo, will you?"

Ella grabbed a white china bottle from the stand beside the tub. "From what I overhead in the kitchen, nothing else in the world has changed. No boy babies and the FAE is still holding strong on the whole noninterference with the Female Curse thing. I wish we could get our hands on the broadsheets."

Susannah decided not to tell her how to gain access to the tabloids their mother forbade them, and anyone else in the castle, to read. She was surprised Ella didn't already know. "The curse on the princes wouldn't affect the upper land, necessarily." She poured shampoo in her palm and handed the bottle back. She struggled to lather her hair without raising her arms above her head.

"Does the book mention that FairFairy Oath thingamabob?"

"No, and it's my turn to ask questions," she said while sudsing. "Is Jon Tom in a snit because of our ruined slippers this morning?" The thought of her mother ringing a peal over the detective's head gave Susannah a surge of pleasure.

Ella propped a hip on the rim of the tub. "He's testing the grounds for secret passages."

"Yet another tunnel search? What does this make, the fifth?" Susannah smirked. "Did you see him yourself?"

"I overheard a conversation Cook had with the fairy astrologer this morning. Madame says she can feel him using a depth finder."

"So he does have magical assistance," Susannah grumbled under her breath. She hadn't noticed any surges, like she sometimes did when the fairies came to renew spells. "Certain enchanted items would be a challenge. We tricked Mother's magic mirror, but it makes me wonder what else he has. He had a permanent ink pen in the interview."

Ella grinned. "I can search his belongings."

"We're not that desperate yet. What else did you hear?"

"He grew up in Pavilion, and his family runs a pastry shop. He left home when he wasn't yet twenty and solves cases for fairies because they pay well." Ella giggled. "Cook heard he doesn't have a sweetheart, but his female clients always fall in love with him. Do you suppose one of us will—"

"Don't even finish such a ridiculous sentence. Of course we won't." Susannah spat soap out of her mouth.

"Maybe we'll see him during our leisure activity on Sixday." Ella corked the shampoo bottle. "I wonder what Mother plans for us this Sixday?"

Susannah drew in a deep breath and ducked her head underwater to rinse—and cool her head. She detested that she, a grown woman, was completely under the thumb of her parents. The Queen planned their work days and their leisure days. The princesses had little authority and even less say.

But that was the way of things in the Middle Kingdoms, worsened by the Female Curse. More and more women fled their unwedded, unbedded and corseted fates, took up with lower-class men, troupes of actors. Despite her displeasure with the social structure, she wasn't inclined to toss aside her family and her kingdom in useless rebellion.

Her breath staled in her lungs. Susannah surfaced and water streamed from her head and tangled hair. She rubbed a tendril between two fingers. Still soapy. She slid forward and water sloshed over the side of the tub.

Ella scrambled sideways. "Hey, dry person here."

"How did you escape work?" Susannah dunked the back of her head in the water and shook her hair around. Not many girls in the aristocracy labored like Susannah and her sisters. The Queen, before marrying their father, had been a poor baron's daughter. She believed in the salubrious effect hard work and constant occupation had upon character. If her mother was right, all twelve of them should be angels, yet Susannah knew they weren't. Far from it.

"Cook sent me to the herb garden. I detoured." Ella glanced at the ornate cuckoo clock on the wall. "Esme will probably tell on me. Why is she such a carp?"

"I don't know." Susannah shrugged, and the movement tweaked her aching shoulders. Would she feel like this every day when she grew old?

Ella cocked her head to one side. "Maybe she's a changeling. I can understand why the fairies wouldn't have wanted her."

"It won't wash," Susannah said. "Esme is the spitting image of Grandmere."

"Emphasis on spitting." Ella replaced the shampoo on the shelf. "I also overheard Cook say the Hinterlander incursions in Orzo have increased because they didn't have enough gold to pay the fairies to renew the wards. Isn't that the kingdom where the Queen and princesses got stuffed in jail because they tried to rule themselves? Treason and such?"

"Yes. King Nobbyknees died without issue," Susannah said.

"What a stupid name," Ella said.

Susannah grunted. "Don't you remember any of your Middle Kingdoms history? It was Malady's christening gift to him, to have unattractive knees." Susannah forced her parents to keep her, as the sort-of heir, abreast of the current political situation and disseminated the information to whichever siblings were curious.

Ella wasn't usually one of them. "That won't happen to us."

Their own country, Foresta, was the closest to Oldtree Forest, and on the other side of that lurked the Hinterlands, but their kingdom was prosperous enough to keep the wards fresh. For now. If they had no leader trained in kingdom management, they had no stability. If they had no stability, they had no income. If they had no income, they had no gold for the fairies. If they had no gold for the fairies, the fairies would cease to ward Oldtree Forest.

Susannah rubbed her temples.

"You're going to rant about the Kingdom Laws now, aren't you? Ugh. Time to go. What does caraway look like?" asked Ella

"Tiny leaves, pale pink flowers. You should pay attention in the stillroom. Herbs, potions and other focus objects clarify my power. Even fairies use them sometimes."

"I won't need all that rubbish when I find my magic." Ella rolled her eyes and slipped out the door of the bathing chamber.

Susannah didn't share Ella's conviction. Had she been that brash as a teen? Perhaps her years of fruitless struggle to save the kingdom had beaten down her spirit.

She slumped into the tub so only her head stuck out of the water. Why kid herself? She'd been sullen and snappy as a teenager, angry about her fate and angry about the world. Ella's optimism had never been a part of Susannah's personality.

She did, however, understand Ella's drive to work magic. In her early twenties, she'd unearthed a dusty fairy primer in the library and tried the exercises. That day was as fresh and clear in her memory as if it had been this morning. Joy had surged through her when she realized she could work magic, the same feelings she experienced when she used her power now.

The water had cooled, so she ran the hot spigot, reluctant to leave the tub.

Finding her power had been like breaking a secret code. Dibs and dabs of spells hidden in the texts of songs, poems and fables leapt out at her. Nina helped, even if she'd displayed no glimmerings of magic. Nor had Ella, which was probably for the best.

Several months ago, she combined a transportation ritual from a child's prayer book with a wish-fulfillment spell. She planned to access Ulaluna and petition the fairies directly. The result had been the stairway to the twilight land of the princes. Not the fairy realm, exactly, and not the fulfillment of the wish, exactly, but certainly fascinating. It had been the biggest spell she'd ever tried. All other attempts to access Ulaluna had fizzled.

After the fact, it occurred to her the fairies would hardly be pleased a mortal could access their homeland. The magic use she could conceal with the wish spell, but breaking into their realm—not her finest idea. Desperation wasn't complementary to good sense.

Susannah rubbed her eyes and finished rinsing. After squeezing her hair and winding it in a knot atop her head, she rang the silver bell.

Emily came through the door a moment later, carrying a mug in one hand and a bundle of fabric across the other arm.

"My tea?" Susannah, arms and shoulders loosened, pushed herself out of the tub. Water slopped onto the floor.

"Yes, Princess. Do you want it now or shall I help you dress first?"

"I'll take it now." She wrapped a towel around her like a toga and stood in the middle of the warm bathing chamber, her toes paddling in the water on the floor. She sipped the bittersweet tea gingerly.

Emily said, "I had Cook add sugar to the tea, but nothing covers the taste of willow bark."

"My currant-grape jelly would cover it. Too bad I didn't have you put the tincture in a scoop of that."

Susannah pinched her nose with one hand and drank down the whole mug. "Ugh!"

"It will help your aches, milady. Now let me get you into a clean night rail and brush your hair for you."

"Let's go to the bedchamber for the hair brushing." After Susannah stepped into a clean pair of pantaloons, Emily tossed the white flannel over her head, which settled around her legs, and Susannah did up the buttons. Then she followed the maid into the hall, lethargic from the hot bath.

The stones of the hallway were chilly beneath her bare feet. Except at the peak of summer, the castle's hallways and most of its rooms remained cool.

"Princess Susannah!" called a man's voice behind her.

She whipped around, and her wet knot of hair tumbled down and thumped against her back. Jon Tom strode down the hallway with a smirk upon his handsome face.

"Bull stones!" she hissed. Her hair hung in a clumpy tangle nearly to her waist and dampened her gown. "What do you want, Detective?"

Jon Tom held out his hands placatingly. "A moment of your time, Princess."

"I'm not properly attired. Your questions will have to wait."

"Your sleeping gown is modest enough, milady. I can't see an inch of your flesh."

Susannah crossed her arms over her chest. "I can't stand about in the hallway talking to a man while in my nightgown. Are you entirely unaware of the limits of propriety, sirrah?"

"I'm aware enough to know the quickest way across the line." The man's black eyes twinkled, and if he'd had a moustache, she had no doubt he would have twirled it. However, his tan face was unmarred by stubble. Very well groomed, was the detective.

"Then you're aware that you're crossing the line now. I'm not even wearing a robe!" She backed against the corridor wall so he couldn't see the wet part of her nightgown.

"Princess Susannah, you're a woman grown."

"Mr. Tom, I'm the daughter of a king with certain standards of decorum to maintain."

The corner of Jon Tom's lips twitched, and he took a step forward. "I'm sure you work very hard to maintain those standards in the wee hours when you send your sister for juice in makeup, earrings and satin dancing slippers. And Ella, if I'm not mistaken, a child barely past her woman-time, was out in the hall in something that greatly resembled a chemise."

"My sisters like to experiment with their clothing. Try new styles." Susannah's face grew hot. He might think he was onto something—and in fact he was—but his knowledge amounted to nothing. Perhaps he assumed any odd behavior exhibited by the sisters stemmed from herself. Perfidious man.

Jon Tom took another step closer and loomed over her. "In the middle of the night? I don't believe you."

Susannah inched to one side until his arm came up to block her way. She would have to duck under it or brush against it to get away.

"Unhand me."

"I don't have a hand on you," he said. Something puckish flashed across his face, and dimples appeared in his lean cheeks. "Shall I remedy that?"

He was enjoying this far too much. She looked around for Emily but the child stood in the bedchamber doorway, her mouth agape. Susannah heaved a disgusted sigh to show him she was annoyed, not unnerved. "Don't force me to call the guards."

"Your special guard is right in front of you, Princess. There's no need to call me." The man's velvet voice rubbed her skin with an almost physical sensation.

Susannah tilted up her chin. "I'll call the guards, Detective, I swear it. Your behavior is reprehensible."

"Milady," Emily squeaked, "your hair is making a puddle on the floor."

Jon Tom backed away and gave a courtly bow. "I concede! I don't suppose now would be a good time to test your bedchamber for secret passages."

"What do you think you can find that nobody else has?" The thought of him in her room, sorting through her things, gave her a shiver.

"I imagine I can dig something up."

"Stay out of our bedchamber. Mother and Father checked it thoroughly, and you have no business retracing their steps. You don't even have Wilbur with you."

"Wilbur?"

"The magic sniffing pig. They've tried everything and found nothing because there's nothing to find. There's no need for you to enter our chambers. In fact, I forbid it."

"Your mother gives me my orders, Princess." His eyes sparkled as if his assignment were nothing but a frolic. Nothing that would damage his reputation should he fail. Did he expect them to topple like his other clients? Did he expect her to fall in love with him?

Would he, in fact, encourage it?

She wanted to wrinkle his poise like a sheet of unwanted paper, and she couldn't think of a single way to do it. All she could do was stare.

As if aware of her thoughts, Jon Tom smiled. "I heard you were ill and I imagine you need your...bed. Thank you for this delightful moment of your time."

"I didn't give you a moment of my time," she replied and then frowned because she had. "Does this mean you won't need another moment?"

"I intend to be around for a long time. I'm sure there'll be many moments between us."

Susannah raised a nervous hand to her collar. There he went again, his insinuations tracing fingertips down her spine. Why couldn't she control her reaction to this man? Or was it an automatic response to a virile male, a healthier specimen than the enchanted princes?

Dragon knows she hadn't been around many of those.

Before she could reply, Jon Tom brushed past her. She walked to Emily, placed her hand upon the girl's shoulder and watched him disappear around the corner.

"I cannot like that man, Emily," she said, more to herself. "He has no respect for propriety."

"Indeed, milady," the maid agreed.

Chapter Eight

For the next several nights, Susannah and her sisters slept the sleep of the innocent. If Susannah was troubled by the feeling that invisible men watched over her bed, she said nothing to her sisters. Instead she reminded them to dodge Jon Tom if he sought to interrogate them. "Pretend ignorance of anything save your jewels, your hair baubles and your gowns," Susannah instructed. Such a task would be easier for some than others.

However, the man had a homing device fixed upon her. He could scarcely have had time to spy on anyone else. He popped up at the most inconvenient times to ask questions and wrack her nerves with his dark, knowing looks. The day she was assigned to the garden, he held her spare clippers and commented on her well-rested appearance. When she was sent to the weaving room, he pointed out the flaws in her cloth. And when she cheated her mother's schedule and escaped to the library, Jon Tom was there, reading over her shoulder and selecting books for her off the shelves.

Why had he fixated on her? If Susannah had been a normal woman, she might have suspected a partiality on his part, and certain of her sisters suggested it, but that was absurd. He was a spy, and she was the puzzle. The butterflies in her stomach when he looked at her were from exasperation and nothing else. Any pleasure she took in making him laugh was imagined.

After several days of Jon Tom's constant attendance, Susannah convinced her mother to assign her to the library with Calypso, Peter and Hortense. She didn't tell them about the invisible prince, but they speculated quietly about the enchanted princes' behaviors.

"The princes are not themselves." Susannah ticked off examples on her fingers. "Humbert became distressed by my wet gown, Yarrow caught whatever illness he had, Daemon tried to seduce Calypso in the Divan Room and Theodorix tried to make love to Hortense's hair." Then there was Prince John, but she didn't mention him. "What have we done differently than in the previous months?"

"He didn't try to make love to my hair," Hortense said. "He wanted to loosen me up."

"What a joke!" Calypso said with a laugh. "Maybe one of us was kind to a fairy in disguise. Anybody given their last bit of bread to an old fart lately?"

"I think it's like men to be inconstant," Hortense said. "If given a task, they were bound to cast it off sooner or later."

Calypso brushed paper bits off the table with her quill pen. "If men always fail in their tasks, doesn't that make them constant failures?"

Hortense heaved a disgusted sigh. "You know what I mean."

"It's not their personalities. If one of us had been kind to a fairy, she'd have given us a wish," Susannah said. "It's almost as if the spell were wearing thin. Like some of the curse strands have snapped and the curse is in a transition phase. We could be in danger."

"You being the expert on spells, of course," Peter said with an eye roll. "You have some trick you want to try and Hortense won't approve if you can't convince her it's necessary."

"I have to learn, if I'm to break one of these curses," Susannah said. "And no, I don't have a trick I want to try."

Peter shook her head, and the fading sun from the skylights struck blue sparks from her smooth black hair. "You've been looking for an excuse to stop visiting the princes since we started. First it was cruel to them, then it was cruel to our parents, now it's dangerous."

"All those things are true," Susannah insisted. "I need to research what happens when a large curse begins to wear off before we can go again." She wouldn't say *if* they went again, because she didn't welcome the spat such a proclamation would trigger.

"Don't do any needless experiments," Hortense said. "I

agree with Peter on that."

"Of course you do." Although she abided by the safe list, her sisters' fears were like a broken music box that only played three notes. She'd heard them all before in varying combinations until a single tone roused her hackles. So she rose from the table and wandered into the stacks, selecting the books she had secreted in various places. No matter their other thoughts about her magic use, her sisters wouldn't mind that *Unsightly Uses of Invisibility* was one of her choices. It was considered a joke book.

She returned with a selection of tomes to find Jon Tom, dressed in black leather breeches and a dark blue tunic, loafing on the edge of the table, whispering to Peter. He bit into a large red apple and the crisp sound of it echoed through the quiet chambers.

Her stomach clenched in a way that had become habitual at the sight of him. She hadn't yet encountered him today and had been wondering where he was.

"What are you doing here?" Susannah asked. Her father had approved the man's request to be unchaperoned with the princesses. The Queen in particular took great delight in his activities and allowed him to dine with the royal family. Susannah hoped the preferential treatment caused Jon Tom trouble in the guardhouse where he slept—if he did sleep. No, wait, she knew where he slept—he slept on a pile of cushions outside the princesses' bedchamber like a man unconcerned with keeping his job.

"Shh, milady." Jon Tom put a finger to his lips. "Your strident tones are out of place in the library."

Calypso and Hortense had had the presence of mind to spread their books and papers across her magical research. How could she explain the manuscripts in her hands? The sly detective was bound to notice, and what Justice Chamber issue could she claim demanded she read a joke book about invisibility?

Peter laughed, a silvery tinkle of sound. "My sister hates for her studies to be interrupted. I'd rather be in the orchard amidst all the birds and bees myself." She took the apple from Jon Tom's hand and nibbled it, matching her mouth to the place where his had been.

Susannah considered marching right back to the shelves, but that would look suspicious. And he'd follow her, asking his strange questions, which seemed to have little to do with any sensible investigation. Why on earth could he need to know her favorite books or whether she preferred vanilla to chocolate? Instead she walked to the far side of the table and thumped the books down beside Calypso.

"Here are the books you asked for," she said. Calypso grunted and set the stack on the floor. "Do you need any more?"

"A little something about Kingdom Law 212," Hortense requested with a glare at Peter. "Peter could use the Gardialli tome on Kingdom Law 333."

"The Kingdom Law regarding unions between nobles and members of the lower classes, if I'm not mistaken," Jon Tom said with a smile. "Princess Peter, is the Justice Chamber question you study a romantic issue?"

"She needs Appendix D in particular, which states a commoner or peasant who importunes a person of noble birth can be banished from the kingdom." Hortense pursed up her mouth and sniffed. "With the Female Curse, troubles of this type are unfortunately abundant."

Reassuring that at least one of her sisters held Jon Tom in as much distrust as she did. Susannah had begun to worry the rash partiality many of the princesses had formed for the detective might cause them to relax their guard.

"Ah, if only love could be ruled by Kingdom Law." Jon Tom held a hand to his heart. "Wouldn't the world be an easier place?"

"It would be an unexciting place," Peter murmured. She trailed her fingertip on the moist white inside of the apple and licked the juices in a suggestive manner. From her vantage point, Susannah saw Calypso kick Peter under the table.

Jon Tom didn't appear to hear the muffled *thunk* or see Peter flinch. "I came in here to ask if any of you—"

Susannah cut him off. "You're always prying. You had your chance to interrogate us, and this constant hounding keeps us from our duties." She used a harder tone and harder words than she felt, because much of what he'd done the past week hadn't been prying. It had been more along the lines of companioning.

"The good detective always seeks opportunities to cross examine the culprits," Jon Tom replied. "Surely you know that much, Princess, from your own...investigations." He picked up *The Seven Habits of Highly Effective Curse Fairies* from beneath Hortense's stack of shepherding resolutions and flipped through it idly.

Susannah doubted he could read Ancient Dullish, but nevertheless she tensed. In a show of unconcern, she raised her eyebrows. "As the only detective in the world, how could you know what a good detective might do?"

Jon Tom placed the slim volume back on the table. Susannah's spine slumped with relief, thankful he didn't dig amidst the parchments on which she was translating the text. Even Peter observed Jon Tom less like a piece of ripe fruit and more like an unpredictable stallion. Peter wouldn't wish anything or anyone to interfere with their nocturnal activities.

Unexpectedly, the detective licked his fingertip and held it aloft, as if seeking a draft. "I detect some tension in the air." He smirked when all four sisters' eyes widened. "See there? I'm a very good detective."

On that note, he bowed to the princesses and strolled out of the library.

"That man is a bother," Hortense said, rearranging her papers into a semblance of order.

"That man is dangerous," Susannah agreed. She collapsed into the chair beside Calypso with a *whump*, oddly disappointed he was gone.

"That man is too smart." Calypso leaned over the table and dragged Susannah's work across it.

"That man turns me on," Peter sighed and rested her chin upon her hands.

"I came back to our room to change into a clean frock," Ella told her sisters that night, "and who do you think I found in our room, knocking on the walls and cupboard doors?"

"Who?" Rosa gasped. "The giant badger?"

"No, silly. Mr. Tom! He was in our room, poking about!"

He had done such a thing, when she asked, no told, him not to? "That bloody..." Susannah bit off an extremely crude name and instead gnawed on her thumbnail.

Her sisters chattered about the detective while Susannah destroyed her cuticles. All men annoyed her today, all useless men who just made things worse. After her encounter with Jon Tom, she'd hassled her father about Kingdom Laws 134 and 333. He'd pretended to be too busy with a Justice Chamber decision Hortense had already resolved, which meant he hadn't called an emergency Consortium to discuss the inheritance laws as he'd promised. As he'd promised a hundred times he'd do.

Over the past thirty-five years, the only thing applicable to the Female Curse to come out of the yearly Consortium summits had been the definition of great feats that allowed commoners to become noble. The Consortium's majority vote was the only way Kingdom Laws could be changed. All thirteen kings, thirteen law-trained archivists appointed by the Emperor, and the Emperor himself comprised the group.

Emperor Hubert Halbert Houston the Fifth, otherwise known as Ice Face for reasons unknown to Susannah, was an old and not very bold man. He possessed a son to follow in his footsteps, Halbert, otherwise known as Halbert the Stench, which was more than most of the current Middle Kingdom rulers could claim. The fact that the Emperor, her father and the other kings had cooperated long enough to banish Malady amazed her. If they'd had the fortitude to expel one of the most powerful fairies in Ulaluna, why couldn't they see a legal revolution was required to save the Middle Kingdoms from anarchy? Why couldn't they modify the inheritance laws? Allow ladies to rule. Allow them to marry whom they pleased. If nothing else, allow nobles to marry landed gentry. Better to change the laws than let bedlam prevail.

Though some were in worse shape than others, all the kingdoms had been touched in ungentle ways by the Female Curse. What she wouldn't give to force at least one man, somewhere, to admit the status quo was a status quandary.

She couldn't force her father to lobby for law changes, but Jon Tom in their room, defying her and probably deliberately getting caught, so she'd know he defied her—that was something she could affect.

"Sisters, don't worry about the detective. I warned him to stay out of our room. I'll set a trip spell for him. He won't be so anxious to sneak around in our bedchamber if he's doubled over with the flux."

"Certain magics against other humans are unethical," Hortense reminded her. Her lips tightened in a familiar gesture. "A trip spell isn't a mere sedative or harmless illusion."

"Perhaps you could ward the room," Ella suggested. "Didn't you say *The Sneaky Fairy Book* mentioned wards? I could help you figure out how to do it."

"I think not," Hortense said sharply. "We can buy a legitimate fairy motion detector and let it do the work."

Wards weren't a bad idea, despite Hortense's automatic dismissal. They gave trespassers the urgent need to be elsewhere, and could be focused on individuals or species, like the border wards. Perhaps she could look something up tomorrow.

"I have a notion, but it would require a personal belonging." Susannah's "to be researched" stack grew higher every hour, it seemed—the Female Curse, the enchanted princes, humans who possessed magic, the wearing away of spells, the truth about invisibility and potential devices used by one very annoying detective. Now she had to suss out magical wards.

"I could get something personal from him," Peter said. "And I won't need magic to do it. But I might need to practice on our little princes first."

When Peter suggested visiting the princes, Lilly stopped brushing her hair. "We haven't seen our princes in forever. All work and no play is making me a dull girl."

"A couple of nights isn't an eternity." Susannah exchanged glances with Calypso and Hortense. Although Hortense had thought it best if they remained above for some time, Calypso wanted to investigate the strange happenings. Susannah, absorbed so completely by Jon Tom that the invisible prince hadn't disturbed her dreams, knew the enchanted realm was stranger than her sisters imagined.

However, it irritated her that Jon Tom had invaded the sanctity of their private chambers. Perhaps she'd tell her father that Jon Tom had been skulking in the princesses' room. On the other hand, her father probably knew of Jon Tom's search mission, and her mother probably told him to do it. Just because they'd struck up an odd sort of relationship didn't mean he'd cease to do his job. She shouldn't feel so disappointed.

"Well?" Lilly asked. "Are we going or not?"

"I don't see why Susannah chooses whether we go or stay, anyway," Peter complained. "There are eleven of us and one of her."

"For the obvious reason nobody else can open the door, you ninny." Calypso tossed a pillow across the room at Peter.

"It's not a good idea." Susannah scuffed her foot against the stone floor.

Did she want to take such a chance, just to snap back at the detective? They could fake an excursion by rubbing holes in their slippers. It wouldn't be difficult. Fashionable dancing shoes had wafer-thin soles. They were pretty much wear and toss. The princesses had discussed sturdier dancing slippers to hide their revelry but hadn't gotten around to implementing the project, considering how their mother would react if she heard what they'd requested from the cobbler elves.

But why give up a night of drinking and dancing? Why give up a chance to interrogate Prince John? The longer Jon Tom remained at the castle, the closer he'd come to realizing she wasn't the typical princess. And the closer she'd come to wanting to keep him around.

Dangerous indeed. She needed more distance from him.

Ella said, "If we go tonight and your prince deserts you, you can ride back with me. I'll row if you drive off my prince as well."

"I didn't drive off my prince," Susannah said. "You all know strange things are afoot in the land below. If we go, we must be wary and observant. Don't be alone with any of the princes, even if they seem normal. Pretend the standard rules for chaperonage apply."

Peter yawned. "Are we going, then?" She shot her eldest sister a challenging glance. "It would serve Jon Tom right for breaking into our room. The man is delicious, but he's as pesky as a gadfly."

Susannah smiled again. The cocksure detective sprawled in front of their door had no way to stop them. "Perhaps we should humble Mr. Tom by bringing him one step closer to his dismissal."

"I like Mr. Tom." Rosa frowned. "I want him to stay."

"We cannot like him," Susannah insisted, as much to herself as her sisters. "Mother hired him to spy on us. Pray keep that in mind."

Rosa pouted. "But Calypso said he ought to work in the Justice Chambers so she no longer had to. Then he could stay and not be a spy."

Ella rolled her eyes. "He can't stay, not unless you want him to find out Susannah has fairy powers, and then she'll be locked away. Face it, Rosie, Mr. Tom's got to go."

"They wouldn't lock Susannah away just because she's special," Rosa said. "Besides, Ella, they'd have to lock you away, too, when you discover your powers."

"We can't know for sure what they'd do, sweetheart," Susannah said, "and it's best if Ella doesn't try to discover any powers of her own until I understand them better."

"I think we can be pretty sure what would happen." Esme uttered a mean laugh. "They'd accuse you of treason or something and cast you from the kingdom, if the fairies didn't tear you limb from limb."

Susannah hastened to soothe Rosa. "Mother and Father would accept me, but fairies are jealous of their status. You know how competitive they can be."

"If we're going, let's go." Calypso pretended to jig with a partner. "My, Humbie, what broad shoulders you have! Of course you can take off your vest if you're too hot."

"Everyone keep mental notes on anything unusual," Ella said. "Who knows what detail will provide the clue to crack this case?"

"You sound like Jon Tom. Crack the case, indeed." Susannah couldn't resist another magical glance through the wooden door at the detective, and the power curled her toes the same way his stare did. His dark hair gleamed in the dim light of the lamps, and he shifted into a more comfortable spot on his stack of cushions. The ties on his shirt had come undone to reveal a slice of smooth, tan chest. Even in repose his lips held a slight smirk.

He wanted to search her bedroom, did he? Wanted to

invade her private space? Susannah wished she could invite him in, but not for the reason he might think. She'd like to watch him search the walls and armoires while she looked on, laughing at him and knowing the frustration he was going to be feeling on the morrow.

Chapter Nine

Although he'd been foremost in her thoughts for days, the image of Jon Tom dissolved, replaced by a different anxiety. Susannah's gut tightened as they reached the bottom of the stairs. Everything seemed normal—the flowers with their fragrant blossoms, the grass under their feet, the jewels glistening and tinkling upon the trees—but then, everything had seemed normal the previous trip. Susannah suddenly regretted concentrating her research on detection devices instead of invisibility, but Jon Tom had seemed the greater threat.

"You're nervous as a cat in a kennel," Calypso said to Susannah when she twitched at the sound of a branch snapping.

"Of course I am. Who knows what we'll encounter? I'm worried." How she wished she could tell Calypso about the invisible prince! Two heads were better than one when deciphering a puzzle, but she believed him when he said something dreadful would occur if she spoke of him. That was a common characteristic of curses involving secret lives.

It probably wasn't wise, coming here tonight. Yet Susannah couldn't stay away—not when it would rid her of Jon Tom before he could find anything out and before she grew too accustomed to him. And not when it would satisfy her curiosity about the changes in the enchantment and the enigmatic new prince.

"The doubts you had when we first started coming didn't make you this jumpy," Calypso said. "Is there something you're not telling?"

Calypso had known her too long. Susannah gave her a half-truth. "It's no secret. The younger girls know how to defend themselves from unwanted attentions, but they trust these young men. They won't be alert."

"We warned them enough times—how could they be anything besides alert? Even Peter agreed to remain in the ballroom, the banquet hall or the front lawn tonight."

Prince Siselwade waited beside Susannah's boat. His vest and pants hung limply on his aesthetic frame, their red color garish against his skin. Unlike most of the other princes, his tongue tripped over itself and his rowing skills were little better than her own. The boat dropped behind, as did the boat of Rosa and her escort, Prince Ludo.

Ludo, whose body hair bristled out of every opening of his white vest, was tall and husky, so why should his rowing be as slow as Siselwade's? Did the princes suffer from some sort of malaise? The rest of the escorts rowed in typical manly fashion, heave-hoeing and flashing big, happy grins. She'd have to speak with Prince Ludo, see if he was feeling under the weather or if he even knew what weather was.

"I...I read a lovely book today, Princess," Siselwade stammered. He clasped her arm and helped her up the beach and into the castle. "It was a book of poetry."

"What sort of poetry?" Susannah dusted off her slippers before mounting the broad steps to the castle. Would Prince John approach her when she was with another man or did that violate his version of the curse?

The young man coughed and Susannah turned to him. He blushed from hairline to neck and all the way down his thin torso. "Love poetry," he whispered, as if the very utterance would offend her sensibilities.

Susannah didn't question him further, afraid she'd send the boy into a tizzy. As it happened, Siselwade wasn't a good dancer. Nor was he a possessive escort. In contrast to the night she stood alone, Susannah's popularity was phenomenal. The others realized Siselwade would allow them to cut in, so they did. Even if he and Susannah had just taken the floor, even if he had just gotten her back from a reel with Prince Ufta or a stroll about the rooms with Prince Bertram.

Susannah barely had a chance to catch her breath, much

less search for Prince John. She asked several princes, gingerly, if they knew anyone named John, but none did. Her sisters stuck close to the dance floor, aside from an episode rousting Esme and Prince Vladimir out of the Divan Room.

"I'm going to be nearly as sore as when I rowed across the lake," Susannah said to Hortense between sets. Siselwade held her goblet of wine while Yarrow headed her way with a certain look in his eye. Susannah groaned.

She took Siselwade by the arm. "My prince, won't you take me for a stroll on the moonlit balcony?"

Hortense narrowed her eyes, and Susannah put a finger to her lips. "I'll be as safe as Rosa with Ufta," she whispered. "Just don't tell any of the girls or next thing you know they'll all disappear." She tugged Siselwade in the direction of the nearest balcony. Prince Yarrow, deprived of Susannah, swept a very startled Hortense into his arms for the waltz that was beginning.

Breathing deeply of the cool outside air, Susannah dropped her escort's arm and accepted her wine with a smile. She leaned upon the white marble balustrade overlooking the palace's gardens. The grounds to the left of the castle teemed with flowers, exotic fruit trees and ferns. The grounds to the right were comprised of cleverly arranged rocks, crystal-clear pools and statuary. Blocks of hedges dotted the landscape and moss grew thickly between the stones. Susannah gazed over the dimly lit stone gardens, and fairy lights played off the pools as if the sky were below as well as above.

"Tell me, Prince Siselwade, about the love poetry you read today." It had probably been long enough for him to have calmed from his earlier embarrassment. In truth, Susannah would have liked the prince to disappear and leave her peacefully absorbing the night air, but he stood there so awkwardly she felt sorry for him. He seemed much younger than she, roughly the age of her sister Temple, at best.

"But I read no love poetry today." Avoiding her gaze, he adjusted his ill-fitting red vest. "I read of a dashing prince who conquered a dragon."

"Earlier this evening you told me you read a volume of love poetry."

"Princess, I know not of what you speak!" His pointy

features contorted in a confused, desperate expression that reminded her of Humbert after he splashed water upon her chemise, so Susannah forced a laugh.

"I'm thinking of my sister. You must think me a silly woman!" She'd no wish to be deserted by her escort again. Better this child-man row the boat. Perhaps the enchantment would heal him if the task made him sore.

The youth's face quit twitching, and Susannah raised her glass. "Would you be a dear and fetch me another measure of the peach nectar?"

The young man stiffened at her request, as if saluting his superior officer. "I shall fetch you a refreshing ice as well," he declared, and fled her company with indecorous eagerness.

As soon as her escort left, a husky voice on the other side of the balcony spoke. "Bravo, milady. I'm impressed with the way you handled that rabbit boy."

Every nerve in her skin prickled. Mysterious whispering, no body—must be that sneaky Prince John. Had he been here all this time?

Susannah resisted the urge to raise her hands into a defensive stance. "Where are you? How long have you been watching me?"

"All night. You certainly made up for your lack of dances the night we met."

"I told you I came here to dance." Susannah tossed back her dark ringlets, suddenly conscious she was wearing one of her old red shifts and not a newer, more flattering one.

The voice spoke again, much closer to her. "Then you should dance with me." She felt a touch on her bare arm.

She edged away. "Prince Siselwade will be back any moment."

"You'll be lucky if Prince Sissy comes back at all."

Susannah stifled a laugh. "That isn't true. He's been an excellent companion."

"Some escort—leaving you out on a dark balcony at the mercy of any passing prince."

"At your mercy, you mean? I think not."

"I could be upon you before you knew what was coming," whispered a warm voice in her ear, but when she reached to fend him off, he wasn't there.

"I had little trouble with you last time, as I recall." Susannah flattened herself against the balcony railing so he couldn't approach her from behind. The cold marble chilled her lower back through the silk of her garment. "I wish to interview you."

"Your pulse races at the base of your neck." A quick finger stroked her collarbone. "Is that not fright?"

"No." She turned her face away from a touch upon her cheek.

"Are you frightened to be alone with me?"

"You don't frighten me."

"Then what do you feel?"

Susannah crossed her arms over her chest. If the prince was going to use his invisibility as an excuse to fondle her, she wasn't going to make it easy. She'd come here to interview him, not flirt with him. "Fatigue, of course. From all that dancing."

A leg brushed her calf. "We can go to the Divan Room, where you may rest in comfort."

"My prince will look for me here," she protested, even though the thought of sinking into a cushioned sofa was tempting. Perhaps Prince John would rub her feet, as the other princes sometimes did.

And perhaps not.

"He's already forgotten which balcony he left you on." Susannah glanced through the elegant glass doors into the ballroom just as Siselwade wandered past, a silver chalice in his hand. Light from the chandeliers that graced the ceiling of the ballroom poured through the doors in a perfect yellow square, but she stood to the left, in shadow.

"I've no wish to row myself across the lake again tonight, sir. I should remind him where I am, unless you'll man the oars yourself?" She smiled sweetly.

"Alas, I'm not allowed," the prince replied. Susannah scooted along the balcony toward the light to call for Siselwade.

A strong arm held her back. From the position of the arm and the hand at the back of her neck, from the warmth in the air, Prince John must be standing right...in front...of her.

Susannah closed her eyes, and every nerve along her body

tingled with awareness. When one relies upon sight, the other senses fade. Now she could feel the outline of the man, inches from her body. Now she could smell his scent, a peppery tang, with fruit on his breath.

"Ah, Susannah." A pair of warm lips feathered along her brow. "Don't call him. Stay with me." His cheek pressed against hers, and the hand clasping her neck threaded into her thick, heavy hair.

"I didn't tell you my name," she whispered. "I've been meaning to ask you—"

The tentative touch of his mouth upon hers cut her off mid-sentence. He rubbed softly against her lips, once, twice and lingered the third time with a moist pressure. When his tongue parted her lips, she tasted apples.

How long they stood on the balcony, with their mouths and tongues touching, with his palm cradling the back of her head, she didn't know, but it was long enough for her heartbeat to quicken and her nipples to tighten, long enough for her to fantasize about further indiscretions. She stroked his velvety face. His hair was silky, with locks across his forehead.

Prince John took her hand and halted her tentative exploration. "Princess," he said, his voice even huskier, "let me take you somewhere more comfortable. We'll fetch wine and fruit and talk."

"Talk," she said. She opened her eyes and saw nothing. A flood of cold air rushed along her front, restoring her sanity. "Yes, I wanted to talk."

"Then we shall."

She hadn't conversed with men one-on-one much in her life until recently. Jon Tom talked to her. He listened as well. The princes, on the other hand, did not.

"The princes never want to talk," she said.

"I'm not like—"

"The other princes, I know. You told me last time. Or do you remember?"

"I remember every moment I've ever seen you, in detail. I love to watch when you don't know I'm there."

His quiet intensity jolted her. She crossed her arms over her chest again to hide her taut nipples. "How...disturbing."

He chuckled. "We should definitely talk."

"What do you want to know?"

"I want to know how you came to find me, my dove. How you came to find the enchanted land and all the princes in it. What drives you to return, night after night."

His questions had a familiar tang. They reminded her of the questions she herself had asked the princes, back when she thought she could get a reply.

They were not, however, questions she cared to answer. And it was late. "The night is half-gone already. We must return to our own castle by a certain hour."

"Tell me other things about you. How do you spend your days in the land above?"

"You know about the land above?" she asked, intrigued.

For a moment he didn't respond. Then he said, "I know it exists but little else. My memories were erased by this damned curse."

"Why do you think you're different from the other princes?"

"Perhaps in my other life, my life before the enchantment, I was a truly wicked man." He traced a fingertip down her forearm and ended at the back of her hand.

"Fairies don't have the same concept of wickedness as humans. Their motives cannot always be comprehended." Such as, why would the fairies have trapped all these men here in the land beneath? And why would they allow the Female Curse to ruin the Middle Kingdoms, which supplied most of their gold?

The prince took Susannah's hand and squeezed it gently. She stared into the emptiness as the press of his lips warmed her knuckles. "Come," he murmured. "Why do you resist? You've nothing to fear from me."

She'd just kissed a man she barely knew, a man who might be dangerous, and enjoyed it a great deal. Even with the other princes, she didn't allow familiarities until the end of the evening, when a goodnight embrace might be shared. Most of her sisters did the same. Susannah had suspicions as to how far down the primrose path a few had traveled. Considering the princes' incapacity, they hadn't reached the end, at least not with the princes.

The princes forgot by the next visit, anyway, as if the kisses had never happened. Prince John showed no signs of forgetting. Perhaps he wasn't as harmless as the others, either. Where was her common sense?

Prince John placed a light kiss on her palm. Her fingers curled around it. "If you tell me about the land above, perhaps I'll remember why I've been banished. Or are you frightened to find out?"

"I told you already, I'm not afraid of you. I'm afraid of—"

"Are you afraid of what you might do, alone with me?"

"Don't be silly. It isn't wise to tamper with unsolved curses. Exchanging information might be harmful—like telling people I met you."

"How do you know so much about curses and fairies, my flower?" The prince tugged her hand and she followed, reluctantly, across the balcony and down the steep, winding staircase into the rock gardens. A brick-bordered trail lined the side of the castle, though it went no farther than a wall near the back of the palace.

"I do research for my father's Justice Chambers and sometimes the cases involve magic." She supposed it was necessary for Prince John to hold her hand. She couldn't see where he was going otherwise. Either way, she was more comfortable knowing where he was.

"I see," he said, which made her smile a little, since she could see nothing.

It was her turn to ask a question. "How do you eat and drink here without any of the other princes noticing cups and plates flying about by themselves?" They passed beneath another balcony. "How do you sleep without fearing another will lie down upon you?"

"The enchantment must cause the other princes to be oblivious. No one besides you has ever noticed me."

"I fail to believe that could be true. A minor incident set Humbert off the other night and nearly disrupted Siselwade tonight."

"You're very observant." He guided her up a set of twisting stairs back into the castle. She picked up her skirt and clung to his arm for balance. If she didn't look at the hand that gripped nothing, it wasn't as disorienting. The circular steps led to the Divan Room balcony.

"It couldn't be that they don't notice minor differences," she continued once they reached the top. "I would say, more, they can't cope with change, especially not lately."

"Perhaps our perspectives of the situation are too different," he said.

Velvet-upholstered fainting couches and divans lined the walls of the room. Beside each couch perched a tiny lacquered tea table, and plush throw rugs littered the parquet floor. Jewel-toned tapestries depicting romantic scenes insulated the walls. The prince deposited Susannah on a velvet divan in the corner of the room. After stroking her cheek, he stepped away from her, or so she assumed.

His invisibility made communication with him difficult. "Where are you going?"

"I'll fetch us the refreshment your escort promised," replied his voice from the doorway.

The music from the ballroom filtered into the chamber. Susannah stretched her legs out on the divan, tucking her chemise around them, and leaned onto the arm with a sigh. Would her sisters notice she was gone when Prince Siselwade drifted unpartnered about the ballroom? Hopefully not. It wouldn't foster obedience if she were caught doing exactly what she warned the rest of them not to do. However, it's not as if they would actually see her with anyone.

In a short time, a plate of food and a brimming goblet materialized before her eyes, and she flinched. Prince John chuckled.

"You can make things you're holding disappear?"

"If I concentrate." He didn't elaborate. He just extended the goblet until she accepted it. The plate floated down to hover a few inches away from her leg, and his lower back pressed against her thigh.

She should inch away from him. As a lady of the nobility, men weren't supposed to touch her out of turn, especially not in areas other than the hand and arm, but she didn't impose that restriction on the men here. It was pleasant, nice, to allow an arm about her shoulders or let her leg rest against a man's. So far there'd been no repercussions.

She sipped the fizzy wine. He'd chosen champagne, not one of the innocuous beverages. A selection of fresh fruits, sweetmeats and petits fours garnished the silver plate. A strawberry moved away from the plate to disappear in two fascinating bites. She heard his teeth make short work of it.

Another piece of fruit floated from the plate toward her, a plump cherry. "Open your mouth," he said, but she shook her head.

"I'm not hungry." The sight of the food flying about was unsettling. The thought of Prince John feeding her was even more unsettling.

Fabric swished in what might have been a shrug before the cherry disappeared.

She took another drink, this one longer. Was he looking into her eyes? Did he have blue, green or gray eyes? Was he dark or fair? She knew he was tall and strong and smelled of spice.

"What do you look like?" Perhaps he was swarthy, with dark hair and dark eyes. Perhaps he favored dark tunics and tight breeches and had a smile like the very devil.

"I don't remember." He twirled another cherry in the air by its stem before it vanished.

She was being silly. This wasn't a time to think about Jon Tom. She needed to concentrate on quizzing him about the enchantment.

"Have you ever tried speaking to any of the others?" she asked.

He popped three diminutive petits fours in his mouth and swallowed before answering. "Something cautions against it just as it cautions me you must keep my secret. You did, didn't you?" He took the champagne from her hand, raised it to his invisible lips and drank.

"Of course," she said. "Do you remember how long you've been here?"

"It feels like an eternity. The days bleed into each other with numbing sameness—except for the evenings when you grace us with your presence."

From his sing-song tone, she'd swear he knew more than he revealed. Susannah rolled her eyes. "Why haven't you spoken with me before?"

"I feared I would startle you." The prince methodically

demolished the goodies on the plate and offered her the occasional tidbit. He brushed her bottom lip with a honeyed treat, and she batted at his unseen hand.

"Why did you change your mind?" She licked her mouth. "Why did you speak to me and not one of my sisters?"

The prince ate the last strawberry. Susannah grew impatient with his noncommittal remarks, his concentration on the plate of food. Was he being evasive or was he unable to answer her questions? If she could see him, she'd tweak his nose.

"There's something about you I find irresistible. I've noticed that since the first moment I laid eyes on you." He hummed, as if remembering something tasty. "It was like a tornado caught me up and curled me into knots."

"Very evocative," she said with a snort. "Me, a force of nature, twisting poor fellows into knots." Perhaps he wasn't all that different from the others, if he uttered ridiculous sentiments like that. "Why did you untwist yourself enough to say hello?"

"I could no longer restrain myself."

Susannah rolled her eyes again. "Have you sensed any changes in the enchantment lately? Any differences?" Could he sense things or was he, too, caught up in the twilight brainlessness of the other princes? Susannah wriggled on the divan, moving her bottom into a comfortable position. She grasped the stem of the goblet he held, her fingers covering his. When he didn't reply, Susannah took the goblet away from him. "Answer me."

She'd bet her quarterly allowance something in the curse had shifted, and it was imperative she discover the cause and predict the ripples. Was it something she was researching? Was it the enchantment itself, wearing away over time? Was it tied to this man's presence?

"Forgive me," he said, his voice jagged. "Your beauty distracts me." A warm finger outlined the scooped neck of her chemise.

Susannah slapped him away with her free hand. "Mind yourself!" She tugged the neckline of her chemise up and shoved him with her knees. "More of that and I'll return to the ballroom." She didn't want to, really, since she hadn't finished questioning him.

"As you command."

She took a cool drink of champagne. "Do you remember what it was like before we found you?"

The pressure of his body against her thigh vanished, and the plate soared through the air to settle upon a table. The hairs on her neck and arms prickled as she gazed into the empty space beside her. Where was he?

Prince John sat again with his back pressed against her midriff instead of her leg. He tweaked one of the curls on her shoulder. "You're a curious little squirrel tonight, Princess. I should be questioning you to see if you jar my memory."

He'd pinned her between himself and the cushioned back of the divan. Where were his hands? If she gave him the goblet, she'd know where one was, but then she couldn't hold it between them like a shield. "I trust my answers will be as helpful as yours," she quipped.

"How do you spend your days? I've imagined it, many times, but I'd rather hear it from you."

An account about her restrictive, cloistered life would surely keep his mind off anything frisky. What harm could it do to list her daily tasks and how busy her mother kept her? She kept her answers generic, light, not mentioning names of kingdoms, places or people.

Noble females were only schooled until age ten, except for household management, but her mother's program included advanced training in many areas. She described the weaving, gardening, accounting, star charting, shopkeeper visiting, researching, hunting, and even the fencing she and her sisters did. All good tasks toward developing each of them to be at the kingdom's helm, or behind its helm. Susannah sought additional instruction in Middle Kingdom and intercontinental politics to the extent her parents would allow it.

All of which didn't leave much time for parties, balls, gossip and falling in love with court jesters, jeweler's sons or detectives.

"Even our entertainment is designed," she explained. "That's why it's so wonderful to come here, escape our schedules and have time to ourselves."

The prince didn't molest her during her near monologue, so

she relaxed. She drank all the champagne and more. He laughed at her descriptions of her sisters' antics, sometimes catching one of her hands and placing a feathery kiss upon the knuckles. Genteel. Safe. The champagne buzzed around her head since it had no need to halt in her very empty stomach. Perhaps she should have eaten a croissant. Where had that second glass come from? Or third?

Prince John's soothing voice washed over her cottony ears. "Surely there's more to your life than planned activities. What about personal ambitions?"

Such a respite, to speak—to complain—to someone who wasn't her sister. Someone who wasn't frustrated with her, didn't disapprove of her and didn't expect her to save the kingdom. She squashed the impulse to tell him she wanted to end curses with her magical powers.

"Our kingdom's citizens are healthy and productive. The same cannot be said for all the Middle Kingdoms. One of them," she said with a sad shake of her head, "has been overrun by Hinterlanders. I mean, barbarians. Bad guys." She'd used an exact name.

"That's politics. Is there a special man in your life?"

An image of Jon Tom sitting on the library table, swinging his leg, leapt into her head, and she ignored it. "No," she said.

"Surely you want to fall in love?" The prince had begun, about halfway through the second goblet, to hold her hand and stroke the knuckles. Now he moved his attentions up her bare arm, across her shoulder, fingers caressing her collarbone. One of the wide chemise straps drooped on her shoulder.

She couldn't bring herself to stop him. His touch was tranquilizing. These princes couldn't threaten her chastity. She tilted her whirling head against the arm of the divan as goose bumps whispered across her flesh.

"Love," she said, "is useless to hope for. There aren't any men in our lives. No men, no children and no one to inherit."

"Ah, but there are men in your life," the prince said. "Hundreds of them." He set the empty goblet on the side table. Her eyes grew heavy as he massaged her shoulders.

"They don't count. We can't marry the poor fools. We can't even..." Susannah stopped herself and closed her eyes. A blush rose from the tips of her breasts to her ears.

Prince John, from his voice, was smiling. "You can't even what, my sweet?"

Didn't he know what the other princes—what he—couldn't do? The others forgot each time, though Susannah had forbidden her sisters to bestir the men to that point. She certainly halted any kisses before the situation escalated. It was possible Prince John, never having wooed a princess, wouldn't know the extent of his curse.

She didn't want to be the one to break it to him. With his memory, he wouldn't conveniently forget he was trapped here for reasons unknown and half a man to boot.

"You don't want to know." She shivered as his hands moved from her shoulders to her flushed cheeks. Fingertips learned the curves and planes of her face and tickled along her lips.

"I want to know everything." His voice had grown lower, or was that her imagination?

Cloth rustled as his cheek grazed hers. "How did you discover this place?" he whispered.

"I read something in a book." His lips trailed along her neck. She didn't know what to do with her hands so she placed them on his shoulders, covered by a coarsely woven material.

"What kind of book?"

"A historical volume." Susannah's body floated in a pool of liquid. Champagne, no doubt. One of his hands dropped to her rib cage.

His tongue tasted her earlobe and sent coils of delight down her spine. "Yes, but how did you find us, my love? How did you unearth this fairy place?"

Susannah's head lolled against his arm when he slipped it behind her. "Not a fairy place. This can't be Ulaluna. We've eaten the food and drunk the wine. I think it is another plane, though. Perhaps it's like my bottomless reticule that expands to fit whatever's in it."

She couldn't think straight. Everything whirled. The hand on her rib cage inched up to cup her breast, and Susannah gasped. Instinctively she arched her back. Her hands tightened on his shoulders.

She had to stop him. This was wrong. He'd grow excited and realize he was impotent.

Such thoughts fled her mind when Prince John rolled her nipple between his fingers. Susannah whimpered and dug a hand into his silky hair, dragging his face down to hers.

Against her face she felt him smile. His hand left her breast and a finger tapped her lips. "You haven't answered my question."

"What question?" Alcohol and arousal blurred her memory, and all she could think was how badly she wanted him to kiss her.

"How did you come to find this place?" His palm dusted the tips of her breasts in quick succession. She shifted her legs against the divan restlessly and brought one knee up so it rested along his back. Her head spun, and she couldn't concentrate.

"Magic," she exhaled. His touch felt better than any spell, more thrilling than using her powers. She moved her hand to his neck and drew her nails along his skin.

In a rather strained voice, he continued, "What magic? Did a fairy give you a charm?"

Susannah knew further caresses in this vein were cruel to him, but she craved his hands all over her body and hers all over his. Her bones oozed with molasses.

"Enough talk," she demanded. "Kiss me."

When her hand fisted in his hair, he complied. His lips were hot against her open mouth and his tongue met hers hungrily. An ache built in her loins, echoing the heat already there. She pulled at him to join her on the divan.

Without breaking off their kiss, he shifted her onto her side and stretched out beside her. He was not, to her disappointment, dressed in a skimpy vest and loose trousers. He wore a cloak and what seemed to be a linen shirt. His hand slipped around to stroke her buttocks.

When he bent his head and took her nipple into his mouth through the thin silk of her chemise, she moaned aloud as tight spirals of desire overwhelmed her. The hand on her buttocks inched up her skirt. Cold air tickled her legs and brought a measure of sanity into her swirling head. This was as far as she should let him go.

Her head felt heavy, hot. "Wait."

The touch of his hand on her bare thigh, between her

stockings and her loose pantaloons, nearly brought tears to her eyes. No man had ever touched her there, and the sensation was exquisite. Susannah squirmed closer to him and threw her bare leg across his body.

"Susannah!" His big hand cupped her bottom and crushed her to him. A hard ridge surged against her woman's mound, and when he rotated his hips, it rubbed a spot that sent a sweet, sharp jolt through her.

"What are you doing?" Her breath came in short gasps and her eyes flew open. Seeing nothing in front of her yet feeling every inch of his body was a contrast her conscious mind could barely handle.

"Making love to the most luscious woman in the world." He kissed her, and she fought to free her lips.

Her hand moved between their bodies and she grabbed the hard thing below his waist.

With a groan, he yanked her chemise to her waist. When her pantaloons wouldn't slide down her hips, he ripped them in half.

The long, hard thing she clutched through his trousers burned into her hand. "What is this!" she yelled and squirmed frantically in his arms.

"My jack of all trades," he said, "as if you didn't know."

By the time he'd finished his sentence, Susannah had clambered over his invisible body and leapt from the divan. She came to a halt in the center of the room.

His manhood! His fully functioning, fully hard manhood! Indeed, he wasn't like the other princes. The edges of her vision blackened with a massive wave of panic. She watched as her torn underpants flew to the end of the divan, and a pair of warm hands saved her from crumpling to the floor.

"Darling, what's wrong?"

"Your manhood," she babbled.

Prince John gave a pleased chuckle. "It's not so large and frightening as all that, is it? With all the times you've visited here, you knew what to expect."

"I don't!" she exclaimed. "I've never... They can't."

"I've seen your sisters disappear into private rooms, Susannah, and many kisses exchanged. You can't tell me you never."

"I can tell you I never, if I never." Susannah knew her words made little sense. "It doesn't go this far. It can't. The other princes can't."

"The other princes can't make love?"

"Their...their groins don't function. We assume it's part of the curse."

"I told you I wasn't like the other princes. So every one of those dandies out there is impotent?" Prince John dropped his hands and laughed. "'Tis a horrible curse indeed!"

"It's not funny." Susannah swung a fist toward his laughter and made contact with him.

"They must have done something terrible to merit this punishment." He restrained her fist easily.

"And what did you do?" Susannah pulled her hand, but he didn't release it.

"Obviously nothing as bad as they did." Abruptly he yanked her against his body. Standing, he was a good bit taller than she and more intimidating than when they had lain together on the divan. "And now, my sweet, where were we?"

Susannah trembled against him, torn between desire and fright. His arms slipped around her, and he nibbled her jaw.

"Stop."

"You don't mean that." His hand slithered up her ribs to cup a heavy breast in his palm. "You're ripe for it. A sensualist, Princess, just as I suspected."

A sensualist? What did he mean? Susannah craned her head away from his treacherous lips. "I thought you'd be like the other princes."

The prince licked the corner of her mouth. "I'm not. But I'm eager to show you what it's like to be with a real man."

"You're not a real man, you're an invisible man. An invisible, enchanted man."

He laughed softly. "I'm real where it counts the most." His manhood pressed against her soft belly, as if in emphasis.

"I can't do this." Her eyesight blurred with tears. "I only allowed you to kiss me because I thought you were like the others."

He froze. "You allowed me to make love to you because you

thought I was impotent?"

"Yes. No! Not exactly." Susannah jerked her head, and her hair tumbled about her shoulders where he'd loosed it from its coiffure. "It was only supposed to be kisses."

"Was this some freakish punishment? Did you mean to torment me with the knowledge I'm unable to complete the act?"

"Not to torment you. I just wanted—"

"Did you hope I'd satisfy your lusts like a harem boy? Is this how you use the others?" He gave her a little shake.

"You have it wrong." She pushed against his chest, her heart pounding. She should never, ever have come here alone with him. She was such a fool! "We don't let things go this far. Please, you have to believe me!"

"Are you sure you aren't the wicked fairy who bespelled these princes? Your own herd of eunuchs to service you."

"How can you say such things?" She twisted in his iron grasp. "I'm mortal. I can't do magic. And if I could, I wouldn't hurt people with it."

"You worked your magic on me, truly enough." He trapped her lips in a punishing kiss. Susannah felt herself sliding down, down his body, down to a place where she'd give him whatever he wanted, but then he released her.

"You're a cruel woman, Susannah." His angry voice shifted toward the balcony. "You're cruel to add to the princes' torment by flaunting what they can't have. What sort of game do you think this is?"

"It's not a game." It was serious. More serious than she'd realized.

"Yet you keep playing. It's in your nature, I suppose, to entice men."

Susannah pressed her shaking hand to her throat. "Because I'm a woman?"

"Because you're you."

"You don't even know me," she protested. A slight breeze blowing through the open balcony doors was her only reply. Again.

Chapter Ten

Five sisters had no escorts by the time Susannah emerged from the Divan Room and had to row themselves across the lake, but Susannah wasn't one. Siselwade, oblivious to the fact his date had disappeared, shuttled her across the water.

"What happened after I left? Did all the princes go wild?" Susannah whispered to Hortense as they stood on the far shore and awaited their unescorted sisters. Lilly, greatly offended, lagged far behind everyone. They could hear her complaints across the water, but none of Susannah's sisters rowed as poorly as she had rowed the other night.

"Rosa and Ufta got into a fight because he cheated at dice, like you can tell with that ridiculous game. Ella and Temple upset their princes when they tried to cast a spell to restore their memories. Calypso ran her escort off herself when he refused to allow Rosa to accompany them across the lake."

"Should I ask what happened to Lilly's prince?"

Hortense flicked the hem of her chemise to dust off the sand. "Lilly egged Prince Cuchalain to battle Prince Jordan for her company."

"The princes actually fought?" Susannah winced. "Have they become violent?"

"They might be." Hortense linked her arm through Susannah's as they turned toward the eternal staircase. "My escort was mannerly, but I alarmed him several times. It's like everything is coming apart at the seams."

Susannah squinted up the stairs, which wound up and around the dark rock face, taking the princesses out of the enchanted realm and back to the ordinary. "I agree."

"I don't think we should come back. Ever. It's not as if it's our duty to free these men."

"We can't leave them. Who else will save them?"

"It's not our duty. We have other duties." Hortense lowered her voice until Susannah could barely hear her. "Why were you gone so long?"

Susannah answered in kind, not wanting the others to hear. "I was exploring, and, ah, testing a new spell."

Hortense dropped Susannah's arm with a sniff. "You spend too much time practicing magic when you don't know what it will do."

"I'll never learn if I don't practice."

"You're a bad influence on the younger girls. You should be more discreet, not give them ideas. Your knowing how to do magic is bad enough."

Since the beginning, Hortense had been Susannah's harshest critic. She'd insisted Susannah abide by the safe list. She worried the most about consequences. She'd worry even more if she knew how stimulating it was to use the power. "Did Temple and Ella actually cast a spell?"

Hortense mounted the first stair. "Oh, no. That was just another misfire to add to the farce that was tonight."

"I'll speak to them." Susannah scowled. "They have no business mucking around like that."

"And you do, of course." Sometimes Hortense was unnervingly astute, and that was when she annoyed Susannah the most.

✧✧✧

The Queen didn't disturb her daughters until long after the cock's crow the next morning, a Sixday. In fact, perhaps mollified by several mornings of cooperation from her brood, she sent Emily to wake them instead of coming herself.

"The Queen says you're supposed to put on your boating gear for luncheon on the barge." Emily made her way down the bed row, tickling the sisters' feet with a feather duster. "You have the morning to yourselves, but breakfast is already cold on the table."

"The barge!" Ella jumped out of bed. "Great!" She slammed open the heavy door so it banged against the wall and ran from the room.

She was quickly pursued by several others, who hurried upon bare feet to the bathing chamber down the hall. Luncheon on the barge meant the King and Queen would host members of the local gentry and merchants. Access to enchanted princes didn't detract from the appeal of other young people, both male and female.

For Susannah, the idea of making polite chitchat with merchants and sheriffs and jewelers who all expected her to do her duty, to marry the next baronet to come along and keep the kingdom together, brought a scowl to her face. The thought of seeing her father, who'd lied to her about bargaining with the fairies again, deepened her scowl. The memory of Prince John's opinion of her turned her scowl into a sour grumble. Men!

Oblivious to Susannah's bitter meditation, her sisters readied themselves for their turn in the bathing chamber. It soon became evident one maid, however skilled, wasn't enough to find all the earrings, tack up all the drooping ruffles, fetch all the skin potions and curl all the hair.

"Emily, perhaps you should ring for another maid if we're to be ready in time for luncheon," Susannah suggested as Emily gathered clean robes and pantaloons for the princesses already in the bathing chamber. Dressing for an event in the above-ground world was more complicated and time consuming than dressing to visit the princes. It involved considerably more layers of clothing.

"The Queen wouldn't like it if you were late." Emily rang a different bell on her girdle, this one connected to its twin in the kitchens. "She also said all of you were to come to the lake and no one was to be sick." She winked at Susannah before leaving the room with the princesses' clean clothing.

"They're going to use all the hot water," Esme said. She rubbed at her eyes with her fists and yawned.

"The magic spigots create all the hot water anybody needs," Susannah pointed out. "The only time we ran out was when Ella left the faucets running to see what would happen."

Esme grimaced. "They'll take so long in the bath there isn't time for the rest of us."

Susannah ignored her. Esme always found something to gripe about.

Peter stood before her wardrobe sorting through her gowns. A polite knock on the door preceded two more maids, come to help the princesses at their toilettes.

"Constance!" cried Rosa. The freckled chambermaid was the youngest princess's bosom buddy whenever the girls could escape their duties long enough to play. The two began chattering like magpies. Constance, it seemed, had been to the stables and seen one of the riding mares give birth.

Susannah sent the other maid to the bathing chamber and asked Constance to gather robes and fresh pantaloons for any remaining princesses who wished a bath. Constance rummaged through the princesses' wardrobes lackadaisically. At least she was doing as Susannah asked and she didn't have to reprimand the girl.

"I don't want a bath," Rosa said, after a whispered debate with her friend. "Can I just wash my face instead, Susannah? Then I can see the new baby horse."

"I don't think Mother would appreciate you coming to the luncheon smelling of the stables," Susannah said. "When you're dressed, play in the solar until it's time to go to the barge."

Rosa grabbed her robe and clean pantaloons, and Constance draped the articles she'd gathered across Susannah's bed. The two adolescents wandered out the bedchamber door, heads together. Susannah doubted they'd go to the bathing chamber and hoped the Queen didn't find her youngest roaming the halls in her nightgown, toting a fresh pair of panties.

She could force Rosa to wash up, but she was distracted this morning, her thoughts in turmoil. Besides, what harm would it do Rosa to play with Constance for an hour or two? The lives of the princesses were mostly work, and the playing they'd been doing lately with the princes...well, it wasn't the same. She'd relish the chance to unshoulder her responsibilities and stresses. Go for a picnic. A vacation. But she had her future, her sisters' future and her kingdom's future to cement, and she'd never solve the Female Curse loafing around.

Rosa didn't return in an hour, although Susannah was too busy dressing and having a quick, hard word with Ella and

Temple about last night to search.

The princesses donned pantaloons, camisoles, corsets, corset covers, stockings, special petticoats and split-skirted boating gowns. Susannah's outfit was a high-waisted maroon skirt combined with a white blouse and maroon spencer, a short, tight jacket. It flattered Susannah's special proportions, accentuating her deep bosom without giving her a pigeon's figure.

When everyone else was pressed and primped, Rosa raced into the bedchamber, wearing her robe and minus her extra pantaloons, with very dirty feet and straw in her hair. Constance was nowhere to be seen.

"Rosa!" Hortense shook her finger at the girl. "We have to be at the lake in twenty minutes, and it takes fifteen to walk there. Mother will give you laundry duty for a week."

"I could cast a cleaning spell," Susannah began, but Hortense cut her off with a glare.

"We can take care of it without that." Several of the sisters converged on the child, tongues clucking, and whipped her into a reasonable facsimile of clean and dressed just in time to meet their escorts to the lake. Two red-faced young guards in the royal gold uniforms waited for them, plus an unaccountably solemn Jon Tom in black.

Susannah, at the head of the column, fell into step alongside Jon Tom as they made their way out of the palace. Her spirits lifted slightly at the sight of him. Perhaps he'd distract her this afternoon with his quips and observations. She'd be interested to hear what he had to say about the local gentry.

They traveled through the bustling courtyard, where soldiers paraded, maids dusted carpets and vendors waited to sell their wares to Cook, and set off toward the orchards, en route to the lake. It felt natural to walk with him, their arms nearly touching, the sun warm on their heads. It felt right to walk with this man at her side.

And that was not a good thing.

"What are you doing here?" She tried to color her tone with displeasure. In a short time, he'd become a fixture at the castle. A fixture in her daily routine.

"You're always asking me that, Princess. In case you have

forgotten, I work here." His voice was cool, and he didn't meet her eyes in the challenging way she'd grown accustomed to.

Unlike Prince John, the detective was visible. The detective was present, hovering more than she'd like instead of exiting at a crucial moment. Unlike Prince John, she knew what to expect from the detective—sly innuendoes and a rousing argument. He was consistent, and she liked consistency.

Susannah tried again. "I don't suppose I could forget when you follow me everywhere."

"Indeed," was all he said. He didn't offer his assistance when she lifted her skirts to descend the steps leading to the orchard, and he made no teasing comments about her appearance, though she'd dressed carefully. Her hair, in particular, had been obedient this morning.

Was he miffed because they'd evaded him a second time? The sisters' late snooze and ruined slippers had doubtless been reported to the Queen, and Mr. Tom would have heard as well. As much as she might like to, it wouldn't do to taunt him, for that would be an admission of guilt.

She felt enough guilt today, after the invisible prince's disgust with her last night. One moment she was sure he'd been unfair, and the next she found herself agreeing. They had been treating the princes like their personal harem, using them to stave off frustration. Not only that, but their secret mutiny, even though she was doing the right thing, never sat well with her conscience.

Eleven chattering princesses, a brooding Susannah and their silent guards walked through the palace meadows along the lake trail. The sun gleamed, and butterflies danced in the light breeze. Daffodils speckled the higher grasses beside the closely cropped trail, and scarcely a cloud marred the sky.

"It's a wonderful day for a luncheon on the water," Peter declared. "Mr. Tom, have you seen our castle lake yet?"

Susannah's sister oozed past her and took Jon Tom's arm with a feline smile.

"No, I haven't." Jon Tom, the devil, flashed Peter a bold grin and patted her clinging hand. "Why don't you tell me about it.

Susannah supposed his crotchets were over, now that Peter demanded his attention. He reserved his crotchets for her.

Peter tossed her gleaming black hair. "It's fed by Dragon

River and numerous springs—one of them a hot springs. It's private. Very private. Bathing there is an experience not to be missed."

"If you don't mind the mineral smell," Susannah added.

Jon Tom ignored her. He helped Peter unnecessarily around a rock-strewn patch in the path. "If you mount an expedition to the hot springs, pray seek my escort. I'm nearly as fascinated by nature's mysteries as I am by human ones."

Why was he charming to her sisters and brusque with her? One would think since he sought her out more than the others, he preferred her company, but he was nicer to the others. To Peter. Susannah frowned. The actions of all twelve of them would cause his dismissal, not just her actions, so why single her out for snarls and snarks?

Why single her out period?

Susannah's grumps and Peter's wiles were interrupted by the arrival of Rosa, a smudge of stable still on her cheek. She took Jon Tom's other arm.

"Mr. Tom said my pony Sir King was very handsome," she said, "and the new colt was going to be a fine, fast runner. Didn't you, Mr. Tom?"

Jon Tom smiled down at Rosa with the same degree of affability as he'd directed at Peter. "Your pony is very handsome. Soon you'll be big enough to ride the new colt, once Blackie is grown."

"You named the new colt Blackie?" Susannah asked.

Jon Tom defended his young admirer. "He's quite black. Princess Rosa, Constance and I selected the name together."

"I'm glad you can detect the color of horses, at least." Susannah's snide comment had no impact on the man soaking up the attention from her sisters. Yes, she concluded, he was deep in a sulk today. But she couldn't shake the feeling it was more than that. He wasn't the kind of man to mope because he'd been bested. He was the kind of man to try harder.

If she were correct, something else bothered him. But what?

"Madame Sourpuss got up on the wrong side of the bed this morning." Peter leaned against Jon Tom's arm and brushed him with her royal bosom. Lesser men had been known to catch fire after such a maneuver, but the detective was apparently flame resistant.

Rosa skipped to the side of the path, picked a daffodil and put it behind her ear. She offered another to Jon Tom, who slid the stem through the top buttonhole of his black vest.

"Thank you, milady," he said with a gracious nod of his head. Rosa proceeded to ask nonstop questions about mythical creatures Jon Tom had encountered, in particular giant badgers (existed) and alicorns (didn't exist). Peter couldn't turn the conversation back to more seductive topics.

Her beautiful sister missed the superior glance Rosa tossed her way, but Susannah didn't. The sight of Rosa besting Peter for the attention of a man was amusing, but it had serious implications. Who would Rosa be able to court in earnest, or would it always be in vain—like Peter? Of all of them, Peter was the most frustrated and bitter. Her natural inclination to admire and be admired grew warped with the lack of a husband or lover, with the lack of available men in general.

If any of the sisters rebelled, Susannah had no doubt it would be Peter. That was one of the reasons Susannah tried to overlook some of her behavior with the enchanted princes. Before they discovered the realm beneath, Peter had been ready to take up with the next attractive guard or tailor who fell under her spell. Had taken up with a tailor, if truth be told. The princes took the edge off Peter's desperation, and all the sisters slept better at night. Better sleep, if less sleep. Not even the Queen's scheduled social events dulled the ache of unrequited urges like visiting the princes did.

At least, it had at first. For Susannah the efficacy of the visits had waned. Had the visits waned for Peter as well? Not good, especially not at a time when Susannah had grave doubts about opening the door to the enchanted realm again.

The way Peter hung on Jon Tom suggested both waning and waxing. A waning of her complacency. A waxing of her interest in potent men. The detective was more exotic and virile than the jeweler's son, and it appeared Rosa shared Peter's preference for exotic men.

As her baby sister continued to dominate the conversation, Peter's face took on a sour cast. Susannah's mood soured for different reasons. She never enjoyed these social outings as much as her sisters. She was uneasy with the sons of the middle class and wondered how she would have fared with noble youths had there been any to meet. The last male offspring of the noble families before the Female Curse, Prince Halbert, had chosen Princess Gibralta of Stonedell when he came of age. Susannah had secretly been relieved. Marriage to Halbert, a stupid man birth-gifted with "periodic bouts of foul body odor" by Malady, might have been worse than spinsterhood.

The dark blue lake glittered like a sapphire in the surrounding green of the countryside as they descended the final hill. It wasn't a vast lake, more of a long, wide spot in the river created by the sawmill dam, but this portion was private and well tended. Several carriages were parked next to the boathouse, and the sounds of merriment carried across the air from the barge.

"Looks like there's a large crowd," Lilly observed. She sounded tired and disinterested in the opportunity for male companionship. Susannah had noted her sister's lack of color this morning. Though she was a good bit younger than Susannah, the rowing had probably stiffened her up.

"Mr. Tom is going to be my escort," Rosa declared.

Peter, who'd been exhaling periodically throughout Rosa's discourse, pursed her lips. Susannah slid her arm through her sister's with a chuckle and tugged her away from Jon Tom.

"You've been outmaneuvered by a budding femme fatale," Susannah whispered. "A man adores a woman who asks him a million questions about himself."

"She just wants to know about that idiot badger," Peter muttered.

"Buck up, Petes. You'll be the belle of the barge." Susannah hoped the jeweler's son was here to pacify her sister's offended pride. It wouldn't do if Peter harried her to go below tonight. With all the craziness in the enchanted realm, who knew what would happen? Would Prince John turn the princes against them? Sink their boats? Seduce one of her sisters?

No, they absolutely couldn't return to the land beneath.

"Yoo-hoo, Mother!" Ella waved to the Queen, seated astern on the bi-level, royal barge beneath a shade awning. Their mother couldn't possibly hear, and Susannah concluded Ella just felt like yelling.

The open, flat-bottomed sternwheeler was white hulled with blue accents. Lacy scrollwork decorated the gunnels, the upper deck supports and the railings, and a giant white and blue paddle wheel dominated the stern. The King was topside, near the bow and surrounded by townsmen. Susannah could just make out his salt-and-pepper head above the crowd. He would be surrounded by townsfolk all afternoon, so Susannah wouldn't even get the chance to scold him about calling a Consortium.

With one last glare at Rosa, Peter accompanied Lilly to the barge. Several younger townsfolk milled about the front of the boathouse and called out happily when they caught sight of their royal friends. Although the hot springs wasn't as well equipped, it had the titillating reputation for being haunted.

Which was exactly what Rosa was telling Jon Tom. "Two star-crossed lovers, a royal princess and a handsome peasant with curly black hair, were discovered by the princess's cruel parents at the bathhouse and drank poison instead of being separated. It was vastly sad."

Rosa, who'd yet to display romantic interest in any particular male, gave Jon Tom a coy glance. Susannah didn't like the look of it. Was the sly child approaching her woman-time? She hadn't started her monthly courses, but interest in the opposite sex often preceded physical maturity. Susannah needed to relay this tidbit of information to her mother, that Rosa might require closer watching.

"That's quite romantic, milady. Have you ever seen the ghosts? I hear ghosts are very nice creatures."

"We used to go swimming at night to look, but we never met them."

If Jon Tom had been a dog, his ears would have perked up at Rosa's innocent comment. "You've been in the habit of creeping out at night?"

"We were accompanied by guards." Susannah butted into the conversation with a lie. "Our parents knew, and we were never in any danger."

"I was going to say that." Rosa's pretty face grew a shade paler when Susannah gave her a searing glare. She'd wring the girl out like an old rag later.

When Lilly had first tested her romantic feet, she'd been a

giggler, not a prattler. The difficulty for Susannah and the Queen, who relied upon her eldest to help chaperone the younger girls, had been the butcher's boy. Secrets that might change the world had not been a concern. If the King and Queen—and Jon Tom—found out about the enchanted realm, they'd probably find out about Susannah's powers, and that would be when the worst trouble would begin.

Susannah squeezed Rosa on the shoulder. "Dearest, run ahead and make sure the sheriff isn't ruining Father's day over the state of the jail cells. I'll make sure no one steals your escort." Susannah smiled sweetly, but Rosa was familiar with the expression and obeyed.

Having led the procession all the way to the lake, Susannah and Jon Tom were now in the rear. "If I'd known you were this anxious to be alone with me, I'd have made an appointment," Jon Tom commented.

Susannah was relieved to hear the suggestive tone back in his voice. Now things would be normal again, and this strange feeling she'd disappointed him in some new way would vanish.

She looked up at him and shaded her eyes. "Rosa is becoming too attached to you. I don't want to see her hurt when you leave us."

"I'll invite Rosa to visit my new mansion after your father bequeaths it to me. I plan to request the nearby Darby house."

Susannah stopped walking. "Why, that's to be my dower—"

"Princesses who won't be getting married have no need for dower houses, now, do they?"

After the exchange of only a few sentences, Susannah wondered how she could have ever missed the man's normal mode of communication.

"You're a vicious troll," she snapped.

"Some of my best friends are trolls." Jon Tom's teeth flashed insolently.

"I see you've taken on the manners of your friends."

"And yours are so much better." He gave her a discourteous half bow. "My...lady."

Susannah stamped her foot in anger. Stamping one's foot did little to relieve stress, but it was better than socking the man in the jaw. Plus her long skirt hid the motion. "You're being ugly because my father's going to fire you," she guessed. "You've no leads and you're taking your frustration out on me."

"I've made a lot of progress, Princess Susannah," he replied. "My conversations with your sweet sister Rosa have been interesting, to be sure."

"Is that why she's been talking about you nonstop? Have you been seeking her out and encouraging her affection for you?" Susannah set her jaw. This conversation was different from any of the others they'd had. They'd wrangled, yes, and bickered, but it had never felt this personal. "I misjudged you. I didn't think you would stoop that low. You're ghastly to mislead a young girl in that manner."

"How do you harm the child, Princess, with your nightly carousing?"

The pit of her stomach dropped. What did he know? How could he know anything? "We don't—" she began.

"Save the excuses. I assure you, I'll decipher this mystery and am well on my way to doing so. A good detective—"

"You're a bad detective," Susannah interrupted.

Jon Tom smiled. "If you've never known another detective, how can you be so sure I'm a bad one?"

"Whatever you are, it's bad." She felt as mulish as Esme and as mature as Rosa. "Sir Magnus was a good detective, but you haven't detected a thing."

"You apparently didn't read my resume. Besides, the man was a myth."

"So were giant badgers until a week or so ago." Susannah wanted to cry out, *Point!* like the enchanted princes did during that strange dice game, but restricted herself to a pat of her curled hair.

"I'm flattered you've been researching my livelihood. Sir Magnus isn't a well-known character. To think you spent so much of your library time contemplating me." He put his hand to his chest. "It fair makes my heart flutter."

"I happened across the book when I was researching a Justice Chamber issue," she lied. "Long ago. I have a very good memory."

"If you knew about Sir Magnus when I was hired, you'd have mentioned it."

A small group of princesses and townsfolk had remained outside the boathouse to watch this volley of insults. Her sisters had witnessed prior spats with Jon Tom, but the locals had not.

She lowered her voice and crossed her arms. "The only thing that matters is whether you're taking advantage of an impressionable child."

"The lies you've told you parents matter. Not to mention the lies you've told me."

She had definitely wronged her parents, but why did she owe him honesty? He'd been hired to spy on her. He wasn't her brother, her father...her lover. If she thought he'd become somewhat of a friend, she'd been softheaded.

Susannah drew in a steadying breath. "Sometimes a suspicious person might hear a lie when he's being told a truth."

A cough sounded from the boathouse, and Jon Tom turned to view their spellbound audience. "Touché, Princess," he murmured. "Let's cease making a spectacle and take up this quarrel in private. There are things I need to discuss with you. Nor would I have you think I'm abusing Princess Rosa in any way. Perhaps tonight, after your sisters are in bed?"

A clandestine meeting with Jon Tom? She'd recently been clandestine with another man, and that had been a mistake, but Mr. Tom wouldn't attempt to seduce her. Would he? A shiver passed through her that had little to do with the breeze tweaking her pomaded curls into disorder.

"Are you serious?" Susannah asked.

"I would seriously like to speak with you alone."

"You don't need my cooperation. Petition my mother to set up an interrogation session."

"I'd rather come directly to you."

She lifted her chin. "Hunt me down in the library."

"We could be interrupted there. You won't want to be interrupted when you hear what I have to say. Tonight."

The detective seemed so confident. A twinge of unease hit her. What did he think he knew? She flicked Hortense a beseeching glance. Her sister herded the others to the boathouse with a few sharp words but stayed behind herself.

Aware of Hortense's disapproving glare, she dropped her

voice to a whisper. "If I were to meet you, it would be in the daytime. If." As she spoke, a spicy scent tickled her nose and stirred a memory, but not enough for her to put a finger on it.

"We need to reach a truce. I've no wish to feud with you ceaselessly." Jon Tom raised his hand as if he were going to touch her.

Susannah's breath caught in her throat. She stared at his long fingers, the calluses on his palm. Would he do it? Brush her cheek? Touch her hair?

"Susannah, everyone is waiting," Hortense called. Jon Tom dropped his hand to his side.

"What would I get out of this meeting?" she asked. "It's not proper to seek to be private with you." She needed to find out what the detective knew, but a secret assignation was out of the question. It wasn't as if he were a harmless, enchanted prince.

It wasn't as if all the enchanted princes were harmless.

Jon Tom quirked a mobile eyebrow. "One thing I'm sure of, Princess, is the chaperonage laws aren't something that worry you."

She blinked. Perhaps part of the truth would distract him. "You're right."

He smiled, until she continued.

"It isn't bending an archaic law that worries me. It's the company I'd be keeping."

"I have given your esteemed mother my word I wouldn't harm her daughters." His teeth flashed in a knowing smirk. "Hmm, what does that leave? Are you worried you wouldn't be able to control yourself if you were alone with me?"

"Be silent!" Susannah spat out.

He rocked back on his heels and regarded her insolently. Prince John had made similar comments about her supposed lack of self-control. About her sensual nature, her desires. Was she giving them an immodest impression? She who couldn't convince a man to marry her even though the kingdom was prosperous?

Actually, she hadn't attempted to convince anyone to marry her since she'd found the enchanted princes. No newly minted baronets or widowed earls had toured Foresta lately. Was it possible, in the interim, that her increasing use of magic had altered her nature? Fairies didn't abide by the same social or sexual strictures as humans. They were, to put it bluntly, licentious. Had their magic made her the same way?

She'd been so tempted by Prince John last night. No man had ever aroused her that much. His touch on her body had been a hot brand she'd have trouble forgetting. Except— something about the detective consumed her attention as well. But he'd never kissed her. He'd never touched her intimately. She must remain calm.

He made it difficult. He leaned over her. "It must be nice, to be a royal princess and have men do as you command. What if you encountered one who wasn't inclined to obey?"

"I've never noticed you feel so inclined."

"And what will you do, Princess, now that you've met me?"

"Susannah!" Hortense's voice was sharp with anger. "Mother will wonder what's keeping you."

She whirled on her sister and held up her hand. "A moment, Hortense."

She didn't mind the distraction. It gave her a moment to find a retort. "What will I do? I'll have you put out of the castle. Clandestine meetings, indeed. Very unseemly. I think not, Mr. Tom."

Jon Tom's expression darkened like a threatening storm. "What do you know of what's seemly? Your mouth speaks such prim words, but your nature betrays you."

"Do not speak to me in such a way!" She trembled as ire washed over her like ocean waves. Her nature? He pinpointed the exact part of her she was questioning after last night. She opened her mouth, shut it, opened it again. What under the stars could have driven him to say such a thing? Did he believe it or was he needling her? How could he have guessed her secret, and very recent, fear?

He was no mind reader, else his case would already be solved. Something else had inspired him to speak it. Something like her nature. If she hadn't been so angry and shocked, she might have burst into tears.

Heedless of Hortense waiting nearby, she ranted at him. "You can't imagine what I go through every day, knowing I'm the one who's supposed to marry and save my kingdom, knowing I'm the one who may never do so. Knowing that even if

I do, I won't bear male children. I'm trapped by unfair laws and a curse no one can break. A curse that, indirectly, is my fault! My fault for being born. If you want to help, apply your skills to the Female Curse, not how twelve hopeless women put holes in their slippers."

Susannah's throat closed. Her eyes grew hot. She never spoke her true mind with such emotion to anyone outside of her family, and sometimes not even then. It was not in her nature. She turned from the detective, who had the grace to look ashamed. He raised a hand to her and stopped himself. Again.

If he'd laid his hand upon her arm, if he'd touched her, she might have thrown herself at him. Would she have clawed at his eyes or wept upon his chest? Susannah didn't want to know the answer to that. Without another word, she fled across the grass to Hortense.

Chapter Eleven

The barge was roomy and built for comfort, not speed. Cushioned benches lined the sides on both decks while the magic-powered stern wheel propelled them slowly across the lake. A string band played on a tiny stage downstairs in the forward bow. On the bottom deck, the wind tousled Susannah's hair. Gold-coated waiters moved among the guests and served finger sandwiches, fruits, crab cakes and sticky figs, washed down with lemonade or iced chocolate. Benevolent parents observed their children mingling with the royal daughters, and even the Queen smiled.

Susannah sourly wondered if any of the townsfolk had hopes one of their sons would perform a great feat and be able to inherit this barge, this whole kingdom. More likely, the young men would perform piddling feats that did no good or try to slay dragons and get themselves eaten. The youths in their kingdom had enough sense so far not to hurl themselves at the task of achieving nobility. In some kingdoms, middle-class lads were growing rare as well because they'd all been killed attempting great feats.

Peasants hardly ever chased after the dream. They had too much sense, less ambitious mamas and papas—and were more likely than the bourgeoisie to dumb-luck into a title. Perhaps the influx of hardy farmer stock would dilute the idiocy of the Middle Kingdoms' rulers. By the time the new baronets achieved Consortium majority, Susannah would be too old to enjoy the results.

If the Consortium, and the Middle Kingdoms, even existed for the baronets to repair.

A sharp whack snapped her out of her reverie, and a blue ball clacked onto the bench beside her. Ella trotted up. "That was supposed to go through the wicket," she said. "Do you mind tossing that here?"

Susannah threw her sister the ball. "Don't hit them into the water like you did last time. You'll end the game too early."

"Come play with us." Ella leaned upon her croquet mallet. Her hair, like Susannah's, had defied its pomade and haloed wildly. Her gown had water splotches. "You're dumpy today. You can be on my team."

"And lose for sure?" She forced a smile and waved away Ella's offer. She couldn't bring herself to pretend enjoyment of the expedition. She preferred to lick her wounds alone. Parental chaperones milled everywhere, so Susannah had no responsibilities besides leaning on the gunnels and staring off into the distance. She didn't feel like informing her mother about Rosa's womanly development, and if she stayed where she was, she might not lay eyes upon Jon Tom at all.

In addition to his taunts about her nature, the detective's jibe about lies had sliced into the careful shell that allowed her to defy the King and Queen. To drag her sisters to an enchanted palace, and not tell them. To have magic, as a mortal, and not tell them. A great deal of guilt oozed through the cut. The princesses' activities brought much unhappiness to their parents and the unfortunate guards who volunteered to watch them.

Yes, she had idle time, but as usual, Susannah gnawed her cuticles and churned her worries and fears in her mind. If her magic were revealed, their kingdom might be ostracized. Boycotted by the fairies. Who knew what else? The rules for human-fairy interaction certainly didn't cover her situation. Foresta's citizens could live without the modern conveniences fairies supplied for them, but without fairy warding, the wild, primitive Hinterlanders would pour through Oldtree Forest and overwhelm them. Foresta's military was disciplined but small, like the kingdom itself. Growing, of course, as were all armies in all kingdoms, but still too small.

If she gave up her magic this instant, the kingdom might be safe until they had no one to rule it. Their parents would be happier. Jon Tom would go away.

But how could she give up the magic now that she'd found it? Once she'd broken through the barrier as a teen, her thirst for knowledge, for cures to the curses, had turned her into a driven woman. But had the heady power changed her spirit, her character? She didn't know.

Jon Tom and Prince John would lead her to believe it had.

Another issue was how to convince her sisters to give up the princes temporarily. She herself couldn't bear to give them up forever and resign herself to failure. She'd blossomed with magic for a reason, hadn't she? The princes' situation paralleled the noble ladies in the Middle Kingdoms—no one to love, no one to marry and limited activity with which to fill their lives.

Solving the Female Curse came first and releasing the princes second, but she'd made the most headway with the princes. She'd found them, and now after all these months something had caused them to misbehave. Yesterday in her surreptitious translation of *Seven Habits*, she'd shuffled through a bit in the second chapter, in the text after the first guideline, about fulfilling the paradox of a curse.

Or maybe it had said wrap it in cotton cloth and bury it under a stump for seven nights, she wasn't sure.

Lilly slid onto the bench next to Susannah with a sigh and interrupted her crotchets. "I'm tired, and I don't like rowing boats one bit. How long before your shoulders quit hurting?"

Susannah raised an eyebrow. "I can still feel a twinge, but you're younger than me, and you rowed much better than I did."

"Definitely," Lilly said with a giggle. "I was hoping..." Her sister's musical voice trailed off and she looked down at her slim fingers anxiously.

"What were you hoping? That Mother would ask you to sing so you could enchant all the men?"

Lilly shrugged and winced with pain. "I was hoping you could do that thing. You know, when Ella sprained her ankle jumping down the garden stairs?"

Most of the sisters, while they accepted Susannah could open the door to the enchanted realm or peer through a solid rock wall, were leery of Susannah's magic. It was hard to break eons of conviction that mortals couldn't perform spells. Lilly asking for a magical curative was something of a breakthrough.

It probably wasn't wise to use the power for something nature could fix, as Hortense always insisted, but the opportunity to prove herself delighted Susannah. "We'll have to go somewhere no one can see us. I know how much the aftereffect of rowing hurts."

"Oh, thank you!" Lilly's face brightened and she rose from the bench in a flurry of skirts. "I didn't want to fuss this morning because no one else seemed to be ill."

"Your stiff upper lip is commendable. Where shall we hide, the ladies room?"

"Oh, I know a better place. Behind Mother and Father's thrones is the wheel room. No one is ever in there during one of these luncheons."

Susannah and Lilly wove through the partygoers with that "Going to the powder room" aura to ward off conversation. The necessary was also in the stern.

"How do you know about this secret wheel room?" she asked her sister.

Lilly opened her lavender eyes very wide. "Sawmill Archie and I—"

"I don't want to know!" Susannah held up a hand. "You're one and twenty. That's old enough to draw your own boundaries with your paramours. But do keep in mind the local lads are not enchanted."

"He just explained the principles of the fairy wheel," Lilly said with a toss of her blonde hair. "I know how to handle these boys."

"Just so you don't handle them the way you did the princes last night." Susannah couldn't help herself. It was as if an internal mother took possession of her every time she fell into conversation with one of the younger girls.

When Lilly's face scrunched, Susannah regretted her nagging. She wanted to make amends, show how thankful she was that Lilly appreciated Susannah, magic and all.

"I'm sorry, Lilly." Susannah slipped her arm around her sister's tiny waist and squeezed. "I'm sure you noticed my little argument with the detective. It's made me snappish."

Lilly shrugged but didn't slide away from her arm. "You've been snappish all your life. Peter says it's because you're not popular with men."

"Why should I be? You know my curse." Susannah sighed. "I won't marry a man of my own choosing."

"You don't even try. You're not even nice to them."

"It's not easy for me to talk to fellows. My talents lie in other areas."

"That's what Hortense says," Lilly agreed. "But what does she know? She's not all that nice to men herself."

"Men aren't the only important thing in life." Susannah couldn't believe they were having this conversation. She'd just reminded herself to be kinder, yet they were already arguing.

They reached the bottom deck and sidled along the railing to the stern where the broad paddle wheel spritzed them with lake water. Nearly as wide as the barge, its blue-painted spokes blurred together as the wheel turned ceaselessly. It rose to the level of the top deck at its peak.

Lilly, who didn't seem bothered by the discussion, opened the narrow door built into the back wall. They stooped to enter the room, which was dominated by the splashing wheel. Moldy and tight, the chamber contained wet rope, dim fairy globes, a pile of tools and a ladder that climbed to the upper deck. The fairy globes, sensing their presence, brightened. The edge of the rolling wheel formed the back of the chamber, and sunlight glittered at the top. A clumsy move would cause a nasty accident and tangle someone in the churning wheel.

Susannah studied the ladder dubiously. They hugged the wall away from the wheel and splashing water. "Surely you don't want to climb up behind the thrones?"

"You're right. That would hurt my shoulders. Can you do it here? The room up there is dryer, but it's behind Mother's throne and she might hear us."

"Sure," Susannah agreed. "Turn your back to me. This will feel warm." She placed her hands over her sister's shoulders. "Is this where the pain is?"

"Yes."

Susannah concentrated, opening the barrier in her mind so power trickled down her arms, out her palms and into Lilly's stiff muscles.

"Oooh, that feels good." Lilly hummed with pleasure. "It's like sunshine."

In addition to the electric feel of the magic, Susannah's shoulders twinged as she soaked the ache away. When it disappeared, she removed her hands. "I'm done."

"That's it?"

"That's it." Susannah shook out her fingers. "My hands tingle but there shouldn't be aftereffects."

"But that was so innocuous."

"Do you think fairy magic is evil, Sister? Or that I would use it in an evil way?"

"No, but Peter said…" Lilly stopped herself and smiled in a self-conscious fashion.

Susannah laughed. "Peter also said she'd be married by the time she was twenty-five and the sole heir to Father's kingdom. You'll notice she's thirty and unwed."

Lilly hugged her and kissed her cheek. "I shouldn't have said you were bad with men even though you're beastly to Mr. Tom."

Susannah wanted to say, "He starts it," but instead she said, "Mr. Tom is a different case. He's dangerous. And I'm not convinced he doesn't have a magic mirror or truth spell under his cap."

"Yes, dangerous." Lilly winked at Susannah, who frowned in puzzlement. Then she continued. "You're truly afraid of him finding out, aren't you?"

Susannah wasn't the only one in danger, though her danger was more profound than her sisters. "He's come closer than anyone else. He seems to think he knows something."

"He can't possibly." Lilly waved a slender hand. "He would have told already."

The two sisters were silent for a moment, and then Lilly rushed through the spray of water and climbed the ladder to the upper deck. "As long as we're here, you might as well see the wheel from the top."

As silently as possible, they ascended the narrow ladder and stood in the upper chamber, similarly snug but dryer. Through a hole in the floor, Susannah looked down upon the wide wheel as it made its watery circuit. A slight tingle in the air let her know this was the seat of the magic that drove the wheel.

A Spell for Susannah

"This is where the fairies come to refresh the power," Lilly whispered. "Archie told me. His father wants to install a fairy wheel at the sawmill for dryer seasons."

"I feel the magic," Susannah said. "It's residue from the spells. I feel the same thing in the bathing chamber when the fairies renew the spigots, and sometimes I notice it when the spigots are in use."

"That's creepy." Lilly shuddered.

A double thump from the opposite wall of the chamber sent Susannah and her sister into a mouse-like silence. Muffled voices came after the thumps. If Susannah guessed correctly, the noises came from the small, raised throne dais on the other side of the top wall.

Lilly pressed her ear against the wall. "I bet it's Mother and Father. Let's listen."

"Eavesdropping." Susannah tsked, but she pressed her ear against the wall all the same.

The voices remained muffled but one of them was the Queen's and the other had a deep, husky timbre that sounded like Jon Tom.

Susannah, here in the tingling power room, decided to try something new. "Hold my hand," she whispered to Lilly. "I'll try my listening spell on us both."

Perhaps because of the residue of magic and perhaps because of Susannah's increasing talents, when she cast the spell, the sudden clarity of the voices took them aback. In fact, they didn't have to have their heads pressed against the wall to make out the conversation. Lilly, fascinated, seemed no more frightened by this than she'd been of the healing spell.

"...if you could tell me more about it," the Queen was saying. Her dry voice crackled with sarcasm, and Susannah could picture the skeptical look on her mother's face.

"My argument with your eldest daughter was minor, Your Highness. Nothing to concern yourself about."

So he was hiding things from the Queen, Susannah mused. He wanted his assignation with her to be secret. What did that mean?

"Encouraging her to act the harridan in front of several local families is not a minor thing, Mr. Tom."

125

"It required little encouragement from me," he muttered. Susannah scowled while Lilly swallowed a giggle.

"What was that?" the Queen asked.

"I said, your daughter's a very headstrong woman."

"She takes after her mother," the Queen said with relish. "However, I don't understand why you're going about your task so abrasively. You could catch that fly better with honey than vinegar. I thought we discussed this."

"I have a plan, Your Highness."

"You only have one more chance, my good man. Have you made any headway?" Susannah had no doubt her mother's bright gaze pinned the man to his chair.

"I'm confident I'll be able to tell you where you daughters have been going these many months when the time comes."

Confident, was he? There was no way he could know unless he had a magic mirror that penetrated Susannah's glamour on the beds. Even then it wouldn't reveal the enchanted realm itself, just the ladies' absence. Susannah and Lilly exchanged a baffled glance.

"How have you come across this information?" the Queen asked.

Jon Tom cleared his throat. "I have a mole amidst the princesses. If I apply the right pressure, I can get her to tell me everything I want to know."

Was it Rosa? And what did the horrid man mean by pressure? She met Lilly's gaze again, and the girl shrugged, equally mystified.

"Who is it and how are you getting your information? You don't appear to be doing what I told you to do."

The conversation made little sense. How had their mother instructed Jon Tom to find out? If she had some method in mind she thought would work, why hadn't she done it herself?

"Some of my techniques must remain the confidential province of the detective." Jon Tom appeared to be regaining his footing with the demanding Queen. "Trade secrets, you understand. Telling you would be like revealing the secret ingredient in a chili recipe."

"It's cinnamon," the Queen said. "Everyone knows that. Enough swanky dancing around the topic. You say you'll be able to tell me where they've been. What about how to keep them from going?"

"Was that part of the original agreement, Your Highness?"

"I don't care if it was. I'll know how to control my own daughters and you'll tell me, or you won't get your reward." They heard the same thump that had alerted them to the conversation. Susannah realized it was the Queen striking the floor with her cane.

"I can pull out the written contract," he said.

"I can order you hounded from the kingdom," the Queen responded. "And my husband will do as I say."

There was a strained silence before Jon Tom chuckled. "I see where Princess Susannah gets her strong will, Your Highness."

"Is Susannah the mole?"

"I can't tell you."

"I've also noticed you spend time with my youngest."

There was a scuffling sound, and the Queen continued. "You thought I had no idea what you did with your time. You're not the only talented observer, my cocky lad."

"If you were in the business you'd give me a run for my gold," he said. "I'm glad you're a Queen and not my competition."

"About Susannah, Mr. Tom. Goading her won't work. Miss always appears to be on the verge of falling into a screaming fit, but mark my words, she never does. You can't be so squeamish. Do as I told you, and all will be well."

"I don't think I'll need to resort to that."

"Squeamish," the Queen repeated. "You have my royal pardon in advance. This is what I hired you to do."

A royal pardon in advance—it sounded as if the Queen wanted Jon Tom to act the thug—cheat, steal or murder. But that was ridiculous.

"It's not necessary, Your Highness. I've been provoking her so she'll grow angry with me and take steps to see me dismissed. If she's cross, she'll be incautious."

Susannah pressed her lips together. Forewarned, forearmed. She should have known he had some ulterior motive for spending time with her. And she had, but part of her had hoped... Oh, it was ridiculous.

"So she is your mole!"

"I didn't say that," he denied. "That's just one avenue of research."

"She's sharp-tongued but not hot-tempered, and her reaction to you hasn't been typical. If you want to goad one of my daughters to lose her temper, try Peter, Esme or Ella."

"I told you," Lilly whispered. "You're not so bad as all that."

The Queen spoke more. "With Susannah, it's a defense mechanism against people who threaten her or men to whom she's attracted. With you it's both, hence the strength of her response."

Susannah's jaw dropped open, and Lilly stifled a hoot of laughter.

"I wouldn't hurt her," Jon Tom said stiffly.

"I've seen the heated looks you lay upon her. You're foolish to do this the hard way. She's half in love with you already."

Lilly chortled with delight. "That's just what I thought!"

"What was that?" Both the Queen and Jon Tom went silent.

"It sounded like voices." The sisters heard scooting wood and then a knock upon the wall next to their heads.

"It's probably one of my girls canoodling with that jeweler's boy. Who's missing?"

The Queen's cane thumped again, and Susannah dumped the listening spell. She and Lilly scrambled down the ladder, through the spray in the bottom room and out onto the narrow deck near the paddle wheel.

Eavesdroppers rarely heard anything good about themselves. Susannah's face burned as Lilly stifled more laughter. Her mother, now Jon Tom, thought her attracted to him. She had a sinking feeling she knew her mother's original orders for the man. Half in love with him already—and he should finish his job the easy way. With trembling hands, she shook her dusty skirts and water droplets flew off to land upon her sister's lavender gown.

"Cut it out!" Lilly wiped at her bodice, but the darker patches stood out against the delicate material.

"Take my hand. Mother will toss us to the mercy of the laundresses if she finds out we were doing something as uncouth as eavesdropping. I've never tried a drying spell, but—"

Lilly stepped back. "Well, don't try one now, you'll send us up in flames."

Rebuffed, Susannah dropped her arm. Before she could decide what to do next, the Queen and Jon Tom rounded the corner of the walkway, the Queen's mouth thinned to a narrow line.

"Did your beaus jump into the lake?" The Queen cracked her cane against the walkway's wooden railing.

Susannah scratched behind her ear where a water droplet had made its way through her thick hair. She very carefully did not look at Jon Tom. "What are you talking about, Mother?"

"Why aren't you with the rest of the party? What are you doing back here?"

"Watching the paddle wheel," Lilly replied. "We came out here to cool off. And talk." She linked arms with Susannah. "Girl talk."

Susannah had an idea. "Mother, can we have a moment alone with you?" She squeezed Lilly's arm to her side in thanks.

"I'm sure Mr. Tom would enjoy knowing what girl talk had you two ladies up in the wheel room eavesdropping on your mother," the Queen said.

Jon Tom, behind the Queen on the narrow walkway, watched Susannah as if he could read her mind and figure out what she'd overheard.

With new eyes, she stared at him, horrified at what she was seeing and how much she liked it. Her mother's words forced her to acknowledge what had been growing inside her since the moment she saw him, a deep attraction to his lean, dark face and raffish air, to his mobile lips and tall, straight body. She had never giggled and gushed about a dream man, but if she had, with his intelligence, his humor, his face and form—he would be it.

He had everything she wanted in a man except nobility.

Butterflies, nay, canaries, flapped in her stomach. Prince John had done this to her. The use of magic had done this to her. She was no longer herself but a madwoman who lusted in her heart and body until she was thick with it.

"Susannah, I said, please tell me what you were doing in

the wheel room," repeated the Queen. "Snap out of it. Woolgathering isn't like you."

"I wanted to know what was behind the door." She gripped the railing. "How could we have been listening to anything over the sound of the paddle wheel?"

Slightly behind the Queen, Jon Tom quirked a devilish eyebrow and wagged his finger back and forth.

"You, sir," began Susannah, but Lilly jabbed her in the ribs.

"Mother, we need to talk to you alone," the younger woman insisted.

"Mr. Tom, give me a moment," the Queen said. "I'll find you where Esme is, I'm sure. I recommend you start there."

"Start there doing what?" Susannah asked, even though she could guess. But she didn't want them to know she'd heard the Queen claim she had feelings for Jon Tom.

"Don't ask foolish questions." The Queen jerked her head, dismissing the detective.

Jon Tom bowed and left, but not without giving Susannah one final mocking glance. Susannah watched him edge around the corner, her gaze unfocused.

"Emily told me your new dancing slippers were in a sad state this morning. Would you care to explain how they got that way?"

"Emily is a snitch," Lilly grumbled. "We were up late practicing a new rumba." She shuffled in the narrow space of the deck. "One, two, three, one, two, three."

"That's an old rumba," the Queen said.

"Yes, I can't seem to get it right."

Susannah shook off her trance. "Mother, I think Rosa is about to reach her woman-time. She's been flirting with men."

"What men, the men she danced with last night?"

"Mother!" Susannah blew out a breath. "With a man from the castle."

"You're jealous," Lilly whispered.

"What was that?" the Queen said. Their mother abhorred whispering and secrets.

"I said, you're not very observant." Lilly smiled. "Rosa has been attempting to charm Mr. Tom since he got here."

Susannah must not be very observant, either. She'd only noticed it today.

"You're sure she's not just happy to have someone who'll admire Sir King?" the Queen asked. "My baby is too young. It cannot be time already."

"I was twelve." Lilly straightened her skirts. "Rosa is twelve."

"You also started flirting with men when you were born, and it had little to do with your woman-time. I'll arrange for a visit to the court healer," the Queen said. "If it's true, we have a celebration to plan. My baby's woman-day celebration." Their mother gave an unaccountable sniff. "I suppose it's the last happy event I'll be able to commemorate since none of you can marry."

"Someone will marry into the family eventually," Lilly said. "It just might not be happy."

Susannah flapped her drying skirts. "If you'd reason with Father about Kingdom Law 134 and 333, all this could change. He won't listen to me, Mama. It's the only solution."

"Susannah, I know it's a pet project of yours, but there's nothing we can do to budge the kings in the other lands. And you've got to cease hounding your father to organize a supplementary Consortium. It would accomplish little and annoy the Emperor. You know His Splendor is against changing the inheritance laws. Even with harmony crumbling before their eyes, the Emperor and his kings prefer to wait for middle-class men and peasants to perform great feats and marry their daughters."

Susannah spread her arms helplessly. "But why, Mama? You've always taught us women can think as well as men. Rule as well as men. Why does no one else see it?"

"I don't want to rule a country," Lilly said. "That's just you, Susannah."

"Ah, Lilly. My pretty flower. It shouldn't be for men to run the world, but whoever is best suited." The Queen leaned on her cane with a sigh.

Susannah echoed it in a moment of rare accord with her mother. Her mother agreed with her about the inheritance laws, though she'd long ago grown weary of debating it, but like the Queen said, it helped not at all. Susannah and her sisters had the benefit of a broader education than most of the nobility, males and females alike. They were considered irregular, practically bourgeois by some, and their beliefs about womanly competence radical.

Perhaps that was another subtle aspect of her personal curse. The independence of the Foresta princesses frightened away new baronets and old widowers. Susannah would never marry because she was so cursed independent.

Lilly looked from Susannah to the Queen, and Susannah saw sparks of mischief in her sister's eyes. "I heard some of the kings have taken to sending Malady tributes in hopes she'll reverse the Curse," she said.

"Where did you hear such a thing? You aren't allowed to read the broadsheets," the Queen said. "I won't have my children getting their information from those pulps. They mix too much hearsay with facts."

"We shouldn't send that bitch anything," Susannah growled.

"Watch your mouth." Susannah could tell the Queen's heart wasn't behind her reprimand.

Lilly giggled. "She's a mean old bitch. She probably likes women, if you know what I mean, which is why she wanted so many of them in the world."

"Lilly!" The Queen's heart was firmly in that reprimand. "You have been at the broadsheets!"

"Liking women wouldn't make her a bitch," Susannah countered. "But she's a bitch anyway."

The Queen threw up a hand. "All right, she's a bitch. It's why we convinced the other kings and queens to outlaw her. She put a reek in christenings for a hundred years, at least."

"Mama," Lilly said, "what could we do if she decided to seek revenge? Mortals have no defense against magic unless other fairies help us."

The Queen clasped her hands over the head of her cane. "It's economics, my dear. Who do you think pays the fairies their delicious gold? You know that's one of the few substances they can't enchant, alter or create for themselves, which is why they crave it so dearly. They can't even touch it unless it's been properly smelted. We can, so the fairies want to stay employed by us. They enforce Malady's banishment, even if they cry professional ethics and refuse to lighten her curse."

"What about the FairFairy Oath?" Susannah asked. "Doesn't it say anything about what's fair and what isn't? I mean, "fair" is the first word."

"It's never been proven what the Oath says."

"What if people could..." Lilly bit her tongue when Susannah punched her. "Mmph!"

The Queen turned around on the narrow walkway and marched toward the main part of the boat. "Come along, girls," she said over her shoulder. "It's nearly time to dock. What if people could what, Lilly?"

"Nothing." She took Susannah's arm and held her back a little. She placed her lips next to Susannah's ear. "If humans could do magic, we wouldn't need the fairies. They'd be willing to fix the problem Malady created."

"And I wouldn't have to be so afraid all the time. I wonder if other humans can work magic? Surely we'd have heard about it."

"Not if they're as sneaky as you and don't want to get caught."

"True," Susannah said with a sigh. "I certainly don't want to get caught."

Chapter Twelve

During the fourth course at dinner, Susannah's father confirmed the news her sisters had heard at the lake. A young peasant in Kingdom Rasta had performed a great feat, elevating himself to the ranks of the nobility, and was making his triumphal tour across the Middle Kingdoms. Commoners and middle-class men who succeeded were made baronets, a nonhereditary title that required marriage into the "true" aristocracy to reap further benefits. If a baronet chose to marry beneath himself, or if he were already married, he wouldn't bestow nobility upon his offspring. The baronets didn't receive lands, only their title and any sweeteners from prospective fathers- and mothers-in-laws.

Few of the new sirs married their childhood sweethearts, though a couple had taken the bribes and run—usually into the Hinterlands, because they quickly fell out of favor in the Middle Kingdoms.

"Why haven't you told us of this prospective mate?" Hortense demanded. "We could have issued invitations, prepared for his visit and brushed up on our court etiquette."

"I doubt a lad who used to be a farmer's son is savvy about etiquette," Calypso said.

The sisters all turned on the King. "Yes, Father, why did you keep this a secret?"

Their father, seated at the head of the table and hiding behind a huge goblet of wine, winced. Only his salt-and-pepper hair and bristling beard showed around the rim of the cup. He was the epitome of strength and wisdom in his Chambers, in dispensing justice to his citizens, but when faced by his family, their Papa had the courage of a noodle.

Considering their much greater numbers and the habitual ferocity of her mother, who could blame him? Susannah had tried all day and couldn't even rile herself to protest the Queen's seeming betrayal of her own child. She was, after all, in opposition to what the Queen thought best, and her mother was almost as determined as Susannah to do the right thing, despite the consequences.

Almost.

Jon Tom, the only other man at the table, obviously considered it necessary to defend the King. "Such animation over a boy. Princesses, he might not even be to your liking."

"That wouldn't matter, if it meant one of us could secure a legal heir to the throne," Hortense said. "Whichever one of us he chose would do her duty."

"Hortense loves to have duties," Rosa whispered to her hero, seated between herself and the Queen. "I think she'd love to have a husband more. I know I would."

Susannah exchanged a pointed glance with her mother. She then cast Jon Tom a glare for allowing Rosa to flirt with him, affected as she always was by the contrast between his swarthy skin and white teeth. The knowing look in his eyes, now that she understood what inspired it, unsettled her less.

"How long have you known a new baronet was made?" Hortense asked the King.

"It isn't fair you keep us secluded from the rest of the world," Peter added. "It's enough to make one want to subscribe to the broadsheets."

A statement Susannah knew to be erroneous, because Peter already read the broadsheets.

"Gossipy trash." The Queen snorted. "You learn all you need of the world when you take your lessons in kingdom administration."

Peter got the broadsheets from Cook, but not all the princesses knew Cook indulged in them despite the Queen's castle-wide ban. Susannah found them enlightening herself but hadn't seen this news. Well, she'd been a tad busy, these past six months.

"Law isn't the only thing important in this world, Mother," Peter drawled. "Men are important too, very important. Especially fresh, new, noble men."

How long was her father going to drink from the wine goblet in order to avoid his daughters' comments and hurt looks? He probably wasn't even drinking anything—just holding the cup there, the faker. Well, he'd brought this on himself.

"Dang it, Papa, you always spring a guy's visit on us at the last minute," Calypso said. "Remember the new baronet who showed up when we were being punished with laundry detail? You'd think a guy whose Mum had been a laundress would have been more understanding."

"I wasn't working in the laundry." Rosa licked honey off her knife blade and earned herself a raised eyebrow from her mother. "I was a good girl even then." This she said with a glance under her lashes at Jon Tom, observing the royal-family byplay with fascination.

"You were three," Esme pointed out, "and a squalling brat." She stuffed another glazed coin of pork into her mouth and smiled nastily at Rosa down the table.

Susannah watched the attacks upon her father with little sympathy. Despite the fact his goblet routine amused her, she wished he'd mentioned Sir Hanson earlier. The most stress to catch the boy fell upon her shoulders, christening curse or not.

"Shall we be having many parties?" Lilly inquired. "I need to plan my wardrobe."

Parties! Balls! Picnics! Susannah detested the sporadic visits from elevated nobles, even though she tried earnestly to win herself a husband. Perhaps flaunting her aging charms for a twenty-something boy who was the greatest prize in the Middle Kingdoms might take her mind off her troubles, but she doubted it, not even with her magically inspired wantonness. A crotchety earl who'd lost his wife was more her speed, though that type tended to marry locally. That type also tended to expire long before their wives.

Which was, when you considered it, a blessing in disguise.

"He'll marry one of King Gargantua's daughters, you just watch. Kell's as plump as an autumn turkey with land and wealth." Calypso gestured with her fork. "The lads never stay here for long. Our kingdom is too small and too close to the Hinterlands."

"What did he do, Papa? What was his feat?" Ella asked, but the King had not emerged from his goblet yet.

"I hear he fetched water from the Fountain of Youth for Queen Derryberry and now she looks younger than Princess Stasia. That must be a smashing story!" Calypso's waving fork nearly speared Hortense.

"These baronets have stories to tell, I can see, but what about widowers?" Jon Tom asked. "What about the last sons of the nobility before the Female Curse?"

Was he truly curious or trying to trip them up? These were questions he'd not asked Susannah individually. No, his questions of her had all been much more personal. Designed, perhaps, to foster intimacy between them—with the Queen's blessing. As if that would cause Susannah to confess.

It would not work.

She rolled several tiny cabbages across her plate until they came up against the pork. Maybe she should hide them under her rice so her mother wouldn't notice she was off her feed and prescribe a purge.

"Same difference." Calypso shrugged. "The Middle Kingdoms have always been short on sons, and now there aren't any left. The geezers choose the youngest, richest and most beautiful girls available. And that's not us."

"Speak for yourself," Peter said.

"Princess Calypso, don't underestimate the charms of yourself and your sisters." Jon Tom's dimples flashed. "You boast among your number some of the finest flowers in beauty, wit and deviousness to be found anywhere in the Middle Kingdoms." He raised his glass in a general toast, but Susannah was the one seated across the table from him.

"Deviousness isn't a charming quality," Rosa said. She set her chin upon her hands and gazed up at him. "Not like sweetness of nature or asking a man a lot of questions about himself." Her plate lay neglected in front of her. She had, throughout the meal, been asking Jon Tom questions about himself instead of eating.

"Is the baronet coming here or not?" Hortense demanded.

"When is he coming? Why didn't you tell us? Why?" The princesses pressed their father until the Queen rapped on the table with the butt of her silver knife.

When all eyes were upon her, she stated, "Your father didn't want to get your hopes up."

"They always come here, even though they don't stay," Calypso pointed out. "If it's not the way Papa runs his Justice Chambers they want to know about, it's the hunting in Oldtree Forest. Not that I blame them."

"Some visit for other reasons," Peter said in a voice that sounded suspiciously like a purr.

The Queen pointed her knife at Peter. "No one here is so desperate this young baronet should be coerced, by foul means or fair, into choosing any of you for a bride." Her meaning was quite clear. "Your father and several kings are entering a new round of negotiations with the Fairy Alliance to find a solution to the Female Curse. The inheritance troubles are a long way away for our family."

"More negotiations? You've been in negotiations for years." No matter what Susannah did, her father wouldn't do the reasonable thing and pressure the others to revise the Kingdom Laws. No, they waited for suicidal peasants. She often felt she alone, in all the land, sought a real solution to the Curse. A tide of annoyance crashed over her.

She pushed her plate away. "Why call a Consortium to snivel to the FAE when you ignore the fetid stench of Kingdom Law 134? Nothing ever comes of negotiating with the fairies. Not in thirty-five years have you gained an inch. What do you offer this time, your firstborn? Do you send me to the fairies?"

"Wish they would," Esme grumbled.

The King quickly raised his goblet to his face, after setting it down when his lady wife reigned in her daughters.

"Papa, put down that goblet. I know you aren't actually drinking."

The King peered over the rim of the cup at her, down at the other end of the table. He made a slurping sound. The Queen cast her fine gaze at the ceiling.

"Your eldest is vehement in her beliefs," Jon Tom said. "I too have heard little is to be gained from negotiating with the fairy folk. I don't do business with them unless I get a contract signed in gold ink they can't manipulate."

Susannah, used to Jon Tom countering her every move, raised a suspicious eyebrow before she realized that was a habit she'd picked up from the man himself. He winked at her, a habit she didn't think she was in any danger of adopting.

"Not all fairies are wicked like Malady," Rosa said. "Budbud is quite nice. She blesses our faucets without fail."

"Don't say that old biddy's name," Calypso said. "What if it made her show up and curse us all with bad gas or something?"

"Budbud wouldn't do that!"

"No, the b...witch, Malady."

"Calypso, that's enough," the Queen said.

"She wouldn't have to curse Papa," Ella said, giggling. "He's been in the port again."

"You little devil!" The King chucked a half-eaten roll at his squealing progeny. An impassive servant caught the badly thrown bread with one hand as if it were nothing unusual.

Because, in fact, it wasn't. Susannah used to be a dab hand with peas, but hadn't been carefree enough to indulge in years.

"My family is a disgrace." Rosa sighed and shook her head. "I do hope you'll overlook them, Mr. Tom. Very unsophisticated."

The dessert course was a cool strawberry syllabub served in iced bowls shaped like different birds. Jon Tom stroked a long finger down the neck of his glass swan. "You must have a talented glassblower on your staff. I solved one case where a dishonest glassblower used fairy ice for his creations so they disappeared in three days, and he with the buyer's gold."

Susannah accepted her syllabub from a maid and exhaled. "Don't you ever get tired of boasting? What about cases you've lost?"

"It's difficult to say. There've been so few." He said this with a straight face, but she knew him well enough to sense when he was teasing. "I failed to discover who'd stolen a giant's singing harp once."

"I'm sure Mr. Tom will perform his assignment to my satisfaction," the Queen said. "No one can expect to succeed at everything."

Jon Tom inclined his head. "Or hide everything they wish to hide."

Did he have to gloat in such a fashion? He had a pre-pardon to beguile her, and her own mother was of the opinion she was half in love with him already! Even the way he ate his dessert was gloating. Tonight his gaze had an even more superior quality, like he knew something that would put her at a disadvantage.

Which he did. Susannah flushed as pink as her syllabub.

And, of course, he was watching her, that infuriating smile upon his face. He licked a dollop of cream from his forefinger and deliberately let his gaze drop to her bosom.

Her mother, too, had a funny smile. What exactly was her pact with him? Was he to charm Susannah...or more? Did the Queen intend to sacrifice one daughter's honor, one daughter almost too old to bear children, in order to buy fewer slippers? To satisfy her need to control the whole kingdom and everyone in it? Why did her mother think a seduction would provide any information beyond the fact Susannah was more than half in love with Jon Tom?

"Quit weighing that roll like a shot put," the Queen snapped at Temple, which startled Susannah off her tangent. "And you, put the syllabub in your mouth at once." Ella, who'd aimed a huge spoonful down the table, gagged down the oversized mouthful.

The King slumped back in his chair and patted his stomach. "Another delicious meal down the hatch." He stifled a belch. Ella swallowed, took a gulp of water and echoed her father's belch without the stifling attached.

The Queen placed her linen napkin on the table. "Your Highness, I blame the girls' behavior entirely upon you."

The King's eyes widened, the picture of innocence. "See what I have to put up with, Jon? Henpecking from all quarters."

"To be pecked by such hens," Jon Tom said, "is to be the happiest rooster in the Middle Kingdoms."

Jon Tom's lips were reddened from the syllabub. Susannah sucked the last of the confection off her spoon, reminded of the sweet wine on the tongue of the enchanted Prince John. These distracting surges of physicality hadn't bothered her before...

Of course! The insight hit her like a bowl of syllabub in the face.

She'd been practicing magic for years without side effects. It wasn't the magic. Her libidinous urges were due to the slow burn of the enchanted princes, the quick blaze of Prince John. He'd awakened her physically and intellectually, and Jon Tom could sense her hunger.

Susannah was no green girl. She knew about sexual frustration. Sex was an itch one scratched or, if an unmarried noble female who had no wish to be banished, learned to ignore. Her nature did call out to Prince John and, perhaps, Jon Tom, but it was human nature, not some unwholesome lust. Her body had unfinished business.

Nothing to be ashamed about, unless she made rash decisions to alleviate it. Susannah's throat tightened with sentiment, and she pulled a thread out of her napkin to disguise her relief. Identifying the problem was half the battle.

She forced her gaze to remain on the crystal bowl and contemplated Kingdom Law 134 or even 333, those unfair, stupid rulings. If they were changed in the Middle Kingdoms' time of need, she could have any John she wanted as a spouse. *If* she wanted a spouse. An overhaul of Kingdom Laws would allow her to inherit without one.

But a husband—ah! A virile husband with whom she could progress beyond the restrictions of the single maiden. A husband with dark hair and eyes, a husky voice and smooth, delicious skin...

Blast! She definitely needed to talk politics with her father. Why couldn't he see how much more sense it made to improve Kingdom Laws than to debate with fairies?

Though how much sense did it make to lust after commoners who were a threat to her in more ways than three?

The Queen rose and signaled the end of dinner. The King and Jon Tom stood, as did her sisters, but Susannah remained seated.

"Susannah?" the Queen said. "The meal is finished. Are you glued to your chair?"

Susannah smiled, showing teeth. "I wish to speak with Father."

Her sisters leapt away from the table and rushed the door. They'd no wish to be subjected to another debate between herself and the King about the inequitable aspects of the Middle Kingdoms' laws.

"Why don't you go with my sisters?" Susannah suggested to Jon Tom and waved her hand in the direction of her fleeing siblings. "I'm sure you'll be more entertained in the drawing room than you will here."

"I'm sure I would not," Jon Tom replied.

"Jon and I have been in the middle of a fascinating discussion about one of his cases," the King said. "He can't possibly let me wonder about the outcome for another night. He must tell me how he solved it. Now, in fact."

"Papa, I wish to speak with you. I won't leave your side until I do." Susannah stalked down the table to her father. She planted her fists upon her hips in an unladylike fashion. "You have some explaining to do about this Sir Hanson. And your rotten talks with the FAE. You promised me you'd call a different sort of Consortium—without fairies."

"Didn't we have a nice chat about this the other day?" the King quibbled.

Susannah tapped her foot. "I'm your heir, so to speak. I'm the firstborn you're probably about to trade to the fairies. I deserve to be heard."

"I doubt the fairies want you, Susannah," said the Queen, who'd remained beside the table.

The King begged his wife. "Dear? Honey? Don't you need to instruct Susannah about something?"

"Mother, would you prefer I speak with you about the inheritance laws?" Susannah fluttered her eyelashes. "The stress of the Female Curse preys upon my spirit and I need the counsel of my beloved parents."

"Not really," her mother said.

"His Highness has been anxious to hear about my case with the Fairy Beatific." Jon Tom rounded the table to loom over Susannah. "He thinks it might reflect on your situation, Princess. I argued a case using the FairFairy Oath. Perhaps you've heard of it?"

"Rumors only," she said, intrigued despite herself. "So it exists? Mama, did you hear that?"

"The fairies don't wish to make it public. It could be used against them when they overassert their powers. They do, mostly, stick to it."

The King nodded. "Yes, that case. The one with the, ah, fairy thing."

"The conflict was between a human family and a fairy

wherein the fairy was accused of gifting a child in an inappropriate fashion and was forced to pay another fairy to cast a softening based upon my presentation to the FAE. That's why I think it would interest you, considering your own fairy gifts."

Susannah's stomach lurched. For a moment she thought he meant her magic but realized he meant her christening blessings—and her curse.

"How impolite to bring my curse up," Susannah said, thinking of her other blessings—canniness, sharp vision, a way with jams and jellies and a bounteous bosom.

"Your identity is no secret, Princess. You're the last noble child visited by Malady before the banishing." Jon Tom tilted his head, acknowledging her significance.

"Don't be missish." The Queen picked up her ever-present cane. "On that note, I believe I'll repair to the drawing room."

"Go with her." Susannah tossed her head at Jon Tom. "Your case is bogus. Christening gifts are covered under the rules for human-fairy interaction in the subsidiary-effects section. Mortals can refuse all gifts or accept all gifts, with the understanding fairies don't seek to do their offspring harm. Well, except Malady. Did she cast that spell?"

"No, and it was a softening the humans requested, Princess, not a retraction. All quite legal and covered in the rules. Or at least in the Oath. Perhaps you might like to keep me on retainer in order to plead your case to the fairies."

No rules she knew about, and she'd researched thoroughly. "I don't think we'll need you on retainer. And I don't want to hear about your case." Actually, she did. "I'm sure you lost it."

"On the contrary, milady, I won it."

"Now my father knows what happened and you can leave. In fact, I order it."

"At your command, Princess." Jon Tom bowed gracefully and departed after the Queen.

"Susannah, why are you so rude?" the King asked. "Didn't we teach you any better than that?" He inched toward the door as he spoke.

"*You* certainly didn't." Susannah moved to stand in his path. "Mother might have, but she's not here."

With a rapacious smile, Susannah slid her arm through her father's and patted her hand upon his embroidered tunic. Now that her mother was gone, her father was at her mercy. His primary defenses against his daughters were fleeing, frolicking and hiding behind the Queen, and she was in no mood to frolic.

"Now, dear Papa, tell me of your recent discussions with the FAE and why you've been hiding them from me..."

Chapter Thirteen

As it transpired, Sir Hanson confirmed a visit to their castle in a week's time. Susannah was grateful for the distraction because the frantic bustle meant her sisters were too busy to complain about Susannah's refusal to take them beneath. The main flaw in her crammed schedule was it left her no uncensored library time. When she had occasion for private study, she inevitably ran into Jon Tom, or he ran into her. The fear he'd put two and two together and get something greater than three and less than five curtailed her investigations.

She couldn't even accuse him of stalking her. Her mother, in addition to the task she thought Susannah didn't know about, had openly assigned the detective to "help" Susannah research Sir Hanson. They were supposed to inventory what might make a lad from Kingdom Rasta tick, but Jon Tom spent a good portion of time off topic. She took pains to hide any hint of attraction when they worked, unchaperoned by any but the archivists who popped in and out.

Studying with Jon Tom was both enlightening and exhausting. When they weren't bickering, he was a tease and a reprobate and he made her laugh when she didn't want to. It was a battle to restrict their conversations to business, a battle she often failed. If he offered her a bite of his apple, she refused. If he stretched, catlike, and displayed his form to advantage in one of the dark tunics he favored, she didn't look. If he complimented her appearance or wit, she scoffed. If he offered to rub her aching shoulders, she reminded him of the impropriety. She was all that was decorous with no trace of the woman who was, perhaps, halfway in love with him already.

On the bright side, he remembered everything he read and compiled information quickly. His was a keen mind that challenged hers. His laughter rang out easily, and each time it did a glow of pleasure warmed her.

Instead of being unforthcoming, as he had until now, he opened up about his past, his preferences and everything else under the sun. His tales about his youth in Pavilion intrigued her, as did the descriptions of his cases. Often the discussion had little to do with him and more to do with information he just happened to possess. He was a master of trivia, large and small.

If only her father had hired him to assist in the Justice Chambers, to study ways to work around the inheritance laws! Some kingdoms had the post of Chief Attendant in Chambers, though the princesses had jointly served that function since Susannah had been seventeen. She could respect the detective in an arrangement like that, she could admire him, like him, were he not a threat to her in ways he couldn't even imagine.

"Cows," Jon Tom observed one day, "are the most tedious creatures. Imagine living in one field your whole life, your only occupation the production of milk and calves. It would be worse than running my parents' bakery."

"Yes, imagine," Susannah said, her voice dry. They'd read every book in the library about animal husbandry and hadn't had a disagreement, a situation too good to last. "Imagine not being able to leave home because you're unmarried and there's no one for you to marry. No bull, as they say. Imagine being locked up nightly with eleven cranky women for no reason."

"They wouldn't be cranky if they were locked up with me."

"I'm cranky, and I've been locked away with you every morning and afternoon for days. Endless days." She threw down her book with a sigh.

"If you'd allow me to—"

"I know what you're going to say. Mind your tongue." Susannah offered the reprimand with only half her usual firmness. She, too, was tired of studying cows, and she didn't want to fight with Jon Tom. "Let's research woodcarving. The broadsheets Mama gave me claim Sir Hanson whittles in his spare time."

Jon Tom set his chin upon his hand. "May I ask you an

impertinent question?"

"You need my permission now?"

The detective twirled his black quill pen between his fingers. He was dressed in dark gray today with silver buttons and fine white lace at his throat and cuffs. "How can you do it, Princess Susannah? Abide by these laws? Offer yourself on a platter?"

"What would you suggest I do, run away from home instead? And support myself how? Who'd hire a disgraced princess for anything but a position of disgrace?"

"Merely a philosophical question, milady."

Susannah shifted upon her chair. She wasn't going to be able to avoid a quarrel, so she answered him honestly. "Do you know what it would mean for all the nobles to die out? To lose my parents and be unable to preserve the kingdom because I'm unmarried, and a woman? To watch it all fall into disrepair?"

"An end to certain laws you detest," he suggested. "Perhaps it would be for the best."

"The Middle Kingdoms aren't a phoenix, to rise from the ashes purified and whole. It's not a simple job to guide a kingdom, Mr. Tom. That's why it's best if people trained for it are at the helm. The royal offices and their executive branches maintain Justice Chambers, and for that, and other services, the citizenry pays their taxes. Foresta requires a steady influx of gold to fund the border wards. Or do you fancy Hinterlanders roaming about the countryside, raping, pillaging and chopping off heads?"

"Sir Hanson isn't trained to rule."

"But I am." She straightened her dark green skirts with a decisive flick.

"He might be a man who won't listen to his wife. He might think women are weak."

Susannah laughed. "And you don't?"

"How could I think that, now?" He set down his quill and took her hand in his own. Actually took her hand! She was so shocked she didn't withdraw it. He often threatened to touch her, or massage her shoulders, or do other things, but he never followed through.

"Now?" She tried to act like his warm palm, his grasp,

didn't affect her.

"Now," he murmured and leaned toward her. There was a small table between them, but if he stood, he could kiss her. "He might be a man who doesn't love you."

She knew he intended to overset her, hinting of love and emotion. He was close to succeeding. Verbal repartee she could ricochet, but if he took it further, she'd lose her footing. "What does it mean, to be in love?"

"It means you burn to feel your lover's body next to yours. It means you think of her night and day. It means you would give up anything to please her. A kingdom. Your life." He caressed her palm with his thumb, slow and mesmerizing.

She did think of him night and day—when she wasn't thinking of the Female Curse, her magic or cows. And right now, at this very moment, she burned to feel him against her. But she wouldn't give up her kingdom or her life, not when her mother seemed to have encouraged Jon Tom to act the lover.

"What nonsense," she forced herself to say. She snatched her hand back. "I'll never fall in love. I can't afford to."

"Don't be so sure." His husky voice—did it hold a hint of passion, or just a hint of design?

It was time to put Jon Tom in his place, far across the table from her. She knew just how to do it. "Have you ever been in love?"

He smiled. "I'm unattached, Princess."

Susannah hunched her shoulders. "I suppose being single serves your investigations well. Would you make love to a woman so she'd reveal where the bodies were hidden?"

"I'm sure I'd never fall in love with a murderess. A temptress, a trespasser or even a liar, but not a murderess." Jon Tom inspected his nails casually, but his jaw shifted.

Her turn to lean forward, palms on the table. "I didn't say anything about falling in love. I spoke of attacking the problem using all your...tools."

"Such a high opinion you have of me."

"I've heard things about your past cases. Or should I say conquests?" Usually women used their allure as bait, not men. If the rumors were true, the enterprising detective had begun to exploit the nobility's absence of males. It should come as no surprise he was willing to seduce her at the Queen's behest, yet it saddened her each time she reflected upon it.

"You don't strike me as the kind of woman to give credence to gossip." He held up a hand, fingers spread. "I had five sisters who ordered me around and a mother who supported the family almost without my father's help. Would I dare use a woman in that fashion?"

"You take great pride in winning your cases. What if it made things easier?" she asked, echoing the Queen's words on the barge.

"I respect women. I respect the acumen of the female mind. Some of my most mystifying cases were perpetrated by ladies, and I love a challenge."

"Then you must be mad for me," she said, daring him to answer. "How will you feel when you can't solve this case, Mr. Tom? Will you be mad for me, or just mad at me?"

"Now it's you asking impertinent questions." Jon Tom laughed, but it sounded forced. He paused a moment to gaze at her with inscrutable eyes. "What if I were mad for you, Princess? Do you only soften for someone the law allows you to love?"

He seemed uncertain, as if considering the truth of the matter himself. How did he manage to give that impression? His talents were indeed wide-ranging. She needed to end this conversation before he sent her heart vaulting over a windmill.

"I wouldn't throw the Kingdom Laws at you, Mr. Tom, just this book." She shoved a large volume about woodcarving across the table. "I'm mad for you to tell me what the lads in Rasta are whittling these days."

No matter his demeanor, no matter his apparent candor, she had to gird herself—gird her loins, in truth. She was a case to him. A challenging case. He might acknowledge her intellect, but he didn't chase her heart, only her answers.

❖❖❖

Susannah presented their findings nightly to the family at dinner while Jon Tom observed without comment. Each time he looked at her, Susannah knew how mercenary he thought them.

Two days before Sir Hanson's visit, her mother called Susannah, Peter and Calypso to her office. Over the past week, the Queen had devoted herself to preparing the castle and grounds to tempt Hanson to forge a bond with their tidy little kingdom. Her schedule kept her from pointed discussions with her daughters about expectations, but the furrows between her brows as she sat behind her desk, fondling her cane, indicated the hiatus might be at an end.

Jon Tom sat to one side of her, hands crossed in his lap. His brow was not furrowed.

The Queen thumped her cane like a gavel. "As the three eldest princesses, I've decided you should rehearse your courtly arts before Sir Hanson's visit."

"Aw, Mother!" Calypso exclaimed. "Dancing's all right, but the flirting and the manners and all that nonsense? It's a drag. Why do we have to practice that?"

"Because you'd like to solve our inheritance dilemma?" The Queen leaned her cane against the side of her chair and clasped her hands on the table.

"Susannah and Calypso might need polishing, but I can hardly be described as ignorant of a lady's most elegant weapons." Peter touched her fingertips lightly to her breastbone.

The Queen ignored Peter. "You'll spend several hours a day in simulated flirtation. Jon Tom has agreed to act the part of a noble male to facilitate your efforts."

"Really!" Peter's hand fluttered at her breast. Normally the Queen selected innocuous individuals to masquerade as eligible men when training her daughters in the social arts.

Susannah glanced at Peter. Her sister's skin glowed with pleasure and anticipation, and her rosy lips bowed in a perfect smile. The detective would have to be blind not to notice Peter's exceptional beauty. Something akin to jealousy curdled her insides.

Calypso smacked her hands together. "It beats Emily trying to act like a horny baronet. I mean, they aren't all horny but some of them are a piece of work."

"Calypso," their mother warned.

Calypso continued, undaunted. "The best way to seduce a

farm boy would be to moo and, you know, milk a cow." She made an indecent gesture with one hand.

At that the Queen squawked. "Calypso! A little delicacy, please."

Jon Tom stifled a cough behind his hand.

Susannah trapped her opinion behind her teeth. If it weren't for Peter and Calypso, she'd say this fell right into her mother's plan—throw Susannah and Jon Tom together until her old-maid heart grew squashy with infatuation. It wasn't working so far, and it wouldn't work in the next two days, not even with simulated flirtation. What a joke.

Her sisters adjusted quickly to the startling news. Peter vibrated with excitement at the chance to ply her arts on the detective. Calypso gave him a cheeky thumb's up.

"I must be mad." The Queen, uncharacteristically, rubbed her fingers upon her temples in a gesture of frustration.

"Your Highness, the plan is sensible," Jon Tom said. "The princesses need a real man to practice on if they're to learn anything."

Susannah didn't look at him, but she felt his gaze trail across her body. A real man? That phrase had become inherently aggravating.

Peter was so willing and beautiful. She was ripe to fall in love. Lilly? Susceptible to flattery. Esme? Vengeful and temperamental. Any of them would have made a better weak link than Susannah. Even Rosa, she had to admit.

Yet Susannah was her mother's choice and Jon Tom's target. His innuendoes grew more devious every day, as if he weren't performing but following his natural inclinations. His presence grew more to her taste. He'd held her hand and spoken of love. He and the Queen thought she was enthralled, vulnerable, and they were flat wrong.

She wasn't vulnerable. She was, in fact, officially angry. This was preposterous.

The Queen sighed. "Susannah, have you nothing to add?"

"Yes, I do. Jon Tom isn't a noble man and I doubt he knows how to act like one. Sir Hanson won't act like one, either. What good is this going to do besides tickle a certain overweening castle employee's perverse sense of humor?"

The Queen pulled some of her hair out of its neat bun. She squeezed the toad on the head of her cane, propped against the side of the chair.

Susannah wasn't done. "If you want us to grow comfortable around a farmer like Sir Hanson, look to our stables, not Jon Tom. Or would that not serve your purpose, Mother?"

"It would serve my purpose if you do what I say without protest. And I say you will practice your social skills. Every little bit helps, Susannah."

"As a detective, I do have experience in the gentlemanly arts." Jon Tom leaned back in his chair and placed one leg over the other, clearly enjoying himself. "Happy to be of service."

Susannah waved him off. "It's not as if we'll forget who you really are."

"I've also been trained in the art of disguise. I can change my appearance and my voice so you wouldn't even know me." He adopted the clipped, nasal tones of the Emperor's Court with startling accuracy. "Is this enough of a gentleman for you?"

"Bravo!" Calypso applauded. "Do the Emperor's son Halbert. You gotta laugh at the guy—sounds like his mouth is full of cheese. Smells like it, too."

Jon Tom smiled. "Perhaps later."

"I know what you're trying to do," Susannah said. "It's a waste of time."

"You mean impressions?" Calypso asked. "I thought it rather clever. Better than my impression of the dairy cow. Ha!"

The Queen leaned forward. "I've changed my mind. It's clear to me who's in the most need of etiquette lessons."

Susannah nodded in agreement. Calypso's forthright nature and lack of decorum had been a problem in the past. In Jon Tom's absence, she could finally translate the next guideline in the *Seven Habits* book.

"Susannah is the only one in need of your tutoring, Mr. Tom," the Queen continued.

"What?" Susannah put her hands on her hips. "After Calypso brought up cow milking and horny baronets in the same conversation? You're joshing me."

"Calypso has her own unique charms and Peter has, well, the obvious ones. From what I can see you're lacking in both."

Susannah dreaded the expression on Jon Tom's face. She saved herself the pain and glared at the Queen, who merely raised an eyebrow. Her mother wasn't wrong about her attraction to Jon Tom, but she wasn't a slave to it. Nor would it sap her brain so much that she spilled her secrets to Jon Tom. She just had to avoid physical contact. And champagne and divans. And libraries. And probably a few other places.

"This is absurd," Susannah said. "I have work to do. I can't mess with this silliness. I promise to be as sweet as syllabub to Sir Hanson, even if he's a buffoon."

"If you can learn to be civil to Mr. Tom, I'll have faith in your progress."

"I'm not a Hinterlander, Mother. I can be civil."

"Mr. Tom, has she been civil to you?" the Queen inquired.

Susannah opened her hands in entreaty. "We didn't fight all the time."

"The princess was a dedicated research partner but not what I'd describe as syllabub."

"Mr. Tom is wasted on Susannah. You should let someone with the best chance of catching Sir Hanson polish her skills." Peter waved her hand up and down her body. "That would be me."

"Peter, your vanity does you no service." The Queen scribbled something on a parchment and ended it with a decisive splat of her quill. "I'm quite decided."

"No offense, Jonny, but I'm glad to be off the hook." Calypso shrugged.

Jon Tom inclined his head. "No offense taken, Princess."

Peter uttered a sound in between a gurgle of shock and a cry of protest. She sounded like a parrot. "Mother! I need to practice!" She cast a languishing glance at Jon Tom.

"Peter, you and Calypso may return to your scheduled occupations." The Queen's tone brooked no argument.

When her sisters left, Susannah turned to go as well.

"Susannah, have a seat. We have matters to discuss."

"What's to discuss? I told you, this is a waste of time. Put Jon Tom to work solving the inheritance troubles. Funny you and Papa haven't thought of that, if he's supposed to be such a good detective."

Susannah thought she heard a snort from Jon Tom but his expression was impassive, without a hint of his wretched dimples. Only his eyes betrayed his amusement at the whole situation.

"Teaching you to keep a civil tongue in your head might be what's needed to solve our inheritance troubles. The baronet will look to you if he wants to marry into this kingdom. As the eldest daughter, you're best dowered and first in line for rule."

"I'll do my duty, but I don't see why this one will be any different."

"My dear, you don't even know the boy. You might have studied his lifestyle this past week, but that doesn't tell you everything about him."

"This won't change anything!" Susannah threw up her hands. How could her mother expect her to cooperate with this sham?

"Sir Zavier was interested in you. And Sir Duper. They'd just needed more of a nudge than you gave them." Sir Duper had been an overweight, former chef who'd caused a great deal of excitement when he focused his attentions on Susannah, but he only wanted her jam recipes.

"They're all alike, all the new baronets, and I have no trouble being civil to any of them." Susannah felt her face grow hot with anger, and she blasted her mother with one of her deepest fears. "It's never enough because I'd choose to get married—to just about anybody! Even that weirdo Zavier would have saved our kingdom. But thanks to Malady, I'm not to marry a man of my choice."

"Then you must let the man choose you." The Queen's eyes narrowed. "And that is why you must become more civil, so one of them will."

Jon Tom contemplated his neatly turned cuff, the mocking expression on his face gone. In fact, Susannah could have sworn he looked discouraged.

"May I speak, Your Highness?" he asked.

The Queen nodded.

"Princess Susannah, if you'd marry anyone to secure your father's kingdom, surely you can stomach two more days of me? We've gotten along well enough in the library, haven't we?"

"There. He admits it." She turned to her mother. "We've

gotten along all week because I was civil. There's no need for this."

"I will not be swayed," the Queen said.

Susannah clenched her fist until she could feel the sharp bite of her fingernails in her palms. "How far will this tutoring go? I want to know the terms and boundaries."

The Queen tapped a finger on her lip. "How hard will it be for you to adopt a sweeter manner with a fellow human being?"

"How shall he measure my ability to be cordial? Shall I make him laugh a certain number of times? Or ask him questions about himself? If I disagree with him, do I lose points?"

"Susannah, don't push your luck."

"I merely want to know what you expect," Susannah said, pushing her luck. "Is he to reciprocate? If I'm to flirt, shouldn't he flirt as well? Or will he just take notes?"

Susannah trained her gaze on her mother, watching for any signs of guilt. It was one thing to encourage Jon Tom to seduce her on the sly and another to send them off with instructions to "practice flirting". Had this been her plan from the beginning, with Calypso and Peter included only to make it less blatant?

The Queen sighed. "It will do little good if Jon Tom acts only as judge. I've asked him to guide you in the little things that flatter a man."

"Peter can teach me that."

"Peter would teach you things I've no wish for my daughters to know before they're married," the Queen said sharply. Susannah wondered how much the Queen knew about Peter's proclivities and then shrugged. There was only one thing the Queen didn't know—and that's why she was foisting Jon Tom upon Susannah, in hopes he'd discover Susannah's secret.

"Mother, two whole days when I could be—"

"Two days is hardly enough! I should have thought of this long ago." Before handing the paper in front of her to Jon Tom, the Queen scribbled on it some more. She whispered to him, and he rose gracefully.

"I've set up a schedule of your activities and amended it to activities appropriate for two. You won't be playing bridge, you'll be happy to know."

"Does Papa agree with this?" Susannah sidled away from Jon Tom when he came to stand beside her, too close for comfort.

"He realizes what's at stake."

Her mother meant more than her ability to engage Sir Hanson. Already she hated that young man! She hoped Peter did seduce him. Surely her sister would have the sense to keep Susannah on as first advisor when she inherited?

But then she, Susannah, wouldn't be the one in charge, the one making the decisions, the one fulfilling her life's purpose. Every single thing appeared to be out of her hands, a state of affairs that set her teeth on edge.

"Why does he get the schedule?" she asked. "I might have some opinions on it."

"Doubtless," Jon Tom murmured.

The Queen closed the oversized ledger beside her and rang a silver bell for a maid. "Because he's the man, my dear. The man is in charge of activities planning."

"Hogwash. You did the planning. Papa doesn't choose your activities. Or his own."

"When we first met, I allowed him to," the Queen said. "One thing you must learn is to let a man think he's in control."

"I suppose their pebble-sized brains thrive on a sense of power," Susannah agreed nastily. "He'd feel less of a man were he were forced to admit a woman knew what was best for him." Jon Tom chuckled, and his arm brushed against hers.

"I know many individuals who thrive on a sense of power. Not all are men." The Queen arched an eyebrow.

Susannah protested. "I do not thrive—"

"Let it drop, Susannah," the Queen interrupted, "and focus on the task at hand. During courting, the man is responsible for showing his lady love an amusing time."

"I'm not his lady love."

"You're not a lady, that's true," Jon Tom said, too low for her mother's ears. "But you're mine for the next two days."

Susannah shot him a disgusted look. They'd developed enough of a rapport during his time at the castle that he ought to know such blandishments would only annoy her.

A maid entered the room to fetch the ledger and whisk it

away to the library. The Queen clasped her hands on the table and addressed them. "Your first activity will be the hot springs. I suggest you go change."

"I can visit the hot springs in this dress." Susannah gestured to her wrinkled brown gown with its full skirt and high, concealing bodice. "It's perfect for stalking across the countryside."

"It's not perfect for swimming." Jon Tom pointed to the first item on their list and Susannah widened her eyes. Swimming, in bathing wear, at the hot springs with Jon Tom? It was painfully contrived. Did her mother really mean for them to...

"I don't think so," Susannah said, to the Queen, to Jon Tom and to herself.

The Queen tilted her chin down. "I do."

Susannah stalled. "Who are you sending with us? She'll need to get ready as well."

"You're a grown woman, and I have no one to spare. I trust you and Jon Tom to conduct yourselves honorably. During official periods of courting, Susannah, a young couple is allowed time alone to explore their compatibility, even royals. You know that."

Jon Tom stepped closer to Susannah, his arm again brushing hers, and she swallowed hard. This was one of those heated situations she needed to avoid if she didn't want the Queen's plan to succeed.

"My reputation will be ruined. This isn't an official period of courtship, and Mr. Tom isn't a noble."

"Where's my crusader for women's equality now?" the Queen said with a sigh. "For a woman who swears she could rule a kingdom alone, you're certainly reluctant to try something as uncomplicated as courting."

"It's not courting, Mama, it's a farce. The hot springs? Could anything be more obvious?"

"I obviously wish you would cease complaining about it," the Queen grumbled, but she averted her gaze.

"If you're so angry you wish to banish me, just do it," she said, testing a theory. "There's no need to manufacture an affair."

The Queen stared at her. "Susannah, of course it's not my

intention to banish you!"

Susannah leapt into the gap. "Then I would suggest boating, not the hot springs. I'm sure Mr. Tom would enjoy paddling me about, and I promise not to push him into the lake."

Jon Tom quirked an eyebrow at her.

"I promise," Susannah insisted. "Let us practice toasting one another with champagne. Let him carry my basket while I clip roses. He can compare me to a summer's day or something."

"More like a stormy winter night," Jon Tom whispered.

The Queen, if she heard Jon Tom, gave no indication of it. "According to your research, Sir Hanson has a farming background, and country folk spend time with their lovers in rural settings. It wouldn't do for you to be hesitant. The lad was able to find the Fountain of Youth. He may be interested in our hot springs."

"I'll tell him all the stories of natural phenomena and the benefits of mineral water he could ever hope to hear."

"I'm sure he'd be dumbfounded by your vast knowledge, Princess." Jon Tom placed his hands behind his back and rocked on his heels. "My first lesson for you will be not all men appreciate a clever female. It takes a very special man to do that."

"I'll tell him the same rubbish Rosa told you about the ill-fated lovers," she snapped, "and I'll bat my eyelashes and wear something frilly. There's no need to invite scandal. Mother, be reasonable."

Something she'd said or done seemed to have firmed the Queen's resolve. "No one will gossip about a daughter doing exactly as her parents command. If they do, I'll take care of it." A frown played across her countenance. "Do as I say. That's an order from your Queen."

Susannah stumbled backward, away from Jon Tom, away from her crack-brained mother, shaking her head in dismay.

"I'll be at your chamber door to escort you in thirty minutes." Jon Tom folded the dreaded schedule neatly into quarters and slid it into a hidden pocket. "Do wear a red bathing costume, Princess. Scarlet looks so well on you."

How did he do it? He was like a cat who'd land safely on his feet no matter what building he was thrown from. If she could be the one to throw him from the castle ramparts, she'd dearly love that opportunity.

Chapter Fourteen

She had to be as ugly as possible. Ignoring the fact she didn't look glamorous on most days and it never stopped Jon Tom from plaguing her, Susannah kicked out of her brown workaday gown, petticoats, corset, chemise and stockings. Clad in her drawers and camisole, she glanced at the serving bell by the door of the princesses' bedroom. It would be easy to ring for a maid. One silver chime would bring Constance or Emily pattering through the hall to aid whichever of the sisters needed her. Either one of them would be happy to accompany her and Jon Tom to the hot springs.

However, the Queen could only be pushed so far, and the slipper mystery already shoved her to the edge. Defiance of her mother's latest command would put her in hotter water than anything Jon Tom could create. Besides, she needed no escort. She could overcome her attraction to the raffish detective if she remained annoyed, and she had little doubt she'd remain annoyed.

Why was her mother doing this to her? But she knew the answer to that. The Queen had tried everything and hadn't managed to reign in her daughters. She had no proof besides worn slippers and her daughters' exhaustion that anything abnormal was even happening. When Susannah considered the situation in that light, she could argue that the Queen was overreacting.

But the Queen also possessed a considerable amount of intuition. In short, the Queen was no fool.

Susannah had only done what needed to be done. She'd sought answers to the Female Curse and found something other than what she and her sisters had expected. Should she be censured for trying to save the poor princes as well as the Middle Kingdoms? Her mother, in Susannah's tattered slippers, would have made the same choices.

Feeling righteous and deceitful at the same time, Susannah dug in Esme's wardrobe for a particularly hideous yellow swim shift. It was the sleeveless, clinging style most ladies favored, but it fit her like a sack. She grinned at her unsightly reflection in Peter's cheval mirror.

He wouldn't even be able to look at her in this. She swished the skirt and enjoyed how the lemon color turned her bilious. The fabric hung straight from her breasts and concealed any hint of her waist. It was a mystery why Esme liked it.

Susannah threw a red summer cloak over the suit. Sometimes the princesses changed at the bathhouse, but she preferred to remain fully clad the entire time she was with Jon Tom. Next she bunched her hair into a swim net. Then she took it off. The wildness of her uncombed hair was less attractive. It was likely to get sticks and snarls in it and reek of minerals. She pictured the wet, snaky tangles hanging about her face, stinking, filled with twigs, and imagined Jon Tom trying to flirt with her. He could never run his fingers through that mess. Too bad she couldn't nip down to the library for an anti-lust chant, but it probably fell in the category of healing spells, something she couldn't effect on herself.

A knock at the door startled her. Had it been thirty minutes already? She ignored the knock and the sudden discomfort in her midriff.

"Princess Susannah," Jon Tom called from the hallway. "Your suitor for the day awaits."

Very annoying butterflies took flight in Susannah's stomach. If she didn't answer, perhaps he'd think she'd already departed for the hot springs.

"I know you're still in there," he called again. "Lesson number one. It's unmaidenly to keep a suitor waiting."

"I'm not ready," Susannah replied.

"Milady, you'll have to speak louder. Such a thick door to protect the royal princesses."

Susannah bunched the yellow hairnet in her fist. She suspected he'd heard her perfectly well. "Go on without me. I'll meet you in a nonce."

"A gentleman never leaves a lady unescorted."

"I'll forgive you this once." She walked to the door and laid a hand upon it. Exerting her magic, she saw he wore the same dark tunic and trousers from earlier—no bathing costume or robe—and a smirk upon his handsome face. Did he plan to bathe naked?

"But you're not..." Susannah thumped herself in the forehead with her other fist. She'd almost revealed she could see him through the door.

"What's that, Princess? What am I not?" His black eyebrow quirked upwards toward his hairline in that familiar, infuriating way. It was good to know he made that gesture when alone, that it wasn't solely designed to annoy princesses.

"You're not serious." She rested her forehead against the door. "Surely, Mr. Tom, you don't mean to go through with this travesty."

"It would help me greatly if you'd open the door."

"Can't you detect all you need through a mere door? If this door stands in your way, how can you profess to discover what we do in here at night?"

"Oh, I check in on you periodically."

"Do you have a magic mirror?" She hadn't seen him use one. She hadn't seen him do anything besides sleep when he guarded the princesses.

"A good detective never reveals his secrets until he's paid to do so." One side of Jon Tom's mouth twitched, and his eyes gleamed with a stray thought. To Susannah, it looked like a naughty one.

She was glad other mortals didn't possess magic, or what would stop Jon Tom from gazing through walls and doors at her whenever he chose? She'd never used her powers for pleasure, but she could, if she wanted. Did he bathe with the guards? Did he have his own chamber? The thought made the tiny hairs on the back of her neck prickle.

Jon Tom shifted positions and rocked back on his heels. With a shake, he ran a hand through his hair. It fell back onto his forehead, dark as a raven's wing. Suddenly Susannah felt like a voyeur. She dropped the magic and yanked open the door.

Jon Tom took a small step backward. She skewered him

with a glare. "Let's not play games with one another, Mr. Tom."

"That's exactly what the Queen has ordered us to do, milady. Play games."

Susannah grimaced. "I don't want this and you can't want this either." His blandishments wouldn't undo her, not even when he uttered them with that twinkle in his eyes.

"You can't imagine what I want, Princess. In fact, I'm not sure you know what you want yourself." Jon Tom's gaze raked up and down her form. Amusement brightened his face as he took in her mussed hair and tattered cloak showing a glimpse of her yellow bathing costume.

The arrogance of the man! He had no idea what he interfered with, just by his very presence. He had no idea what she was capable of and what it would mean if her magic were discovered. What it would mean if she weren't allowed to continue her studies and break the curse upon the land. Her heart darkened with the need to put him in his place.

"Pigswill." Susannah slammed the chamber door behind her.

"Tell me what you want, Princess." She knew he meant his voice to be low and seductive, but instead of responding, she stalked off down the corridor.

"I want to marry a man who'll enable me to secure the kingdom and my family's inheritance. I don't care if he's a peasant, a pig farmer, a chef or a doddering old fool so long as he's a legal mate. Does that sound like I don't know what I want?"

"What of love, Susannah? Princess? Don't you want a grand love to warm your days and nights?"

Susannah was on such a roll she didn't care Jon Tom had stumbled over her title. "I love my sisters, my family and my kingdom. That's enough love for anyone."

"What of the special love between man and woman? Don't you want to experience it?"

"These times and the blasted Kingdom Laws don't allow for love. Thus you see why this façade of lovers is a waste of my time, why pretending to court a trumped-up palace guard is a waste of time."

They reached the outer courtyard and continued down through the gardens toward the lake, Susannah in the lead.

Thankfully, they didn't encounter her sisters along the way.

"The Queen believes spending time with a trumped-up palace guard will help you achieve your goal," Jon Tom replied somewhat stiffly.

Good. She'd yanked him out of his playacting. If she could keep him out of that mode, the day might pass more easily, and more sanely. "My mother doesn't know everything any more than you do."

"She wishes the same thing you do, and as her humble employee I wish to help the Queen. Don't think it's a hardship to spend time with you."

Susannah sighed. It didn't take him long to recover ground. How spiteful did she have to be? No amount of spite and bickering had taken him aback so far.

"You do realize I know exactly what the two of you plan, don't you?"

From the corner of her eye, she saw Jon Tom smirk. He fancied himself the better player in their battle of wits. Remembering her mother's advice with delicious irony, she decided to let him continue to think he was in control of the situation.

"Your mother wants you to present your most polished face to Sir Hanson and realized I could aid in that endeavor. To aid in your endeavor, Princess."

An idea blossomed in her mind, as warm and sudden as opening herself to the magic. He thought to flirt her into compliance. Her mother had requested she adopt a sweeter manner. And they both intended for her to fall in love with Jon Tom.

They didn't intend for her to turn their plan to her advantage.

"How many cases have you lost, total?" she asked.

Jon Tom didn't answer immediately. They came within sight of the lake, the stone of the boathouse pale in the afternoon sun. The top story of the white and blue pleasure barge rose behind it. Susannah led the detective down the path toward the nearby forest and the hot springs at the edge of it.

"Not many," he said. "I've met few mysteries I couldn't solve. Why do you ask?"

"Because I wanted to know. Why else would I ask?"

"Do you fancy this case will be one of them?"

"You know I do. What a silly question!" Susannah laughed. Her red cape fluttered open and she wished she'd worn an attractive swim dress instead of this yellow thing. However, it wasn't her appearance he liked. It was the reward money and her dower property.

"Even silly questions can be interesting." Jon Tom smiled too, whether in response to her own smile or in amusement at her certainty—or her ugly swim shift—she didn't know.

She slowed her pace and furrowed her brow as if in thought. Well, she was in thought, but not the thoughts he thought she thought.

She would be charming, but not too charming. She'd soften toward him, laugh more and provoke him less. She'd allow him to think the plan fruitful and report to her mother all was well. And whenever she chose to strike, she'd kick him in the rear, right out the door of the castle. Even if she and her sisters feigned a trip beneath, abraded their slippers on sandpaper, one more failure and he was finished.

It was so simple and so obvious. Why hadn't she thought of it before?

"Mr. Tom," she said, keeping a hint of acidity in her tone, "let's drop the matter of who shall push and who shall pull. I'm weary of the brick wall that is your head, as I'm sure you've grown weary of mine."

"Princess, your head is made of the most enchanting bricks—"

"Please! Drop the flowery talk. We both know it for what it is. No!" She tapped his arm playfully, but hard enough to sting. "Don't tell me what you want, or what I want. Just tell me what you think will capture the attention of Sir Hanson. We've learned enough about his country, his life and his cows. What will interest him as a man?"

"What's with this about-face?"

Drat, he'd noticed instantly. "I'll level with you. As you claim to be a student of human nature, you know I can't help but resent your presence. You regard me with suspicion, you interfere with my daily activities and you patronize me. If I'd barged into your life, wouldn't those things annoy you?"

"I've never appreciated interference and skepticism of my abilities. I see your point."

"My frustration with you shouldn't prevent me from taking advantage of something that could help me. You're right, Mr. Tom. You might not be able to help me impress Sir Hanson, but perhaps you can and I'll secure the inheritance of our kingdom."

"Perhaps I can," he agreed.

"If we crumbled, there'd be no one to protect Foresta's borders so you could enjoy that fortune you think you're going to get." Susannah flipped Jon Tom a cheeky smile and shook her hair out of her face. She'd seen Peter do that to great effect. "You might have to concede your designs upon my dower property, though, unless there's some other way you think to obtain it." She directed her gaze toward the hot springs and bathhouse at the edge of the forest and let her smile melt into something more secretive.

Pleased when his grin faltered, she allowed him to take her arm and help her down the smooth granite steps. Her head filled like a balloon with her tiny success. How amusing to suggest naughty things! No wonder Jon Tom always looked as if his life were a party.

Even in spring and summer, a mist rose from the bubbling hot springs, surrounded by ferns and evergreen trees. A stream trickled out of the far end of the irregularly shaped bowl and disappeared into the woods. The water cooled before it reached the lake, but the year-round warmth made for some interesting aquatic life. Transparent salamanders and bright minnows lived in the stream, and birds often came to the springs to bathe. White flowers with fringed petals thrived in the steamy, sulfuric heat, and amidst the ferns thick at the edge of the bowl were tiny purple toadstools, not to mention tiny purple toads. The small bathhouse was built of the same gray stone as the steps and the contoured seats beneath the surface of the water.

"Tell me," she mused, "if you were Sir Hanson and I brought you here, what would you be thinking?"

"I'd be thinking this is a lovely place, Princess Susannah," Jon Tom said. "I'd take one look at the privacy and know what you had in mind. I'd be looking forward to seeing you with your wet hair tumbling around your shoulders and beads of water on your lips and lashes."

Jon Tom would have to be quite close to see those tiny droplets of water. She swallowed a compulsion to flee. He was a master of this game and she was a novice. But she had something in her favor—he didn't know she'd decided to play.

"Should I bring Sir Hanson here, just the two of us?"

"I can only advise you what thoughts would be in a man's head at this moment."

"We're discussing Sir Hanson, not just any man. Sir Hanson and me, in particular."

"Yes, of course." Jon Tom smiled. "But the question is, do you want those thoughts to be in his head? Do you want him to envision what you'll look like wet from the springs and flushed with heat?"

"I don't know yet." Jon Tom wasn't thinking those things, was he? He toyed with her. "I'll gauge that situation when I come to it. Perhaps I will."

When Jon Tom's brow creased slightly, she lowered her lashes. "Perhaps I'll want to think of him that way."

"Do you often think of men that way, Princess?"

"None of your business." She sat on a marble bench between the bathhouse and the springs. "I've certainly never brought a suitor here, not even the fat chef. Until now." She made herself smile at him while her cloak slipped off her shoulders.

Even here in the shade, her swim shift practically glowed. "An interesting swim shift, Princess," he said. "It's glorious to behold." He was to be congratulated for not squinting in the glare of the brilliant yellow garment.

"I chose it with you in mind, Mr. Tom."

"I'm positive you did. It's very definitely not red. It's good to know you think of me when you're dressing...and undressed."

Susannah shook her head with a sigh. "We agreed there was to be no more of that."

"I don't recall shaking on that agreement," Jon Tom countered. "I recall you telling me how things were to be."

"It should be the same difference, when a lady makes a request. Especially when a man is courting a lady and wishes to please her." Susannah unlaced her slippers and set them beside her on the bench. The thin wool of her shift slid over her calves.

"Do you..." Susannah found her mouth suddenly dry. "Do you plan to bathe, Mr. Tom? I don't see a suit."

"Oh, yes. It's rare that a commoner such as myself has the opportunity to enjoy a royal hot springs."

"But your suit?" Susannah persisted. Despite her current upper hand, this scenario could detonate if Jon Tom didn't have a suit.

He gave her a slow smile and unbuckled the black leather belt around his tunic. "What suit?"

Susannah leapt up from the bench and shook her finger at him. "Oh, that is too much. The suit you're going to march into the bathhouse and put on," she scolded. "Mama insisted we be here alone, but it wouldn't be proper for you to swim in the buff, not even for a courting couple."

"I think you'll find a courting couple has little concern for propriety. An opportunity like this wouldn't be wasted."

"Waste it." Susannah stomped down the bank to the edge of the springs. "Instruct me verbally on what I should do were Sir Hanson to attempt a nude bath. I'm a quick study." She heard his belt clatter onto the bench where she'd just been sitting.

Gingerly, she stuck her foot into the springs. Moist heat curled up her leg, beneath the yellow shift.

Fabric rustled behind her. She didn't look. Instead, she stepped forward into the springs. The water rose to mid-calf, to her thighs, the worn stones smooth under her bare feet as she made her way to the center of the pool.

"You'd best be leaving something on your bottom," she called out, still not turning around. Her only answer was the sound of sliding fabric, whispering across the water. Perspiration beaded on her forehead. With wet hands, she scrubbed her face. Tendrils of hair were already beginning to curl into ringlets, and she shook them back, this time not thinking at all of how Peter might do it.

"Mr. Tom, answer me!" She reached the center of the spring and heard a splash behind her as he entered the pool without saying a word. Quickly she waded to the opposite embankment where her favorite stone seat lay hidden near the egress of the springs. The water was clouded with tiny bubbles and the bank low enough that she could clamber out handily.

"Princess Susannah," he said from much too close behind her, "surely a woman like you isn't intimidated by something as vulnerable as a naked man."

He'd reached a part of the pool where he'd be concealed from the waist down. Susannah's toe bumped against her seat and, pretending nonchalance, she dropped into it. The water crested the tips of her breasts.

In the middle of the pool, Jon Tom waited with steam curling around his bare shoulders. He was tanned and nearly hairless, and the smile on his face should be against Kingdom Law. Mimicking her, he rubbed wet hands across his face, then slicked water through his hair.

"I'm not intimidated," she said. "I'm uncomfortable and insulted. I don't see what I'm supposed to learn here. If I tell my mother you skipped the swimsuit but not the swim, she'd throw you right in the dungeons. You're not that precious an employee."

"If you tell her that," Jon Tom said, "you might incriminate yourself."

"I didn't tell you to go naked, and I have on a very proper shift." She kicked her foot up so her calf came out of the water with the yellow material stuck around it.

"A very large shift." Jon Tom laughed as the material billowed around her in the bubbles of the spring. Susannah tamped it under her legs.

"Don't come any closer," she warned. How had the situation degenerated so quickly? "Instruct me from there."

"You must learn to be charming under pressure," Jon Tom said. "I'm pressuring you."

"I'm not pressured," she lied. She waved her hand above the surface of the pool, splattering droplets. Ripples lapped against his tan chest. His nipples were dark, his upper body defined. She'd seen men's chests before—swimming with friends from town, dancing with the enchanted princes—but those men weren't a threat to her. Her heart pattered so fast she was surprised it, too, wasn't making ripples.

"Then I'm not trying hard enough. What would test your poise, Princess, and make you aware of the special peril a potential lover represents?"

"Nothing you could do," she retorted. "I have no wish to see the entirety of you. Isn't this how I should act, were you Sir Hanson? Would he respect my maidenly sensibilities?"

"Sir Hanson will be no stranger to the delights of the flesh after his tour of the eligibles, if he ever was to begin with." Jon Tom paddled at the surface of the water before continuing. "He might interpret your sensibilities as missishness and search for a greener pasture."

"Although pasture is appropriate for our dear Sir Hanson, you can't possibly be recommending I—"

"I recommend nothing. I'm just advising you what might be in his mind."

"Surely you're not so ignorant of the Grand Tours you don't know what the new baronets want?"

"A good time?" His dimples creasing his cheeks, he flicked his hair off his face. "Fine hunting? Jam recipes?"

Susannah rolled her eyes but didn't blush, although the heat of the hot springs had increased her temperature everywhere. Jon Tom wasn't making any movements toward her. She could handle this. She trained her gaze on his face. "Unless they were already in love with some noble lady and sought the great feat to win her, the new baronets shop for the best deal, not a plunge in the pool, so to speak. You haven't experienced these tours like we have."

"I've never given much thought to attempting a great feat myself." Jon Tom's dark gaze drifted away from her and she sighed, tension ebbing out of her body.

"With your interest in fame and fortune, I'm surprised you never considered it before."

"I've always been happy with my lot in life and have never wanted for money. I tour all the Middle Kingdoms for my cases, taking in the wonders and sights. My family in Pavilion is thrilled to see me when I go home for visits, and I dandle nieces and nephews on my knee. I've been to the Desert of Colors, to Seelan, to the Arataki'it Islands. What more could I want?"

"A kingdom to rule, same as anybody." Susannah wiped a drop of water off her cheek.

"A kingdom to rule and a princess to wife. I suppose that would have advantages. What are they like, these baronets?

How are they treated by the nobility? Are they accepted as equals or patronized? What gifts are they given, besides aristocratic daughters?"

Susannah shoved her hair, floating in the water like weeds, behind her shoulders. Her decision to eschew the hairnet had been unwise. "They're frequently young and stupid. They never start their tours here, so by the time they arrive in Foresta, they're full of themselves. They expect to be waited upon hand and foot. You have heard of the phrase, 'fairy's gift to women'? They realize that's exactly what they are."

Jon Tom stretched his arms up above his head in a lazy fashion. "Have none of the local lads succeeded in a great feat?"

"They aren't encouraged to try," Susannah said tartly. "Our young men are more valuable to their families alive. The ratio of young men who survive isn't high."

"You're awfully young, Princess, to be so cynical."

"Not funny, Mr. Tom. You know quite well I'm not young."

"You're younger than I am."

"And probably less cynical. Give me time."

"You're not less cynical than anyone." He trailed his arms through the water and grinned at her. "Were I made into a baronet, I wouldn't search for a rich kingdom or a powerful position. I'd search for a lady whose family I could laugh with, whose temper was sweet and even and who delighted my senses."

"If you manage to achieve a great feat with one of your silly cases, be sure and notify me whether you continue to feel that way," Susannah said. "The pageantry with which most of the Middle Kingdoms greet the baronets would go to your head, same as anyone's. If you think we're mercenary and extreme, perhaps you haven't heard what Kingdom Chimea did to capture Sir Goldenhair. That sort of treatment might even go to my head."

"Actually, the treatment of the new baronets reminds me of my original point, your missishness and how you should overcome it in order to beguile Hanson." Jon Tom dropped into the water and ducked underneath. He came up wet and shaking his head.

Susannah waited until he wiped the water from his face. "How circular of you. Here I thought our discussion might yield some results after I enlightened you as to what manner of men we're faced with, and you turn the argument back where you want it—a critique of me."

Jon Tom chuckled. "You asked for my help, Princess. To capture the interest of this baronet, you must be more enticing than the women who offer material wealth."

"Me? Me be enticing?" Susannah threw back her head and hooted with laughter. "Mr. Tom, let's not kid ourselves. I can manage to be polite, somewhat quiet and a good listener. I can ask the baronet questions about himself and project an aura of goodwill. My curse notwithstanding, his decision will be based on what the kingdom can offer, not me. Then there are my assorted sisters, one to appeal to any man's taste."

Jon Tom splashed water over his chest and shoulders before rubbing the back of his neck. As he didn't automatically reply, Susannah had to wonder what he was thinking. He must think her grasping. He must think her horrid. He must think her impossible.

No, she'd lost sight of her goal. He must think her so dazzled he'd tell the Queen she was on the verge of succumbing.

"Do you know where I'd begin my Grand Tour if I were elevated to the nobility?" Jon Tom finally asked. "Where I'd begin it and end it?"

"Those are the kinds of notions that send many young men to their deaths. I'd stop them in their tracks, if I were you. It would be a shame to lose the Middle Kingdoms' only detective to a dragon."

She wiped another droplet from her cheek. He sought to unnerve her, and she knew it. If she kept assuring herself knowing was half the battle, would she only need to struggle half as hard?

"You can't look me in the eyes, milady. You know the answer already, don't you?"

She knew the lie, at least. "I'm sure I don't know what you're talking about."

"I'd have to make an exception for the sweet and even temper, but there might be other benefits involved. Perhaps it's time to test my hypothesis that you lack grace under pressure."

Chapter Fifteen

With a raffish grin, John Tom asked, "What would you do if Sir Hanson came toward you like this? If you were alone at the hot springs with him, and he was six, five, four steps away?" As he counted, he drifted closer to her through the steamy pool. "Show me how charming you can be, milady, under a strain like this."

Susannah shifted on her seat and strove to appear unconcerned by the direction of his conversation or his approach. He was almost within arm's reach and the water level inched down his torso. Down his rib cage. Down his abdomen, a hint of black hair trailing below his navel.

"Don't come any farther out of that water!" Susannah leapt out of her seat and nearly propelled herself into his arms but managed to retain her balance. "I know how to defend myself from overfriendly men, sirrah, and I'm not afraid to prove it."

"That reaction isn't going to win Sir Hanson," Jon Tom said with a laugh, but then his eyes widened as they took in her dripping form. "Holy goddess!"

"What is it?" Susannah said. "A water snake?" She stared at the bank but the ferns were serpent-free.

"Ahhh!" Jon Tom sighed and held his palm to his heart.

"Don't tell me you're speechless." She lifted an arm to shove at her annoying hair when she realized Esme's yellow swim shift clung to every inch of her torso and every generous line of her hips—and was two shades away from transparent.

With a gasp, she dropped into the curve of the stone seat. Waves sloshed into her face and around Jon Tom's tight belly. She slumped in the water and wished it were icy, to cool her humiliation.

"Not speechless," he said. "I'm astounded. Amazed. There's a difference."

She smacked her palm on the water and sent droplets arching onto his face. "I shan't bring Sir Hanson to the hot springs. That will solve the whole problem."

Jon Tom took another step closer. The cloudy, bubbly water dropped to a dangerous level, and Susannah forced her spellbound attention away from his midriff. She didn't like the subservience of her position, her head level with his navel, but if she stood, he'd see...everything. Again. Susannah now realized why Esme favored this garment. How in all the civilized lands had she found indecent wool?

He reached out and tweaked a floating tendril of her hair, gazing down on her with unsettling awareness. "A man, when confronted by such riches, cannot help but want a bit for himself."

"If Sir Hanson has been blessed with riches throughout his Grand Tour, there's nothing here he couldn't resist." Water tickled her neck and her breath quickened. Any notion of retaining the upper hand when she was this close to Jon Tom's unclad form slipped right out of her head. She was going to have to get away before he...

Jon Tom lifted an arm to push aside his hair, which pulled his body that crucial inch farther out of the water. A pair of dark, wet trunks clung low on his hips like a second skin.

At that, Susannah did leap out of the water. "You're a beast!" She splashed water into his face. "Letting me think you were nude."

"Entirely your own notion, Princess, spawned from your wicked imagination."

With a mighty shove, Susannah thrust Jon Tom into the hot springs where he stumbled and fell beneath the surface. He rose, spluttering and laughing.

"No, I don't think Sir Hanson is going to be seduced by your sweetness of manner. You'll have to concentrate on some other attraction." His gaze roamed across her form with an appreciative glint. "I could suggest a few."

Susannah's eyes narrowed and she glided through the pool. The water forced her to a much slower pace than she'd have liked. "That's it. You'll have to be gotten rid of. I simply have to drown you."

Jon Tom stood his ground. When Susannah reached an arm's length away and glared up at him, he chuckled. "You have no sense of humor. Men like a sense of humor."

"Men like it when you laugh at their stupid jokes and pretend they have greater wit than they do."

"Then why aren't you laughing at my stupid joke?"

"Ha, ha, ha." She punctuated herself with another shove.

This time he didn't stumble. He grabbed her hands and splayed them against his chest. His skin was hot. His heart beat firmly beneath her fingers.

The annoyance gushed out of her, replaced by something warmer. She'd never touched him except for the most innocuous contact, though she'd fantasized about it. Her hands tingled. Her body tingled. She felt as if she were immersed in the underground lake with its fizzing water.

"Be careful, Princess. I might shove back." He squeezed her hands.

Desire sizzled through her like a lightning strike. She wanted to kiss his chest, his neck, take his scent and his taste inside herself.

One tug, one shift of his weight, and Susannah would tumble into his naked—nearly naked—body. Small bubbles popped all around them.

Perhaps attacking him physically hadn't been wise.

"You shouldn't approach or address a princess of the royal house in an unseemly manner," she breathed. If she closed her eyes and let herself float away in the water, would she wake up in her bed and be dreaming? "No man should touch a royal princess except to help her from a carriage or escort her in a dance."

"The Queen gave her consent to typical courting behavior between a man and a woman. Though I'm not noble, I'm a man."

Oh, he definitely was! She couldn't forget what was at stake here, what game she played. She took a deep breath and hoped he'd keep looking at her face, not the racing pulse in her neck. He must imagine her to be succumbing, but she mustn't actually succumb.

She lowered her lashes. Drops of water had condensed on them. "I somehow doubt this is typical. Perhaps I should just embroider your face on a satin pillow."

"Will you sleep with my face beside yours at night, dreaming of me?"

"Actually," Susannah said, tugging her hands, "I'm a terrible seamstress. You'd come out looking like the giant badger."

He slid her palms across his chest, forcing her to learn the curvature of his muscles. His skin was wet silk to her touch. "Sir Hanson would be charmed if you touched him like this."

"And are you?" She swayed an inch closer. Her breasts brushed his chest. "Are you charmed?"

Slowly, Jon Tom drew her hands around his waist and pulled her against him. His hands trailed through the water along her arms, barely touching her. Steam coiled around them, through her, and Jon Tom's hard body pulsed in time with her own.

He didn't answer. Susannah kept her eyes closed and her face lowered. Her hair brushed across his chest.

"I'm suddenly very glad you're wearing a swim costume," she whispered.

"I'm suddenly very disappointed you're wearing a swim costume," he replied, his voice husky. Were his lips nuzzling her hair?

"Don't say that." Beneath the water, she hadn't allowed her lower half to meld to his. Jon Tom wasn't like the enchanted princes, with their limits. Their safety.

No, he'd be like Prince John. The thought of him made Susannah wince inwardly. It was one thing to waltz across the dance floor with enchanted princes a couple nights a week, but it was another to be intimate with two men and be unpromised to either. To be this confused by both of them, tied into sensual knots only they could untangle.

This man, though, Jon Tom. He was no enchanted prince. He exasperated her and excited her. He was here, now, pressed against her with the knowledge and consent of her mother. How far, she wondered again, did her mother's consent extend?

"This shall be your next lesson, Princess," he murmured against her damp hair. "When a man you wish to charm takes you into his arms, resist at first if you must, but give in."

"It isn't proper."

"Don't think of propriety."

"Should I think of my kingdom? My duty?"

"Think of nothing but the man you're with. Think of me, Susannah." And with that, he tilted her face up and kissed her.

If Susannah had been ice, she would have melted. If Susannah had been stone, she would have turned to lava and covered his body. As it was, she was merely flesh, and she sank into Jon Tom's kiss without a thought for how she might return to the surface.

His tongue, tasting faintly of the minerals of the springs, faintly of the warm spice of his skin, stroked her willing lips, parted them. He raised his hands to cup her face and then the back of her head. Susannah sighed and lifted her hands to his broad shoulders. Bubbles tickled their legs, fizzed beneath her skirt. She pressed against him, reveling in the feel of his wonderful, complete masculinity.

"Susannah," he groaned, "you're turning me into a madman."

"Don't talk to me," she whispered. "I'm obeying my mother." She buried her face in his neck and licked water from his skin.

In turn, he explored the curve of her waist and hips. Even in the heat of the springs, his touch scorched her. When his hand grazed her breast and his manhood surged against her, Susannah knew she was going to have to halt to this delicious torment or...

There was no *or*. No matter what sanction her mother had given, Susannah couldn't let herself surrender. Was it possible to die of lust? He cupped her breast in his hand and grazed her neck with his teeth. Possibly it was, and shame.

Lowering his head, he took her nipple into his mouth and sucked it through the yellow fabric. Susannah shuddered and twined her legs about his hips. His manhood strained against her intimate mound as the skirt of the swim shift drifted around her waist.

She was losing it. Losing control. She was going to lose something else too. Could she stop this? She had to. Shivers of pleasure buzzed through her as he rocked his pelvis and mouthed her other nipple.

In desperation, Susannah twisted in his arms. He mistook it for passion and grasped her buttocks. His fingers were dangerously close to her core, and he reached between her thighs.

If he touched her there, she'd be lost.

If he didn't touch her there, she'd explode. How could this be happening? Her mind screamed at her to stop, even as she helped him lift her swim shift over her head, even as he bared her whole body to his touch.

"We shouldn't do this," she said.

"We should." He rubbed his palm over her hard nipples, and her legs buckled. He caught her against him.

Susannah grasped his shoulders, buried her face in his neck and said nothing.

"We should do this as well." He lifted her out of the water and placed her at the side of the pool. The soft ferns bowed on either side of her, and her heart raced with fear and anticipation. Would he undress? Would he take her now? She looked up, up, past the steam, past the green treetops. The sky was endless.

He brushed her intimately, just enough to make her moan. She tried to roll away, but he trapped her. "I've dreamed of being with you like this," he said. "I've wanted you a long time."

"Please, Jon," she whispered. "I know there are other ways we could please each other. I don't want to reach a point of no return."

"You think we haven't raced past that point already?" he murmured. "Sweet girl, we can't return from this."

Helpless, she lay back while he rubbed his face against her lower belly, his lips far hotter than the spring water. When he spread her thighs, she whimpered. The touch of his tongue against her core, the suckle, the pull... Spears of delight radiated outwards from her center. An ache built in her cunny that was nearly painful. Deeper. Warmer. His fingers and tongue stroked until she could hardly breathe. Her hands grasped the ferns on either side of her, her nails dug into their stems.

He paused, blew heat over her skin and continued loving

her, one long finger sliding inside. The ache blossomed, crested. She stuffed her fist against her mouth to muffle her cries.

Jon Tom kissed his way up her torso, finally reaching her mouth. He tasted of passion and musk. He laid his head upon her shoulder, and his weight pressed her into the soft bed of ferns. "You're extraordinary."

Susannah couldn't speak. Following the path carved by sensation, emotions coursed through her, filling her heart but closing her throat. She'd denied it before but now she knew— she was in love with Jon Tom, a man who wanted to ruin her life.

Jon Tom kissed her neck and caressed her nipple with his hand. With a jolt, something inside her sparked back to life.

"Gods." Her voice cracked. "Tell me this was my mother's idea so I can hate you for it."

"This definitely wasn't your mother's idea." He laughed against her skin, his breath a moist tickle. "But it's been mine since the moment I laid eyes on you, in that green dress, your white collar so properly buttoned, your beautiful gray eyes flashing. I knew then I'd do anything to have you."

Susannah struggled to sit up, and Jon Tom rolled onto his back, pulling her over him. Her legs straddled his hips. So far, Jon Tom had touched her, had kissed her, had pleasured her. Tentatively, Susannah traced the line of his strong jaw with a trembling finger. So smooth. She touched a lock of his crow black hair where it curled on his forehead. If he had her, then she had him as well.

"Susannah, I want you even more now." His eyes darkened as he looked up at her. She leaned toward him, her lips parting. Her hair fell around their faces and blocked the sun.

In the partial dark, their gazes locked. Though she'd just experienced pleasure beyond her fondest dreams, Susannah knew more could be had—if she joined with him.

She wanted it. She wanted the risk. She wanted him, completely. Her mother knew they were here. Her mother sent them here. She'd promised to protect Susannah's reputation. She could enjoy the lovemaking, and it didn't have to change anything else.

It didn't have to mean he and the Queen would win.

Jon Tom squeezed his eyes shut and smiled wryly. "You

aren't mine to have, are you?"

But she was! At least in body. "I was wrong. We can—"

"No, you were right. It need go no further."

Susannah bit her lip and stared at the hollow of his throat. In a small voice, she said, "I want to."

Jon Tom pulled her down for a kiss. "How much?" he said. "Tell me how much."

Susannah kissed him, her tongue slipping between his lips to tangle with his. She placed her hand near his wet trousers and her fingertips danced across his belly. "How much do you think?"

Jon Tom nudged her legs apart and caressed her. Susannah gasped as he spread her body's moisture across her pearl. It was so sensitive she tried to jerk away, but he held her fast.

"We shouldn't." He inserted two fingers, stretching her hotly, and she whimpered with eagerness.

He froze. "You're a maid."

Susannah squeezed her inner walls around his fingers, adapting to the oddness of the sensation. "Of course I am."

Jon Tom wouldn't meet her gaze. "Susannah, this isn't right. I have a task to complete, and we're on opposite sides of it. Falling in...into something with you complicates that. Complications I never expected. If I could finish my case, things would be different. I'd be in a better position."

"I thought you wanted me. Wanted to have sex." A growing sense of dread began to overwhelm her passion. Could it be true? Was he using her body's desires against her? Would he slake her lusts if she told him her secrets?

She hadn't truly believed the gossip about him, but it fit too perfectly with their compromising position.

He kissed her hand. "I want to make love to you more than I've ever wanted anything."

"More than you want to solve your case?" It was one thing for her to realize she might love him, but if he claimed feelings for her, they wouldn't be true.

"If I make love to you, will you help me?" His gaze molten, he dragged her down and kissed her. Even as her pulse raced, her heart fell.

She had her answer. It was her mother's plan, or his, or some combination of the two. His seduction was meant to wring answers from her. He was aroused by her, challenged by her, amused by her, but there was no tenderness in his heart.

The deliberation of his sensual assault froze her desire. She was acting the fool. Even though he seemed to enjoy her and want her, she couldn't take what he offered and remain unchanged. She was too aware of why he offered it.

"I have to get dressed." She clambered off him and slid into the pool, tears threatening. The yellow swim shift was easy to spot in the cloudy water.

"Susannah, you misunderstand me."

"I understand everything." She sloshed to the bank and yanked the gown over her head. "I understand the hot springs are a risky place to bring Sir Hanson, if the thoughts in his head will be anything like yours."

"Hanson!" Jon Tom growled and splashed behind her. "Do not bring that boy—"

"I'll do as I wish with that boy. Thanks to you, I have a few more tools in my arsenal." If he came up behind her and took her into his arms, could she withstand the temptation?

"You can't pretend this didn't happen." His voice was tinged with anger and something else. "You won't be able to shove this into a dutiful little compartment like the rest of your emotions."

"I can," she said. "I will. You don't realize what's at stake."

"Why do you think we argue like we do? Why do you think I can't stay away from you?"

"My mother ordered you to stalk me." She dropped to the bench to don her shoes. Silk slippers, and not worn at all. He reached the edge of the springs.

"Dammit, Susannah!" He smacked a fist into his palm. Water ran down his chest and legs and pooled on the steps. "This has been inevitable since the moment we met. I know you sensed it. How can you set this aside now that you've tasted what it could be like?"

Susannah was drained to exhaustion from their encounter and from the hot water. Grabbing her cloak off the bench, she draped it across the front of her body.

"I have to marry and save my kingdom, if I can. I can't dally with some man who strikes my fancy. No matter what my mother gave you permission to do, it's too uncertain. I could be banished. What would I do, cast adrift upon the world? Who'd employ an old maid trained to run a kingdom? Could I support myself as an overly educated whore?"

Jon Tom's face blackened with a scowl. "You'd never be cast adrift."

"It's Kingdom Law. My parents honor those laws, however unfair they seem. My mother has deceived you if she said otherwise." She was too tired to appreciate the picture he made with the water trickling down his body, his hair slick and his body tight with unreleased passion. "Would you take me in, Jon? Surely a disgraced princess in tow wouldn't help your business."

Some spark of insight flashed in his eyes, relaxed his tense face and he opened his mouth to speak.

"Don't answer that," she sighed. "Don't lie to me any more."

She secured her slippers with messy knots and began the long trek toward the palace. She left Jon Tom by the side of the hot springs and didn't see him for the rest of the day, despite whatever schedule her mother had intended them to follow.

Chapter Sixteen

"Mr. Tom tells me you behaved admirably during your practice courtship yesterday," the Queen praised Susannah at breakfast. The King had departed and only the women remained. Obviously Jon Tom hadn't told her mother the entire story or that tone of approval wouldn't tint her voice. Or had he?

She stared at the poached egg quivering on her plate. How much did her mother know? Did she know Susannah had nearly lost her virginity? Did she know Susannah had locked herself in her room the rest of the day?

Dresses rustled and forks ceased to scrape on plates as her sisters honed in on the conversation. She could feel them bite off their questions between their teeth. She was lucky Jon Tom wasn't sharing this meal with the royal family. She wouldn't have been able to retain her composure had he been watching her, imagining her nude with pictorial accuracy.

"Only one more day for lessons," the Queen said. "Sir Hanson is due tomorrow, and I have hopes one of my daughters will captivate him. It should be you, my dear."

Her mother's mention of Hanson broke the silence. Rosa was first to the gate. "If she never marries, he could wed any of us and still become king."

"He'll look to her first, goose." Calypso, beside Rosa, rapped her plate with a spoon. "She's first in line. Someone else could marry her and be king instead."

"If he falls in love, he won't care about that." Rosa batted Calypso's spoon away.

"If he were going to fall in love, he could have done it in another kingdom," Peter said. "He could have done it when he was a farmer. This isn't about love. This is about power and money. And I still say it should be me brushing up on my womanly skills."

Esme snickered. "You just want to brush up against Mr. Tom."

Glad the attention was off her, Susannah tuned out the morning bickering to consider her activities for the day. Perhaps Jon Tom had no intention of seeking her out. He'd made no move to last night. The idea of a whole day to herself, a whole day without him in it, was both a relief and a disappointment. She could slip into the library for some research, in particular the *Seven Habits* volume. She'd neglected her studies since his arrival.

With the deterioration of the enchanted princes' curse, the next visit below would be pivotal. Curses didn't wait upon the breaker once their strands had begun to snap. You had the one chance, or the three chances, and that was it.

And then Jon Tom had awakened in her yesterday a wish that...a wish she could live someone else's life. A wish to be done with curses.

She'd made no progress solving the Female Curse, not in the many years she'd studied, but if she could help these young men, it would be something. Her toil, her secret skills, would have benefited someone. There was so much she didn't know but so much she suspected. She wondered if Jon Tom ever felt this way, frustrated, unable to solve a case but positive he was inches from a breakthrough.

She'd ask him.

No, she'd avoid him.

"Has Mr. Tom informed you of your plans for the day?" Rosa asked Susannah, which brought her attention back to the breakfast table. "Are you to take a tour of the ghost castle on the other side of town or a romantic picnic in the center of the Floramaze?"

"I don't know."

Her sisters fell silent in case Susannah revealed any more details. She'd refused to speak about the detective the night before. Her nose had been stuck in her *Seven Habits* notes. A passage about cures for curses lured her to study today, that and the temptation to hide from Jon Tom. He never failed to find her in the library. Perhaps she'd try a different room. The formal dining room was rarely occupied. She could fetch the Dullish dictionary...

"Susannah, answer me," Rosa demanded.

"I did answer you. I said I didn't know."

"You're not listening. I asked if Jon Tom was a chivalrous or a passionate lover."

"Rosa!" Susannah exclaimed. "What sort of question is that?" She looked to the Queen, who eyed her youngest child askance.

"I'm not a baby anymore," Rosa said. "I know about lovers."

"I'm betting passionate. She's in a daze of passion already, can't you tell?" Esme again. Several of the sisters sniggered, but Calypso and Hortense regarded Susannah with worried eyes. The Queen's expression changed to something more enigmatic.

"Did he hold your hand? Did he press his lips to yours?" Rosa asked.

Wasn't the Queen going to reprimand Rosa? Little Miss Knows-about-lovers, indeed.

Annoyed, Susannah said, "Mr. Tom did exactly as Mother told him to do." She glowered at the Queen and then remembered she was supposed to exude goodwill. The plan to turn the tables on Jon Tom, and thus her mother, had leached out of her mind in the heat of the hot springs. There were so many significant events coming to a crux, her head couldn't hold them all.

"Borrrring!" Esme mocked. "We all see the way he smolders at you. It was Mama's idea he pretend to court you, so she won't be cross if you tell us what happened. We've a right to know, poor, manless maidens that we are. We have to get our jollies vicariously. And you're to get the new baronet, too. It doesn't seem fair."

"Susannah doesn't automatically get the new baronet," Peter said. "The new baronet will choose whomever he fancies."

Esme made a rude noise with her lips and tongue. "The fellows always pick the lady with the land, Peter. Give over. Look at the fat chef. He could have had Susannah but went to Kingdom Tennubia and married nasty Princess Gethsemene because her fortune was bigger."

"You would know," Peter said, inspecting her nails, "being so nasty yourself."

Esme smirked and continued to harangue Susannah for details.

Instead of answering, Susannah picked apart her breakfast pastry, turning it into a pile of crumbs. Princess Gethsemene was ugly as a bulldog and shrill as a shrew, and Esme's backhanded compliment was simply the truth. The new baronets chose with money in mind. Why would Hanson be different? She wasn't some temptress to take a man's mind off his aspirations. Jon Tom, for example, chose his job over her, and she'd been naked and willing, two things men supposedly adored in a female.

Heavens. She could only pray Hanson considered their kingdom the best of the current offerings and herself the best of the available princesses.

She also prayed her curse didn't interfere. The fact she might love someone didn't matter. She should, in fact, twist her useless feelings to her advantage. If she dreamed of marrying Jon Tom, if she convinced herself the detective was the man of her choosing, could she hoodwink Malady's gift horse?

Susannah paddled her fingertips in her crumbs as she toyed with the idea. An interesting proposition, one that wouldn't have stood a chance before she'd fixed her affections on someone. Perhaps it could work. It certainly wouldn't hurt.

Meanwhile, her sisters' questions turned more personal, and Esme made several more lewd comments. She glared at them all and wished she could pinch their behinds with magic. Suffering through Hortense's lecture would be worth it.

The Queen placed her napkin on the table and motioned for the maids to take away the plates. "Esme, have I mentioned what you'll be occupied with today? It's far too late to polish you into an elegant young lady, so you're helping the laundresses clean and iron your sisters' ball gowns."

"What?" Esme's fleshy face purpled like a beet. "That's punishment duty."

"So it is," the Queen observed.

"I've done nothing wrong." Esme glared at the Queen before turning her hateful gaze on Susannah, who blanked her face and stared at her plate. She didn't want to incite her sister further. As much as Esme frustrated her, Susannah didn't wish her ill.

Much.

"Hamish will be in the laundry today," the Queen continued, "to oversee. Or you could muck out the stables. Hamish said he would be happy to oversee there as well."

"I'll iron." Esme speared Susannah with another baleful look. "But someone might be sorry for this. Someone might owe me."

"None of that, Esme." The Queen rose from the table. "Ladies, attend your assigned duties. You may take off two hours before sunset and have the rest of the evening to prepare for the festivities tomorrow. And please, my darlings—get a good night's rest."

When she found out the formal dining room was being cleaned, Susannah took the servant's backstairs to the library and settled in a dusty corner in the philosophy section with *Seven Habits* and the Dullish dictionary.

Susannah wished she were quicker at synthesizing the rules for Contemporary Dullish with the Ancient Dullish in the *Seven Habits* text. Ella was excellent with languages, but she dare not involve that imp in her project. She opened the book to the passage she was translating in the second chapter. The faded faces of the men in the illustration mocked her, as if she should be able to cast a spell to make them talk. Well, that would be easier than thumbing through this confusing and very obscure dictionary.

Wiosahgiuo yo asiogh saiioh po lisagh io ieiond lisagh lislis. The first word meant "discover". *Yo* was a multipurpose adverb/preposition that took its meaning from context. She already knew from the first guideline in this chapter that *saiioh* meant cure. So, she had the nonsensical sentence, "Discover adv/prep *asiogh* cure *po lisagh io ieiond lisagh lislis.*"

She'd seen *lisagh* before. Where? She flipped her translation papers and scanned her crimpy handwriting. There it was. It meant curse, but a specific kind of curse—a big, intricate curse. "Discover adv/prep *asiogh* cure *po* big curse *io ieiond* big curse *lislis*." This was about cures for big curses, just as she'd hoped!

Susannah wriggled with excitement. She paged through the dictionary to the "P" section. *Po* sounded like a multipurpose word like *yo*. There it was, a preposition with the definition of "for, against, within". "Discover adv/prep *asiogh* cure within curse *io ieiond* big curse *lislis*." The cure was within the curse? That didn't make sense.

Maybe *yo* meant "for". "Discover adv/prep *asiogh* cure for big curse *io ieiond* big curse *lislis*." Since *po* and *yo* were so similar, they might be a prepositional pair and would both mean "for". Yet another weirdness of the Dullish language. She'd go with that, for now, though it was also possible *po* was a separate adverb or preposition.

Which gave her, "Discover for *asiogh* cure for big curse *io ieiond* big curse *lislis*." That couldn't be right.

She didn't remember the nitpicky language rules well enough to do this. She needed a break. Susannah slammed the dictionary shut, and a cloud of dust puffed into her face. She sneezed violently.

"There you are, Princess Susannah."

Susannah, eyes watering and a hand covering her nose, tried to jump out of her seat but bruised her knees on the end table she'd dragged into the corner to use as a desk.

"Jon!" she exclaimed. "I mean, Mr. Tom. I didn't hear you come in."

"Hidden in this nook and surrounded by such fascinating, and thick, literature"—he slid a tome, nearly half a foot thick, from the shelf—"I'm not surprised. I didn't hear you either, until you sneezed."

Damn dust. She studied his black, shiny boots.

"What are you doing, cramped away in this corner? You usually study at the center table."

"I...I was distracted by a reading I thought would only take a moment," she said. "In this book." She held up the dictionary. "I do love a dictionary. I just open it to a page and soak up the knowledge." She knew she sounded guilty. Her pulse raced at the sight of him.

Jon Tom took the large volume from her hands. He wore dark red today with his usual white undershirt and fitted black trousers. Through the must of the books, she could smell the spice of his light cologne.

Here she was again, sitting at the man's feet, eye level with his navel.

He let the book fall open and peered at the text. "*Wexmes, wexma*: to put a curse upon someone. *Wexmix*, feminine, *wexmixim*, masculine: a being capable of putting a curse upon someone." He glanced at Susannah curiously.

"I adore the Dullish language." If he'd give her the book back, she'd put it atop her research, set the lot on the floor and he wouldn't have a chance to see what she was doing. She scooted the end table away from her and stood, nearly bumping into him in the narrow corridor between the high shelves. "It's musical."

"Musical, is it? I'm not familiar with Dullish," Jon Tom said with a smile. "Sing something for me."

"I can't sing. You'll have to address Lilly for that."

He smiled again and flipped a page in the dictionary. His casual attitude made her suspicious after seeming so frustrated with her yesterday. Had her mother given him a pep talk about having another go at her?

"Would she know a Dullish love song? Perhaps some lyrics about a frustrated...what was it, *wexmix*, whose love charm worked so well her suitor couldn't leave her be?"

A love charm was definitely not on her safe list. Which reminded her she had wanted to seek a de-lusting charm for herself. She needed it badly, because right now she longed to bury her face in Jon Tom's neck. Lick the corded muscles of his chest, his lower abdomen. Taste the part of him she'd never seen. She could see his pulse beating in his neck, though not so fast as it had yesterday when he'd been wet and hot, kissing his way down her body.

Susannah shook herself. What had he said? Something about an overactive love charm. "That does sound like a curse. A man you wish to avoid trailing after you everywhere and poking in your business."

"Am I so monstrous you're reading dictionaries rather than spend time with me?"

Susannah met Jon Tom's gaze fully for the first time since yesterday. His dark irises were practically indistinguishable from his pupils. She couldn't begin to read his thoughts.

"You aren't monstrous," she said, "but I am avoiding you."

"Dullish isn't a favorite study of yours? What are you doing, then?" He moved to pick up the papers on the end table, but she stepped in his way and bumped his arm. A tiny shock rattled through her at the contact, and he jerked away.

"Dullish takes my mind off things."

"Well, Princess, put your mind onto this. Your Mother has scheduled us to picnic in the center of the palace maze today."

"That's a less provocative choice than yesterday." Susannah rolled her shoulders back and forth. She'd been hunched over her books longer than she'd thought. "What were we to have done last night, lounge by a fire and feed one another strawberries with whipped cream?"

Jon Tom chuckled. "Nothing so blazing. Just read one another scenes from a play. I told the Queen we muddled through it and trusted you to remain out of sight. I didn't think you'd want to see me again so soon."

"You're right. I didn't."

"And you still don't." Jon Tom leaned against one of the tall, sturdy shelves and watched her. "I can understand that."

Why could he understand? Because he didn't want to see her, either?

"The play was *Two Loves Lost*," he told her.

"Melodramatic fluff." Susannah dismissed it with a wave. "Do you know it or should I brief you in case Mother asks?"

"I'm familiar with the plot. The heroine can't choose between two men, one her equal and one her inferior, so she loses them both."

"Like I said, melodramatic fluff. The main character is a ninny. It is obvious she should choose—"

"Her equal?" Jon Tom's expression deadened.

Susannah cleared her throat. He seemed to be drawing a parallel between the plot of the opera and the plot of her life—himself and Hanson, she supposed. Only for her, it should be *Three Loves and One Kingdom Lost*, if she counted Prince John. For that matter, it could even be titled *Who Knows How Many*

Hundred Loves and One Kingdom Lost, expanding the plot to include all the enchanted princes. Her lips quirked.

"You find the choice of her equal humorous?" Jon Tom asked. "Let's see what the word for "ninny" is in the Dullish language."

"It's ninny, and she should have chosen the cloister." She grabbed the dictionary and set it on her notes and the *Seven Habits* book. Although she felt a breakthrough in translation was close, she didn't think Jon Tom would let her spend another of their assigned rendezvous in study. Moreover, she didn't want to explain why these particular studies were so important. And she was hungry. Hungry and stiff.

He followed her out of the stacks. "Why do you believe neither suitor was for her?"

"Her equal was a brainless snot, and her inferior only wanted her money." Susannah shook dust and cobwebs from her blue skirts and wondered if she should change before their picnic. Her corset and brocade bodice pushed her breasts toward the round neckline of her blouse. However, it wasn't comfortable to picnic in a corset if it involved sitting on the ground. The corset would have to go. What a shame.

"That isn't how I read the play. Is it all about gold with you, Princess?"

"Is it not with you?" she retorted.

Jon Tom swept forward to hold the tall library door. "Not always. I've never lacked for funds since my detective business became successful. Fairies in particular pay well. I get the most useful items from fairies." He smiled, and his eyes grew distant. "Some jobs I choose for the entertainment value."

"I hope we've kept you entertained."

"Princess Susannah, that's something I want to discuss with you." Jon Tom caught her by the arm and turned her to face him. They paused in the long corridor outside the library door, next to the tall, thin windows facing the inner courtyard. After yesterday it would be priggish to complain of Jon Tom touching her. She noticed, though, his hand didn't linger.

"Yesterday shouldn't have happened the way it did. I'd like to offer my apologies." He stared into her eyes. "I was uncouth."

Susannah didn't answer right away. Did he regret their tryst—or his failure to secure her secrets? Did he fear for his job? Had her mother not given him permission to seduce her after all?

She could respond in one of two ways. If she remained her usual grouchy self, he'd have a harder time if he intended to seduce her further. If she flirted with him, it might keep him off balance and ensure favorable reports to the Queen. It was nice to be in her mother's good graces for a change. She just had to keep in mind that when she'd tried this yesterday she'd ended up naked and begging.

She curled her finger around a tendril of hair and twisted it. "Uncouth wouldn't be my choice of words."

"Uncivilized? Coarse? You've called me so many names." His earnest mood lightened.

She smiled. "Vicious troll is my personal favorite."

"Surely you wouldn't have let a troll—"

Susannah dropped the ringlet and held up a hand. "Enough."

If she kept her distance from him, she could do this. She'd lost the upper hand yesterday because of their lack of clothing. And the other parts. If she were careful, she could maintain her poise while giving him the impression she was aflutter for him.

This would be easier than charades, considering it wasn't make-believe. She was aflutter for him.

"We'll go wherever you want," he said.

Susannah pressed a hand to her breast in feigned astonishment. "Anywhere I want? I heard a rumor the lady wasn't meant to plan the activities during courtship. How else can I judge you based on how well you're able to predict my desires?"

If she played the coquette, she could tempt him and tell him secrets designed for his ears—and her mother's. And she could, just a little, enjoy his company and fantasize things were different. Fantasize about choosing him as her husband, which would hopefully dupe her personal curse.

"I suggest we start with the picnic, but if you have any better suggestions, I'm willing to consider them." Jon Tom held out his hands in an open gesture. "I'm a new-fashioned man. And after yesterday, I owe you some breathing room."

"It depends." She cocked her head to one side. The weight

of her hair in its hasty knot pulled her scalp. "What lesson will I be learning today? How to accept a man's apology when he obviously doesn't mean it?"

"Not everything is a lesson, Princess. I know I've caused you pain. I'm truly regretful yesterday happened the way it did."

Susannah shrugged one shoulder. "You should be. That last trick, when your inner cad took over, was inexcusable."

"I was wrong to importune you at a time like that. If I could erase it all—"

"I wouldn't let you!" she exclaimed, and realized she was telling the truth. "I don't regret the first part, you understand."

Jon Tom quirked both eyebrows at her vehemence. "You don't?"

"Not exactly." No matter if her mother had arranged for it, his enjoyment of the tryst had seemed authentic. She refused to believe the witty man she'd come to value could fabricate arousal, even if he could fabricate other things. Even if he was a threat to everything she hoped to achieve.

She hid a heavy sigh. "We should be frank with one another—about this, at least. Importuning aside, you're the one who said our encounter was inevitable. You said you wanted to be with me. Was that a lie?"

"My interest in you is no lie." Surprise and desire warred in Jon Tom's countenance, and he glanced up the corridor. Sunlight through the yellowed glass windows played in his hair, gilding the ends. "I treated you with disrespect. I did things to you I had no business doing."

"But you stopped," she said. "We almost went somewhere I can't go, and you stopped. But I don't hate what I experienced." She blushed.

She tread a fine line between honesty and deceit, but the fact they were not arguing would throw him off guard. She placed her hand on his arm. "Do you understand what I'm saying? There are places I can't go."

Jon Tom's dark gaze assessed her and she suddenly became aware of a smudge of dust on her hand, of hair tickling her neck. She was pretending to be infatuated with him but she was actually infatuated with him. It was time to see how good a detective he really was.

Slowly, he placed a finger under her chin and tipped her

face up. "Are there other places you want to go?"

"I hear Pavilion is lovely this time of year." She held his stare, unflinching. Daring him.

Jon Tom lowered his head toward hers, and she shut her eyes with a sigh. Yes.

No! Voices echoing down the corridor had them jumping apart to a decorous distance.

"Perhaps we can travel to some of the places you want to go," murmured Jon Tom, not looking at her. "I'm told I'm an excellent guide."

"Perhaps," she said. "And perhaps we could start with a picnic in the maze."

"Anything you desire."

Two maids pushing a cart bristling with mops and buckets clattered around the corner. One of them giggled when they saw Jon Tom and Susannah.

"Princess, Mr. Tom," the maids said, bobbing quick curtseys.

Susannah bowed her head and her hair nearly tumbled loose. She raised a hand to her disintegrating chignon and bit back a smile when Jon Tom's gaze dropped to her bosom. His hunger couldn't be manufactured by her mother, which was both gratifying and dangerous.

"I didn't eat much at breakfast," she said. "I'm starving, but I need to change. Shall we meet in the courtyard in thirty minutes?"

Chapter Seventeen

Susannah traipsed ahead of Jon Tom and twirled a lacy parasol. She was very aware of him behind her, toting the overflowing picnic basket as if it were no heavier than a loaf of bread. For his benefit, her low-cut underdress was pale pink with the same blue brocade bodice he'd admired outside the library. She'd secured her hair in a soft twist on top of her head.

"Have you visited our maze?" she said over her shoulder. "I'm sure it would offer a detective such as yourself no challenge."

"No, I haven't, though several of your sisters have offered to lead the way to the center." Jon Tom reached ahead of Susannah and opened the wrought-iron gate. She tilted her parasol out of the way and brushed him as she passed through. Her shoulder slid against his chest.

"I suppose I've beaten them to it." She gave a breathless laugh that sounded silly to her ears. She wouldn't be able to maintain her composure if she didn't keep her distance. A flirtation could be conducted from several yards away, with the flutter of a fan or the steps of a minuet. Too bad she didn't have a fan or a string band handy. She'd think of something, something other than having him for lunch instead of whatever was in the basket.

One thing she could definitely do was control the conversation and make sure he didn't spice it up with distracting innuendoes.

A lecture, then. "Our maze is the largest in the four surrounding kingdoms," she explained, "and the most intricate. None of the others have anything to compare. It's shaped like a cabbage rose and boasts several hundred twists and turns."

They crossed the smooth lawn, dotted by tiny yellow cinquefoil the gardeners left for color. The boxy gray palace rose behind them, turrets soaring in an aqua sky. Ahead, the maze's privet and boxwood hedges made for a tall and silent border. Curves that represented petals burgeoned out from the sides. Along the tops of the hedges flitted numerous small birds.

"We can climb the observation tower before we enter the maze. It might help you solve the puzzle if you see it from above first." She gestured to the sturdy platform that rose twenty feet in the air and yielded a bird's-eye view of the labyrinth.

Jon Tom shaded his eyes against the sun as he peered to the top of the tower. "I'll solve the puzzle from down here." He motioned toward the greenery. "I see a cupola. Is that the center?"

"A gazebo surrounded by a fountain, the Dancing Waters. They run at the top of each daylight hour. Perhaps we'll make it to the center of the maze before they come on." She slid her gaze sideways to Jon Tom. "And perhaps not, if I allow you to lead."

He turned to her, his eyes twinkling. "Allow me to lead, Princess? I wouldn't know where to begin."

"The front gate would be a good start."

"Surely you'll have pity on me until after our meal." Jon Tom hefted the basket. "I wouldn't want to carry this for the length of time it would take me to find the path."

The entryway to the maze was an ornate gate in a high wall of green hedge. Iron curled to form the words "Floramaze" across the top. Susannah pulled a key from her pocket. Through the bars of the gate she could see three pathways, the center one leading directly to another iron gate. When the princesses wanted to picnic at the pleasant, and very private, heart of the maze, the center path was the direct route, provided they had the proper key.

"You're a detective, not a strongman, I suppose." She folded up her parasol and tapped it against the ground. "The center path leads straight to the gazebo."

"Many thanks, milady. You did mention you were famished."

Susannah twisted the key in the lock until she heard a click. She swung the open gate, the creak of hinges raucous.

Startled birds flapped away from their perches around the gate, and insects buzzed. With mocking gallantry, she skimmed a little bow to Jon Tom.

"I'll lock the gate. We never leave it open so people won't wander in and get lost."

"It's that complex?"

"Actually, yes. We have fairy bells in several spots so maze-goers can call for help. They're mostly for Fay's benefit. She gets lost every time."

Jon Tom waited while she drew the gate closed and locked them within the concealing hedges. His eyes alert, he peered down the other two paths, intrigued. Carefully kept stone vases of blooms, blossoms and herbs at every split in the path gave clues to the intrepid explorer, were he able to break their code.

She plucked a tiny asparilla bloom from the plant at the first intersection and crushed it between her fingers, relishing the sharp scent.

Jon Tom turned his attention back to her. "Here we are. Alone again."

"We're usually alone," she said, "thanks to my mother."

He placed her hand on his arm and led her up the primrose path to the gazebo. Their shoulders brushed against the hedges, against each other. Her awareness of him mushroomed. He covered her hand with his and interlaced their fingers.

Susannah's kid boots tapped against the smooth stones of the walkway. The rest of the trails in the maze were packed dirt. It was easier for the gardeners to tend than grass or small stones, and it was also easier to tiptoe about the maze in silence. If any of her sisters wanted to creep up on their picnic sound unheard and sight unseen, they could. Most of the princesses had the labyrinth paths memorized and all of them had their own keys.

If the afternoon went as planned, peeping Thomasinas wouldn't be a worry. The flirtation would be mild, but enough to keep Jon Tom reporting auspiciously to her mother and enough to keep him believing any secrets she let slip. Now she just needed to make some up.

Jon Tom stroked her palm in tiny circles. She pulled free as soon as they reached the next gate and shook off a frisson of alarm. How could this be as persuasive as the hot springs? Jon

Tom was fully dressed. She was fully dressed. Her sisters knew they lunched in the maze, and interruptions were possible. The close-cropped lawn around the gazebo boasted several benches, but the maze, with its prickly hedges, bees and pungent scent wasn't as conducive to lovemaking as the steamy springs.

Of course, she'd never been here with Jon Tom.

"Are we going inside or lunching here?" He tickled her under the chin with a flower, and the sweet scent brought her back to earth.

"Inside."

The gate sank into the thick, squared-off masses of privet. It wasn't as tall as the entry gate, only head-high to Jon Tom, and clematis wound through the bars. Susannah unlocked it with the same large key and he preceded her through.

"The fountains are finishing the program," Susannah noted.

He set the picnic basket on a marble bench outside the gazebo, and they admired the play of water and the statues of the dancers. Fifty jets shot up alternately, some in arcs and some in sprays, in a moat most of the way around the gazebo. Gracefully carved marble dancers lined the moat. The splash and splatter of water on water and on the heads of the statues was like a shower of spring rain.

"Your Dancing Fountain is delightful," Jon Tom said. "Literal, too."

The pale, elegant gazebo had a domed top. Crystalline windows set in orderly embrasures caught the sun's rays and turned them into prisms on the stone floor inside.

When the fountains stopped, Susannah put down her parasol and sat beside the basket. "Shall we eat?"

Jon Tom sank to the ground and lounged upon the thick sward. She pulled out thin ham and tiny crescent rolls, pats of cool butter, chicken slivers and lentil salad, pear slices and cheese, herbed crackers and mint chocolates, pots of raspberry jam and clotted cream, condensation dripping down the sides of the jars. To drink they had fruit juice and white wine. While he watched, she arranged everything on the long bench and served it on delicate saucers with clean white linens.

"It's almost too lovely to eat," Jon Tom said, but he was looking at her, not his artfully arranged food.

Susannah folded a piece of ham onto one of the crescent rolls. "I think you can manage." Next she had cheese, mild and creamy white, the perfect match for the pears. They ate in silence for several minutes.

It was awkward without conversation, though. "Tell me more stories about growing up in Pavilion," she suggested.

Jon Tom propped his elbow on the bench. A swag of hair fell over his forehead, making him look boyish and carefree. "What do you want to hear? We covered my parents, siblings and old, mean grandpa when we researched Sir Hanson."

Susannah itched to brush that lock of hair off his forehead. "I still feel like I know next to nothing about you."

"You know everything you need to know about me. I'm honest, hardworking, intelligent and handsome."

"Tell me another one!" She waved her knife at him. "Honest?"

"Ah, you don't disagree I'm handsome." He pretended to preen in the reflection of his spoon.

"You know you are. Do all men in Pavilion have so little facial hair?"

"It's one of the many unique things about us. Pavilions are passionate, dark and rarely need to shave." Jon Tom leaned toward her, his arm pressing her leg. He lowered his voice. "They say the ladies have legs as smooth as babies' bottoms. I wouldn't know, since I left Pavilion when I was just a lad."

"I thought you were eighteen?"

"Surely you don't think I was familiar with the legs of ladies at that age?" Jon Tom's eyes twinkled up at her, and dimples creased his cheeks.

Susannah gestured in disbelief, nearly spilled her drink and set it beside her. "Surely you don't expect me to believe you weren't?"

Jon Tom placed his hand against his chest and widened his eyes. "I was innocent in the ways of love until I ran away to seek my fortune in the big city."

"You said your Mama gave you a pouch of coins and begged you to go before you bedeviled her to death."

"Princess, your recall is too fresh. How am I supposed to amuse you with tales of my misspent youth if you remember everything I told you the first time?"

"I like your tales." Despite her dire warnings to her sisters about letting Jon Tom squirm under their guard, she could listen to him all day, not to mention argue with him and kiss him.

"And I like your...tale." He winked and took another helping of chicken.

Susannah laughed and stirred the pot of raspberry preserves. "I know this sounds strange, but try jam on the cheese."

"Show me."

She slathered the preserves on an oval of cheese and held it out to him. Instead of taking it, he leaned forward and ate it from her fingers.

"Oh!"

He caught her hand. "I missed a spot." He licked a dollop of red raspberry from her finger. His impish expression dared her to protest.

"So you like the jam." She hid her face behind her drink and mixed her second beverage with no alcohol. She topped his glass with pure wine for good measure.

Jon Tom grinned, a flash of white, and spooned lentil salad onto his plate. "Now I see why the basket was so heavy." He ate at the bench as if it were his table, his shoulder bumping Susannah's knee. "We have everything in here but the kitchen washtub."

"Cook thinks we're skin and bones."

"You're perfect the way you are." Jon Tom held up his glass in a toast. "Though you'd be just as perfect with a few more pounds."

Susannah rolled her eyes. "I bet you say that to all the fat princesses."

"Don't be silly." Jon Tom leaned back on one arm. "I had little occasion to speak with princesses before I took this job, much less any fat ones."

"Are you saying—"

Jon Tom silenced her with a hand upon her knee. It burned through the layers of skirts and petticoats. However, mischief still lurked in his gaze. "You don't realize what an incredibly...gifted woman you are, do you?"

She suspected she knew what he referred to, and it wasn't her magic or her christening curse.

"I suppose you verified all my christening gifts at the Office of Community Records?" She'd never discussed her body this frankly with a man and wasn't sure what to think of the direction their conversation had swerved.

"Hm, let's see..." Jon Tom ticked her christening gifts off on his fingers. "Susannah has some nuptial issues. We'll skip that one. Susannah has a way with jams and jellies. I agree, especially when they get on her fingers. Susannah is canny. Oh, yes. You're living up to your potential there. Susannah has excellent vision. I've no proof, but fairy giftings rarely lie. And Susannah has nice—"

"That's quite enough." Susannah felt her face turn red.

"But I have two fingers left," Jon Tom protested. He waggled his hand in front of her. "Two more christening gifts, both of which I'm thoroughly grateful the fairies saw fit to give you." He dropped his gaze to her chest and waggled his brows.

Susannah looked down as well. The tiny ruffles edging her pink underdress framed the tops of her breasts, pushed up by the bodice. The cleft between them was a rosy shadow.

"It's rude to discuss a person's attributes when she's sitting right here."

"I have it on good authority it's worse when she isn't there. It's called gossip."

"I'd rather not continue this conversation." If she did, she'd also continue thinking about how he'd kissed her breasts at the hot springs. "Let's talk about something else."

"You're the one who mentioned your gifts, my dear. I was merely expressing my deep appreciation for each and every one of them."

"So you appreciate that I cannot marry a man of my own choosing?"

"I appreciate that you aren't married."

Susannah threw a cracker at him. "I'm sure that wouldn't stop you."

"On the contrary, I have a great respect for the bonds of matrimony." Jon Tom picked the cracker from his sleeve and flipped it into the grass nearby.

"Then why aren't you married?" It shouldn't be a surprise, after yesterday, but knowing he admired her bosom did funny things to her insides.

Jon Tom cocked his head to one side. "I've never wanted to be married. I've never been in love before."

"The other day in the library you described love as a burning. How else would you know? Were you lying then or now?"

"Knowing what it's like doesn't mean I've ever felt it...before."

"Never? Not once?"

"Never before," he repeated.

Slowly, Susannah spread raspberry jam on a piece of cheese and ate it while Jon Tom waited. She realized she was supposed to note his recurring use of the word "before" and ask about it. He was dropping hints he was in love, now, to tenderize her, like a steak.

If only it were true, she'd be as soft as the melted butter on her croissant. But he didn't love her, and even if he did they couldn't marry. She was his assignment, and she'd do well to remember that.

"That's unfortunate," she said, finally. "Love is a many splendored thing."

"I've heard that." He sipped his drink and his gaze never left her face. "Do you have plenty of experience with it? You told me love didn't enter your equation."

She lowered her lashes and sighed. "I hope to marry Sir Hanson. Someone. But no baronet will be my true love."

Ironic that she was telling the truth. She was pretending to have feelings for Jon Tom while hiding her true feelings—which were the ones she was pretending to have. It was as convoluted as a theatre plot, only in the theatre Jon Tom would be a noble in disguise and they'd marry and live happily ever after.

This wasn't the theatre, even if her skills as an actress increased by the minute. She would continue the repartee as long as she was on the bench and he was at her feet.

Jon Tom popped a mint chocolate in his mouth and sucked on it. "Do you think you'd have married for love had the Female

Curse never been cast?"

"Perhaps," she said, "if you discount my christening gift and go on the theory there are many men a woman can love. I believe there's only one man best suited for me."

Jon Tom raised one eyebrow, and for good measure, the other. "You believe in mates of the soul? That surprises me."

"It just proves you don't know everything about me." She bit into a ripe pear. She could understand why some of her sisters thrived on dalliance. The play of words, the occasional brush of shoulder against shoulder or hand against hand—it yielded a charge like no other.

"My goodness, it's warm today." She waved her napkin in front of her face. The trick was remaining unruffled. The trick was not letting the incident at the hot springs duplicate itself. She had to lead, not follow, and keep him off balance. She ran a finger under the ruffle at the neck of her dress and lingered over her breasts.

"It's hot," Jon Tom agreed, his voice a little hoarse. He cleared his throat and drained the rest of his golden tumbler.

Susannah held up the bottle of wine and shook it. "Would you like more?"

Jon Tom set down his tumbler. "I'd like more raspberry jam."

"Help yourself." Susannah handed him the pot and the serving knife.

"I prefer a different utensil." He grabbed both the pot and her hand and slipped her finger into it. Susannah tried to pull away, but he was much stronger. With a wicked glint in his eye, he closed his lips over her finger.

His slick mouth woke her body like a fire alarm. She drew a quick breath and tugged her hand.

"Ah, ah, ah!" he said. "I'm not finished." This time he turned her hand and placed a dollop of jam in her palm. After nipping her fingertip, he licked the sticky jelly from her like a cat.

Ribbons of sensation snaked up Susannah's arm and through her body. Jon Tom smeared jam on her wrist and kissed it from her skin. Farther up, near her elbow, he repeated the procedure, licking and rubbing his face against her arm.

"This is the best dessert I've had in a long time." The sleeves on her gown buttoned tightly at the elbow and he slid the tiny pearl from its loop. Susannah sat immobile, tense yet curious. How could kisses on her arm tighten her nipples and echo inside her core?

It was only a few kisses on the arm. He was still at her feet and she was still on the bench.

After rolling up her sleeve, he scooped jam onto his finger and placed it in the crook of her arm. His teeth grazed her skin as he licked her arm.

"You'll get the bellyache if you eat much more jam," she said. Yes, she sounded relatively unmoved. In the position of power.

"Worth it." He traced his fingertips along her arm.

"That tickles." Still calm. To show him how unmoved she was, she took up her golden tumbler with her free arm and sipped, as if he were merely the after-dinner entertainment. "Do you want any cheese with that?"

Suddenly Jon Tom yanked her arm and dragged her off the bench, across his chest.

"What the devil?" Her drink flew through the air, the remaining liquid splashing in an arc across the ground. Wrapping his arms around her, he pulled her backward onto the thick grass, she atop him with their bodies touching from chest to hip, from hip to toe. Part of her hair fell from its pins and tumbled into his face.

Beneath her, Jon Tom blew curls out of his mouth. "No cheese," he said. "No hair, either." He rolled until he was on top and her hair splayed behind her head.

His hips pressed against hers. She could feel his arousal and one of his hard thighs nudging between her legs.

I shouldn't have played with the ruffle on my dress. That was her last coherent thought before he kissed her.

He nibbled her lips and parted them with his tongue, teasing her, opening her. He tasted of raspberries and chocolate, and she met him with demands of her own. Their breath mingled while their tongues danced and lips clung.

He rolled onto his side but left his leg across her hips, trapping her. With expert hands, he undid the tiny buttons of her bodice. The wide neckline of her underdress and chemise offered little barrier. He untied the strings of both and they fell open like the petals of a flower.

Once her breasts were bare, he gave a sigh. "Beautiful. Luscious." He bent to kiss one rosy tip and then the other. "But not as sweet as they could be."

The pot of jam lay off to the side. He sank a finger into it and, as she watched in bemusement, rubbed the cool jam across her nipple. Heat pooled in her loins as he rubbed around and around before he grazed his teeth across the other nipple. Susannah gasped at the sensations—slick jam and raspy teeth, his tongue, his hot mouth.

When she whimpered, he switched breasts, licking off the preserves. His hand dropped to her waist, then her lower belly, and his knee prodded her legs. She moaned and brought his head up for a sweet, urgent kiss. Fumbling only a little, she found the buttons on his tunic and slipped them free. She ran a hand inside and found his flat, male nipple through the white shirt, just as hard as hers.

A new warmth whispered along her legs, the sun on her stockings. He drew her skirts to the top of her thighs. With a teasing finger, he brushed aside her cambric underwear, searing her inner thigh before climbing higher.

Through her rising passion, she heard a rustle and a stifled gasp. Susannah's eyes flew open. Peter and Esme stood in the front gateway of the maze, the shock on their faces evident. Seeing her on the grass with her skirt hiked up around her hips and Jon Tom kissing her bosom couldn't have been what they expected.

"Susannah!" Esme shouted.

Jon Tom surged to his feet and drew her with him. He placed her behind him. Tension thrummed through him, and Susannah marveled at his transformation from lover to protector.

"Peter, Esme, what a pleasant surprise." Jon Tom bowed mockingly. "I'm afraid you're a bit late for the picnic."

Susannah adjusted her chemise and underdress and buttoned her bodice. "What are you doing here?" she asked, as if she had every right to be half-naked with their bodyguard.

Esme cackled. "Arriving too late to chaperone your virtue."

"We don't require a chaperone." Jon Tom reached behind

him and patted Susannah on the hip comfortingly.

What he didn't realize was she wasn't frightened of repercussions, and she wasn't humiliated. She was furious.

"I can't believe you're sneaking around and doing this." Her fists wrapped around the bars, Peter shook the iron gate. "I doubt Mother had this in mind for your practice courtship."

"It's what you had in mind," Susannah said.

"Yes, but I—"

"Shut up, Peter."

"This wouldn't have occurred with anyone besides Susannah. No offense, ladies." Jon Tom inclined his head to Peter and Esme. "I'm sure you realize your sister holds a special place in my heart."

"I just bet she does." Esme's round face was pink with excitement. "Special places seem to be the order of the day. This is fantastic. No more ordering me around, Sister, or I let the pussy out of the bag."

"No, you won't." Susannah finished buttoning her bodice and whipped her skirts around her legs until they draped correctly.

"You can't stop me."

Susannah stepped from behind Jon Tom and fury sparked in her heart. Her pulse raced faster, harder than it had when Jon Tom had caressed her inner thigh. While it was for the best her latest indiscretion with Jon Tom had come to an abrupt halt, that didn't mean she was grateful. Or pleased.

She raised an eyebrow at Esme. "You're mistaken. I can stop you."

She'd never threatened any of her sisters with magic, but Esme immediately knew what she meant. Knew it bore little relation to the harmless sleep spells or illusions on the safe list. Peter gaped, shorn of words, and Esme's face turned as red as a ripe tomato.

Susannah stormed to the gate. Her hair stood out from her head in a crackling mass. "This is not the time or the place to discuss this," she hissed. "And might I point out this is no worse than what I've caught you doing with you-know-who?"

"But they can't—"

"Shut up, Esme," Peter and Susannah said at the same

time.

"And Peter," Susannah continued, shaking her finger at her sister, who jerked back as if struck. "The tailor. Need I say more?"

"No," Peter said.

Jon Tom cleared his throat. "Since both of you ladies are past the age of prankish spying, why did you follow us when the Queen ordered we have no chaperone during our lessons?"

Peter worried a fleck of rust on the iron gate with a fingernail. "Is this one of those detective questions I have to answer?" Unaccustomed humiliation marred Peter's beautiful face.

"It would be very polite to answer," Jon Tom said.

"Sir Hanson is expected to arrive tonight and Mother said we could quit working for the rest of the day. Susannah included."

"I see. And you believed Princess Susannah needed to know this without delay."

"I'll speak with you tonight." Susannah, still furious, rubbed her index finger and thumb together, as if they had fairy dust on them—the primary component of several interesting spells. "Now get out of here."

Even though they were both grown women, Peter and Esme fled like children.

Susannah turned back to Jon Tom. He'd rebuttoned his tunic but hadn't otherwise moved. "I think our picnic's over for the day."

"It was just getting interesting."

She squeezed her eyes shut. Every time she looked at him, she wanted to see him without his clothes. She quickly discovered closing her eyes didn't help because it was even easier to picture that smooth chest, that dark trail of hair.

She opened her eyes. "It's a good thing they interrupted us. Jon, I just can't. I want to, but I can't. You make me forget who I am."

He stepped toward her, stopped a pace away. "Is that such an awful thing?"

Susannah smiled dryly. "It is when you're the bad guy and I'm the good guy." She plucked her tumbler from the grass and dropped it into the picnic basket. Then she packed away the remnants of the food, leaving the crackers for the birds. "Didn't we discuss this 'will we, won't we' yesterday?"

Jon Tom fastened the last button at his collar. "Perhaps you misunderstood my intentions. I was under the impression you wanted to go to a different sort of place. I was, I am, happy to oblige. I'm not at liberty to explain at this time, but I owe you that."

Susannah flinched with embarrassment. "You make it sound like I'm using you for your..." She couldn't bring herself to say his tongue, his hands.

"For my what? My skills?" Jon Tom chuckled. "Is that what you're doing?"

"I don't know what I was doing. You make my thoughts fall to pieces like bread crumbs." She slumped down on the bench beside the basket and wrung her hands.

Jon Tom touched her chin with a finger and stroked her cheek. "Susannah, you cannot think I get nothing out of such a bargain."

She jerked her chin out of his grasp and stared fixedly at the gate. "You shan't get what you wanted yesterday. You said we couldn't continue unless I cooperated."

"I was wrong, yesterday, to give you that impression." Jon Tom frowned and rubbed his hand across his chin. "That's not what I meant. I said it would be less complicated if my case weren't between us. Making us enemies."

Was he sincere or attempting to cover his gaffe at the hot springs? She should tell him she knew of his plan, so he would finally drop the façade. What would lay behind it?

She emptied his tumbler and dried it with a napkin. Keeping her hands busy steadied her. "I know what my mother wants you to do and why. I know that's why you're making love to me."

"No." He shook his head slowly. "This thing between us, it's separate from the case. But it's still between us."

"There are two ways the case can be made to go away," Susannah pointed out. "Your way and mine. Why should it be yours?"

"If it's yours, I'll be banished for my failure and you've already made your intentions clear on what you plan to do with the rest of your life. I don't think it's spending time with a failed detective. My way, and I stay."

"If it's yours, I'll be banished and..." Susannah threw a fork into the basket. "What am I saying? How can it be yours? There's no case."

Jon Tom lifted her from the bench and turned her to face him. His grip on her upper arms was hard. "Can we, just for one minute, quit playing games?"

Susannah looked up at him. Her head barely reached his chin. "What games?"

"Do you want me gone? Do you wish you'd never see me again?" He bent his head and kissed her, lightly, then more deeply. She allowed it. Reciprocated. Her head whirled.

He moved his mouth to her ear. "Is there someone else you'd rather be kissing?"

"My husband," Susannah whispered. "My lawfully wedded husband."

Jon Tom's eyes flashed with dark fury. "No one besides me should ever touch you."

"You should never touch me."

With a growl, he pressed his hips against her. He pulled her hair until her head bent backward and nipped her exposed neck. She cried out, and he muffled her cries with his mouth, hard and possessive.

Shock flooded through her at the ferocity of his onslaught, yet it was paired with a sharp spike of desire. The wild sensations coursing through her body terrified her even as they thrilled her.

When she was pliant and gasping, he raised his head. "Do you think Hanson will make you feel like this? Do you think Hanson will want you so much he wrestles the compulsion to throw you down and ravish you his every waking minute, even though he knows it's wrong?"

She couldn't meet his eyes. "I don't care."

"You throw yourself on the altar of duty when it doesn't have to be you."

"But I want—"

"Shh." He silenced her with a light kiss. Susannah could feel his ire fade as he cradled her against him. Gently, he straightened her bodice and caressed a love bite on the swell of her breast.

"You're mine," he said, his voice tender yet fierce. "Don't forget that when you meet this baronet."

Chapter Eighteen

Peter and Esme shot her hateful glances all evening. They began during dinner, blasting her with silent resentment as the family bickered. Later, in the billiards room, they turned their backs on her in indignation whenever she walked near. All twelve sisters were dressed up and keyed up since Hanson was due to arrive, but the tension between Susannah, Peter and Esme was palpable. Their mother seemed to sense something was amiss, but she rarely interfered in inter-sister squabbles unless they spilled into her daughters' overall behavior.

Susannah, for her part, didn't count this afternoon as one of her proudest moments. She'd threatened to use spells against her sisters and nearly succumbed to Jon Tom. Again. She had to face facts. She stunk at playing love games, even when her kingdom was at stake.

Not to mention her heart.

As soon as their mother sent everyone to bed, Peter and Esme spearheaded a push to visit the princes. Most of Susannah's sisters joined in.

"We might not get another chance if Hanson sticks around." Calypso tossed a red croquet ball into the air, caught it and picked up another to try to juggle.

"It's too peculiar there," Susannah said. "You all know that."

"Probably because we aren't going enough," Esme said.

"I don't think so. Who knows how long they were there before we even found them?" Susannah lay back on her bed and kicked off her slippers. One of Calypso's croquet balls dropped to the floor with a crack.

"You think, but you don't know." Peter, on the next bed, fluttered her fingers. "You don't know much, do you? Maybe I should tell everyone something I know."

Susannah threw her legs over the side of the bed so she and Peter were face-to-face. "I know somebody's got their pantaloons in a twist and they'd better quit threatening me."

"I believe the threats began elsewhere," Peter said. "Unnecessary, unpleasant threats. Like I would have told."

Peter's blue eyes snapped with anger and hurt, and her lips pursed in a sulk. She might tell the other princesses, but maybe she wouldn't tell the Queen. Of everyone, she best understood the temptation to go beyond the pale with a man.

Esme, however, was a different story. Susannah's magic was a secret none of the sisters would use against her, but now Esme had different ammunition. What would she do with it?

Their sisters observed Peter and Susannah with undisguised interest. Muting spells were simple, so Susannah leaned over and pinched a feather out of her pillow. As it fluttered to the ground, she cast a small dampening bubble. The feather allowed her to focus and ensured the spell was light and natural. The other ladies recognized the trick with the feather, and several flung themselves back on their beds in disgust.

Peter sat unmoving, staring daggers at her. When Susannah reached for her hand, she tried to pull away, but Susannah was stronger, or at least more determined.

"You aren't going to cast a spell on me, are you?" she asked with a flip of her hair.

"I just wanted a bit of privacy." She tilted her face so only Peter could see because Ella read lips. "You won't tell Mother about Jon Tom?"

Peter tugged at her hand again, this time not as hard. "What good would it do if you were mad at me? I don't see what Jon Tom wants with you when he could have..." She cut herself off and took a deep breath. "I wouldn't have told."

"I'm sorry I threatened you. That was ugly of me. I was flustered." Susannah glanced at Peter with a smile. "Do I have to apologize to Esme?"

"No, and she'll use the information against you, too." Peter squeezed her hand. "Do you know what I've had to give her to keep her from telling Mother about the tailor?"

"Whatever you gave her, I think you can take it back." Susannah recalled the Queen's comment in the study two days ago. "I think she knows."

"Mother hasn't said anything to me about it." Peter's eyes narrowed before she shrugged. "I guess she isn't going to. That's a relief."

"What's a relief?" asked Ella.

Susannah jerked around in surprise. Why could that little pest hear what they were talking about? The spell was in effect. Well, she hadn't used any fairy dust. It mustn't have been very strong.

"It's a relief Susannah and I made up," Peter said.

"Why were you fighting?" Ella bent to pick up the feather Susannah used for the dampening spell and bounced on the bed. She tilted her head and blew the feather into the air.

"She said some hateful things to me."

"And to me," Esme said from across the room.

Peter smiled at Susannah. "To show she's sorry, she should take us to see the princes."

Peter never missed a trick.

"I don't think so." Susannah dropped her sister's soft hand. Ella's feather fluttered across Susannah's line of sight, and she grabbed it.

"Please, let's!" Lilly said. "Think of it as practice flirting with Sir Hanson."

Esme snickered. "I don't reckon Susannah needs practice, what with all the training she gets with Mr. Tom."

"Yes, Susannah, you get all the live ones." Lilly heaved a dramatic sigh.

Esme snickered again. "You have no idea how right you are."

Susannah's fingers clenched around the feather. Esme was going to be difficult.

"It's not going to happen tonight." She stood from her bed and fisted her hands on her hips, glaring at her pudgy sibling. "I need to research what happens when spells wear away. Remember that countess who had toads and spiders coming out of her mouth? I'll see how long it lasted." She smiled at

Esme meaningfully. "Perhaps that will give me some ideas."

She sometimes wondered if Esme were adopted, but the fact was she looked and acted exactly like their maternal grandmother, a malicious old lady who resented her marriage to a poor baron. How Grandmere had birthed their hardworking mother was a mystery.

Too, most bushels of apples had a rotten one hidden at the bottom.

Peter picked up some lotion from her bedside table and smoothed it over her calves. "If the princes are out, I have an alternate suggestion. Cast us a magic-mirror spell so we can see Sir Hanson. He's bound to be here by now."

"That's outright spying!" Susannah exclaimed. "We'll see him tomorrow."

"You spy on Jon Tom enough." Uncowed, Esme crossed her arms and glared up at her. "And I know why. Come on, let's see the baronet."

When Esme mentioned Jon Tom again, Susannah wandered to the door—the one through which he rested only a few paces away. "I can't cast a magic mirror. We'd have to be standing outside his room and I don't think Mr. Tom would allow us to do that." She almost giggled at the thought of the twelve of them, lined up against the cold wall outside Sir Hanson's guestchamber, their faces pressed against the stone for a gander at the boy, who'd probably be in the middle of picking his teeth.

"If she can't do it, I don't want her trying just because you're a bunch of peeping Thomasinas," Hortense said. "She might cause an explosion or transport Hanson to the enchanted land. It doesn't sound ethical, either."

"I wouldn't do it so badly as that," Susannah grumbled, insulted. "I could use a mirror and some variation of the spell that lets me see through walls."

"Then do it," Esme demanded. "Let me look first. Maybe he'll be naked."

"Definitely not," Susannah said.

"Why should you be the only one who gets to look at naked men? You and Peter, I mean."

"Hush your mouth," Susannah said.

"What do you mean by that, Esme?" Hortense asked. Ella, still on Susannah's bed, twisted around to see the exchange.

"I mean, she and Jon Tom were in the maze today, half-naked and—"

Without thought, Susannah flung up her hand with the crumpled feather and let her surge of anger channel her power and smack a dampening bubble over Esme. The other woman's eyes bugged out when she realized she was bitching in a vacuum, that Susannah had, indeed, used magic on her in a less-than-beneficent fashion.

Her sisters stopped whatever they were doing and evaluated Susannah with consternation.

"If Esme has something to say, I want to hear it." Hortense rose from the bed and stalked to Susannah, her face twisted with anger. "You've no right to be using your aberrant powers on us like that. You've no right!"

Emotions washed through Susannah: confusion, shame and still that heady sense of power, that thrill of magic coursing through her body. The instant explosion of it, the instant release, was like...

Well, not so much like that. She leaned against the door, slumped to the floor and closed her eyes.

Gods, what had she done?

With a cheer, Ella bounded off Susannah's bed and ran to her side. "Teach me to do that!"

"She'll do no such thing." Hortense grabbed Ella by the collar and pulled her away from Susannah.

"Hey, hands off!" Ella squirmed out of Hortense's grasp and dropped to the floor beside Susannah. "You're sure to solve every curse in the Kingdoms now, Susannah. If you can shut Esme up, you can do anything."

Behind Hortense, Susannah heard a few stifled giggles, but only a few. It made her feel no less guilty. Using her power on someone unequipped to counter it was like beating a puppy or a child. The sleep spells she'd sometimes cast on maids or guards were one thing. This was something else, something precarious and unforeseen.

"I...I..." She couldn't force any coherent words out of her mouth. She drew her knees up to her chest as hot tears seared her cheeks and fell on her nightgown.

Esme stumbled off her bed and crossed the room, moving her mouth without sound. She picked up a hairbrush and threw it at Susannah. It struck the door with a bang and clattered to the floor.

Next she reached for a pot of cosmetic, but several princesses intercepted. "Take the spell off her," Hortense said. "I'd be interested to hear about you, Mr. Tom and the maze."

Susannah scrubbed her eyes and met Peter's gaze. With a tiny smile, her beautiful sister shrugged and picked up an orange stick to buff her nails. Was that her way of saying she was sorry Susannah was in this position? Or how she knew the story would come out all along, which was why she hadn't been planning on telling? And maybe it was just Peter's way of saying, glad it's not me.

"Jon tried to... I mean, we..."

"The spell, Susannah." Hortense swooped up the hairbrush and smacked her palm with it.

Susannah inhaled a deep breath to calm herself and open the magic. For a moment, she was empty. The bud of her power was gone, as if the misuse had dissolved it forever. Panic rose and her throat closed up.

Ella patted her on the arm. "Just tell me what to do and I'll do it."

"You can't," Susannah said, her voice shaky. "You don't want this in your life. Look what it's done. Look what it's done to everyone." Fresh tears streamed down her cheeks and Ella offered her a flannel sleeve.

Suddenly the room was filled with a violent shriek as the spell wore off. The profanity Esme had been spewing this whole time inside her soundproof bubble assaulted everyone's ears like a team of ironworkers.

"Bloody witch!" she shouted. "Stinking, troll-warted, whey-faced hag!"

"Put it back on her, Susannah," Calypso groaned. "Please!"

"Dung eater! Toilet-bowl scraper!" Esme jumped up and down in her anger. "Sneaking, slimy whore!"

"Come on, Es, she's not a whore, we stopped her from that." Peter stood from her bed with a lazy stretch.

"Keep your yap down. Ears outside." Calypso put a not-entirely-loving arm around Esme's shoulders. "There are other ways to shut you up, Sister, and nobody will be angry with me if I use 'em."

Esme growled. In a lower voice she continued, "Our slut of a sister was rutting with Jon Tom—"

"Not rutting, surely," Peter interrupted her.

"Rutting with Jon Tom in the maze. She threatened to use her bloody perverted spells on us to keep it a secret."

"Susannah, is this true?" Hortense asked. The frown on her face carved lines in her forehead so deep Susannah wondered if they would ever come out.

"It's true." Susannah leaned her head against the door and sniffled. "I failed to keep him at arm's length. But I didn't tell him anything, I swear it."

Hortense smacked the hairbrush on her palm again. "I don't care about that. What about the magic? Who will you use it on next? Ella, when she rips her gown? Fay, because she can't make up her mind? Are we safe from you, Susannah?"

"Susannah won't do that!" Ella wrapped her arms around her sister. "She didn't hurt that stupid cow."

As Ella trembled beside her in anger, a strange pressure cottoned Susannah's ears, as if they needed to be popped. She shook her head. It must be residue from using the magic in anger instead of careful deliberation.

"It won't happen again," she promised. The loss of control had frightened her, frightened her more than any strangeness in the enchanted realm. Frightened her more than the fact she was in love with a cocksure detective who might, even at this moment, have his ear pressed to the door.

She resisted the urge to check. She didn't think this would be a good time to use one of her spells, not even one as innocuous as that.

"Sure you won't, until next time," Esme said.

"I might beat you soundly with a stick, but I won't use magic on you again, not like that. I'm sorry, Esme."

"You owe me." Esme had recovered from her fit of fury and an acquisitive gleam lightened her eyes. "Massively. Show me Hanson."

"You have the most one-horse mind of anyone I know."

Calypso gave Esme an ungentle shake. "Susannah's right. We'll see him tomorrow."

"I don't think Susannah needs to be casting any more spells tonight," Hortense said. "Maybe not ever."

"How else are any curses going to get broken around here?" Ella demanded. "Takes magic to break magic."

Hortense smoothed a hand over her dark hair even though the braid she wore down her back was a perfect, smooth twist. "With steady research and bargaining with the FAE, I'm sure our rulers will come to some sort of understanding."

Ella scrunched up her face. "Sure, the men are going to let women rule and marry commoners. I don't think so. Those old coots aren't going to give up their power, no matter what Mama tells Papa to do."

"Here, here!" Calypso clapped her hand enthusiastically on a bed frame.

"Starting now, I'm going to help." Ella dragged Susannah to her feet and practically shoved her to her bed. "You need someone who understands magic. That way if you're allowed only one curse, I can break the other one."

Susannah sighed, exhausted. If Ella hadn't been dragging her, she might have had to crawl. "I don't think that's a good idea."

"I can research. I can read the books and find other spells in places they're hidden, you know, in nursery rhymes. Maybe I'll find another book like the one you're translating."

"Using magic the wrong way was too easy. You get mad and throw things enough as it is. You saw with Esme what can happen when you lose your temper."

"She deserved it."

Susannah took Ella's hands in hers. "Nobody deserves to have magic used on them as a weapon, not if they can't defend themselves."

"It wasn't a weapon, you just shut her big mouth."

"Maybe humans aren't meant to tamper with magic. Maybe we can't handle it. It was too easy to cast that spell in anger."

"Like taking candy from a baby?" Ella asked.

Susannah shook her head. "Whoever said that didn't know much about babies. I do. I remember all of you as babies and none of you were easy to take candy from. I've got to be an example for the rest of you. That wasn't a very good example."

"Using magic isn't a good example," Hortense said. "She's right, Ella. You shouldn't tamper with it. She already is, but you don't have to start. And she'd best not violate the safe list again." She placed the hairbrush on a dressing table with a clack.

"Rutting with Jon Tom in the maze is the kind of example I want to follow." Esme plopped on the bed beside Susannah. "We know what you two have been doing. You can't lie any more. So spill."

"Um, spill?" Susannah was baffled by Esme's about-face, but people were often furious with Esme and she with them. Perhaps she was used to it.

"Spill the details. What's he like under all those black, tight-fitting clothes?"

"I can't kiss and tell!" Susannah blushed hotly as several of her sisters clustered around. "Little pitchers?" She glanced around for Rosa but saw the child was, unaccountably, sound asleep on Ella's bed despite the hubbub.

Calypso noticed the direction of her gaze. "There's no excuse not to tell us every last juicy bit," she said cheerfully. "What's it like to be with a real man instead of one of our lame ducks?"

Susannah rubbed a hand across her forehead in embarrassment. Though she'd often listened to her sisters tell tales of the young men they flirted with, the enchanted princes they kissed, she'd never been the center of the gossip. It was a novel sensation, and not entirely unpleasant.

"Well, it's like this..."

Chapter Nineteen

Susannah stood at attention by her mother's throne in the grand audience chamber and wished she were naked. Her burgundy court gown itched, and the accompanying steeple headdress squeezed her skull. The gold designs smattering her skirt and myriad ruffles along the hem weighed her down like well stones. Her several petticoats didn't ease her load, either. The cloying scent of plumeria, which Ella had spilled while they were dressing, tickled her nostrils.

The six elder princesses queued beside their mother while the six younger stood on the other side, next to the King. Long receiving lines of nobles and their daughters lined the carpet in the center of the vaulted chamber, waiting anxiously to meet the Middle Kingdom's most eligible bachelor. Red and gold ribbons that matched the carpet twined around the pillars supporting the ceiling.

"Why did we wait until this afternoon to meet the baronet if he arrived last night?" Susannah asked the Queen softly. She and her sisters had stayed up late, talking, but the friction caused by her misused magic hadn't dissipated. Her sleep had been uneasy, filled with dreams she was being spied upon.

"We wanted to give our dukes, barons and earls a chance to welcome the lad as well."

"And their daughters," Calypso cut in. She pointed at the anxious, giggling young ladies dressed in their flashiest finery. "Why ruin our odds, Mama? Like twelve isn't enough to pick from. I figure Susannah and Pete are in a dead heat, though Lilly might be a contender if you don't handicap her."

"This isn't a horse race, Calypso," the Queen said. "Don't be vulgar."

"Sure it isn't. And you haven't tricked us out like prize fillies. All we lack is a wreath of oats and roses around our necks."

"I don't see why we have to wear full court regalia," Susannah added. "Semiformal would have been more appropriate for a day presentation." Semiformal would have negated the ungainly headdresses that, even though paired with frontlet loops to balance the load, made one's scalp, neck and shoulders ache. And how, she wondered, were two-foot-tall hats attractive to a man, anyway?

Susannah was conscious of Jon Tom at the head of the left visitor line and wondered what he thought of her, dressed up like a doll. Had he overheard anything during the upset in the princesses' room last night? The low din of conversation in the audience chamber prevented her from hearing his comments to the earl beside him, not that he'd have been telling the man about the royal daughters.

"Sir Hanson has been on his Grand Tour, and the other nobility treated him with all due ceremony," the Queen said. "We should appear just as grand, and that includes you."

"If you ask me," Calypso commented, "the chappie would probably welcome a break from all the pomp."

"I didn't ask you," the Queen said.

Susannah noticed Jon Tom smirk at Calypso's comment. Apparently he could hear their conversation, even if she couldn't hear his. He must have sharp ears. She'd rather he not be present at her first meeting with Sir Hanson, but the Queen had informed her he'd asked to come.

That didn't sit easily with Susannah. The man she'd kissed yesterday, the man who'd exhibited a possessive streak and the man she'd like to marry? It was not an auspicious combination.

"Hush, ladies." The Queen stared at the far end of the domed audience chamber. "Our gentleman caller is due at any moment."

As if conjured by the Queen's assertion, a gong sounded and the footmen beside the doors yanked them open. Even the staff felt the tension of this Grand Tour, since it was rumored the newly made baronet hadn't favored any noble ladies at his previous stops. This was the last kingdom on his route. The Foresta princesses had been continually passed over by the various eligibles, but something in the air hinted this time would be different.

And it could be different, if Susannah could concentrate on charming him—without choosing him—to mislead her dratted curse. Confessions of true love, as everyone knew, had broken curses before. Would she be forced to reveal her feelings to Jon Tom in order to marry Sir Hanson?

Due to the excessive zeal of the footmen, the doors whipped open and banged against the walls. A slim young man stood there, fair-haired, silver circlet askew, clad in a blue tunic and trousers—and scratching his bottom.

Giggles swept the parallel receiving lines, and Susannah's own lips tipped up in a smile.

The announcer put his megaphone to his lips. "May I introduce Baronet Hanson Gillywether, of the kingdom Rasta and the town of Bremen."

The young man dropped his hand and strode through the doors, up the long carpet. A friendly grin spread across his face as he nodded his head to the individuals lining the runner. The shiny silver circlet denoting his rank tipped even farther to one side.

"Sir Hanson," Susannah's father boomed, "welcome to our little piece of the pie."

Calypso groaned, earning herself a reproachful look from the Queen. "I hate it when he says that," she whispered to Susannah.

"Greetings, Your Highness and Your Highness." Sir Hanson executed a respectable bow, swinging out his right arm gracefully.

He must have hired a tutor. Many of the young men did, but most bumbled through all royal courtesies, secure in the knowledge of their desirability.

However, the young baronet stayed in a lateral position a moment too long, and his silver circlet popped off his head. It bounced on the thick rug underfoot and rolled to the feet of Jon Tom, who quirked an eyebrow in response.

"Drat." Sir Hanson straightened and brushed a self-conscious hand over his tousled hair. "Can you toss me that crown, good fellow?" He turned to look at the King and Queen with a shrug. "Awful thing is always falling off. They should make them with little combs on the side to hold them on your head."

"There stands our once and future king," Calypso whispered. The Queen rapped her cane on the throne. To Calypso's right, Susannah heard Peter heave a disappointed sigh.

Jon Tom picked up the crown and strolled forward to hand it to Sir Hanson, who jammed it back on his head, crooked. As the detective returned to his spot in the line, he glanced at Susannah with a dark, sardonic gaze. She knew how he viewed her plan to ensnare the young baronet. She didn't care. She couldn't care. It wasn't as if she could marry the detective.

But why did the cynicism in his gaze make her feel small and grubby, like a stable hand after cleaning day?

"Wake up and say hello." Calypso elbowed her, and Susannah realized her father had just introduced her. She curtseyed and gave what she hoped was a youthful smile. The baronet had an unlined face. The broadsheets claimed he was but twenty-four.

Over ten years her junior. What could she possibly do or say to interest a boy like that?

She'd have to start somewhere. "I'm happy to meet you, Sir Hanson," she said. "We have many fine activities planned for your stay."

"Many activities, you say?" The baronet smiled, a little woodenly, and bowed again. Miraculously, his circlet stayed on his head.

Obviously a list of activities wasn't going to entrance him. The baronet's gaze lingered on Peter but flickered back to Susannah once or twice. No doubt he felt like a monkey on display, but he'd been feeling that way since he began his tour. He should be used to it.

Because he'd started a precedent with Susannah, Sir Hanson bowed twice for each princess, up and down, up and down, like a crane drinking water. His crown fell off after his introduction to Hortense, and he held it in his hand for the rest of the sisters. Lilly went on a bit too long about the honor involved in meeting such a great hero, and Ella stumbled during her curtsey, but all in all, the introductions went more smoothly than any Susannah could remember. It helped that

Hanson's eyes glazed over after the first several princesses. He didn't seem to notice them whispering, their court gowns rustling, their tall headdresses bobbing.

After Rosa's introduction, the King walked down the three steps to Sir Hanson's side. He clapped the baronet on the shoulder, and the poor man nearly fell to his knees. Most of the rulers in the Middle Kingdoms were more conscious of their dignity than Susannah's father. The look on Sir Hanson's face was bewildered.

"What do you think of my litter, eh?" the King said. "I daresay that's the longest bout of introductions you've ever had to bow through."

"I hate it when he says that, too," Calypso muttered. "What are we, hound pups all thrown from the bitch at once?"

"Mother," Susannah whispered, "don't let Papa start in on the many magnificent aspects of our kingdom. It's not the time for his sales pitch. The boy is fidgeting, bored and probably hungry. And now he's scared to death."

The Queen stamped her cane onto the ground. "Banquet," she commanded.

The King twitched. "My lady is hungry, and I suspect my daughters are eager to get to know you. What do you say we sneak off to the banquet first and have a man-to-man chat before the women take over?"

"Certainly, Your Highness." The baronet cast his gaze about wildly, lighting on Susannah as if to beg for rescue. Why would he beg her for rescue when she was probably the thing he wished rescue from? Strange young man. Maybe she reminded him of his mother. Susannah made a mental note to counsel her father against coming on too strong.

"Come, we'll take a short cut." The King took Hanson's arm and towed him to the doors behind the throne dais that led directly to the servants corridor and thence to the banquet hall.

"Let me tell you about the magic barge on our private lake." The door snicked off the rest of the King's spiel. The Queen's lips tightened in a familiar manner.

When the King and his prey disappeared, the Queen clapped her hands together. The footmen opened the audience chamber doors. She rose and marched regally down the receiving corridor, and the princesses fell into lines behind her.

Susannah risked a glance at Jon Tom.

His face was shuttered. Inscrutable. He was, of course, watching her, but she could gauge nothing from his blank expression. Tradition ruled that the entire royal family must leave the audience chamber and seat themselves before anyone else, so Susannah didn't see him again that evening.

Despite Susannah's attempts to converse with Sir Hanson, her father monopolized the young man's attention during the formal banquet. The baronet handled the many glasses and plates with aplomb. He ate a good deal with the tiny banquet spoons and nodded at the King, who sat at the table's head along with the Queen. The hundred or so other nobles and, she supposed, Jon Tom, were seated at other tables in the room, the roar of conversation muted but lively. Who was Jon Tom seated beside? If it was a noble daughter, she was probably twisted around in her seat for a glimpse of Sir Hanson.

Through the apricot compote and the broiled garlic artichoke hearts, through the almond-crusted halibut and the cucumber peas, through the buttered mussels and the pepper-cheese flowers, an army of servants whisked the miniature plates and bowls onto and off of everyone's placemat. The King rambled on and on. Susannah finished her puff pastry and wondered why her father had taken such a liking to Sir Hanson. Perhaps he was just doing his part to ensnare an heir.

"Sir Hanson, don't you like your cheese pastry?" Susannah asked him. "The filling is made from the milk of the Reston cows common to your homeland."

The baronet gave her a weak smile and gulped down his pastry. The current style for formal banquets was to serve as plentiful a selection as possible, necessitating tiny portions of each in miniature dishes. One was meant to sample everything offered, and if it wasn't to your taste, at least the spoons didn't hold much. The crystal thimbles of wines and liqueurs with each course were voluntary, and Susannah drank water during the meal—in a regular-sized glass.

The baronet sat to the King's left and Calypso to the Queen's right. Susannah dined between Sir Hanson and Peter and traced a pattern on the damask tablecloth with her spoon. Because she had only Peter to speak to and Peter was in a sulk, Susannah ate more than she normally did. She squirmed in her rigid, formal corset. She wished she could go upstairs, take off her stupid court headdress and brush out her hair.

Her father waved away a second serving of chocolate trifle. The Queen caught Susannah's gaze and narrowed her eyes, tilting her head slightly to indicate the baronet. Then she engaged her husband in conversation.

Susannah took a deep breath, then another. Perhaps it would make more room inside her corset for all the food. What might Hanson like besides cows? "My father mentioned the superior hunting in the Oldtree Forest, I'm sure. Do you enjoy hunting?"

She pitched the question loud enough for Calypso to hear. Although it wasn't the thing to converse across the table, her family didn't stand on absolute ceremony. Besides, her father wasn't obeying the rules of polite discourse, so why should she? If she could get Calypso chattering about horses and hounds, they'd give their father a run for his coins.

"Not really, Princess Susannah." The tablecloth rustled near Hanson's legs, and she realized he was nervously tapping his foot on the ground.

Poor fellow. She widened her eyes at Calypso and inclined her head toward Hortense. Hopefully Hortense wasn't still so disgusted with Susannah she refused to answer the call of duty. They needed to yank the conversation away from their father, or their mother would lambaste them.

Hortense tinked her spoon against the trifle bowl, as if by accident. Hanson glanced up. "Has our father described our Justice Chambers?" she asked. "He resolves a higher proportion of citizen complaints than any other kingdom."

The baronet nodded and licked chocolate from his tiny spoon. Little curls had sprung up all over his head and bushed around his circlet, making him look even younger. Across the table, Hortense pursed her lips.

Unaware of the byplay, Hanson quaffed a thimble of hot vanilla liqueur. "Jon said the Justice Chambers were a marvel of efficiency."

"Mr. Tom?" Susannah nearly crumpled her spoon in her

fist. "When did you have the opportunity to speak with him?"

"He took me about this morning. Showed me the lay of the land." The baronet's cheeks were flushed, probably from the amount of alcohol he'd consumed over the course of the meal. The thimbles were deceptive, Susannah had learned long ago.

"The lay of the land." Susannah didn't know how to take that and ignored Calypso and Hortense across the table, both making "shush" faces. "So Mr. Tom spent the morning with you. He didn't mention it to me."

"Why would he? If he's here to sneak about and investigate you, it seems as how he wouldn't tell you what he's up to all day long."

"How do you know he's investigating us? Did he tell you that?" What was Jon Tom doing, filling the baronet's ears with spite to ensure she couldn't carry out her plan? In what way did her courtship of Hanson interfere with any of his plans?

She didn't understand the man. He criticized her for researching Hanson's background but helped her do it. Despite the Queen's command, he could have slacked off. He hinted she should shirk her duty and let one of her sisters marry but didn't offer her an alternate life. He made love to her but didn't love her. Why should it matter to Jon Tom whom she married? Surely he didn't want their kingdom to crumble into pieces, not when he aspired to settle in it—in her dower territory, no less.

Hanson stifled a little belch. "Jon told me because I asked. He said he was a detective, so I asked if he was here to solve the mystery of the twelve dancing princesses and if so, why he was still on staff. And then he said something strange that I didn't understand."

"What could be stranger than an occupation as farcical as a detective?" Susannah put down her spoon before she hurt herself squeezing it. What else had the man told the baronet?

"He said he wasn't here for twelve princesses, only one."

Across the table, Hortense and Calypso exchanged a glance Susannah didn't miss. She had little doubt what Jon Tom meant by that, but she wasn't about to explain it to the baronet.

She changed the subject before Hanson questioned her. "He's a strange man. You can't believe half of what he says, and the other half is shifty. How did you know we're being investigated? I thought you came here straight from Kingdom Tennubia."

"The kingdoms are thick with gossip about you. It's one reason I came here last."

"I'm not sure I understand you." The headache that had started when she donned her headdress stabbed Susannah's temples. He'd saved their kingdom for last because of something he learned via gossip. Did he think they had blemished reputations and were his last choice? They were known for eccentricity, thanks to the Queen's inclusion of them in running the kingdom, but not wantonness, surely.

"I'm sure I don't understand you, either." Hortense's mouth was a grim line. The expression on her face combined with her black cone headdress gave her the appearance of a storybook bad fairy.

"Do you mean that you dreaded our reputations?" Susannah tilted her head back, and her headdress dragged her hair and pulled her scalp. The silk-tented ceiling of the banquet hall, however, held no inspiration. No broadsheets she'd found time to read had cast aspersions on their family, so discovering they were the subject of wide-ranging gossip was unsettling, to say the least.

Sir Hanson widened his nervous grin to include all the diners at their end of the table. "Nay, I don't fear your reputation. You sounded the most fun."

If they were the subject of ugly speculation, it was all Susannah's fault. All her fault. "Everyone speaks of us? Everyone? Even in Pavilion?"

Calypso thunked her goblet onto the table. Susannah snapped to attention. "Susannah, has your big, fat head been in the lake these past few months? How many times have the Duke of Orange's daughters begged us to tell them how we sneak out of the castle? If we knew any single men in the area?" When Calypso rolled her head, her peaked headdress swayed like a double-masted sailing ship.

"That's just town gossip. We wouldn't be a topic in other kingdoms." Susannah motioned to a servant with a tray of liqueur and took two, downing them in sweet, fiery succession. Tears sprang into her eyes, and the pit of her stomach blossomed with warmth.

Through the blur, Susannah noticed her parents listening avidly to the conversation. "What baseless rumors," she claimed, after blowing out a long breath. She dabbed her watering eyes with a napkin. "Perhaps you could describe this tittle-tattle."

"Oh, you know, it's the usual. You hear it all the time about noble ladies these days." The baronet turned pink. "It ain't for me to say in the presence of ladies. Jon Tom assured me the rumors about you are unfounded."

"Gossip is food for idle minds, young man," the Queen cut in. "You should be ashamed for even questioning the honor of my daughters. They might be willful, but I should hope I've taught them how to go on."

Sir Hanson cringed. "I mean no offense, Your Highness. Princess Susannah asked about the rumors from other kingdoms."

Susannah fanned her face with the napkin. The servants padded around the tables with selections of fruit slices and nuts. "Were these rumors what brought you to the conclusion my sisters and I would be the most...fun?"

The King shifted in his seat. "Now, see here," he began.

Susannah waved him to silence. She didn't want to alienate the baronet, but if he'd come here expecting that sort of a good time, it would definitely change her planned course of action.

Hanson shook his head vigorously. "No, no! I have several sisters meself, you see, close as peas in a pod. I know the shenanigans sisters get up to, you see? They're more fun than a hog in a pantry. And there's twelve of you." The baronet's speech patterns reverted to their native dialect in his anxiety. She could taste the burr of the farm in his rolling vowels. "I never gave a thought to your reputations."

It had to be true. If he were here for a roll in the hay, would he come an inch from admitting it during a formal banquet? So, the lad had several sisters and wanted to have fun?

"I'm glad you don't believe the silly rumors," Susannah said, "but I daresay we can still contrive to be the most fun."

"I, um, daresay too," the baronet said and heaved a sigh of relief.

Chapter Twenty

Her mother relieved her of duties for the duration of Sir Hanson's visit, so Susannah spent the next several days getting to know the young man. Her sisters were also on holiday, and the palace rang with laughter and squabbling. They toured the maze, the lake, the hot springs, the rose garden and the outskirts of Oldtree Forest. They spent evenings in the billiards room or the stargazing chamber. Susannah's sisters crashed into bed every night too exhausted to beg for a visit to the enchanted princes.

Through it all, Jon Tom remained in the background, watching, and his dark gaze evaluated Susannah's progress. He made no move to trap her in corners and remind her how he could make her body melt with a single kiss. He didn't appear the one time she slipped away to the library. He ceased to whisper double entendres whenever her sisters turned their backs, and at the table he was the image of gentility.

And it was beginning to make Susannah crazy. She couldn't concentrate on Hanson—she was too busy waiting for Jon Tom's other boot to drop. Her lack of movement with the baronet, due to her distraction, was a rare peeve with her sisters, not to mention her mother. She hoped, though, if anything would confuse her stupid curse, mooning over Jon Tom would do it.

Several days into the visit, Hanson expressed an interest in having his fortune told, so of course it was arranged for a group to visit Madame, the fairy astrologer.

At midafternoon, the sunlight streamed through Madame's stained-glass windows in swirls of yellow, green and blue, which splashed brilliantly across pristine white carpets. Hanson perched before Madame on a purple stool with fat legs. The wizened old fairy spread his hand, palm up, on her divining table, muttering and shaking puffs of fairy dust from her feathered cap.

Susannah and several sisters waited their turn on one of the settees lining the wall of the turret room. Jon Tom, their silent shadow, leaned against the doorframe. He hadn't spoken to Susannah today except to wish her good morn. He hadn't touched her in two days. Four, if she didn't count the polite clasp of hands as she dismounted from the carriage.

She missed his touch. She missed him.

Lilly pressed Susannah's arm. Her gaze were pinned on the young baronet. In a whisper, she said, "I have to ask you something."

"What is it?"

Lilly turned her head so Susannah could see more than her profile. "Do you want Hanson or not? If you don't, let us know so we may have our chance. You're going to let him get away, just like the others, because you can't quit thinking about Mr. Tom."

"Hush, he'll hear you." Susannah cut her gaze to Jon Tom, who hadn't moved.

"He can't hear anything over Madame's chanting. I'd expect Fay to have trouble deciding, but you? You must put him from your mind."

"I didn't mean Hanson would hear you. I meant him." Susannah inclined her head to the doorway, where Jon Tom gazed into space. "His ears are very sharp."

"So what?" Lilly shrugged. "He knows what you had was just a fling and now you must marry your kind. It's the way of things."

"Can we discuss this at some other time?" Some other time when she could think up a new excuse to avoid the conversation. "I can't be expected to decide in four days."

Calypso stretched across the arm of the next settee and cupped her hand around her mouth to speak into Susannah's ear. Lilly slanted herself across Susannah so she could hear as well. "If you don't hurry," Calypso said, "the rest of the unweds in the kingdom are going to dream up excuses to visit, and we'll be neck-deep in vipers trying to snake the bait. We at least have the decency to give you first crack."

"First crack shouldn't be taking this long," Lilly added. "And you should know, some of us aren't willing to wait much longer."

Susannah wanted to shake them both, leaning on her, pressuring her to make a decision. "You're speaking of him like he's an animal. He's a man, not a trophy."

"He's better than the fat chef. You're just stuck on—"

"Did you hear that?" Hanson's clear tenor voice interrupted their fierce, whispered conversation. "Madame says what I want is going to take much longer to find than I expect."

Susannah and her sisters pasted polite smiles on their faces. "Madame is as cryptic as ever," Susannah said. "Once she told me I'd find something no one else has, and unless she meant a four-leaf clover in the lake field, her prediction still hasn't come true."

Madame beamed, her round face wrinkled as a honey pastry. "My girl, if you'd let me study your fortune again, my updated prediction would be more on the spot." The fairy extended a plump arm in invitation.

"Oh, do, Princess Susannah," Hanson said. "It's smashing fun, and then I won't be the only one who knows what's in store." He popped up from the stool and nearly overturned it.

"Hanson, we gave you the use of our first names." Susannah hoped the reminder would distract him. Who knew what the old fairy would be able to sense about Susannah's magic? She hadn't had her fortune told in years for that very reason and professed she didn't wish to be depressed by it.

To Susannah's relief, Calypso volunteered. "I'll go next." She hastened to the stool next to Madame's table. Smacking her hand down on the wood, she said, "What do you see, some horses and hounds?"

Madame took Calypso's hand and smoothed it out before she sprinkled it with fairy dust. As she muttered, Susannah sensed the tang of minor magic in use. She looked at Jon Tom. Had he noticed her reluctance to have her palm read?

The detective watched Sir Hanson with speculation coloring his features. Susannah recognized the expression from the many times it had been turned on her. His eyebrows quirked and his full bottom lip bowed with a subtle moue. What did he think of the young man's fortune? If it was she that Hanson wanted—or the kingdom she represented—how quickly had he hoped to woo and marry someone? It was not as if she planned to put up a fight. It was not as if any unwed princess would put up a fight.

Madame cleared her throat and made her prediction to the room at large, instead of privately. "You're blessed with good health and good sense."

"I know that, that's my christening gift," Calypso said. "What else?"

"You'll make good use of your gifts in the days ahead." Madame cocked her head to one side. "In other words, no change since three days ago when you last came to see me."

To Susannah's surprise, her sister snatched her hand back to her lap. She hadn't known Calypso visited Madame independently. Her hunt-mad sister seemed more caught up in the here and now than the sooner and later.

"Mr. Tom should go next," Calypso said. "All these female vibes are skewing the predictions. Making them dull. I mean, we all know what's in store for us, right?"

Jon Tom executed a small bow. "I'm sure the lives of the ladies in this castle are far from dull. I am equally sure Madame has no wish to waste her time on a commoner like myself."

"Tsk, lad, I can see from here you're uncommon."

"I really don't think—"

"What is it with no one wanting to know the future?" Sir Hanson clapped his hands together and rubbed them. "I love hearing what's to come. It's like watching your favorite play and knowing the end will please you."

"I doubt my future is as bright as yours," Jon Tom said. "It's probably more along the lines of a tragedy."

Jon Tom's negativity surprised Susannah. Did he really think that or was he just trying to dodge a foretelling, like Susannah had these past fifteen years?

"Nonsense." Madame crooked her finger at Jon Tom. "I'm not predicting your whole future with this little spell. More like a cookie prediction. Seat yourself, child."

Jon Tom's eyebrow arched, but he did as Madame insisted. Susannah wondered about the raven black he wore today. Even his undershirt was black, somber against his throat, and the buttons on his tunic were black bone.

"Splendid!" Hanson said. "I love cookie predictions. I always choose the chocolate. Everyone knows it gives the best luck." He plopped on the settee next to Calypso. Lilly half rose as if to shift to his side, but Susannah grabbed her arm.

Madame patted Jon Tom's hand, uncurled the fingers and tapped each fingertip. "A fine, clever hand it is, with the long fingers of a trickster or a lover. Which are you?"

Calypso chortled. "Probably both."

Jon Tom inclined his head. "I'm sure you'll tell me which." He planted his black boots on either side of the small table and leaned on his elbow, as if he and Madame were combatants in a bout of arm wrestling.

The feathers in Madame's hat wavered as she chuckled. "I wouldn't be telling you anything you didn't know."

"Some say even fairies can't predict the future," Jon Tom said. "That their palmistry, astrology and chart casting are gimmicks and their words cryptic enough to be interpreted however the hearer wishes."

Madame turned her head to view Susannah and her sisters, and her eyes twinkled. "You have a cheeky one here, Princess," she observed, but she didn't say which princess she meant. Susannah's sisters turned to her anyway.

What would Hanson think if her sisters kept dropping hints about Susannah and Jon Tom? She looked at the boy, but several shafts of colored light from the windows preoccupied him as he splayed his fingers through them.

Madame chanted and hummed, bent over Jon Tom's palm. Again Susannah tasted magic in the air, stronger than with Hanson or Calypso. Jon Tom straightened on the stool.

"Private or public?" Madame asked.

"Shout it out, by all means," Jon Tom said. "It's today's entertainment."

"You have something you shouldn't," the fairy said. "Your essence is twinned, which means there's two of you or you lead a double life."

Jon Tom was wrong about the fairies and their ability to foretell. Not only did Susannah sense magic in use, but

Madame never mispredicted. The fortunes were cryptic, but they were also true. Susannah had certainly found something no one else had...two somethings, if she counted her magic and the princes.

"I have many things I shouldn't," Jon Tom agreed.

Susannah bit her lip. She'd never determined whether Jon Tom had any special device for his detective work. Or perhaps the thing he had which he shouldn't was her heart. Oh, what a melodrama!

Jon Tom patted Madame's hand and slid out of her grasp. "A double life is one of the hazards of the profession. Though the good princesses refuse to believe it, I'm not the first detective to practice the art. I just have the best press."

"There was that Magnus fellow Susannah told us about." Calypso leaned back on the settee and crossed her legs in an unladylike fashion. "I gather he was better than you, though."

"I don't believe it," Hanson said. "Jon told me how many times he helped fairies. If he figures things out even the fairies can't, he's got to be the best."

So Jon Tom had found more opportunities to fill Hanson's ear with whispers? When? And what did he say? Not for the first time, she wished she knew his mind. As if aware of her gaze on him, he turned and met her stare for a single, smoldering moment.

Susannah's breath caught in her throat.

Madame broke the brief but intense interval. "You intrigue me, lad. Let me cast a more thorough chart for you." She rummaged in the chest beside her armchair and pulled out a crystal ball, a roll of parchment and a sack that held runestones. Well, unless it was the sack with Madame's game of jacks.

Jon Tom held up his hands in a polite veto. "Thank you, but no." He gave Madame a roguish smile. "For one such as myself, eventually my misdeeds will find me, and I'd rather not know the specifics."

Someone was watching them.

Several days after visiting the astrologer, Susannah, Hanson and a guard toured the capital city so Hanson could mingle with the common folk, ask questions and measure how they fared. There were, of course, more cities in the kingdom, but the capitol city was closest to the palace. They'd asked if he preferred to go alone so the citizens wouldn't feel constrained, but he'd requested that Susannah accompany him.

They'd been walking up and down the orderly streets for two hours, and Susannah's neck kept prickling. The corners of her eyes sensed flickers she couldn't identify, no matter how fast she whipped around. There was never anyone there, never any disappearing boot or sliver of fabric. No one lurked behind the blacksmith's huge cooling barrel. No one crouched underneath the threads-and-notions table.

Hanson remained oblivious to her preoccupation. His admiration of the town and shops buzzed through her ears unchecked. She should concentrate on the young man and cement their friendship, but something kept tweaking her awareness. The two of them rubbed along well, even if she felt more like his sister. She was sister to so many, after all.

There it was again. She was certain someone was spying on them! Someone using magic to do it. There was a tang in the air, even through the sugary smell of pastries on Baker's Street, the dust and bustle of Delivery Street.

Who'd spy on her in town? She thought immediately of Jon Tom and halted on the sidewalk in front of the Dandy Fairy Pawn Shop.

"You want to go in here, Susannah?" Hanson was finally comfortable enough to skip titles. He squinted in the afternoon sun at the faded sign.

"I thought I saw someone I knew." She dropped Hanson's arm and darted around the next storefront, peering into a shop that sold musical instruments. No Jon Tom. The taste she'd gotten of enchantment had dissipated.

Maybe it had been a magic flute.

Hanson stared through the front glass at a display of instruments. "I wouldn't be surprised if you did. You seem to know everyone in town. That's a fine thing, right? The other princesses I met only went to town in enclosed carriages and never spoke to anyone."

"Our kingdom's small. It's easier to know more people. If we toured farther from the capitol, I wouldn't know many at all." Should she ask the shopkeeper if he'd seen a devastatingly dark and handsome man lurking about? Best not. She took Hanson's proffered arm, and they resumed their stroll down the boardwalk.

"It's the smallest of all the civilized human kingdoms. The primary export products are flowers, mushrooms, furniture and fancy dress." Hanson smiled when he finished and looked at Susannah expectantly.

"You've done your research." It was almost like giving Rosa a pat on the head for studying her multiplication tables. "Do you like, er, flowers?"

Hanson shrugged. "Sure, I guess." He stared across the street, and his cheeks pinkened. "I like this kingdom."

Was that a hint he intended to remain in it? Susannah switched her full attention to Hanson. "I'm glad you like it. How does ours compare to the other kingdoms? Your tour must have been very interesting."

Hanson tilted his head back. Many of the buildings on Sundry Street were three or four stories, with balconies overlooking the avenue. Flowering plants teemed out of window boxes and hung off the iron rails that lined the narrow porches.

"It's more flowery," he said finally.

"Then I'm glad you like flowers." Really, this was almost like having a conversation with the enchanted princes. "Hanson, are you having a good time? Do you want to go back to the castle and play billiards or croquet?"

"No, I specifically wanted to spend time with you." He shoved his free hand in his tunic pocket and fiddled with some object inside.

He seemed nervous, but not the kind of nervous she'd been all day. Why did he want to be alone with her? Was it what she hoped? Was he considering marrying into their family? She'd best not pressure him. Best not think of choosing him, either.

Suddenly, Susannah caught the flicker of...something...in the corner of her eye and a very distinct tang of magic. She lunged toward the area she thought she'd seen it, at the corner of the next building. Several carriages and wagons trundled along the road.

"Hey!" Hanson stumbled. He quickly regained his footing and hastened after her, clinging to her hand. "Where's the fire?"

Susannah heard the guard trot after them, his sword clattering in its sheath.

"I swear I saw something." At the end of the boardwalk, she whisked around the corner of the building. No one. No doors or windows along the side of the building. The vehicles in the road would have prevented anyone from a quick crossing.

Yet Susannah felt as if she were inches away from something she ought to understand.

If she told the guard she thought they were being trailed, he'd want them to return to the palace. He'd call the constables and have the area searched. She didn't want to cause a stir.

Instead, she said to Hanson, "I have an idea, something you'll really like. Come on!"

She dragged him back the way they'd come, crossed the road between two farm carts, dodged an apple seller and pattered down a side street. The guard jogged to keep up with them but didn't protest. Plenty of experience escorting the princesses had probably taught him not to ask questions. She took another side street, popped in the back door of a jewelry shop and out the front and marched as fast as she could to the next intersection. Hanson latched onto Susannah's sprint as a game. He jogged alongside her, held tight to her hand and helped her whirl around corners.

She giggled, winded, and wondered what in the world the guard was going to tell her mother. He might not complain to the princesses about their behavior, but that didn't mean he didn't report every bit of it to the Queen.

They reached Lady's Street and she slowed. The thick aroma in the air hit their nostrils like a stew of flowers, powder and spice. Hanson sneezed. He dropped her hand to wipe his nose with a handkerchief.

No one could have trailed them this far without attracting notice. Satisfied any spies or thieves had been left behind, Susannah rounded the corner and collided with Jon Tom.

"What the devil!" she exclaimed. Jon Tom steadied her against his chest, and his warm hands clasped her upper arms.

He made no move to release her. She gazed up at him and recalled their last encounter in the maze. Today he wore a brown leather jerkin and sinfully tight leather breeches beneath his shabby brown cloak. Sweat beaded his brow and trickled down his temple.

Oh, how she'd missed him!

"Hello, chap, where did you come from?" Hanson asked, breaking the spell.

"I'd like to know that as well." Susannah stared into his eyes, as enigmatic as ever. "Don't tell me your detective duties extend to my leisure time?"

She heard their guard shift uneasily behind Hanson and clear his throat. It was one thing for her to grab Hanson's hand and run through the town like a hoyden. It was another for a commoner to practically embrace her.

Jon Tom dropped his hands and bowed. "Princess Susannah, Sir Hanson." He dabbed his forehead with the back of his thumb but otherwise appeared to be completely at ease, cool and somewhat amused.

"I asked you a question. What are you doing in town? Spying on me?" What did he think he'd find out about the nighttime mystery if he followed her with Hanson? Or was that why he was following her? They hadn't visited the princes in many nights, though Jon Tom had continued to sleep on his pallet outside their door.

"Spying on you is my job," Jon Tom said. "But no, that's not why I'm here."

"I don't believe you." Susannah wished she could shake the truth out of him. He was up to something. He was too careful to meet and hold her gaze, just hers.

"Why are you here, then? This is Lady's Street." Hanson gestured at the ornate wooden boulevard sign.

Jon Tom finally glanced at the baronet. "Why are you here?"

"Well, I'm with a lady." Hanson smiled. "We've already toured Men's Street and Children's Street and Grocer's Street and, well, all sorts of streets."

"How industrious of you."

"We're headed back to the castle," Susannah said.

"I thought you wanted to show me something?" Hanson asked.

"Er, I wanted to show you Lady's Street, so you could see the flowers. Since you like them." She pointed up, where cascades of ferns, vines and vibrant blooms thronged along the balconies. It was like standing beneath a tropical garden.

"Oh," Hanson said. "In case I didn't mention it, I like meat pies, too."

Jon Tom returned his gaze to Susannah, his eyes half-closed in mockery.

"We'll fetch you one on the way home." Susannah stepped away from Jon Tom and linked her arm through Hanson's, patting him like an obedient dog. Hanson gave her, then the detective, curious glances.

Susannah tossed her hair, just a little. "Mr. Tom, whatever legitimate business you have on Lady's Street, we'll allow you to finish it in peace." She and Hanson left the detective next to the perfume shop, sweating in his long cloak. She heard him murmur something to the palace guard and both men laughed before their guard returned to pace behind them.

The detective knew what she was doing and why she had to do it. Why couldn't he just let her shoulder her responsibilities?

Chapter Twenty-One

That evening, the princesses convened in the billiards room after dinner for fun, games and bickering. Susannah declined all invitations to play and sank into a wing chair off to the side, hoping Jon Tom wouldn't join them. And, at the same time, hoping he would.

The room was dark-paneled and had a brown carpet flecked with red to hide stains. Two billiard tables dominated the front of the room, with comfortable wing chairs and sofas along the walls. The back of the room featured a shuffleboard mat, horseshoe stakes and indoor croquet goals, though one couldn't play all those games simultaneously. Well, one could, but it was...challenging. A large cabinet in the center stored parts for the games and game rulebooks, to dissuade violent battles over rights and wrongs.

Calypso, Hanson, Rosa and Lilly knocked the bright, marble balls into the pockets of the table closest to Susannah. Calypso tried to include Susannah in the conversation. "It won't be long before our neighbors invade." She leaned on her wooden cue. "We should enjoy the quiet times while we can."

"These have been quiet times?" Hanson bent over the table and aimed along the felt at one of the balls. A clack, a crack and a shout of laughter from the other table confirmed someone had, again, sent a ball flying onto the floor.

Hanson grinned and missed his shot. "Can't say it's been quiet around here."

"Take another one, Hanson," Calypso said. "Remember to point at the spot you want to hit and never take your eyes off the ball."

"Why do you think the neighbors will invade?" Rosa asked.

"Oh, you know, fresh meat and all." Calypso shrugged. "Hanson's a rarity I don't think they can ignore for long."

Hanson blushed and flubbed his second shot. His cue tip skidded across the surface of the table and missed the ball entirely.

"Calypso! Don't talk about him like he's not here." Susannah rose to stand beside Hanson, as if her support would prevent him from hearing her sister's words. Her dinner gown rustled with the movement.

"Sorry, chappie," Calypso said. "You know how it is. No new baronet has lasted more than a double quarter without getting snagged. You're coming on the mark."

"I know." Hanson sighed, his face still pink. "I wish I could go somewhere and hide."

"You can hide in our stables," Rosa said. "That's where I go, in my pony's stall."

Susannah pulled at a snip of dark green piping that decorated the bodice of her tight-waisted gown. The huge skirts puffed out from her body like a bell. She'd rather be wearing a workaday gown. Or a chemise.

At least they'd convinced Mama they should leave off the formal hoops. Hanson didn't give a bean about formality.

Calypso bent over the table, executed a flawless bank shot and sent two balls zipping into opposite pockets. "It might not be as bad as the other kingdoms. We've got fewer women who'll be after you. I mean, excluding the twelve of us." She grinned and blew Hanson a kiss.

Calypso looked very pretty tonight, in a plain blue dress with layered skirts and a square neckline. Her auburn hair lay against her neck in a sophisticated twist. Was it for Hanson's benefit? Lilly, too, had on an enchanting silver gown that gave her fair hair and skin an ethereal cast.

Perhaps her sisters had tired of her indecision. Susannah could understand that, but would a concentrated onslaught from all twelve send Hanson into hiding for real? Perhaps she should resurrect the conversation from town about Hanson's affection for this kingdom.

Poor Hanson. The most valuable commodity in the civilized lands and nothing he could do to escape the popularity except marry.

"Mama won't let many visit at once," Susannah promised him. She watched Calypso sink another ball. "How many did you have to contend with in the other kingdoms?"

"It depended on, um, how many princesses there were for me to, um..." Hanson choked on his words and his sentence ended in a hack.

"We have the most princesses," Lilly said, "for you to 'um'." She giggled. "But we're all very different. Some of us are nicer. And friendlier."

That cinched it. Her sisters were no longer waiting for her to make up her mind about pursuing Hanson.

Rosa slipped behind Calypso before her third shot and bumped her cue. "You missed!" she cried. "Now it's my turn."

Calypso tweaked Rosa on the nose and allowed her the cheat.

"Some of us are just immature." Lilly rubbed the chalk against her cue tip and offered it to Hanson with a gesture that made the top of her gown drape.

Hanson didn't seem to notice. He accepted the chalk and repeated Lilly's actions, minus the shimmy. "I like billiards, but I'm not very good at it. I didn't get much opportunity to practice in the other kingdoms. And, well, my Pa didn't exactly have a table in the barn."

White flecks drifted down to speckle the wooden rim of the table, and Susannah brushed them to the floor. "Some of us who've been playing for years aren't very accomplished," she said. "Including me."

"You never try." Lilly halfheartedly took her turn at the table, humming to herself as she aligned her stick and the cue ball. She peeked at her bosom and bent lower so her dress gaped. "There are all sorts of things you never try."

Lilly knocked one ball in but scratched on the second. Susannah stepped back so Hanson could undertake his next shot.

A rap sounded on the door of the billiards room and a gold-clad footman opened it to admit Jon Tom. Several sisters called out greetings, and Hanson waved for the detective to join their table.

"Jon!" he said. "Calypso's robbing me blind. It's not like I can mortgage the farm to pay off my debts. I could use your help."

Jon Tom sauntered across the carpet, a sardonic smile on his face. It was the kind of smile that didn't bring out his dimples. "I'm sure you don't need my help to win any game. Perhaps the princess will let you win?"

"Not hardly." Calypso twirled her stick like an oversized baton and tossed it toward the ceiling, spinning it like a windwheel.

Lilly jumped aside. "You could put my eye out!"

"You've got two of 'em." Calypso snatched the stick out of the air before it clattered to the ground. Jon Tom and Hanson applauded, but Susannah had seen the trick too many times to be impressed. Calypso saluted her audience and concentrated on the table.

Only a few balls remained. Rosa angled toward Calypso's rear, and Susannah grabbed the back of her collar. "No, Miss," she said.

"But she'll win," Rosa said. "She always wins. It's not fair."

"You need to practice more." Calypso rocketed the cue ball into a red object ball, knocking it across the table into a pocket.

"If Calypso's going to run the balls, I quit." Lilly shoved her cue into the wooden holder and flounced off to join a noisy game of charades.

Calypso smirked and popped another ball home.

"Excellent shot." Jon Tom stood on the other side of Hanson. His arms crossed, he wore a dark brown vest over a billowy white linen shirt instead of his habitual tunic. Fawn breeches hugged his calves and covered the tops of his black boots. Susannah was extremely conscious of him, conscious of Hanson standing between them.

Calypso's blue gown, narrow and devoid of frills, restricted her legs when she tried to stride to the other side of the table. "Kraken take this bloody dress," she grumbled. "I hate it."

"It's not as puffy on the bottom as your sisters' gowns. Why do you wear it?" Hanson asked. "I hate my circlet, so I use it for a plate holder."

Rosa took several dainty steps toward the table, pirouetted

and floated back. Her white skirt swayed like a pendulum. "Mama makes her. It restrains her mannish gait. It's not good for a princess to be mannish."

"Oh," Hanson said. "Seems dashed impractical, though. What if there was a fire and she had to run and save somebody?"

"She'd leave that to the men and guards. Jon Tom could save us."

When Susannah glanced past Hanson, she could see Jon Tom's profile. His brows drew together. "The Queen makes many decisions for her children which, I'm sure, are for the best," he said.

"Mama knows best," Rosa agreed.

"The Queen's command is sacrosanct." This time, there was no mistaking the sarcasm in Jon Tom's comment.

Calypso guffawed. With a sharp crack, the last ball hurtled into a pocket. "Feel smothered, Jonny boy? Try being her kid."

"Investigating her children is difficult enough."

"You win, of course," Rosa said to Calypso with a pout.

Calypso crooked her finger at Hanson and he walked to her side, leaving Susannah and Jon Tom without a barrier. She held out her palm to the baronet. "Pay up."

Hanson sighed. "I'm nearly out." He dug in one trouser pocket and pulled out a handkerchief, a rock, a wad of paper and a pocketknife. From the other pocket he dragged a silver coin, wood shavings, a whistle and something small and shiny.

"Whoops!" He stuffed it back before Susannah could see what it was. He laid the rest of the items on the billiards table.

Calypso rubbed her hands together. "What else has he got in his pockets?"

He delved into his tunic and produced a tiny wooden figurine of a cat with its carefully carved tail wrapped around its feet.

"Oooh, I win with interest!" Calypso accepted the cat and tossed it to Rosa, who leaned against the table in a sulk.

"We were right. He does carve," Jon Tom noted with a sideways glance at Susannah.

"He carves well." Susannah opened the string on her reticule and showed Jon Tom the flower Hanson had given her.

Each petal was outlined with a touch of gold paint so the flower glistened with life.

Jon Tom admired the carving and turned it over in his hands. In a low voice, he said, "The first of many gifts, I think."

The urge to deny it, to tell Jon Tom she wanted nothing from Hanson, rushed through Susannah. She must remain hardened to her course. When Hanson first walked to Calypso to pay his debt, she and Jon Tom had been several feet apart. She'd gravitated to his side, or he to hers, and their sleeves brushed.

Rosa pet the tiny animal on the back with her finger. "It's so real, like it could purr."

Hanson ducked his head. "It would take magic to make my carving that good."

Rosa turned to Susannah and opened her mouth but then giggled. She raced off to show her kitten to the other princesses.

Susannah frowned. What had the little devil been about to say? Jon Tom cast her a speculative glance before returning her carving.

Hanson handed Calypso the triangular frame and helped drag balls from the pockets. With an elaborate flick, Calypso racked the billiard balls.

"Who's for another game?"

Jon Tom cleared his throat. "I'll play you. Doubles."

"You, Mr. Tom? We haven't been able to convince you to play this whole time." Calypso propped her hip against the table. "Are you up to something?"

In reply, Jon Tom strode to the center cabinet and chose a cue. He tested one by sighting down it. Then he selected another and measured it the same way. "Susannah can be on my team and Hanson on yours."

Susannah waved her hands in negation. "I'm really not accomplished at billiards."

He smiled at her from across the room, and dimples peeped out of his lean cheeks.

"Easy win!" Calypso stuck her palm toward Hanson.

He stared at it, puzzled. "I don't have any more carvings, Princess."

"Smack my hand. It means, well, whoopee or something."

Hanson patted Calypso's hand like a child's head.

"Yahoo," she said with a laugh.

"Would you like to smack me?" Jon Tom's voice next to her ear made Susannah jump.

"Can I save it for another time?"

Jon Tom bent his head even closer to hers. "You can save anything for me you want."

Susannah blushed. She glanced up to see Calypso eyeing her suspiciously. "What are we going to wager?" her sister asked Jon Tom.

"If he says information, Cal, he'll cheat to get it." Susannah accepted her cue from Jon Tom, and his fingers brushed hers.

"What would you suggest, Princess?" He extended his cue and tapped the triangle of balls on the table, still in the rack. "What do you want from Hanson and your sister?"

"Don't be so sure you'll win," Calypso said. "I took All-Kingdom last year." She elbowed Hanson. "They don't have a chance. Shall we ask for Jon Tom's quill pen and Susannah's bottomless reticule?"

Hanson shook his head. "I don't want a reticule."

"That's for me. The pen is for you so you can illuminate your carvings."

"Susannah?" Jon Tom prompted her again.

"I don't want anything." She chalked her cue. "I'll play, but I don't want anything."

Calypso heaved an exasperated sigh. "Susannah, that's not sporting." She cocked her head to one side. "Do you see, Hanson, why I said never to play games with her? She can suck all the fun out of anything."

Why had Calypso been telling Hanson about her dislike for competitive activities? Susannah frowned at her sister, who patted her hip as if a reticule hung there. Had she been talking Susannah up to the young man...or down?

"I think we can come to an understanding, Princess Calypso." Jon Tom drew her aside and whispered in her ear while Susannah and Hanson exchanged a bemused glance.

"I don't think so!" Calypso said. "Not while..."

She lowered her voice and Susannah couldn't make out the rest of it. The two of them were definitely having an argument.

"All right, all right." Calypso returned to the table and thumped her cue on the ground. "It's not like you'll win, anyway."

"What did you ask for?" Susannah demanded. She didn't want to lose her reticule but figured, since she hadn't verbally agreed to the bet, she could talk her way out of it.

"You said you didn't want anything, but I do." Jon Tom pulled a silver coin from his pocket. "Shall we flip for the break, Princess Calypso?"

"Aye, but I'll have Hanson flip, not a tricky dog like you."

Jon Tom tossed the coin through the air to the baronet with a ting of metal. It spun and Hanson caught it deftly. He kept his palms closed about it. "Heads or tails?"

"Heads," Calypso said.

Hanson opened his palms. The coin displayed the backside of a phoenix. "Tails."

"Blast!" Calypso saluted Jon Tom with a partial salaam, favored in Seelan, from whence billiards had originated. "Break away, Detective."

Jon Tom smiled down at Susannah. "Trusting me would be a good habit to form."

"Trusting me to play billiards with any competency would not." She gestured toward the table where Calypso situated the balls and removed the triangle. "I'm worse than Hanson."

"We won't have to worry about that. Did I mention I spent time in Seelan?" He chalked the tip of his stick, blew it and chalked it again. "Before you ask, Princess Calypso, I was not in a *Polydame's* harem. I'd been hired by one of the lesser Grand *Polydamen* to solve a case. They sent a ship for me in Chimea and we sailed the coast past the Sun Demons until we reached Seelan."

"Didn't the Dame want to keep you?" Calypso leaned on her stick, fascinated.

"Dam Hadzrami summoned me, and I'm sure he didn't want to keep me anywhere near his wives." Jon Tom winked, rolled the cue ball to the end of the table, sighted down his stick and broke. Balls sped toward the bumpers, several dropping into pockets. The cue ball rolled to a stop almost exactly where Jon Tom had first placed it.

"Lucky break." Calypso leaned on her cue. "Let's see what else you've got."

Swiftly, methodically, Jon Tom cleared the billiards table of object balls, never taking more than a moment or two to line up shots. Susannah had never seen anyone play so accurately and confidently, not even at tournaments. By the next to last ball, even Calypso was cheering.

He dropped the final shot like a stone, and the room broke into applause. Her sisters had wandered over during the demonstration, and Esme smacked the table with delight.

"You're not the best anymore," she said to Calypso, who just shrugged. "What did he win?"

"I can't say."

"Oh ho." Esme chortled. "Sounds naughty. Someone's gonna be jealous."

"Don't be silly," Susannah said, too quickly. "Mr. Tom wouldn't suggest anything improper."

A clock on the far wall chimed the hour. It was late. Though the Queen hadn't been strict about rousing them early with Hanson here, she'd be displeased if they slept half the morning away.

"Let's call it a night," Calypso suggested. "I don't want Jonny convincing me to play him again."

The princesses stashed away billiard cues and game pieces, chattering and milling around Sir Hanson. They'd given Susannah another night with next to no competition to snare him, but considering Lilly's behavior, their patience had adjourned. Tricky enough to woo Hanson herself. Trickier when she'd rather woo another. Trickiest of all that she had to find the balance between wooing and choosing, in order to offset her curse.

Mentally she kicked herself. She dropped the chalks into a holder and dusted her hands. Her grace period was over. She had to make her move. What could she do to find out if Sir Hanson would consider her as a wife before her sisters tossed their caps at the poor lad?

As the other princesses shuffled out of the room, Jon Tom restrained her with a hand on her arm. He nodded at Calypso, who shut the door firmly behind her.

They were alone, for the first time in days. Butterflies

emerged from cocoons in her stomach as she contemplated what he might have in mind.

Jon Tom didn't waste a moment of their solitude in idle conversation or, Susannah was almost disappointed to discover, kissing. Without preamble, he said, "He's going to offer for you. He carries the ring in his pocket at all times and waits for the right moment."

Susannah paced from the cabinet to the billiards table. Her thoughts roiled. "How do you know that?"

"He told me. He asked my advice."

She whirled to face him. "What did you say?"

There was no hint of the smug billiards shark about Jon Tom now. His voice betrayed no passion, no emotion. He could have been informing her that the green book she wanted was on the third shelf to the left. "I told him the most obvious way to inherit this kingdom would be to marry you, though it might not be the easiest."

Was that because he, Jon Tom, would make it difficult for Hanson? Or did he just mean she wasn't an easy person to...be with? "If he's going to offer, I'll have to accept. It wouldn't be my ideal *choice*," she said, emphasizing the last word, "but what can I do?"

Jon Tom's face was smooth and cool. After his intensity the last two times they'd been alone, Susannah sensed his missing emotions like a frigid wind. Had he sundered himself of feelings for her? What did she want him to feel?

"I wish you every happiness with the boy." His gaze, no longer impassive, iced over. "I'm sure you'll be fulfilled by ruling the kingdom, as much as your mother will allow it."

"Why are you doing this to me?" Susannah pressed her fisted hands into her stomach, fingernails biting into her palms. "Why can't you understand what I must do?"

"You're doing it to yourself." Jon Tom ran a hand through his hair in a frustrated manner before his dark gaze fell on her. Quick as lightning, he advanced and grabbed her forearms.

Susannah tried to step away, but he held her fast. "Don't marry Hanson. It's not your life's purpose to save this kingdom. Let one of your sisters shoulder that burden."

"Who are you to say what is and isn't my purpose? Surely I'm more of an authority on that than you are."

"You're blinded by the load your mother has placed on you. It will prevent you from true happiness, mark my words."

"What if I told you to quit solving cases and let someone else do it?"

Jon Tom brought her hands to his lips. His warm mouth brushed her knuckles. "It's not the same. I chose that life for myself. I wasn't born into it."

She lowered her lashes and gave a bitter laugh. "It's what I know, Jon. It's what I want. Not banishment or separation from my family. Not a life of dried-up nothingness. What do you propose I do instead? If I give up the rule, what would I do with myself? This isn't my choice, but I'm out of options."

Jon Tom's brow lowered. "I made a poor bargain with your sister."

"This privacy was what you won?" She plucked at an amber button on his vest.

"Yes." Jon Tom gave her a little shake. "Look at me."

"No," Susannah murmured. "You're like a python. You hypnotize me."

He nudged her chin with a long finger, but she closed her eyes. "I'm not so cold, my sweet. Can you tell me, truly, he's what you want? Not someone else?"

"Like who?" Would he say it? Would he say, come away with me? She risked a glance, but his countenance gave away nothing.

"Someone you love. Someone you want to share your life with."

He wouldn't say it. If he felt something for her, if this wasn't just part of his plan, why couldn't he confess? She sensed an edge in herself, as if words of love from him could break her from the curse of her existence.

No, her existence wasn't a curse. It was, it would be, fine. Healthy. This was her first chance to put herself in a position to rule. To change the rules.

"Do you mean someone I want to share all my secrets with, perhaps? This is just another ruse, Jon, to solve your case."

"No. Look at me! Tell me you believe that's all I want from you."

He forced her chin up this time. She fell into his gaze, their gazes twinning. Excitement stirred inside her, his lips a breath away.

"I believe..." She licked her lips and his eyes flashed with passion. "I believe you'd like to have sex with me as well as solve your case."

His face lanced with pain. "I want more."

Emotion thrummed through her. Did it stem from him?

He kissed her cheek and set her away. She watched him walk out of the billiards room with her heart aching and tears welling. If her sisters had declared a free-for-all with Hanson, if Foresta's unweds panted at the drawbridge, she could wait no longer. She must settle the kingdom's future and end this tearing grief that jolted her whenever she looked at Jon Tom.

She had to propose to Hanson, but to do that, she had to be sure he wanted to marry her. She had to be sure her christening curse hadn't twisted things. His camaraderie with Calypso had been significant. Perhaps Jon Tom was wrong and the ring was for another? No reason to put Hanson in an awkward position if he favored another. Her curse might be stronger and more subtle than anyone realized, no matter her attempts to circumvent it.

She'd have to cast a truth spell before she proposed. She'd do it tomorrow, before she changed her mind, before her morals got the better of her. She'd already broken the rules of the safe list when she silenced Esme. A truth spell would just add to her wickedness.

Chapter Twenty-Two

The next day dawned warm and windy, with showers predicted by afternoon, so Susannah set her one-act melodrama for the morning. After creating her truth powder in a practice run with Ella, Susannah charged Calypso with directing Hanson to the lover's gazebo in the rose garden. All Susannah had to do was wait and hope Jon Tom didn't lurk nearby, ready to leap out and accuse her of ruining her life.

The gazebo had been commissioned by her parents as a playhouse when Susannah was three. A miniature of the palace, it had one room and several turrets. Prickly bushes encircled the structure, as well as miniature apple trees. A single trail through the wall of thorns led to the tall playhouse and surrounding benches. Red roses in urns grew around the statue of the sleeping princess inside and white ones around the prince, frozen in eternal astonishment as he spied his ladylove for the first time.

Tiny buds surrounded the bench she'd chosen for the scene of her first marriage proposal, dipping and swaying on slender branches. Bees hovered fruitlessly around them, drunk on the scent but frustrated, for they weren't yet in bloom. She and her sisters had played Briar Rose in the gazebo, taking turns being the princess, the prince and other characters involved in the tale.

Here she was, years later, waiting for her own prince, though she couldn't say he was her true love, or a prince. He certainly wasn't her *choice*. She muttered that aloud and hoped Malady was listening, though she'd read in *Seven Habits* that well-constructed curses were self-maintaining.

Hanson arrived out of breath, his hair askew and a rip in his shirtsleeve. "I was just in the maze with some of your sisters," he panted, "having the most jolly game. Calypso told me you wished to see me. Are you all right?"

"I only just got here." Susannah fiddled with the leather pouch attached to her tasseled girdle. The cool marble bench numbed her behind, but she didn't intend to stay on it long. She'd worn a full-skirted dress in a ruby shade with blue brocade trim. The fine linen of her underdress peeked through the slashes in the sleeves and around the deep neckline. The linen was very white against the gown and drew attention to her chest.

Hanson glanced at her bosom, then away. Her future husband, perhaps. He had pink cheeks and merry lips, like a child.

"I'd like to discuss something with you." She gestured to the bench. "Please, sit beside me. You'll give me a crick looking up at you."

"Aren't we supposed to be chaperoned?" Hanson glanced around the gazebo. Since no banns had been called, normal chaperonage rules hadn't been relaxed for Hanson and the princesses.

"Some things a lady wishes to do in private." She reached for Hanson's arm and tugged him beside her. His limb beneath the sleeve was lean, well muscled. Fine golden hairs poked incongruously out of the rip.

Hanson's eyes widened as he eyed the rose bushes, the tall hedges and the miniature apple trees surrounding them. Clouds scudded over the sun and cast shadows across the ground, as if warning him to beware of shady dealings. He scooted to the end of the seat, away from her, but it was a small bench.

Hiding her movements amidst an adjustment of her ample skirts, she reached into her pouch and withdrew a handful of the powder. She divided it into each fist and took a deep breath. This was not her most honorable of moments.

Susannah knew truth spells, having mastered ways to circumvent them long before they found the land beneath. Her mother was fond of springing them on her daughters. A discreet sprig of ensorcelled rosemary carried in the pocket had allowed the princesses to evade certain questions. But she'd never cast one until today.

Now or never. The dust clutched in her palms, Susannah kneeled in front of the baronet. Her skirts ballooned around her, and the grass on the lawn tickled her ankles. "I know I'm supposed to wait for you," she said, "but I can't. Time has run out for us, Hanson."

The baronet tried to stand, but she leaned against his legs. She spread her hands across his knees to cover the sparkle of the fairy dust and rosemary. Closing her eyes, she let her power trickle into the baronet.

She said the ritual words and hoped he wouldn't notice their singsong quality. "Tell me the truth, Hanson, and nothing but the truth. Tell me the whole truth and no truth by halves."

"Why would I lie to you?" Hanson appeared to be puzzled. The magic faded quickly, much more quickly than when she'd practiced the spell on Ella. She must be getting better at hiding her energies.

Susannah kept her hands carefully over the fairy dust on his legs. "Sir Hanson, are you planning on asking for my hand in marriage?"

"I d...don't know what to say." The stammering baronet adjusted the collar of his shirt where it was slightly unlaced. "I thought I'd stay another month and get to know you. You and your family."

"Wouldn't the end result be the same? A proposal?"

The baronet screwed his head around as if seeking rescue. "I'm not good under pressure, milady."

With little motions she hoped he'd interpret as caresses, Susannah swept the fairy dust to the ground. A convenient wind scattered it into the soft grass. "I know you carry the ring in your pocket."

"It's the most expensive thing I've ever owned. I don't want to lose it."

"Aren't you just waiting for the right moment? This is it. I've done the work for you. There's no reason to waste time."

"Is there a reason to rush?"

Why wouldn't he comply? Was the spell miscast? It was supposed to ensure he answered her questions. He'd told Jon

Tom he planned to ask for her hand. Her sisters were going to murder her in her bed if she didn't catch Hanson—that, or slip into his bed and catch him themselves. Then there was the threat of visiting maidens.

"Yes, there's cause for haste. The neighbors. My sisters."

"Your sisters are nice." The baronet smiled. "Jolly, in fact."

"Did...did you want to ask someone else? Are you fond of one of my sisters?" Her heart sank. It would save the kingdom, but how she longed to rule herself! It was what she'd been raised to do. It was all she knew.

Hanson took a deep breath and pulled her onto the bench beside him. He slipped the engagement ring from his trouser pocket, a little gold band with a heart-shaped diamond. "You're right, Susannah. I planned to ask you to marry me."

"You like us, then?"

"Your Ma scares me yellow, but I like your Pa and I like your sisters. I like the castle and the lake and the town and the whole kingdom, really. Plus it's as far away from my Pa as I can get without going over into the Hinterlands." Hanson grimaced. "I want to invite my brothers and sisters to live here. What's five more in a castle full?"

"Your family won't be made noble, you understand."

"Aye, but they won't be living on a run-down farm with my slave-driver Pa. It's too bad I couldn't have done my great feat before my sister married."

The words poured from Hanson with little encouragement from her. She hadn't botched the spell. She tested him with another question. "You sought out the great feat to better your family's situation, not for glory and riches?"

The baronet laughed. "The riches come welcome into my pocket. Most of the kings and a few of the dukes and earls gave me gold and jewels and such, hoping I'd marry their daughters. One gave me a horse. Bribes, you know."

"I heard baronets on Grand Tours were subjected to improper treatment." Susannah shook her head, and her hair tickled her neck. One curl looped forward on her bosom.

Hanson inspected that silky curl for a moment before he transferred his gaze to the top of her head. "Some of the money I send to Pa, but some I send fairy courier to my brothers and sisters. In secret, like."

"We've never offered a bribe to anyone, unless you count a jam recipe."

"Oh, I know, Susannah." Hanson nodded emphatically. "You don't have to bribe me."

"What have the ladies tried to induce you to remain?"

He shifted his gaze to his knees. "Queen Derryberry said I should marry one of her gels since I found the youth water for her. Actually, she said she'd off the old king and I should marry her since she looked young again."

"That's outrageous." Her spell lowered his barriers more thoroughly than it had Ella's, and lasted longer. She'd used too much power. Surely he'd notice he was admitting things he didn't want to admit? Was there any way to cancel the effect?

She clenched her fists. She felt horrid enough for casting the spell, even though it was for his own good. She didn't want to frighten him away with an ill-timed proposal.

The baronet didn't notice her distraction. "I did my research, and I picked here. Why marry the littlest princess when I can have the biggest?"

Susannah frowned. "I wouldn't say I'm the biggest." Yes, truth spells definitely had their disadvantages.

"I mean, the one with the biggest dowry. The kingdom. I'd marry any of you, really."

Though she was far from flattered, Susannah resisted the urge to giggle. "Any of us?"

"I asked Calypso and she said to ask you first." He shrugged. "I have my doubts, though."

Jon Tom hadn't mentioned the baronet would be content with any of them. And Calypso, the devil, hadn't uttered a peep.

"You'd rather marry Calypso?" Was this the doing of her christening curse? Perhaps she'd come too close to fixing on Hanson, choosing him to wed.

The baronet tossed the ring into the air and caught it like a bee, smacking his hands around it. "You're a fine lady, but any fool can see you've an eye for Jon. I don't want to marry a lady who yearns for another fellow, even if she has a kingdom attached. Cal was next in line. I mean, Calypso."

"But—"

"What I think is, you should run away with him."

"What?" She spoke of marriage to Hanson, and he told her to run away with another man? "I'd be ruined. Thrown out of the family in disgrace. It's the law."

"When I'm king, I'll change the law and you can come back."

Susannah fingered the hair at her temple, where strands of gray had a distressing tendency to grow, at least until she caught sight of them. "By the time you're king, I'd be an old crone. Papa's not aged, and healthy yet. Besides, it takes more than one king to achieve a majority vote in the Consortium."

"I still don't fancy a wife whose heart is taken."

"How are hearts involved? You don't love me. You don't love any of us."

The baronet shrugged. Fair hair curled around his head in a corona and shifted in the light breeze. "Love will grow in time, if I pick the right wife."

"So love is important to you?"

"Of course."

"Then why choose a kingdom without knowing the princesses in it?"

Hanson stuck the little ring on his pinky. "I had a talk with Sir Gideon—the one marrying that duke's daughter in Bavamorda? He tried to wait and find one he loved, and they snagged him anyway. If I don't pick for myself, it won't be long until someone picks for me. They're not always ethical, you know."

"I hope you realize we won't force you into anything." He was a good-natured, logical man. Life with him wouldn't be terrible. Surely love would develop, just as her attachment to Jon Tom would fade. She already liked Hanson, even if he wasn't her choice. Not her choice!

"I do know that," he said.

Susannah took a deep breath. "I could be the right wife. I know a great deal about running the kingdom. I'd welcome your family here. I like you, and I think you like me."

Hanson rubbed his nose. "What does Jon think about you marrying another man?"

"Mr. Tom hasn't a say in the matter."

"You love him."

"No, I don't."

"I can tell."

Hanson hadn't placed a truth spell on her, but she owed him a version of the story. "I do feel something for him." She placed a hand over her heart. "My sisters and I haven't had much opportunity to meet men, and I've spent a great deal of time with Mr. Tom. But what I feel isn't love." Did she sound convincing? She wasn't convinced, herself.

"You're sure?" He stared into her face, his bright blue eyes piercing. "It's one thing to go into this with our eyes open, and it's another if you're trying to shut my eyes to something."

Clouds covered the sun again, matching her mood. She shouldn't have used that truth spell on him. Inwardly, Susannah shriveled like a spider in a flame. He didn't deserve this kind of subterfuge. But her duty, she had to do her duty.

"I'm sure," she lied.

"Well, then." He picked up her left hand and slid the ring on her finger. "Let's get married."

The tips of Susannah's mouth curled up while her last vestiges of hope drained out. If he'd preferred one of her sisters, if he'd refused to marry her, she'd have been free until the next baronet. But she had her duty, and he was a good lad. A good lad.

Hanson drew her into his arms and kissed her cheek. "You're very pretty, Susannah." The comment widened her smile. It was so far from anything the enchanted princes, or even Jon Tom, had ever said to her.

"I think you're pretty, too." She pressed her cheek against his. The roughness of a growing beard reminded her that this wasn't Jon Tom, with his whiskerless face. It was the face of a man who was to be her husband. Lawfully. She'd done it.

So why did her heart sink instead of buoy, now that she'd solved their kingdom's inheritance troubles? Her family—her mother—would be so pleased.

"You're not supposed to call a man pretty." The baronet placed a self-conscious kiss on her lips, quick and dry. She sighed when he snuggled her closer, but when they embraced a sharp sting emanated from the center of his chest, sizzling her.

She bit back a yelp. Magic!

Susannah slanted away from his awkward clasp, her chest tingling. Around his neck hung a leather string that disappeared beneath his shirt. The necklace blended with his laces, and she hadn't noticed it before. She pulled the cord from his collar.

"What's this?" The bronze pendant, a tiny oak tree, vibrated with a tension she could feel with her magic.

"My anti-charm pendant. I bought it to make sure none of the ladies could cast love spells on me."

No love spells or truth spells! Susannah blinked rapidly, adjusting.

"How wise of you," she said. From the strength of the vibration, she could tell the pendant was authentic. Which meant all the things the baronet admitted about his family, about marrying her, could potentially be lies. Her spell had been blocked.

However, even without magic she could sense the ring of authenticity in Hanson's explanations. He was so cheerful and sincere. He deserved better than her. She could marry, she could rule, she could have what she'd always dreamed of having if she held her tongue.

But he wasn't Jon Tom. He wasn't her choice. She couldn't do it.

Damnable, subtle, terrible curse! It was using her own heart against her.

She couldn't enter this covenant with Hanson. She couldn't even kiss him again, and she couldn't imagine bedding him. She toyed with the pendant, tingles leaking into her fingertips.

"Hanson," she began.

"You're going to tell me you don't think you can love me the same way you love Jon, aren't you?"

"I don't—"

"You do, and I think he loves you. You should have seen his face when I told him I meant to ask for your hand."

Her curiosity overcame her reservations. "What did he say?"

Hanson shrugged, apparently unperturbed by her possible about-face. "That's for you to ask him, Princess."

He squeezed her one last time, patted her hand and drew

the little ring off her finger. "If you won't marry me, can you give me advice? Like a sister?"

"Of course."

He grinned. "It's like this. I'm due to play cards with the princesses after lunch. Which of your sisters should I offer this to next? Whether or not I'm destined to be king, I've a hankering to become a member of this family, no matter how long it takes."

Chapter Twenty-Three

As soon as she finished with Hanson, Susannah raced to the library and searched the nooks and crannies for curious detectives before rounding up her stockpile of magic research. She'd take no chances after Jon Tom's suspicious appearance in the city. Her mother thought she was with the other women and Hanson in the card room, so she ought to be safe for a time. She stacked her materials on the study table and settled in a chair.

As she worked, skipping lunch, the prediction of rain was fulfilled. Fat droplets pounded on the skylights, and their patter soothed her nerves. She did, occasionally, feel the sensation of being watched, which she credited to her imagination.

The last thing she'd translated was that strange passage at the end of chapter two, roughly translated to mean, "Discover for *asiogh* cure for big curse *io ieiond* big curse *lisli*".

The problem with Ancient Dullish was each word could mean several different things and each thing could be represented by several different words. No one had spoken Ancient Dullish in a thousand years, so there was no guide. So far she'd counted twenty different words for "curse". The Ancient Dulls must have been a curse-riddled society. Hopefully their citizenry could break more than one per mortal.

So, to work. She flipped to the "A" section of the Dullish dictionary.

Asioft: Crofter. Hearty bread-like food. Woman with coarse hair.

Asiog: Black earth that eats donkeys and men. See Bog, reverse transl.

Asiogh: Cotton cloth. Field crop. Harvest. Woman with coarse hair. Weave.

Discover for *asiogh* cure for big curse. Discover how harvest the cure for the curse? Discover how cotton cloth the cure? Were there any pronouns or prepositions? Ancient Dullish writing usually dropped those handy little bits of language and articles were a lost cause. She inserted them wherever they felt natural once the bulk of the words had been settled.

She'd try an easier one. *Ieiond*.

Ieion(a): Gem, jewel. A stone tasting of dust.

Ieiond: Cotton cloth. Material.

So, "Discover for *asiogh* cure for big curse *io* cotton cloth/material big curse *lislis*".

While she was in that section, she checked out *io*, but it was as she suspected, a multipurpose word meaning "in, into, through, inside, inner".

Next, *lislis*:

Lislie: Girl's name. Strange person.

Lislim(a,t): Cotton cloth. Silk cloth.

Susannah scratched her nose. How many words for cotton cloth were there? Had the Ancient Dulls been obsessed with clothing? Next word.

Lislitifo: Very pale. Sickly.

There was no entry for *lislis*. Drat! Squinting at the faded writing, she ran her finger down the list again. *Lislie*, *lislim(a,t)*, *lislitifo*. No *lislis*.

A misspelling? An alternate form of *lislim(a,t)*? The repetition of the syllable nagged at her. *Lislis*. Was *lis* in the dictionary? She flipped back a page. No *lis*. *Li* meant "to, from, away, toward, against", but no *lis*.

The word *lisagh* caught her eye again, the "big or far-reaching curse". It started with the same phrase, *lis*. Of course! The repetition of a first syllable, like *lislis* right after *lisagh*, was a self-referential pronoun. She wrote "itself" down, making the sentence, "Discover for *asiogh* cure for big curse in/into cotton cloth/material big curse itself".

Back to the A's. What would fit now that she'd translated the rest of the sentence? Going with the theme of cotton cloth, she tried the infinitive, "to weave".

"Discover for to weave (the) cure for (the) big curse in/into (the) material (the) big curse itself."

Not the wise pronouncement she'd been hoping for. It made more sense when she added a preposition and juggled the meaning of *po*. "Discover (how) to weave the cure for the curse into the material (of) the curse itself."

Finally!

The first guideline in chapter two was: "Create a curse mission statement to use as a frame of reference when clarifying the terms and conditions for the curse, including the cure." It was the word, cure, that had excited her. It had taken months to translate the first chapter, owing to her unfamiliarity with the language, but chapter two had been easier. Slightly. She'd jumped to the other guidelines in hopes of a breakthrough. The second guideline was: "Determine how to make sure your curse creates the smallest possible ripples while the strands remain unified and robust to the end."

The fourth guideline, which she'd skipped ahead and translated, read: "Figure out how the curse will act once the cure has been enacted or has begun, which places the curse in transition." From two and four she gathered that the strands of intricate curses dissolved one by one sometimes, altogether at others. The strange behavior of the enchanted princes seemed indicative the curse was breaking.

Back to the third guideline. "Discover how to weave the cure for the curse into the material of the curse itself." The cure had to be part of the curse—woven into it—yet obviously not something the person or persons under the curse could achieve on their own. Combine that with the tidbit she'd confirmed about fulfilling the paradox of a curse from the first part of this chapter, and what did that give her? To break a curse structured according to the guidelines in this book, one had to find a way to do what the curse made impossible. She just had to hope this was a widely followed cursing system and not the work of a fairy crackpot. It did seem to jibe with the better-known curses she knew of.

What could the cursed nobles in the Middle Kingdoms not do? Simple, have male babies, but she didn't think she should experiment with the birthing process, magically or otherwise.

What could she not do? Wed a man of her choice. If she'd

been able to force herself to marry Hanson, it might have broken her curse, but she'd already have been married to the wrong man.

That left her with the curse on the princes. What could they not do? They couldn't leave the underground realm, but she'd already tried taking one up the stairs. They couldn't remember, but she'd left notes and cast memory spells to no avail.

And the princes couldn't make love. They could pleasure a woman, but they couldn't consummate. Or, at least, none besides Prince John, who'd only shown himself, figuratively speaking, two visits ago.

It was so simple she wanted to beat herself about the head for not deciphering it already. Since none of the other men there were an option, she had to make love with Prince John on her next visit to the land beneath.

Why else would he have revealed himself when the princes had begun behaving erratically? It didn't matter what had started the chain reaction now that it was down to the finale. If the rule of threes rang true, her next visit was her last opportunity before something horrible befell either herself or the princes. One of the dangers in attempting to break a curse was setting it in motion and not following through.

Damn and blast. She ground her knuckles into her eyes. Enough for today. Too much for today! She needed to reflect on the ramifications of what she'd learned.

Susannah scribbled her conclusions on her translation, no doubt in her mind what came next. She replaced the *Seven Habits* book in the jam section and returned to stare blindly at her notes. She'd rather have had the chance to solve the Female Curse, but the enchanted princes seemed to be her single shot at curse breaking. She'd started it, and now she must finish it. If she wanted to free the princes, she'd have to go through with this.

Now that a solution presented itself, she was forced to consider certain realities. When she broke the curse, it would set off an alarm with the fairies. This curse involved so many lives, the FAE had to know about it, and they'd come. They'd want to know everything, all the details, and so would the fairy who cast it. When the big ones went down, there was always an investigation. Fairies claimed curses were made to be broken, but sometimes Susannah wondered.

If she did this, there'd be no more hiding. She'd have to tell her parents everything, including her possession of magic and lack of chastity.

Would Prince John, Dragon forbid, cooperate with her? Should she find a potency spell for one of the others? Take Peter with her to seduce him in her stead? No, there was no way to tell which prince, or sister, she should select. Prince John was the only one with a distinguishing feature, and he'd singled her out. What if he was still angry with her for taunting the princes and himself sexually?

She'd simply tell him she couldn't stop thinking about him. Men loved to hear they were right, so she'd tell him he was, that he was wise and handsomely invisible. That she longed for him, and would he please make love to her. What man who'd professed such ardent desire for her could resist such flattery?

And she'd close her eyes and think of Jon Tom.

"Susannah!" Hanson burst through the library doors. "I'm desperate for your help."

"What is it?" How had he found her? Susannah flipped her papers so only the plain backs were revealed. "Aren't you supposed to be playing whist and cheating my sisters out of their pin money?"

"Your Ma." The lad's eyes grew wide with trepidation.

"You cheated my mother? Are you insane?"

"No, your Ma was dropping hints about how long I planned to loaf about Foresta. About making a certain announcement regarding one of her daughters. She's going to evict me if I don't marry somebody, isn't she?"

"Hanson, don't worry." Susannah patted his arm. "Stay as long as you want. If you tell my mother your intentions to marry into the family, she'll even send for your siblings."

"Talk to your Ma? Can't you do it for me?" The baronet's blue eyes begged her, and he placed his hands on her shoulders. "She scares me silly."

"Mama just wants to save the kingdom," Susannah said with a smile. "She's no different from me. You're not scared of me, are you?"

"Not exactly," Hanson said. "But you'd shine my tail if I

took months to make up my mind. What if I confide in her and she demands I choose now? What if she made me marry Peter? Peter's gorgeous, but she hates me. And Calypso, well, we wouldn't suit."

"Mama won't do that," Susannah hedged. It would be politically unwise to bar the other noble daughters from trying their luck with Hanson if he remained single. All the nobles needed heirs, not just the kings. She didn't tell Hanson that, though. No reason to panic him more. He'd done the tour. He knew the risks. Her eleven sisters vying for his attention, with their various wiles, would traumatize him enough.

"Please say you'll talk to her for me."

"I'll talk to her for you." If she had the chance after she had sex with a stranger, severed an elaborate curse and confessed her actions to her parents. And who knew what explanations the FAE would demand? She bit the inside of her cheek and refused to contemplate that aspect of her future.

"Blessings on you!" Hanson wrapped his arms around her, whirled her and kissed both her cheeks. The waft of her skirt scattered half of her papers to the floor.

"You're welcome." Susannah squirmed in his grasp, afraid he'd see the notes. Her underlined conclusion, "Have sex with invisible prince", was definitely eye-catching.

Sir Hanson kissed her again and set her down. "I'm off to fairy-fone my family," he said, "and tell them the good news." With that, he raced from the library and slammed the door. Susannah knelt to gather her papers with a huge sigh of relief.

A shadow fell across the last paper and she gasped, clutching it to her chest. "The library's an odd choice for a marriage proposal," Jon Tom said, "though not for the bookish Susannah, I suppose." He towered above her, ominous and stormy.

"Were you spying on me?" He must have slipped in after Hanson entered. How had she been so distracted she'd failed to notice?

"Like I told you, spying on you is my job." Jon Tom executed a mocking bow. He wore his brown cloak from yesterday and smelled of fresh air and rain.

"You said you weren't spying on me yesterday in town."

Jon Tom shrugged. "I lied."

"I knew it! You've no business trailing me when I'm with Hanson. It's no mystery what I'm doing with him." Susannah scrambled to her feet and folded her papers so he couldn't read them. Two seconds into her notes and he'd know more about her than she wanted him to, ever. That she could work fairy magic. That she'd lied to him. That she planned to give her virtue to someone besides a legally wedded husband, even though she'd refused him.

"It's a mystery what you see in that boy." Jon Tom stepped closer and she backed into the table.

"We've covered this path." Should she tell him she didn't plan to marry Hanson? He'd want to know why. "What I see is a nice young man I could marry to—"

"Save the kingdom, yes, I know. Always the kingdom."

Susannah slid her papers onto the table, wanting both hands free—to fend him off or wrap around his neck, she wasn't sure. "I should save my breath, speaking with you."

Jon Tom laughed without humor and crowded her. His cloak fluttered around him. "You should save yourself. For me."

I'm afraid a different man will have that honor, she thought, but instead she said, "I'm better off with Hanson."

"You're not suited for a nice young man," he whispered in her ear, sending tingles down her spine. "You'd eat him alive, with marmalade."

Susannah couldn't manage the direction of this conversation. What was the issue at hand? Kisses. No, hiding her research notes from Jon Tom. No, Jon Tom's incessant spying.

"Don't be silly." She snatched up a book and held it between them like a chastity belt. "How did you get in here? You sprang out of nowhere."

Jon Tom smiled. "Perhaps I used magic."

A horrible suspicion crossed Susannah's mind. She'd been nervous as a cat after she sensed she was being watched in town yesterday. Again today her neck had prickled, but she'd assumed it was nerves. How was he always there without being seen? How?

Before she could stop herself, she asked, "Can you do magic?"

"Don't be silly." Jon Tom echoed her words with a sardonic smile. "I'm not a fairy. Humans can't do magic. Why would you even think I could?"

"Half-breed?"

"Princess, what I've told you of my childhood is true, and there were no fairies involved. Half-breeds don't exist." Jon Tom's eyes narrowed as he watched her.

Why couldn't she stop her foolish tongue? Jon Tom was too clever to remain as unsuspecting as the rest of the world if she put ideas in his head.

She needed a distraction. She latched onto the first thing she could think of. "How do you do it? Invisibility isn't possible. Did you get a camouflage spell?"

Jon Tom tilted his head down. "Fairies don't barter with unethical magic. It violates the Alliance's tenets as well as the Oath. Love spells, death spells and certain others are forbidden."

"The FairFairy Oath?"

"The very one."

"I doubt all fairies follow the Oath. Did you get something on the black market?" After her own recent misuses of power, Susannah suspected the fairies were right about mortal ethics, even ones who meant to do good.

"You're making any number of foolish suggestions today." Jon Tom glanced at his feet. "If I had a masking device, I'd have solved this case long ago. I'm just very good at sneaking."

"What, you went to a school for sneaking? Did you learn to pick pockets as well?"

Jon Tom rolled his eyes. "I grew up happy but poor, Princess, two things a bitter..." He broke off and tugged his earlobe. "You wouldn't understand either of those things."

"How dare you! I'm very happy."

"You won't be happy married to Hanson." He took her book away and slapped it on the table. Now there was nothing between them but convention. "You won't be happy with anyone but me."

"You know nothing." Susannah inched backward to give herself some thinking room. Did he want her to be with him? Run away with him? He'd never asked. She didn't understand what drove him, why he hinted he had feelings for her, still, after he knew she wouldn't be fooled. Why, if he had feelings for her, was he willing to betray her?

"I'm going to tell my family the good news," Jon Tom quoted Hanson's parting words. "Wouldn't that be how the tempestuous Princess Susannah accepted his hand in marriage?"

Susannah crossed her arms and glared. "I'm not marrying Hanson."

The detective raised a doubtful eyebrow. "No?"

"He asked me to talk to Mama on his behalf so he could send for his siblings. You should have eavesdropped sooner, or not at all."

"I suppose he hopes his devotion to family will change your heart?" He crossed his arms, matching her, but some of the anger left his face.

He was jealous. A tide of emotion threatened to drown her. She uncrossed her arms and took a deep breath. "Your resentment of the boy is ridiculous."

"Resentment?" Jon Tom opened his arms. "Susannah, I'm jealous of the silk that touches your skin. I'm jealous of the wind that brushes your cheek and the wine that crosses your lips." He bent toward her.

"There's no need to have this discussion again," she said, her eyes wide. "This desire between us has no future." The warmth of him, the spicy scent, surrounded her as the slow patter of rain on the skylights mesmerized her. She yearned to lean into him and become the wine crossing his lips, the wind in his hair. She yearned to make love to him, not the invisible, quick-tempered man below.

"You still call this desire." He brushed her lips with his own, soft as a feather. She closed her eyes. "Why can't you call it love?"

"Why can't you?"

He didn't answer right away. She couldn't choose him over her family, especially when he hadn't offered, and she couldn't leave the princes captive, not when she alone could save them. Those poor men didn't deserve to be trapped there, and who knew what would happen if she didn't see the curse to its conclusion? Would it spread? Would she, her sisters, be drawn into the enchantment as well? There was a reason she'd stumbled across them. There was always a reason.

She'd rather break the Female Curse, but this would have to suffice. Her magic hadn't allowed her to do much else.

Jon Tom touched her chin, tipped her face so their gazes met. "If I tell you I adore you and can't live without you, would you give up your kingdom?"

Was anyone in the library who might see them standing here, tasting one another's breath? Did she even care?

"Hanson will marry one of my sisters," Susannah murmured. "Not me."

"What will you do?" Jon Tom pressed his forehead to hers. "Will you come with me?"

There, he'd asked. Though he hadn't mentioned marriage, it was what she'd wanted to hear. What she'd been terrified to hear. But there was no way he'd let her continue, should she confess to him. And there was no way she could hide her magic from the FAE, maybe not even the Middle Kingdoms, when she broke the princes' curse.

Duty, always duty. Never her choice.

"Certain tasks are still mine alone," she said finally.

"Your overabundant sense of duty again. It comes between us." He was so right. He kissed her fully, coaxed her lips open, stroked her cheek. His exhalation, his tongue, were hot against her mouth. "There should be nothing between us, not even air."

Susannah shuddered with longing. If she could pretend Prince John was Jon Tom, her task wouldn't be as difficult. She broke off the kiss and rested her brow against the skin of his throat.

"Some secrets will have to remain untold," she whispered.

He squeezed the back of her neck in a slow, warm massage. "What will it take for you to trust me?"

"I don't know." How she wished she could tell him! She wished she could take him with her and let him stand in for Prince John, but it might not work, since he wasn't one of the princes, and she didn't want to involve him in that kind of danger. Truth be told, she didn't want to involve herself, but curses were made to be broken. By mortals. By the mortals who had realized how to do it.

"If I promise not to reveal you to your parents, can you have faith in me? Ruin another set of slippers, Susannah, and I'll say nothing. I can endure disgrace if I can just have your trust. Your heart." He spoke next to her ear, and his breath tickled.

Tears welled up in her eyes. "I can't."

"After you complete your mysterious task, after I'm sent away, will you come to me?" He straightened his head and gazed deep into her eyes.

Susannah shook her head slowly. In a few days she'd probably be a prisoner of the fairies, or worse. It was too much to hope she could release the princes and return to her family, or Jon, with none the wiser. And she'd still be afraid, in her soul, to elope with a man who wanted all her secrets without confessing his.

What could she say to him? What would he believe?

"Why do you twist the knife? I'd be wretched without my family."

"We'd make our own family, my love. That's what men and women do."

"I'm too afraid." Tears spilled from her eyes and trickled down her dusty cheeks. She wept for more than he knew. "Please don't ask me again. There's so much I want to tell you, but I can't."

Jon Tom closed his own eyes, and when he opened them they were bleak. "Then I must tell you something. Something I've done."

"It's nothing compared to what I've done and must do." Susannah silenced him with a kiss. "Unless you've murdered and pillaged."

"Deceived. Tricked." Jon Tom swallowed, bowing his head. "Lied."

Susannah gave a watery chuckle. "I'd expect no less. All in the line of duty, my fine detective. Aren't we a pair?"

"I should still confess." He dropped to his knees before her, right beside the incriminating papers on the library table. "Susannah, I—"

"What is this?" called a stern voice from the entryway.

Did everyone in the castle know she was in the library?

Susannah's mother stood at the double doors, an unsympathetic expression on her face. Jon Tom turned to regard the Queen but didn't rise or let go of Susannah's hands.

"Mama," Susannah said, "Jon is about to confess, and I do wish you'd go back out again so he may finish."

"Confess what, his feelings? Child, everyone knows what those are, but they won't do him any good. You're to marry Hanson."

"No, he's about to confess his lies and misdeeds." She didn't bother to correct her mother about Hanson. "So can you go?"

The Queen took two steps into the library. "I most certainly cannot. If you have an affair with a commoner, we'd have no choice but to cast you out. It's Kingdom Law. I am assuming there's no reason to cast you out yet?" The Queen cocked her head to one side, and Jon Tom rose to his feet.

Susannah straightened her shoulders. "I'm not having an affair." If her mother didn't walk into the library, the papers were safe. She tried, very hard, not to glance at the table.

"I haven't trespassed the boundaries you set," Jon Tom told the Queen. "You may rely on that, Your Highness."

Susannah scowled at them both. "How much of this is per my mother's instruction to seduce me for answers? Is that part of your confession? You might as well confess in front of her since she put you up to it."

"You knew about that?" The Queen's brow wrinkled in displeasure. "You don't know everything, though. I didn't give him leave to ruin you."

"Susannah, the case hasn't motivated all my actions. Certain bequests are mine alone." Jon Tom took her by the shoulders and turned her to face him. "You know which ones I mean?"

Susannah smiled, wanly, thinking how useless all this was, how much it didn't matter. "I know which ones you mean."

"That's Princess Susannah to you, sir," the Queen said. "Considering the fact she's to wed another, my encouragement for your intimacy is now at an end. Perhaps I should set a deadline for you to solve this case so you'll have no more reason to be here."

Susannah wagged her finger at her mother. "That would

violate your original agreement with the detective. And you should be aware, Jon, my mother's fond of random truth testing." His expression didn't flicker, but his eyes did, and Susannah knew he understood the hazard.

"He's had long enough. You both have." The Queen stamped her cane on the ground and stalked toward them, anger wrinkling her smooth face. Susannah tipped herself against the table. Her skirts covered the incriminating documents. She didn't think Jon Tom would notice, but he shifted to block any view the Queen might have had of the table.

The Queen halted a cane's swat away. "You probably think your happiness doesn't matter to me. Could you be happy with this man? Could you trust that he loved you for yourself not for the hope of eventual riches?"

Jon Tom studied Susannah's face, as if expecting her to answer her mother when she'd refused to answer him the same things.

"Mother—"

"Let me finish. Would you have confidence leaving your kingdom behind? I raised you to rule in my footsteps...in your father's, I mean. Hanson isn't equipped for it, but he knows to use advisors. If only you'd have been born a man." The Queen's face twisted fiercely.

"If only you'd convinced Father to campaign for a change in the Kingdom Laws," Susannah said, almost gently. She rested her head against Jon Tom's shoulder, not caring that her mother's gaze sharpened. His breath wafted across her hair. "I know what you wish for me. It's not going to happen, but not because I am going to run away with Jon."

"Are you still a maid?"

"As much a maid as anyone my age can be."

The Queen studied the reptilian head of her cane. "I'm not sure I like that answer."

"I'm sure I don't like the Kingdom Laws." Susannah let her unspecific response dangle in the air. Jon Tom shifted uneasily beside her, but she didn't want to leave her mother fraught with anxiety. "Soon, I promise you, most of your worries will be over."

The Queen's head snapped up. "Are you planning

something foolish?"

"No." Susannah sank onto the table. "I just want to finish my conversation with Jon."

"She is, isn't she?" The Queen pinned the detective with a steely glare. "She's going to do something she oughtn't, and it has something to do with the case you can't seem to solve."

"I'll be vigilant." Jon Tom's arm pressed against her shoulder. "She'll spend an uneventful night dreaming of silver lakes and trees that grow jewels, or whatever princesses imagine."

Susannah felt for a moment she would sink into a faint.

He knew. He knew. He knew.

The Queen was oblivious to Susannah's shock. "I can't see you've made much progress guarding the princesses so far, and I cannot approve of your relationship with my daughter. You claim to know deep secrets you can't reveal, but that's probably detective-speak for ignorance. There's one way to find out. I'd like a full report in the morning, Mr. Tom. No more riddles."

Her mother was wrong, so wrong. He knew enough to destroy her. Even if he weren't willing, a truth spell cast on him would be disastrous.

Had one of her sisters confessed? That had to be it. Or he'd eavesdropped on the right conversation at the right time. There was no way he could have opened the route himself. There was no way he could have been in the enchanted realm himself. Wait, there was something she was missing. Something...

Interrupting her, the Queen tapped her cane on the ground. "We should change tactics. What say you spend the night inside her room?"

Neither Susannah nor Jon Tom moved a muscle, staring at the Queen in astonishment.

"With all of them." The Queen rubbed her forehead in exasperation. "I wouldn't spend several painful minutes questioning her virtue only to throw it aside in the next breath. Do you think you could guard her better if you never left her side?"

Jon Tom's eyes gleamed. "I'd guard her well, Your Highness."

"With all my girls there, I've no fear of any ill-timed

confessions on your part. Or anything else. Susannah, come with me."

"I intend to finish my conversation with Jon." She had to find out how he knew about the realm—and if he knew about the magic. If he did, and was still willing to accept her, and the fairies were understanding...

"You will come with me, Miss, and come with me now." The Queen thunked her cane on the hard floor of the library. Overhead, thunder rumbled in the distance.

What about her papers? She shifted off the table and dragged them over the edge with her bottom. They fluttered to the ground behind her skirts. Her books littered the tabletop, so perhaps her mother would think the mess a legitimate research project.

Perhaps Jon Tom would too. Anything he didn't know, he'd find in the documents. Susannah didn't dare look at him. Reluctantly, she accompanied her mother out the door.

Alone in the library, Jon Tom watched the closed doors with an inscrutable expression on his face and bent to retrieve Susannah's secrets.

Chapter Twenty-Four

He knew.

How he'd figured it out, Susannah had no idea. Unless he, like her, was a human with magic, but that didn't bear thinking. Either way, there was no time. No more research. It had to be tonight. For tomorrow, the Queen would have her reckoning.

Though tonight would be difficult. Jon Tom lounged on Ella's bed, playing a game of cards with her, Temple and Rosa that involved a lot of slapping and giggling.

Midnight had come and gone. The rain had stopped and stars twinkled between the bars of their windows, fairy dust against the black velvet sky. Although most of her sisters slept, her youngest siblings whispered and buzzed like they'd never close their eyes.

She'd have to put them to sleep involuntarily. Hortense's safe list wouldn't matter after tonight, anyway.

Susannah fidgeted on her own bed. Underneath her flannel gown, she wore a deep red shift with a plunging neckline. The light silk of the fabric tickled her thighs as she sat, cross-legged, and toyed with the vial of lavender fairy dust that comprised her sleeping powder.

She just prayed the enchantment in the land beneath was unaffected enough that a prince would be waiting to row her across the lake. She had a contingency plan that involved seven-knot flippers but didn't relish attempting it.

Now that she understood how curses were structured, she suspected her absorption of the necessary knowledge had begun the transition period. Something she'd read must have plucked the first strand of the intricate curse and allowed the invisible prince to approach her. After that, a domino effect. Her forays with Prince John, closer to lovemaking each time, further deteriorated the enchantment. It was indeed something she'd done, though not knowingly. But then, some of the most famous curses had been dissolved that way. The prince who kissed Briar Rose awake didn't know it would rouse her. He'd been overwhelmed by her beauty. The children who escaped the gingerbread witch didn't know the oven was the only place to kill her—they just used the tools at hand.

Prince John was to be her tool. She shuddered.

Jon Tom glanced at her across the row of sleeping princesses, as he had been all night. The shadows of low fairy lights lent his features a mysterious cast. He quirked an eyebrow, questioning. He seemed determined to prevent her from journeying beneath, and he'd never had a chance to finish his confession. What had he been about to admit? That he loved her? That he didn't love her? That they should sell timeshares in the enchanted realm to vacationing nobles and abscond with the gold?

He rose from the card game and stole across the darkened room to her side. She clutched her vial nervously.

"Aw!" Rosa whined, stifling a huge yawn. "I was winning."

Ella slid the cards into a little inlaid box. "I was letting you. We need to go to sleep. Don't you want to show Hanson your pony tomorrow?"

"Yes," Rosa said. "Tom Jon is sure to impress Hanson."

Temple stumbled across the room to bed. "Thought your horse's name was Sir King?"

"I changed it." Rosa got into her bed and sighed deeply. "I'm not tired."

Susannah smiled slightly. How did Jon Tom enjoy having a grubby, fat pony named for him? The way the corner of his mouth jumped, she suspected he rather liked it.

Rosa tried one last time. "Where's Mr. Tom to sleep?"

"In front of the door." Susannah pointed to the stack of cushions between the chamber wall and her bed. If she stayed here, if she gave up her quest to free the princes, she'd be sleeping beside a man, all night long, for the first time in her life. And then, tomorrow, she'd watch her mother destroy everything.

She couldn't give up now. She'd be sleeping with a man for the first time tonight, all right, but it wouldn't be with several yards of stone floor between them.

She sighed. "I don't know how much sleeping Mr. Tom will do, though."

"Princess, I detect a note of unease in your voice." Jon Tom motioned to the cushions. "Will you be able to sleep with me so close to your side?"

Susannah tensed at the suggestive nuance. "I suppose so."

"I'll fetch a dressing screen from one of the guest rooms and place it beside your bed."

That would send him from the room long enough for her to put everyone to sleep, open the secret door and flee to the land beneath. He'd have no way to stop her.

"That would make me a great deal more comfortable," she said. "Thank you."

"Mr. Tom is the one who's uncomfortable, sleeping on the floor," Rosa said. "Susannah, you're missish," she echoed the Queen's favorite remark.

"And you're not asleep." She wagged her vial at Rosa and narrowed her eyes. Her sister knew exactly what the vial contained and threw herself onto her pillow. She was grateful the child didn't wake Hortense to complain, but none of Susannah's youngest siblings feared or distrusted her magic, not even after her explosion at Esme. It was only the older, wiser ones.

"You could persuade the birds to quit singing with that glare." A wry grin creased Jon Tom's lips. He picked up the hand that didn't hold the sleeping powder and kissed it gallantly. "Anything to relieve the strain on my most difficult charge."

With a small bow, Jon Tom stepped away and propped the bedchamber door open with a stack of pillows. "Can't have you locking me out," he said with a wink.

As soon as he left, Susannah grabbed the silk bag containing the fins and tiptoed to the open door. No sign of Jon Tom in the corridor. She whisked back into her room, unstoppered her vial and cast a mild slumber spell along with a pinch of the fragrant dust. It took a smidgen of inner strength that filled her with a warm glow. Temple snored and Rosa's droopy eyes fluttered closed, but Ella continued to watch her.

"You're going to try something new, aren't you?" she asked in a loud whisper. "You put everyone to sleep and now you're going down below."

"You're supposed to be counting ponies." Susannah had little time before Jon Tom returned and didn't want to spend it forcing the spell-resistant Ella to sleep. She stripped her gown over her head and shoved her feet into red silk dancing slippers, worn only once.

"Does your sleep spell work if someone knows you're casting it?" Ella pattered to where Susannah stood in front of Calypso's armoire.

"Apparently not."

"Why is a sleep spell okay when making Esme shut up was bad?"

Susannah cracked open the door of the armoire. Why, indeed? She couldn't tell Ella it didn't matter any more. "One was cast in anger and could have been hurtful. The other wasn't, although I doubt Hortense would be pleased. It's about control and conscience. And before you ask, no, you cannot come with me."

Ella sniffed. "I wasn't going to ask. What do you want me to tell Jon Tom?"

"He knows I'm going. Tell him he missed me."

"He knows?" Ella's voice rose in panic. "Is he going to tell Mama? Is she going to call the fairies and send us away?"

"He's not going to tell. If things go well tonight, Mama will have no reason to truth spell him tomorrow. Now hush. I have to get through the door before he returns. He knows about the palace, but I don't think he realizes I can do magic."

"How does he know?"

"I have no idea. Perhaps one of us told. No—" Susannah threw up a hand. "I don't think it's you. And it doesn't matter."

"What are you going to do?" Ella rubbed her bare toe against the foot of Peter's bed. "Are you going to save our princes?"

Susannah hugged Ella's spare form tightly to her. The mild scent of lemons tickled her nose, emanating from Ella's hair and flannel gown. "I hope so. Tell Calypso the notes are on the table where I left them. They need to be concealed."

"I can take care of them."

She stroked Ella's brown hair and sighed, putting the girl away from her. "Cal will show you all the hiding places."

Ella grinned. "How about I show her some hiding places?"

She smiled at her sister, one last time. "Go back to bed and act like you're asleep. Jon Tom could be back with the screen any moment."

Ella raced across the room and slid into her bed. Susannah shoved to the back of Calypso's armoire and opened the flower of energy inside her. It blossomed, spread through the wood and stone and outlined the secret door in faint light. Without a backward glance, Susannah stepped through into the dank first chamber.

Before she could close the door, something jostled her and knocked her against the wall.

"Ella, did you follow me?" No answer. Susannah sniffed the air for her sister's lemony shampoo. She smelled her own rose and vanilla and a fine spice that reminded her of Jon Tom. It lingered on her skin from their embrace in the library. With a sigh, she shut the door, released the spell and descended to the enchanted palace to break the curse on the princes.

The tiny fairy globes embedded in the railing flickered madly as Susannah made her hasty, and eerie, descent. She trailed her fingertips along the rock wall in case the globes guttered out. She'd never ventured to the underground realm alone, and the dark, bottomless silence of the chasm, the distant chill of the ceiling, weighed against her like stone. Could she hear an echo of footsteps or was it her imagination? Her awareness of her solitary progress down the cold, winding stairs deepened. No one could follow her here, or even find her, should anything go wrong. When she hit the green lawn, Susannah was nearly running.

Matching her mood, twelve very unsettled men waited by the shore when she arrived, panting. Beside her boat was Prince Yarrow, tall and lean in a red vest and trousers. The other eleven princes peered into the forest or stared at the soft, black sky. The surface of the lake was as calm and silver as a serving tray.

"Greetings, my prince," she said.

Yarrow helped Susannah into the rocking boat, his moustache quivering, and began to row. His aimless strokes took them first to the left, then to the right. She held the fins in her lap, thankful she hadn't been forced to use them.

Their trajectory led to the side of the island with the stone gardens. Was there a landing beach anywhere beside the front lawn? They'd never located one when they explored the rest of the island.

"I think you want to direct the boat a little more that way," Susannah said.

Yarrow grunted, continued to row, and the course of the small bark shifted.

"Are you surprised to see me tonight?" she asked.

Yarrow didn't answer. His eyes were as glazed as a Wintertide ham, and when Susannah waved her fingers in front of him, he didn't blink. It was as if he were in a trance. She'd never seen one of the princes so unresponsive, but she'd never ventured to the palace alone. Unhealthy princesses had remained behind, but it hadn't precipitated anything as strange as tonight—or the past two visits.

She gave up her attempts to converse. When their boat was nearly across, the princes on the far shore climbed into their shells and rowed just as aimlessly in the direction of the island. She hoped they made it, that the framework of the enchantment would protect them. It had certainly never allowed any of the princesses to steal a boat and row behind the palace. Just like in the crystal forest, some magical twist switched their progress so they always ended up back where they started.

The princes didn't deserve this. They deserved a real life, a mortal life, on the green earth above, with mothers, fathers and sisters, spouses and children—all the things she was giving up for them. If this was her curse to cure, so be it. What else could she do at this point? Tomorrow, it would all come out regardless.

Yarrow beached the vessel and lifted her out of the boat. He ambled alongside her into the castle, tripping occasionally, and she saved him from a tumble down the marble stairs. When they reached the antechamber, he wandered into the ballroom without a backward glance.

No music drifted across the large room, and the princes lolled on floor cushions or chairs with unusual torpor. She paused on the threshold. Would she be safe? She'd memorized a protective spell or two, and there were always the seven-knot fins, but both were untested, and the fins only worked in water. She even had a vial of fairy dust in the silk bag with the flippers.

Why had the night she'd met Prince John been special? What had she done, what strand of the curse had she plucked, to allow him to approach her? How could she find him tonight?

She'd probably never be able to answer the first question, but at least she knew how to break the curse. If she could find her tool. "Prince John, are you here?" she called out.

Nothing. She walked to the center of the ballroom. How did you find an invisible man who might not want to be found? She cupped her hands around her mouth. "Prince John!"

She waited. None of the princes turned, and no would-be lover tweaked her hair or palmed her shoulder. She didn't even want to do this, and here she was hunting the man down like a baying hound on scent. She called again and strode through the ballroom. As she reached the door of the Divan Room, a dry chuckle sounded behind her.

Her heart leapt into her throat. It had never before occurred to her how much he sounded like Jon Tom, though that might be wishful thinking on her part. Without turning, she continued into the room where the wide, cushioned velvet lounge lay in wait, like an altar.

"I've come to apologize," she said to the empty air. "And to make you a proposition."

"I'm always open to a proposition," the voice responded. "And I owe you an apology as well."

She knew the cadence of that voice. She knew the feel of those eyes on her body.

Before her astonished gaze, Jon Tom materialized, clad in his shabby brown cloak. His hand dropped from the brooch at the neck and extended to her in open appeal. "Remember that confession I wanted to make? Consider this my declaration of guilt."

Chapter Twenty-Five

"You!"

"Yes. Me." He draped the cloak on the nearest divan.

She sank onto the velvet lounge, thoughts of seduction and sacrifice blown out of her head by her own blind stupidity. Her arrogance in assuming she'd considered every angle. "How could I have overlooked the obvious? The fairies simply lied about invisibility? A bedamned invisibility cloak. I called it in the library."

"How could I have overlooked the obvious?" he echoed. "My mortal lady can do the magic herself."

Susannah set the silk bag with the fins on the floor. "You couldn't have guessed that."

"It's less likely than my having an invisibility cloak. Not all fairies are oath-abiding, as you guessed, and they don't always tell mortals the whole truth. I can't say for sure which one bargained this cloak with me, as it was done through an agent, but I received it six months ago. I took a job tracking a stolen red phoenix, part of an exotic-pet thievery ring."

"A red phoenix. That sounds familiar. Oh, I can't think. I should be furious with you, but I can't drum up the energy."

Jon Tom settled on the divan beside her, careful not to touch her. "I understand if you hate me for it. But please know, I never use it to titillate my baser urges. Only to solve cases." He flicked his hand in a salute. "Detective's honor."

"Is that an oxymoron?"

He grinned, but she could tell unease ruled him. He was unsure how she would jump—as was she. "Perhaps," he said. "I've only had it six months."

"I don't understand how I never linked the two of you. I'm no green Jenny. We've had guards on us for months."

"I have years of practice going where I'm not wanted, before the cloak. It was a small matter to follow you when there were twelve of you to blame the noises on. Trickier to ride in someone's boat each night, but I managed."

The curse's first strand had been plucked not by her, not by Agravar's words of love, but by the presence of a functional man.

"I thought the boat was too heavy." She'd been so incautious. Such a fool. "Have you known all along I could do magic?"

Jon Tom took her hand. She let him, limp with bewilderment. "I only knew where you were going, not how you opened the door. How many times did I check for secret passages?" He shook his head. "I waited for your lights to go off and slipped inside. No one noticed the door open and close because it was so dark. Plus I oiled the hinges."

"You came in every night?"

He nodded and a dimple appeared briefly in his cheek. "Some nights I just watched you sleep. It's hard for me to believe. Magic, Susannah! Do you realize what this will mean to the mortal lands?"

"Do you realize what this will mean to the Fairy Alliance?" She leaned back on the divan, exhausted. Her emotions roiled inside like a bubbling broth. While it was gratifying to know she hadn't lusted for two different men, she was still intimidated by her unfinished business—business that was unchanged despite Jon Tom's revelation—and more than a little humiliated her womanly instincts had failed to link the two men she'd embraced so intimately.

"When the fairies find out, they're going to cauterize me, maybe all of us. This isn't going to go over well."

"They don't have to find out."

"After tomorrow, there will be no more hiding. For many reasons." Susannah squeezed her eyes shut. "I trust you understand my dishonesty these many weeks?"

"I understood before," he said. "Defying your parents to sneak away, repeatedly, to an enchanted palace full of men isn't exactly a boast-worthy accomplishment."

"You don't hear me boasting." When Jon Tom cast her an arch look, Susannah rephrased her statement. "I suppose I rattled your cage a few times in the beginning."

He cupped her cheek in his warm hand. She curled into it. "You rattled more than my cage. You rattled my confidence. Even with my cloak, I barely discovered everything I needed to fulfill my contract with your mother. I had to establish how to stop you, not just where you were going. You and your sisters are very discreet about what you say and where."

"You don't think I'm unnatural?" She met his gaze, anxious for his answer.

"Come here." He adjusted himself on the divan and pulled her back, her head nestled against his chest. He loosened her hair with an idle hand. "I think you're wonderful."

"Oh."

"Might I ask questions now?"

"Yes, of course." Her head spun. He anchored her. He thought she was wonderful.

"When you first came here, how did you know it would be safe?"

"We didn't, I suppose. My spell was supposed to take us to Ulaluna, to plea bargain. We all agreed to do it, all of us elder sisters. We were willing to take the risk. Originally the younger girls weren't meant to be involved." She smiled. "It's hard to keep secrets when there are twelve of you."

Jon Tom brought her hand to his lips and kissed it. "You kept your secrets from me and your parents. You've been trying harder to solve the Middle Kingdoms' problems than our own kings. You're amazing."

"I'm weak," she said with a groan. "I shouldn't have come back with my sisters, but saying no... I couldn't do it. The princes have occupied their thoughts. Ironically, disobeying our parents helped keep us obedient. Helped keep us all at home, waiting."

"Waiting for a prince to come."

"Yes. And now one has."

Jon Tom squeezed her hand where he clasped it on his chest. "I know. Hanson."

Susannah twisted around until she faced him. She hadn't

brought a timepiece but was conscious of the minutes passing. Whether or not he'd just shaken her world, she had a job to do, and now she could do it with the man who was her choice. "I meant you. I don't know about my sisters, but I've been waiting for you."

"I'm no prince. No baronet, either." Bitterness tinged his voice. "I'm not sure I'm even a man of honor."

"I'm not exactly the pattern card of honesty myself." With her free hand, she stroked his smooth jawline, the lack of stubble, as always, beguiling her. She ran her thumb across his full bottom lip. His nostrils flared as he drew in a breath.

Would he kiss her now? Susannah wet her lips in anticipation.

"I read your papers. Your translations of the *Seven Habits* volume."

"I'm shocked." Susannah worked her hand into his thick hair. The strands trickled between her fingers like silk. Then she wrapped her hand around his neck and tugged.

"I don't think this is a good idea." He straightened, drawing her with him, and trapped her hands against his chest.

"I know more about this than you do."

Jon Tom quirked an eyebrow at her. "I wouldn't say that."

Blushing, Susannah tried to tug her hands free. "I mean, I know more about the curse. The magic. What's needed to free the princes."

"Why is freeing them so important to you? They aren't your family. You don't even know who they are."

"I'm the only one who can free them. With you. Should we ignore that?" She liberated one of her hands and unclasped the brooch on his cloak so she could push it over his shoulders. "This is my last chance before Mother finds out about the princes and my magic. I doubt she was joking about that full report she wants tomorrow. Mother never jokes. If you don't tell her what you know voluntarily, she'll put a truth spell on you."

"You can't protect us?"

"No. She'll check for shields, and carefully. She'd expect you to have one. We've always carried ensorcelled rosemary in our pockets, but she'll be on the alert for that as well. She may even have Madame help."

Jon Tom indicated his cloak with a thumb. "I could disappear."

"And leave me to face her when I admit I exposed my sisters to hundreds of strange men several times a week?" She worked the fastenings of his tunic with great determination.

Jon Tom watched her reveal his white undershirt. It was adorned with tiny blue buttons that had a pearly sheen. "You're using me."

"I'm being expedient. Make love with the man of my dreams, free a slew of innocent people from a curse at the same time." She smoothed her hands across his chest. His pupils dilated when her questing hands traced the closure of his thin shirt.

"You were willing to make love with the invisible prince. You have two men in your dreams?" He tilted her chin up to face him. "Any more I should know about?"

"Don't be jealous of yourself." She planted a kiss on his palm. "The fact of the matter is, I have to do this or they'll never be freed. Why else do I have these magic powers? After tomorrow the fairies will find out, no matter what we do tonight. Do you think Mother will be able to keep my secret? She might not even want to."

Susannah nibbled on his finger and sucked its tip, her sensual actions at odds with her words. "Since I can't seem to do anything else useful with my life, I might as well break the one curse allotted to me. Ironic, don't you think?"

Jon Tom stroked her cheek. "I can think of many uses for your days and nights. What of ruling the kingdom? That's been your goal since I arrived here. Even if one of your sisters weds Hanson, won't you be their primary advisor?"

"My sisters will have to rule without me. I'll be in fairy prison." She smiled dryly. "My life as I know it is over tomorrow. All we have is tonight."

Jon Tom caught her wrist in his hand. "I want more."

"You'll be saving a lot of lives. You'll be a hero."

"I don't want to be a hero." He caught her other hand, wrapped an arm around her and dragged her into his lap. His thighs were hard against her bottom. "You're willing to give everything up, just to break this curse?"

"You heard Mother today. I won't get another chance to do

this." Susannah pressed her forehead against his. "After tomorrow, I'll lose everything. I want to go out with a...you know. Lights and fireworks. Please, Jon." She struggled to free her wrists from his grasp.

"If we leave now, Susannah, we can just slip away. I know places we can go, places your parents can't find us. Your mother can't truth spell me if we're in Bavamorda."

"The princes will still be trapped here, and the curse has begun unraveling. Because you came here. I thought it was me." Susannah nuzzled his neck. "The wheel turns. It may backfire on us whether we make love now or never. Do you choose never?"

Their breath mingled, and his arms crept around her. "If we do this, can we leave afterwards?"

"I have to face my parents, Jon. I owe it to them." Susannah's hair fell past her face like a curtain, and light shimmered through it.

He inhaled and closed his eyes. When he opened them they were black with desire. "What do you owe yourself? You'll have nothing, Susannah."

"I'll have tonight. I'll know I did the right thing." She smiled, a little sad. "One day there will be bedtime stories about me, about the princess who saved the wicked fairy's captives, just by kissing her one true love at the stroke of midnight." She feathered her lips across his.

Jon Tom laughed softly. "If kissing was going to break this curse, the princes would have been free a long time ago."

"Bedtime stories always leave out the juicy parts." She touched the corner of his mouth with her tongue as lightly as a butterfly, and he breathed between her parted lips.

"So you think the prince woke Briar Rose with something more substantial than a kiss?" He rubbed his cheek against hers and kissed her with lush pleasure.

"If it was a kiss like that, maybe not," she said after a moment.

His arms tightened around her body, and he bent his head to her neck, his lips and tongue tracing the hollows. Teeth nipped her skin and he nuzzled her shift off one shoulder.

"Something more like this?" he murmured.

"Yes," she sighed. "More." She ran her hands inside his shirt, popping open the tiny buttons. His chest was smooth and hard. The tiny nubs of his nipples thrilled her palms.

"You're sure about this?" he said.

Susannah took his face between her hands. "I love you, Jon."

Unable to face her candor, his heavy lashes covered his eyes, and he traced the gaping neckline of her shift with a finger. "I know."

"Do you..." No, she wasn't going to ask. "I mean, how do you know?"

He didn't answer. Instead, he buried his hands in her hair and kissed her. Susannah's last rational thought was perhaps he did love her and let his actions speak louder than words.

From there it was all heated caresses, aching passion. They undressed quickly, eager for the feel of one another.

Jon Tom laid her on the divan. He ran his hands up her legs, over her hips and cupped her breasts. He kissed them both before kneeling between her thighs. Susannah threw her head back as he kissed her neck, her breasts again, drew hard upon her nipples with a hot tongue and hotter mouth. When one of his hands inched its way between her spread legs and cupped the wet heat of her femininity, she moaned.

Susannah reached for him, and he stretched out atop her. His manhood nudged against her core. He moved his hips, and the tip rubbed her slick opening until she moaned.

"Now," she said. The ache to join with him rose in her like an oncoming tide. She squirmed underneath him and touched him everywhere she could reach.

"No." He kissed her to silence her. "You're not ready."

"I am!" She wrapped her legs around his hips and tried to draw him into her.

With a deep sigh, he inched forward until he prodded her virgin's skin. The feel of him inside her, even what little he'd given her, drove her wild. She arched against him with a moan and drew his lips down for a searing kiss.

Nipping her bottom lip, Jon Tom raised himself. He adjusted his legs so they supported his weight and slipped his hand between their bodies to stimulate her. His manhood again entered her body. He pressed gently at first, and she squirmed. Her insides stretched to accommodate him.

The sting of pain increased as he rocked into her, increased and pinnacled. She whimpered and squeezed her eyes shut. His hips stilled and he leaned down to kiss her face and stroke her hair.

"Shh," he murmured. "That's the bad part, love. That's all. I promise you won't hurt in a moment." His clever hand stroked between their bodies, and the pain faded, replaced by a deep excitement.

She gazed into his face. His expression spoke of his struggle, his need to overcome her pain. Leaning forward slightly, he cupped her cheek with his free hand. "Are you all right?"

"Better." She kissed his hand and thrust herself against him. Her eyes closed, she increased her rhythm, desire and inexperience making her awkward.

"Susannah, if you keep doing that, I can't guarantee I'll remain in control." Jon Tom's voice was strained.

She needed more of him. She was desperate for it. "Nor I."

Jon Tom stilled her hips and set the rhythm himself. Deep within her, he rocked, brought himself slickly in and out of her body. In and out, in and out, his tempo increased and his fingers played her until she could hardly stand it.

Susannah felt close to something explosive. She cried out, rose against his touch and he groaned. He dropped to his elbows and thrust into her. She wrapped her arms around him, matched her body to his as they coupled in a shuddering release. Ripples of pleasure spiraled through her whole body, sharp and sweet and...

Utterly perfect. Susannah had never hoped to feel a moment this gratifying. Jon Tom buried his face in her neck, and tears leaked from the corners of her eyes. She stroked his moist back and sniffed as he pulsed inside her.

"I love you, too," he whispered, and hot moisture that wasn't perspiration dripped onto her shoulder.

Chapter Twenty-Six

An ominous rumble thrummed in the floor beneath them, and the chandelier tinkled without a breeze.

Jon Tom raised his head from Susannah's neck, his lashes wet. "What was that?"

As if in response, a tapestry fell off its moorings and crumpled to the floor beside the divan. Far off in the castle, Susannah heard a masculine shout and the sound of breaking glass.

"I hate to end this so soon, but we'd better dress." Withdrawing carefully, Jon Tom rose and pulled on his trousers. He kissed the curve of her belly, picked up her shift and draped it across her hips. "I think your treatment is working."

"The curse is breaking? Of course." Susannah wriggled into her shift and stepped into her pantaloons. Beneath her clothing, her womanhood burned with an unaccustomed twinge.

Jon Tom noticed her frown and paused in arranging his clothing. "Did I hurt you?" He brushed her shoulder with a comforting hand.

Susannah pulled her hair from the back of her chemise. "It got better."

"Second thoughts?"

"No." Susannah whirled to face Jon Tom. "No second thoughts."

Cocking her head to one side, she studied her lover, his handsome face, his lean body, his black hair. From the first moment she'd seen him in her mother's office, he'd unsettled her, and now she knew why.

She smoothed his hair out of his face. "I have sixth thoughts. Twentieth thoughts."

"Does that mean you're reconsidering marriage to Hanson?" Jon Tom concentrated on his tunic buttons, although they were already secured.

Could he be that uncertain of her, still? She'd made her bed with him, and now she hoped she got to lie in it, again and again. Her family might disown her, but the kingdom wouldn't fall into inheritance anarchy, at least not from the top.

"I've thrown him to my sisters," she said. "Perhaps I'll run away with you if the fairies don't figure out I used magic to break their palace. But now isn't the time to discuss our future."

Another tapestry tumbled to the ground, and the wind chimes on the balcony trembled, tiny bells ringing with melodious chords. "It might be time to remodel the castle," he said.

"Since the curse took on a physical form, the physical form has to break down."

"Break down?"

"I thought you read my papers."

Jon Tom peered out the door that opened into the ballroom. "Remind me."

"In intricate curses," Susannah lectured, knotting her hair in a hasty twist, "the strands must dissolve for the curse to be lifted. The text in chapter one described smaller magics as yarn and larger magics as cloth. That's what is happening. But effective curse fairies plan for this." She shoved her feet into her slippers, the rumble of the floor making her unsteady.

"That was quite a wave," she said. Surely the fairy who'd created this curse was an effective one, else she'd never have managed it. Susannah tied the laces and straightened. "Talk about sexual aftershocks."

"I don't think this is a joking matter, love." Another quake shook the castle and Susannah put a hand on a side table to steady herself. Upon its heels, a crash of monstrous proportions sounded from the ballroom followed by a chorus of shouts and yells. Jon Tom yanked open the door and a cloud of fairy dust billowed into the room, coating everything in a shimmering haze. Susannah sneezed and wiped sparkles out of her eyes.

Jon Tom fisted his hands. "By the Dragon, the place is falling down around us!"

The tiered chandelier in the ballroom had plummeted to the parquet floor and lay in a million shattered pieces, and the lofty pillars holding up the three-story balustrade rocked back and forth. No princes lay under the central hub, but it was only a matter of time before someone was injured.

The pit of her stomach dropped. "The book said curse fairies were supposed to take the dissolution period into account before they cast a spell. This isn't supposed to be hazardous."

"I mean no insult, but you can't rely on your translation of the book, especially considering you didn't finish it. We should treat this situation as perilous."

Panic welled in Susannah as she considered the situation, the indolent residue from their lovemaking shocked out of her system. Stuck hundreds of feet below the surface, earthquakes coming every minute, the world crumbling around them, there seemed to be no remedy.

"What use is breaking the curse if everyone gets smashed by rubble?" Panic clenched her middle. "Curses are made to be broken."

"We'll debate the ethics of the fairy who cast this spell later. Right now let's get out of here." Jon Tom hurried her out the balcony doors, down the cracking stairs and along the base of the castle. The air was misted with fairy dust. Small bits of plaster and stone pelted them as they ran, and the residue of the stone garden was sharp. Within minutes, her slippers were shredded to ribbons. Rocks sliced her, but still she ran, clinging to Jon Tom's hand like a lifeline.

Princes dropped from balconies and staggered down staircases to run alongside them or ahead of them. They were caught in the flow of panicked humanity. Susannah stumbled, fell, and Jon Tom scooped her into his arms, hardly losing pace.

Susannah wanted to protest she could run, but her feet stung with cuts. She threw her arms around his neck and held on. They rounded the side of the castle to see the silver lake roil violently. White spume flew into the air as stone and other objects rained across its surface.

"The beach looks like the safest place." Jon Tom jogged across the cropped grass and set her down on the sand.

As she clung to Jon Tom, the small island rumbled beneath them and the castle wobbled. Pieces of masonry shook loose and crashed to the ground. With each quake, puffs of fairy dust billowed from the ground, and sometimes from above. Waves from the silver lake grew larger, lapping the beach. Princes streamed out of the castle, wild-eyed, to crouch on the shore. There were hundreds of them, silent and confused. They didn't notice the strangers in their midst.

"The boats are gone," Susannah said. "It's too far to swim across the lake, and I left the seven-knot fins behind."

Jon Tom squinted into the distance. "Can you use your magic to open the door?"

"It's at the top of the stairs." Susannah's voice broke with repressed tears. "All the way across the lake. I'm sure the stairs are collapsing too." To come so close and fail! Why had she assumed the fairy who cast this curse would be in any way effective or ethical? Why hadn't she considered how to get out once the curse was broken? When Briar Rose's coterie woke, their hundred years' sleep hadn't damaged them, and their castle didn't fall down.

However, that castle had been real, and this was a place created by the curse and existing to serve the curse. Now it crumbled into ruin. Fool!

Jon Tom's warm hands gripped her by the shoulders and shook her lightly. Fairy dust puffed into the air. "Don't panic, Susannah, I need you clear-headed."

She buried her face in his cloak and wiped her nose on its scratchy fabric. "I am clear-headed. I simply don't want to die, not now that I've found you."

Jon Tom's gaze burned through the dust, and he hugged her briefly, kissing her forehead. His lips sparkled as the fairy dust turned everything into diamonds.

Susannah sniffed. "If we survive, my family will disown me and the fairies will incarcerate me."

"I won't let the fairies take you. You have my word."

He sounded so firm she could almost believe him. She wished he'd tell her he loved her again. Peter said men needed repeated stimuli to declare their feelings because they liked to pretend they had none. If she were to die, she wanted to hear him say he loved her to her face, not her neck.

"You've become special to me, Jon, and I want to—"

"Shh," Jon Tom kissed her again, silencing her. "Not now."

He was right. Their actions had set inexorable events into motion. With Jon Tom involved in her crusade, the fairies might punish him as well, punish anyone who'd known of her magic and kept quiet about it. He thought to protect her, but in truth she needed to protect him.

"Let's concentrate on getting ourselves and this mad lot of princes out of here." Jon Tom gestured to the young men huddled at the shore of the lake, their vests and trousers no longer exotic but pitiful in the flickering light. Fairy globes drifted around them, exploding in small puffs when they hit the surface of the water.

Susannah wiped dust from her eye. "I don't know what we can do to escape a cave-in."

"You said you opened the door from different rooms in the castle and it always led to the stairs. Can you open a door down here? Now?"

The impending doom loosened its grip on her. "I don't know." She frowned and rubbed more dust from her eyes. "I've always retraced the path of the original spell in my mind. Going home again, the door is there, waiting, and just needs a nudge."

"What was the spell you first used, wish fulfillment plus transportation? Can you forge a reverse path? Do you need special materials?"

Susannah could practically see the thoughts churn through Jon Tom's head. "A couple hours of ritual meditation and something that represents the wish to be fulfilled. The first time, I used a wedding veil for the difficulties the curse was causing, a fairy globe for the fairies we wished to visit and one of my sisters for the humans the curse harmed."

Agravar brushed against her, crying openly, and sank to his knees at the edge of the lake. A cut high on his shoulder drizzled blood down his chest, and the lapping water drenched his trousers. Inspiration struck her. "I don't suppose meditation is possible, but I know something to represent the wish to be fulfilled."

"What?"

"The people I want to save. You—and one of the princes."

She looked around. Yarrow, Agravar and several others were close by. "Him," she said, pointing at Yarrow. "I'll wish to save everyone's life."

"I'll wish for it, too." Jon Tom shifted Susannah away from another stumbling prince, who fell to the sand beside Agravar.

Susannah narrowed her eyes. "I doused the objects with fairy dust, and we're coated already. The spells I know are a matter of concentrating your energy along different paths. Many don't even require materials."

"Try it," Jon Tom said. "What can it hurt?"

He had such confidence in her. Could she measure up to it? "The first time I cast it, I followed the wrong path. What if...what if the original spell created this place? What if I didn't find it so much as make it? What if I try to open a door and it takes us somewhere worse?"

"The first time you wished for something amorphous. To go to Ulaluna. You'd never been there and didn't know what to envision. Now you do. Wish for a special place. And wish hard, Susannah, with all your heart. You're the strongest woman I've ever known. I know you can find the way home."

She wanted to live, she wanted him to live and she wanted all these unlucky men to live. She'd do it.

"I'll need as much silence as possible." She sank to the ground beside Yarrow. "I'll need your hand and his hand, and I'll need you to protect me as long as it takes. Don't let anything disrupt the process, but don't let go of my hand. If I release the energy along the wrong path, I don't know what would happen. I'll ask for a route into the audience chamber at the castle, but where the door will manifest or what form it will take, I don't know. We'll just have to hope we can herd everyone through in time."

Jon Tom settled beside her and shook Yarrow lightly by the shoulder. "Chin up, man, we need you."

Yarrow blinked and rubbed his eyes. "Princess?" he said, his voice broken. His yellow hair was gray with dust. "The sky is falling."

"Would you like to hold my hand, Prince Yarrow?" Susannah took the man's hand and patted it. "I'm afraid of the sky, and this might help."

"Anything for you." He sighed and left his hand in her grasp. His gaze returned to the castle, numb and disoriented.

Susannah took Jon Tom's hand and squeezed it. His presence soothed her, and the warm grip of his palm in hers bolstered her spirits. "Jon, if anything happens, I want you to know—"

"The only thing that's going to happen is you saving all these people." Jon Tom leaned toward her until their faces were close and their breath mingled. "I know you're afraid. I know you're unsure. But think of everything you've accomplished until now. You even pulled one over on the land's greatest detective." He kissed her nose.

Susannah gave a weak laugh. "I'd say you pulled one over on me."

"It doesn't matter now. All that matters is for you to believe you can do this."

Susannah took a deep breath. "I'll go into a light trance state. This took about a quarter hour the first time—the first time it worked, anyway."

Jon Tom regarded her solemnly. "Have faith," he said. "I'm here."

Susannah closed her eyes and willed her power to open. Instead of a tiny flower, she pictured a treasure chest inside her. She opened her mind and was consumed by the glow of ten thousand gold coins. The power flowed through her torso, her limbs, halting at the tips of her fingers where she clung to the hands of the two men. Even her hair crackled.

It wasn't enough. She opened the box further, coaxed more power into her body. The gold coins—she ran her imaginary hands through them, threw them into the air, spread them like seed. Her ears rang with magic. No longer could she hear the splash of stones into the lake, the shuffle of people in the sand, the low rumble of the imperiled island.

The first steps of the spell, she knew. She knew the way to the place for wishing and she burst into it, buoyed by more power than she'd ever called in her life. What did she wish?

Safety from harm. She imagined everyone crushed under a landfall, and the power leaked down some unknown path. Stop it! She had to discipline herself to think only of the place she wanted to go, only of the wish to fulfill.

She willed the power back and pictured the audience chamber, dark and silent, stars twinkling through the huge windows at one end. She remembered the echo of the vaulted ceiling, the cool floor.

There. The audience chamber took shape in her mind, almost solid, almost touchable. She let the first trickle of power slide toward it, reeled it out like fishing wire. A trickle, a spill. Safety from harm. She poured more power into the new path, hesitantly at first and then with confidence. It gushed along the rough bed, eroded the banks and created the way to safety.

The path created, she found she had power left. Now for the transportation. She sent energy over the heads of the men, touched them, drew them into her spell so no one would be left behind.

Dimly she became aware of shouting, of more rumbling, of Jon Tom gripping her hand so tightly her fingers numbed. A chip of stone struck her cheek and water lapped her waist. Her eyelids fluttered, and the path she'd forged receded, unused.

No! She couldn't let it go! Viciously, she wrenched the lid off the treasure chest. The last of the imaginary coins poured into her lap and she threw them in golden arcs down the path to hold it open, then flooded the conduits to everyone in the enchanted land until each was secure. With a mighty wrench, she yanked them all, sent them sliding down the path to safety and fell into Jon Tom's arms.

She couldn't hold the power any longer. She had no more to give. Sucked into a swirling vortex, Susannah spun around and around and Jon Tom was the only solid thing in the world.

Chapter Twenty-Seven

Something hard was under her head, and it didn't feel at all like her pillow. Her bed was even harder, and cold, like a tile floor. Something smelled spicy and warm. Jon Tom.

Susannah opened her eyes and saw Jon Tom's neck. She raised her head, her vision blurry, and squinted at the dim shapes sprawled all around them. Were they dead?

No, it was the audience hall in the castle. The room was silent and dark as everyone lay sleeping. Muted lights twinkled in the fairy globes along the walls. She'd done it! The spell worked!

She shook Jon Tom awake. "We made it!" She kissed his lips, his face, everywhere she could reach. Her energy was drained, her head buzzed, every square inch of her felt like it had been beaten, but she was alive, and so was Jon Tom.

He hugged her tightly and planted a hard kiss on her lips. "It was your faith in yourself that made the difference. Are the princes all right?"

"Sleeping, I think, and not princes, not anymore. Who knows who they really are. At last we can find out." Susannah buried her face in his neck and inhaled. She pressed her body against his, tingling with exhaustion and exhilaration. "Maybe we could let them sleep and—"

Jon Tom's chest rumbled with a low laugh. "I definitely agree with one prediction you made. I doubt the fairies will fail to investigate an exhibition of power like yours, my love." He kissed her again, with more leisure. "Are you afraid? I've faced fairies in my day, and I've some ideas of how this situation may be handled."

Susannah moaned against his lips. "I won't take you where I'm going. The fairies aren't going to like this, and I won't have my punishment come down on your head. Let's not think about that yet. Let's just make sure everyone's all right."

Young men and boys lay strewn across the floor, a smorgasbord of sleeping people of various ages, colors and sizes. The audience chamber was packed. Next to Susannah and Jon Tom, a boy groaned and sat up, holding his tousled head in his hands.

"Why, he looks like Yarrow," Susannah said, "only younger."

"Wha...?" the boy said. "Did you say my name?"

He was Rosa's age, if that. "Child, do you know who you are?"

"Certainly," the boy said. "I'm Yarrow deJardenes."

"But you're too young. There were no children in the enchanted palace."

Jon Tom stood and helped Susannah to her feet. He held out a hand to the boy as well, who hesitated a moment before taking it. "Don't question fate," Jon Tom said. "Let's organize everyone while we have a chance."

"I have to fetch my parents."

"I'll stay here and wake everyone."

Susannah limped through men and boys to the huge double doors and tried to shove them open. They wouldn't budge. The small door to the left was unlocked. Before Susannah stepped through it, Jon Tom laid a hand on her arm.

"Take my cloak," he said. "You aren't exactly dressed for visitors."

"Yes, of course." At least one of them was thinking straight. A whole hive of bees had taken up residence in her skull and were busy making honey. He draped the scratchy brown folds of the garment around her and covered her wet and torn red shift.

"Just don't activate the cloak by pressing the brooch. I don't want to lose you."

Thus clad, Susannah stepped through the door. "Guard!" she yelled.

Within moments a royal guardsman hastened around the corner, hand upon his sword. "Princess Susannah!" he exclaimed. "How are you here?"

"Rouse my parents," she commanded, aware of the picture she presented, her hair damp around her shoulders and herself clad in a shabby cloak. "Bring them here, and make haste."

The guard dashed down the corridor. Susannah waited until she heard the chime of fairy bells waking the palace and nodded. She slipped back into the audience chamber.

Jon Tom, with Yarrow's help, had woken most of the room's occupants. The cuts on her feet stung, but Susannah ignored the pain, helping a child to his feet here or soothing a bewildered young man there. One sweet little fellow, barely able to walk, clung to her skirt and wouldn't let go, so she hefted him onto her hip. They were confused, still under the curse's effects. They showed little desire to do anything but breathe in and out.

Jon Tom noticed Susannah with the child on her hip and smiled. "You picked up a hitchhiker." He brushed the boy's cheek with his forefinger, and the child gazed at him solemnly, his dark eyes round.

Thunder cracked outside the castle, and lightning broke the gloom through the large windows at the end of the shadowy chamber. A wild whistle of wind whipped against the walls.

"Can you do a spell and count everyone?" Jon Tom asked. "We need to prepare for our audience with your parents."

"I don't think I could see through rice paper with the magic right now," Susannah said. "I have limits, and if the feeling in my head is anything to go by, I've far exceeded them."

The storm picked up, and rain battered the thick windows, echoing through the chamber. The squall had blown up suddenly, as if a precursor to some great event. Susannah hugged the child and squinted toward the windows, her hair clinging in damp tendrils to her face and neck.

"I don't like this," she said.

"It's only rain." Jon Tom adjusted his cloak around her shoulders.

"I don't like how rapidly it came up. When we first materialized here, I saw stars."

"Focus, Susannah. We need to get everyone counted." They seated the cooperative, dazed males in lines and came up with an initial headcount of seven hundred and thirty-seven men and boys.

Susannah wished in vain she and her sisters had tallied the princes in the land beneath so she'd know if she'd gotten them all, but she had to trust the magic. Oh, her head! If only she could cast a spell on herself to reduce the aching. She couldn't think straight. She couldn't think how to address her parents. What would she say now that there was no more hiding?

The double doors of the audience chamber burst open, and light blazed through them. The guards who opened the doors stood aside, and the King, clad in a long nightshirt and a tatty robe, strode through, followed closely by the Queen.

"Susannah, the guard said something about..." he began, but shut his mouth when his gaze fell upon Jon Tom, Susannah and seven hundred and thirty-seven unknown individuals.

"What's going on here?" The Queen shoved her husband aside and stalked among the clumps of men. She made her way unerringly toward Susannah, who stood in the center of the room next to Jon Tom.

"I'm here, Susannah," he whispered. "I'm here, and I'll take you in. Don't forget that."

Susannah took a deep breath. "Mother, I'm ready to confess." But she couldn't stop herself from holding the silent child in front of her, a fragile shield. She inhaled the baby-fine scent of his hair like a bracer. She had no idea what was about to happen, how her life was going to change, but there was no stopping this rolling boulder now.

"I should hope so. Whose child is that?"

"I don't know. I found him. I found all these men and boys and released them from a curse. That's where we've been going, Mother."

"You've been going out to steal children? In dancing slippers?" The Queen looked over the sea of heads. The bafflement on her face would have amused Susannah at another time, but not now.

"Hello, young fellow." They stopped in front of Yarrow, who stood manfully next to Jon Tom.

"This is Yarrow," Jon Tom said. "He claims to be a deJardenes."

"My papa is Baron deJardenes," Yarrow said.

"He has that look," the King agreed, just as the Queen sputtered, "That's impossible!"

At that moment, Susannah's sisters tumbled into the room. The guards attempted to stop them, but one glare from Hortense sent them to their posts by the jambs.

Ella cheered. "Susannah did it!" She grabbed Temple by the hands and they whirled around in a caper. "I had an explosion in my head. I do have magic, after all!"

"Why, 'tis all our dance partners," Peter said. "Only, not quite as we remember them." Susannah noticed a moue of distaste on her sister's face when a small boy tumbled into her path, brown-haired and sturdy, with the look of Prince Humbert about him.

"You danced with cursed children? I don't understand." The Queen whirled on Susannah, her face pinched. "Not all of these fellows are children. Jon Tom is no child."

Susannah opened her mouth to explain, but Jon Tom squeezed her hand. "Wait," he whispered. "Just wait."

The storm outside increased in pitch until the Queen had to shout, and a hiss of whispers alerted Susannah that the former princes had snapped out of their daze. They shifted restlessly and gave the sisters, clad only in nightgowns and robes, cheeky glances.

"It's simple." Calypso strode forward. Jon Tom put a protective arm around Susannah, and she leaned into his warmth.

With a wink, Calypso stepped back but remained between Susannah and the Queen. She had no trouble being heard over the storm, over the increasing rumblings from the occupants of the room, adopting what Susannah recognized as her "call to the hounds" voice.

"Susannah can do magic, and she cast a spell to try to get the fairies to ease up on the Female Curse, only we found a castle full of men instead, and we've been sneaking off to go dancing. With enchanted men. It's been great fun, really."

There was a vast, deep silence in between claps of thunder. "That's not simple," the Queen finally said. Thunder boomed and she squeezed the bridge of her nose. "My daughters can do magic? My daughters were unchaperoned how often with how many men?"

Before the Queen could continue, lightning splintered the windows near the ceiling and sliced into the center of the room. The fairy globes along the walls flared. Everyone flinched and shaded their eyes. In a burgeoning glow of light, three fairies materialized.

"You!" Budbud pointed a wizened finger at Susannah through the veil of light. Tiny lights sparked out of the fairies' radiance and winked above the heads of the crowd. "You're coming with us, Miss."

Had Budbud cursed the princes? Surely not—she was just the primary fairy liaison for this kingdom. Regardless, Susannah didn't want to bow to the FAE without a fight.

"No, I'm not." She caressed the child's back and resisted the urge to situate herself in front of Jon Tom. He wouldn't appreciate it if she tried to protect him. Men were funny that way. "I'm staying with my family. In my kingdom. With my lover."

"Your what?" said the Queen. With an unwholesomely evil glare, she focused her gaze on Jon Tom. "Sirrah," was all she said, but her tone held a wealth of foreboding.

"Mama, I don't care if you throw me out. I don't care if you think I'm unnatural because I can do magic. I love Jon Tom and I'm going to be with him. Cal can have Sir Hanson. The succession is preserved."

"Wait a minute," Calypso said. "Don't marry me off just because you've been bit by the love bug. Hanson's too young, and I have scads of men to pick from now." She chucked the child Susannah held under the chin. "I'd pick this one, but he's even younger."

"Pick from these? Marry these strange men in indecent clothing?" The Queen plucked at the child's tiny silk vest but then, unconsciously, patted his soft tummy.

Budbud lowered her pointing finger and stepped out of the fairy glow. Sparks followed her in a trail. "Well, she can, you know. Each one of them is a certified noble male."

"Should I drop the special effect now?" Gary waved his hands inside the shimmering light and it faded.

Budbud spread her arms wide and indicated the young men sitting about the chamber. "They're the sons that the nobles of the Middle Kingdoms would have had, if Malady hadn't cursed everyone. Most of them are twins to some gel who just wants a good man. The curse turned 'em all into adults, temporarily, so they wouldn't need nursemaids."

"Sons?" The King's ears perked. "Sons we would have had?"

"Does this mean the Female Curse is over?" the Queen asked sharply. "Or shall you be stealing our future sons as well?"

"It's over." Budbud waved her hand in the air, and sparkles of light spat from her fingertips. "I don't feel any of Malady's work remaining. This is, of course, thanks to your daughters. Mostly your eldest and her sneaky detective."

Broke the Female Curse? Susannah's aching brain couldn't take it in. Jon Tom squeezed her arm. His pride in her accomplishment showed in the curl at the corner of his mouth and the sparkle in his eye.

The Queen scrutinized Susannah, who studied her mother in turn. She remained defiantly close to Jon Tom, a common male, even though there were now hundreds of nobles to choose from. "Susannah has magic," the Queen said. "She broke the curse. How did she do it?"

"You don't want to know," Susannah said.

"I do."

"No, you don't." Susannah cast her gaze down and blushed hotly.

"I think I can guess." The Queen turned to Budbud. "Am I right?"

Budbud tapped Jon Tom with her fingertip. A white-hot spark tinged with red exploded between Susannah and her lover. "With gusto. But Susannah has to come with us now." She shrugged, and her shapeless brown garment rippled. "Sorry."

The fairies weren't hostile, just brusque. Perhaps they'd only run tests on her. And they hadn't said anything about punishing anyone else.

"What was that you said about sons? We have sons?" The King began peering into the eyes of various men and boys in the room, patting their shoulders and thumping their chests. Little Baron Yarrow ducked out from under his hands and hid behind Calypso.

"If Susannah's going, I'm going." Ella dashed up to stand next to her sister. "I want to learn about the magic, too."

"Susannah's going nowhere," Jon Tom stated. "There's something you aren't considering about the curse and its relationship to Susannah's magic."

"I know everything I need to know." Budbud pointed her finger at Susannah. "She learned to do fairy magic. What more is there? She's coming with us."

"I don't want to go," Susannah said. "I haven't done anything wrong."

"Are you going to dissect her?" Ella demanded. "I won't let you! I'm going to have the magic, too, and if you dissect her, I'll put a curse on the fairies not to have any more boy babies either, you stupid old hoot owl."

"Young lady, hold your tongue." The Queen snatched Ella by the arm.

Budbud stood straighter, to her entire height of four foot eleven. Susannah's heart lurched. "We won't dissect her, just study her. She's unnatural."

Susannah handed the child to Calypso, who jounced him up and down. There was no use arguing with fairies. Jon Tom caressed her arm through his cloak as she fought dismay. How she'd miss him, when she'd only just begun to love him. She didn't regret her actions, though, not when she'd ended so much suffering. Her own life wasn't that important, since it seemed fated to be spoiled by one fairy or another. Perhaps they'd allow her to return, after the tests. Perhaps he'd wait for her.

"There's still the matter of the original curse—" Jon Tom began.

"Hush, hush, man," Gary said, "you'll miss something important."

"There's one more thing we need to do." Pleasentia swished up, with a wink for some of the young men. The King jumped as she waltzed past him, then harrumphed. She pulled a scepter out of a pocket in her flowing gown and waved it over Jon Tom's head.

"Welcome to the nobility, Sir Jon Tom. You enacted a great feat in unraveling the mystery of the twelve dancing princesses and the Female Curse with your utter manliness."

Jon Tom a baronet? Susannah searched his face but it was controlled, bland. Had he expected this? Did it even matter, if she was to be imprisoned by the fairies?

"Right, then." Her mother snatched the King by his arm, pulled him aside and whispered furiously. The King shook his head several times but finally nodded.

"I have an announcement," he said.

"You mean, your wife does," Gary snickered.

Susannah could measure her father's reluctance by the grooves alongside his mouth, but he rarely argued with the Queen when she had that unyielding look. Nobody did. And she definitely had that look.

"As a reward for succeeding in his quest, Sir Jon Tom is hereby bequeathed the Darby mansion and surrounding acreage, a mare and stallion from the palace stables, a covered carriage and driving phaeton, a small barge on the royal lake and boathouse privileges and twelve dozen newly charged fairy globes."

The King cleared his throat and stared at the ceiling. "That's about it."

"It's more than I expected and more than I deserve." Jon Tom executed a humble bow. Susannah wasn't sure she trusted the note of modesty in his voice, but there was no mockery in the curve of his mouth.

"Reginald," the Queen said, her voice dangerous. "Aren't you forgetting something?"

The King sighed and seemed to sink in on himself. "And the hand of one of my daughters in marriage."

"What!" shrieked eleven of the princesses. Susannah stood in shock by Jon Tom's side. No wonder her father had been reluctant to comply with the Queen's wild notion. What would Jon Tom say? He wasn't a man to have his life's choices made for him, not even by her mother. Would he refuse? Could he?

"That's it, Reggie, nail him before he goes on a Grand Tour," Budbud said. "You'll have your daughters in line, the Female Curse broken and your succession stabilized in one fell swoop. You won't miss this one, not with all the excitement." She stamped to Susannah's side and grasped her arm. "You've eleven more to marry off. Make that ten, once Sir Jon decides."

"Take your hand off my arm." Susannah jerked away from

the old fairy, whose hand burned through the cloak.

Jon Tom cleared his throat. "There's something you fail to consider. Perhaps I don't wish to have my future arranged at your convenience."

"Of course you do," the Queen said. "Quit fooling and choose. She can't choose you, so be quick about it."

"I see I won't be given the chance to do this at my own pace," Jon Tom said. Before Susannah's brain could wrap itself around what her mother meant, he swooped her into an embrace and kissed her soundly. "Princess Susannah, I choose you to be my wife. Thank you, King Reginald, for the opportunity to grow old with your daughter."

"The fairies!" Susannah protested. They wouldn't let her marry, would they? That was all she got out before Jon Tom kissed her again.

The King whooped, and Susannah's sisters and all seven hundred and thirty-seven noble males applauded. The Queen made no noise Susannah could hear from inside Jon Tom's embrace.

What about her personal curse? That was it? Had her mother been right? All it required was someone to choose her first, all this time. She supposed it had never been challenged, not even by Hanson, who'd chosen Foresta—not her. Susannah chuckled against Jon Tom's lips.

After another moment, her father cleared his throat. "Welcome to the family, son." He turned to the fairies. "Speaking of sons, don't we have any more of them?"

When the cheering ended, Budbud glowered at the royal family, especially the new baronet. "You'll have to pick again," the crone said. "The lady's future is spoken for. By me."

"Just as I feared," Susannah whispered to Jon Tom. She laid her head on his chest. Perhaps her personal curse was still active, after all. Perhaps she was destined to spend the rest of her years in a fairy poky. "Thank you for wanting to marry me. Thank you for tonight. I'll miss you so much."

Jon Tom smiled. "Don't write us off so quickly, love. Have I mentioned lately I'm the world's greatest detective? You chided me once for underestimating you. Now trust me."

"How about a foreign-exchange program?" the Queen suggested, a satisfied smile on her face. "Train Susannah for six months every year. It worked for Princess Persephone when she didn't want to live in the Hinterlands with her new husband."

Budbud unsheathed her wand from a pocket inside her sleeve. "Who said anything about training?"

"I knew it!" Ella yelled. "You're going to dissect her. I said you cannot have her!" The girl's face turned bright red and she stamped her foot upon the ground.

Susannah felt a peculiar pressure in the air, like lightning about to strike, and suddenly it did! A white-hot bolt shot through the broken window to pierce Budbud straight through the middle. It lifted the old fairy and tossed her twenty feet across the room, where she crumpled like a discarded rag doll.

Chapter Twenty-Eight

It was over as quickly as it began.

No one spoke. Gary and Pleasentia gaped, dumbstruck, at the brown form in the middle of the King's audience chamber. Susannah's legs felt heavy as lead.

Ella started to cry. "I didn't mean it!" she sobbed. "I just wanted her to leave Susannah alone."

The wrinkled mound stirred, and Budbud gave a long groan. "I can see we'll be taking two princesses when we go. Gary, help me up." The male fairy hastened to Budbud's side and lifted her to her feet, patting at her robes and hair until she slapped at his hands.

"I've never called lightning." This was so far beyond Susannah's lack of control when she'd silenced Esme as to render it innocuous. "Ella, honey, that's dangerous."

Ella continued to sob in a combination of fear and bewilderment. Susannah remembered her reaction the first time the powers emanated through her. It seemed Ella's powers weren't the same. She didn't think the delicate flower of force that resided in her, or even the gold treasure box, could create a lightning strike.

"Of course it's dangerous, you little fool. Pleasentia, tie her up in anti-magic bonds and let's go before the rest of the FAE converges on us for wasting time."

"The ladies don't wish to go," said he who had been Prince Fabio, striding forward with a glower. He looked exactly the same, even his age. He crossed his arms over his massive chest and glared at the fairies. Some of the men shook their fists.

"You shall not take a single one of these beauteous ladies from our presence," declared the former prince—or was he a current prince? "They have saved us from a life of gloom and—"

Fabio's speech ended abruptly when Budbud waved her wand. All the young men and boys except the one in Calypso's arms froze in mid-glower. "Seven hundred and thirty-seven pains in my bottom," Budbud said. "I'm glad their families will take over their care and maintenance soon."

"Oh, I don't suppose they're all pains." Pleasentia trailed the drapery of her sleeve across the chest of the immobilized Fabio. "It might be fun to keep one or two around."

Gary smacked Pleasentia's hand before it could reach any lower. "You stop that right now. That boy isn't consenting."

"They weren't consenting when you let Malady lock them in an enchanted palace," Jon Tom said, "but that didn't change anything."

"Fairy ethics prevent interference with another's justly laid curse," Budbud said. "Pleasentia?"

"Boo, you never let me have any fun." Pleasentia sighed and held her fingertips to her mouth. "At least they should be comfortable." She blew a sparkling kiss at Fabio, and he slumped to the ground with a sigh, followed by the remainder of the frozen men and boys.

"Here's a list of which fellow goes to which family." Budbud produced a light blue roll of parchment tied with a black ribbon. The King grabbed for it, but the fairy handed it to the Queen.

"You wish us to arrange the distribution?" the Queen said. She raised an eyebrow. "Seven hundred and thirty-seven lads. That's quite a large project."

"The Middle Kingdoms will see you as their saviors, and you're griping about the job?" Budbud snorted and waved her wand. "Here's a case of fairy-fones to notify their families, and a little something extra in the bottom for your troubles." Several wooden chests appeared on the floor, their contents ringing faintly.

"Will the lads work now? You know, down there?" Calypso asked.

Pleasentia giggled. "With a vengeance, my dear. Some of them have a lot of time to make up for."

"What do you mean?" the Queen asked.

"Never mind." Budbud waved her hand without the wand. "You'll find they know who they are and have a vague notion of where they've been and what happened in the Middle Kingdoms during their absence. But now we must be off. Susannah, Ella, you can come with us calmly or be tied up like sheep to the shearer."

Susannah straightened her shoulders and prepared to leave with dignity.

"I won't go." Ella's lower lip trembled and she threw herself against the King's chest. "You can't make me."

Budbud sighed, deep and annoyed. "Actually, I can. Now be a good girl and—"

Jon Tom, who'd been unaccountably silent, cleared his throat. It was one of those satisfied, pre-announcement coughs when someone is about to change the course of destiny, or at least tweak a nose. Susannah's stomach flip-flopped like a mermaid on dry land. Did he know something?

"There's no rule anywhere which states you're within your rights to take Susannah or her sister," Jon Tom said. "You may feel you're above Kingdom Laws or that this situation warrants special handling, but it wouldn't be wise for you to proceed with this course of action."

"Shut your cake-hole," Budbud said.

"I can prove it's the fault of the FAE that magic sprang up in Susannah and her sister...and who knows where next?"

The humans in the room gawked. Budbud tapped her wand against her palm, emitting a small shower of sparks. "How do you figure that?"

"The mother of invention is necessity. It was necessary for someone to come up with a way to break the Female Curse, and the only way to do it was with magic."

"Not true," Budbud said.

Jon Tom held up a hand. "Let me finish. Susannah couldn't purchase a spell that would allow her to do the things she did. Really, Malady needs remedial training. The curse wasn't well constructed. From what I gather, it must be possible for the average human to break a curse. He or she, working alone, must be able to solve the riddle with the tools and information available. Isn't that what the *Seven Habits* manual outlines?"

Susannah thought how Jon Tom had been her tool and flushed, suddenly conscious she wore a scanty silk shift underneath his rough brown cloak. She clutched the garment closer to her chest.

"We couldn't control what Malady wrought," Budbud said. "Like I keep trying to explain, it's against the FairFairy Oath to tamper with another's spell."

Susannah longed to ask what else was in that mysterious code but held her tongue, unwilling to disrupt whatever Jon Tom had planned.

"Actually, that's not true," he said. "In a case I investigated concerning a young man who'd been turned into a raven, I learned that the Oath states when a curse is found to be unjust, too difficult to solve or detrimental to society as a whole, the FAE is expected to intervene."

"Shut your cake-hole!" Budbud struck her wand against her palm harder and harder, as if she were unconscious of the sparks coming from its tip. The King and Ella, closest to her, stepped back. "What do you think planting *Seven Habits* in the library was, if not interference?"

"Do you mean to say these protestations of being unable to help us with the Female Curse all this time have been balderdash?" the Queen said.

"In a sense, yes," Jon Tom said. "There are several ways fairies are supposed to nudge mortals to break a curse. Dream-walking, animal possession, strategic literature—which we've seen here—kindness tests, endurance tests and so on."

"You put that book there," Susannah said. "I always wondered. What about the magic primer? You must have known someone could use it, someone who could do magic."

"Exactly," Jon Tom said. "If the blossoming of magic in a human was the result the FAE intended in ignoring its moral obligations, then you can't claim this is a special situation and take away the possessors of said magic."

"If this was the result you intended, I resent being an experiment," Susannah added.

Budbud's wand smacked her palm again. "We didn't give you any fairy primer, and we didn't know she'd channel the magic herself. Accurate translation of the volume would have explained non-fairies can use wish spells to access the heart of the *lisiogh*. That would have been in chapter six, which covers the various ways humans break curses. Too bad she's no whiz at Ancient Dullish."

"Inadequate," Jon Tom said. "And what's more, there was no safe way to escape once the remedy was enacted. The palace crumbled and nearly killed us all. As I recall in the chapter about beginning with the cure in mind, one must consider how the curse will unweave itself so the curse-breaker can evade death. I also recall a certain portion of the FairFairy Oath that would concur—the Tinkerbelle addendum?"

"If the detective is correct, a curse that requires several wish spells to solve is also suspiciously mercenary," the Queen observed. "Wish spells cost a great deal of gold, and the ones on the black market are worse."

"The expense is meant to deter humans with nefarious purposes," Gary said. "Should a mortal whose purpose is pure seek a wish spell—"

Jon Tom held up a restraining hand, cutting the male fairy off. It amazed Susannah that the fairies didn't overrule him. Humans rarely got the upper hand with the fey folk. He must be approaching some fact that made them hesitant.

"Susannah had to use magic to open the door every time she went beneath. There was no established secret door. Was she supposed to buy hundreds of wish spells as she evaluated the situation and realized a virile male was needed to break the curse? Was she supposed to know to take an extra spell with her so she could escape?"

Pleasentia giggled. "Generally these things are figured out in three attempts, you know—the rule of three. The girls took their time because they wanted to play around with the boys."

Susannah lowered her gaze to the floor, but she heard a distinct guffaw from Calypso.

"I really don't want to think about that," the Queen said. "You either knew my girls were capable of magic or you brought this on yourselves. Neither avenue allows you to take them. You can only take those who transgress the rules of human-fairy interaction, which are, happily, more public than your FairFairy Oath, and there's been no transgression here. At least, not on the mortal end. It sounds as if you've dishonored the Oath."

"The princes didn't transgress the rules of human-fairy

interaction, either," Susannah said. "They didn't deserve to be locked up like that."

Budbud ignored her. "A human having magic is unnatural. I'd call that a transgression."

"You're entitled to your opinion, but I doubt it will prove to be the case. For one, it's not stated anywhere in the rules of human-fairy interaction." Jon Tom took his quill pen out of his pocket and made a few notes in his tiny detective book. "And two, with both Susannah and Ella capable of magic, it's no longer a fluke. It might, in fact, be inherited." He looked at the Queen and raised an eyebrow, but she only raised her eyebrow back at him.

"Speaking of inherited, haven't I inherited some sons?" Susannah's father tweaked the babe in Calypso's arms on the toe. "I'd even take this tadpole."

Pleasentia cooed at the baby and tickled him with her wand. Harmless silver sparks popped briefly around the baby. "This young fellow is the Emperor's son by his third wife. Not yours, Reggie."

The King glowered. "Which ones are mine? Girls, see if you have any twins here," he instructed his daughters. "That skinny one there looks a bit like Temple."

Susannah glanced at the boy in question and didn't agree, but she'd long been acquainted with her father's desire for sons. She just hoped some element of the curse had prevented the princesses from kissing their brothers.

From the unease on some of her sister's faces, she could see they hoped the same thing. She moved to her father and patted his arm. "Later, Papa. This situation merits our complete attention."

Jon Tom pointed his quill at Budbud. "The challenge was unfair. The curse was too far-reaching and too hard to break, and there are rules for such imbalances."

The three fairies looked at one another. "I just don't understand how you know all this." Budbud said. "Oh, why do I even wonder?"

Jon Tom smiled. Confidence lit his dark eyes and Susannah's chest swelled. This was her lover, this clever fellow who fearlessly debated with the FAE. "I keep my ears to the ground and my nose in the broadsheets," he said. "I'm also sought by fairies for my services and have gathered much information that way. I sometimes barter for information."

"Rest assured I'll be speaking to the FAE about that," Budbud said churlishly. "Besides, the minx had enough help. You underestimated her. She managed it, didn't she?"

"Yes, but my betrothed is a very unusual woman." Jon Tom squeezed her hand and a thrill ran all the way through her.

Budbud rolled her eyes. "Mortals who break curses generally are."

"Madame," Susannah said, "if I may? It's my observation that my magic is different from fairy magic."

"That's why you'll be coming with us, to make sure you aren't doing the fabric of the world irreparable damage."

Susannah shook her head. "Nothing I do is anything you couldn't do, and I leak less power. When you enchant an object, I can feel it afterwards, but when I finish a spell, the magic-sniffing pig can't even detect what I've done. My power source comes from within me instead of the world, which is where fairies get their power."

"That's true enough," Budbud said. Pleasentia and Gary nodded in agreement. "Our mastery is in the ability to control the flow."

"Mine comes from within here," Susannah touched her chest. "And I suppose it's my business, not yours, if I'm damaging the fabric of me."

"You could cause explosions and endanger people, like your twerp of a sister."

From the safety of her father's embrace, Ella shot Budbud a hateful glance.

"She'll learn how to handle herself," Susannah said. "And I'll learn more as well." She stood straighter beside Jon Tom. Hope blossomed inside her. Both she and Jon Tom had valid arguments, strong ones. "I doubt the fabric of the world is your true concern. Do you fear you'll lose business? Your gold?"

"Bah!" Budbud said. "You're no threat to our business."

"Then let us be," Susannah said.

"Or I'll curse you." Ella smirked at the fairies, and the King jostled her.

"We can't let you be. You're going to have to come with us,

and that goes for any of the rest of you who develop magic powers. I don't know what your parents have been feeding you." Budbud glared at the King and Queen.

"The mother of invention—" Susannah began.

Budbud threw up her hands. "Would you shelve this mother-of-invention tomfoolery? Any necessity involved in your mutation doesn't change the fact you must be restrained and studied. Fairy children need years of training before they're safe."

"Maybe they're just dumb." At Ella's comment, the Queen pinched her arm.

"I'll stubble you if I must, child." Budbud pointed her wand at Ella. "With pleasure, too."

"I notice you agree necessity played a role in this situation." Jon Tom flipped to the next page and wrote something down. "I'll take that as an admission the challenge was unfair." He ended a sentence with an emphatic dot.

Susannah peered at the notebook page covered in crabbed golden handwriting. His strong fingers held the tiny quill without bending it and she smiled to think of how recently they had brushed against her body.

"Young man, you're trying my patience." Budbud took a step closer to Jon Tom.

Gary cleared his throat. "Budbud, perhaps we should just level with them."

The old fairy whirled upon Gary and shook her wand. "The FAE will melt our wands if we make that move without consulting them."

"Making it now would save endless rounds of meetings," Pleasentia pointed out. "Nattering on about this pro and that con, drawing up boring diagrams and flowcharts, when we could be doing so many more interesting things." She batted her eyelashes at the King.

"You might as well admit it," Jon Tom said. "The proof of your wrongdoing is clear."

"It's not completely clear to me," the Queen snapped. "Since it involves my progeny, I'd like it spelled out."

"The fairies knew Malady's curse would cause the civilized kingdoms to fall into disarray and did nothing to fix their coworker's misstep. My theory is they hoped the humans would be reduced to begging for help, even promising firstborns." Jon Tom inclined his head toward Budbud, whose jaw dropped. "It's obvious. With mortals that desperate, the fairies could do away with this nasty business of fairy banishment. Perhaps they could even turn us into a servant race, all without entirely violating the Oath most of them subscribe to."

Susannah blew out a long breath. The fairies meant to indenture humankind? Surely not. Few fairies were evil like Malady. When she opened her mouth to question him, he shook his head, asking her to wait. And then he winked.

"Rubbish!" Budbud's face screwed into a purplish mask of anger and she choked on her own spleen. She resembled a boiled prune. "If we wanted you as servants, what could you do to stop us? Nothing, nothing! It was never our intention to weaken humans but to strengthen them. This patriarchal system you cling to in the face of ruin is idiotic."

Jon Tom threw back his head and laughed, and a flash of recognition jostled Susannah. He'd been goading the old fairy into a reckless admission!

The Queen nodded her head. "Excellent work, boy. Needling's a favorite trick of mine as well."

Budbud, still purple, jabbed her wand at Jon Tom. "The detective is spoiled in the head. How can you think the FAE wants to indenture humans? As for your firstborns, I can't imagine anything worse than a passel of squalling, mortal brats when we'd rather have gold."

The King's brow furrowed. "I don't understand. You were cheating this whole time? Why did you want to prevent us from having boys?"

"We weren't cheating." Budbud huffed and her color receded to normal. "We were simply failing to act."

Jon Tom rolled his quill between his fingers so it twirled with a snapping sound, the only outward sign of his excitement. "Violating your own Oath. You let the curse continue in hopes the Middle Kingdoms would collapse."

Budbud made a sound halfway between a growl and a nasty word. "What do you think this is, Mr. Tom, one of your cases?"

"It could be, if the mortals decided to sue for damages." He thumbed through half the book, the pages making a quiet flipping sound. "I've got it right here in gold ink, all the evidence needed. Violating the FairFairy Oath, violating the rules for human-fairy interaction, intimidation, withholding information. The list is not short. Aside from the princes, there are fifteen witnesses, and if you try to spell us into forgetfulness, well, there's my book." He smiled. "Kingdoms Orzo and Pavilion alone could sue you for decades of free spell work, and I can only imagine what you'd owe the princes."

"Subsidiary effects of a curse are covered in the interaction laws, same as subsidiary effects of christening gifts."

"Only if they don't harm innocent victims."

"The human ruling class needs an overhaul!" Gary protested, despite Budbud's glower. "Everyone knows the females of the species are better suited to rule." He indicated Budbud and Pleasentia with a flourish. "Look at how well Ulaluna is governed."

"Yes, observe how well the FAE functions," Jon Tom said, sarcasm evident in his tones. "Observe how well you're able to reach decisions and control your members. You certainly didn't let Briar Rose sleep for ninety years past her curse date while you waffled about thorns."

"That's ancient history," Budbud said.

"It's still a valid and legally arguable precedent. Madame, if you don't wish me to contact each of the beleaguered kingdoms to form a class-action suit, you'd do well to step down in your threat to carry off my future wife. If she says she isn't harming the fabric of the world, she isn't. As for Ella, I suggest you assign her a fairy liaison for emergency training."

Budbud closed her eyes tightly and placed the tip of her wand against her temple. "I know I'm going to regret this," she muttered. "The jackanapes has us."

"Ooh, appoint me to train the kid!" exclaimed Pleasentia. "I like it here."

"No way, this is definitely a matter for the whole FAE. Let them take it from here." Budbud snapped her fingers and the other fairies moved to her side.

"I would suggest you also speak with the FAE about repairing Orzo's border wards free of charge. And I believe Bavamorda could use a touch-up against the Sun Demons."

"We'll talk to them, we'll talk to them. Just don't go off on some crusade. You've got a whole galoot of noble heirs now." To Susannah's parents, Budbud added, "The lads will wake in an hour, and I suggest you distribute them as quickly as possible. Most will require a degree of socialization before they are fit for polite company...or for daughters."

Susannah's sisters giggled, and her mother's eyes widened with a certain degree of alarm. "I don't suppose you could put a spell on my girls in the interim?" the Queen asked.

"Ask one of your freakish daughters," Budbud said. "Except for contracted services, we're through with this family until Ella's trainer is selected. Susannah, I trust, will voluntarily avail herself of the lessons."

"What of Malady?" Susannah asked. "Does breaking the curse mean she'll be allowed back in the human lands?"

"To our knowledge the document your father and his cronies ratified still stands, until it's burned three times with the feather of a red-gold phoenix."

"Then it's finished." Susannah threw her arms around Jon Tom's neck and placed exuberant kisses upon his cheeks. "My hero!" she said.

"My wife," he whispered in her ear, making her blush. "My better half. My one true love." He kissed her back, with increasing fervor, until the Queen smacked him on the back.

"Your courtship might have been unorthodox, but you'll be going by the books now. No more of that until after the wedding."

Susannah sighed as Jon Tom released her and noticed a twinkle in his eye. He tweaked the hood of his cloak where it trailed down her back before moving away.

The cloak—only she and Jon Tom knew its secret. Everyone here seemed to assume she'd taken him with her on purpose. Ella might suspect, but the rest had no idea he'd found the enchanted land on his own. Now they too had a secret, and it would prove useful in the months to come if her mother intended to make them conduct the remainder of their courtship by the very restrained books.

Susannah's father clapped his hands together and rubbed them briskly. "Now that that's settled, can we talk about my other children? Which of these fine lads is mine?"

"Actually," Budbud said, looking over her shoulder, "none of them. You had twelve girls in a row. If you weren't already a king, we'd elevate you to the nobility for that great feat."

And with that, she brought down her wand in a quick movement, enveloping herself, Gary and Pleasentia in a bubble of light, which shrank and shrank until it was the size of a marble. The glowing speck darted up, out the hole in the stained-glass window far above.

And so the King and Queen, Susannah and Jon Tom, Susannah's eleven unmarried sisters and the seven hundred and thirty-seven noble males, seven hundred and thirty-eight including Sir Hanson, lived happily ever after.

From the ceiling of the audience chamber, unnoticed by all the young men, all the boys, all the princesses, the King and the Queen, unnoticed by Susannah and by sharp-eyed Jon Tom, the feather of a red-gold phoenix drifted slowly down, twirling, swirling, caught on one draft or another though there were no breezes. The feather had nearly reached the ground when it winked out of sight in a small puff of flame.

About the Author

Jody Wallace is published in romance fiction under the names Jody Wallace and Ellie Marvel. She has always lived with cats, and they have always been mean.

To learn more about Ms. Wallace, please visit www.jodywallace.com or the cat's website, www.meankitty.com. You can also send an email to jwallace@meankitty.com.

No magic for two weeks? What's a fairy to do?
Go to Vegas, of course!

Survival of the Fairest
© 2008 Jody Wallace

Princess Talista of the fairy clan Serendipity has been sent, like all young fairies, to a remote forest in humanspace for mandatory survival training. But headstrong Tali's got different ideas about where to spend two weeks without magic. What better place than Las Vegas to learn to live like humans, a true test of survival?

Tali might not blend, but she'd like to be shaken and stirred with stage magician Jake Story. Their attraction is instant and electric...and Tali senses there's more to Jake's show than flashy tricks.

Jake always knew he was different, even before he developed an unusual flair for hypnotism. He has no trouble mesmerizing the luscious Tali during act three, but the lights that appear around them when they kiss weren't part of the program.

When the authorities from Tali's homeland track the missing princess to Vegas, Jake and Tali end up on the run. In between magic experiments, evil gnomes and astonishing sex, Tali learns what it really means to be human—by falling in lust, followed closely by love.

But Tali's not human. And Jake doesn't believe in fairies. The truth will either bind them together—or tear the fairy realm apart.

Warning, this title contains the following: Intoxicating sex, misuse of magic, gorgeous cross-dressers and flesh-eating gnomes.

Available now in ebook from Samhain Publishing.

Enjoy the following excerpt from Survival of the Fairest...

From his vantage point on the sidewalk, Jake Story shook his head in disbelief. What the hell did she think she was doing? Instead of running to the median, the woman in Little House on the Prairie outfit screamed and clutched her backpack in the middle of the busy intersection. Car horns blared up and down the Strip, and angry cabbies shook their fists out windows. In the lane where the woman stood, traffic was forced to idle, but in the other, cars sped past. People on the hot, crowded sidewalks rubbernecked, and vehicles on the other side of the palm trees in the median slowed to see what they were missing.

The woman must be a tourist. Vegas attracted every kind of nut. Come to think of it, there was a sci-fi convention in town, Star Cluster or something like that. Maybe she was into all that dress-up crap.

Well, he didn't feel like watching a space nerd get splattered all over the road. "Hey you. Get on the sidewalk!"

His practiced pipes had more range than the average citizen. The woman's kerchief-wrapped head whipped towards him, and he was rewarded by the sight of an angelic face twisted in confusion and terror.

"Get your butt out of the street!" he yelled.

A man in a Mercedes-Benz whose grill was inches away from ramming the lovely dimwit rolled down his tinted window and screamed something a lot less friendly. The woman cringed.

Crud. Time to play the hero. Jake shouldered a pair of gawking teenagers out of the way and strode into the street, holding up his palm in a gesture that clearly said "Halt!" to the oncoming traffic. Amazingly, the drivers obeyed. He reached the damsel in distress, grabbed an arm, and dragged her, stumbling, back to the sidewalk.

The Mercedes pealed out with a screech of tires.

"What's the matter with you?" he said. "Are you on drugs?"

The short young woman struggled in his grasp. "Unhand me!"

He didn't, not until he could confirm she wouldn't head straight into traffic. With her free hand she swung the pack onto her back and peered up into his face with bright blue eyes. "I was momentarily surprised by the, ah, automobiles."

"Cars, of course, being such shocking things." He raised his eyebrows.

She grabbed his wrist and tugged his grip off her with a little twist of her nails in his hand. She had weird clothes, red hair and pale skin, and she looked meaner than a drunk who'd just spilled his last bottle of whiskey.

And she had the cutest little freckles across her nose and cheeks.

"Let me pass," she said. "I need to find Merlin's Cave, and you're delaying me."

The Cave? Star Cluster wasn't at his hotel. "You're looking for a place to stay?" he asked.

"Maybe." The woman jutted out her chin.

"Aren't you Trekkies at the other end of the Strip?" Sci-fi fans were a strange bunch, sorta like programmers—didn't really party, didn't gamble. It's like they were smart enough to know the odds were stacked against them. Why have their convention in Vegas, anyway?

Little Dimwit frowned. "Trekkies?"

She must not be with Star Cluster. A garden-, or desert-, variety tourist, then. From the funky accent he guessed she was from overseas. Might as well help her out and earn his karmic brownie points for the day, just like his mother taught him.

"I work at Merlin's Cave. I just finished an errand, and I'm happy to show you the way."

"You have an automobile?" She shifted her shoulders as if anxious to ditch her pack.

"I didn't drive today. I needed some fresh air."

"If you can call it fresh. It doesn't smell like I expected at all." With a disgruntled look, she wiped her forehead against her sleeve. She wore a white sleeveless apron decorated with flowers over a brown dress plus a shawl.

Definitely too many clothes for Vegas in September. Was she Amish or something? A Wild West re-enactor? Hell, how should he know? He was nothing but a small-time stage magician who'd hardly even been to Arizona, much less whichever funny farm let this one loose.

As if aware of his opinion, she sniffed. "I'm not accustomed to walking. Hire me a cabbie."

So much for doing a good deed. "Catch one yourself, Your Highness." He turned on his heel, but a small hand on his bare arm stopped him.

"How did you know?" She glared at him, suspicion turning her eyes stormy.

"How did I know what?"

"That I'm royal."

Crazy, crazy, crazy! "Look, lady, I don't have time for this. I have a show to rehearse and it's nearly two o'clock. If you want to follow me, fine, but if you don't, the hotel is a block or so this way." He nodded in the direction of the Cave. "When you get to Bally's, turn right."

She cocked her head to one side. "So, I guess you're from around here?"

He nodded.

"Would you happen to know where I could get these changed for paper dollars?" She pulled a handful of antique-looking gold coins out of her pocket.

If those were authentic, this rube had no business flashing them on a busy street in Vegas, even if it was two in the afternoon.

"Put those away," he advised, and she shoved them back into her oversized pocket.

She really did need help. He sighed. How much time could he spare? He only had one show on Thursdays, but his assistant, Jessie, needed another run-through on the floating person trick. He should've driven to lunch today, but he'd needed to blow off steam. This morning, his uncle had—for the millionth time—harassed him about his grandfather, who'd pissed off the cops. Again. Like it was Jake's job to control Pap, not his uncle's. Like Jake, his uncle and the National Guard put together could control Pap.

"You can't just waltz in anywhere with something like that and expect to get a fair deal," he said. "I know a respectable pawn shop whose owner deals in small antiques near Merlin's Cave. Are those doubloons real?"

"Of course they're real. Real human—I mean, real gold. How was I to know gold was no longer accepted as tender in Las Vegas? That's just dumb."

GREAT CHEAP FUN

Discover eBooks!

THE FASTEST WAY TO GET THE HOTTEST NAMES

Get your favorite authors on your favorite reader, long before they're out in print! Ebooks from Samhain go wherever you go, and work with whatever you carry—Palm, PDF, Mobi, and more.

Samhain publishing ltd

Printed in the United States
128620LV00001B/577-585/P